THE TRADER
MAN WITH NO FACE

R.K. MANN

The Trader
Man With No Face
First Print Edition: 2014

Shia Press LLC
2939 Van Ness St. N.W. Suite 1116
Washington, DC 20008
202-363-2113

ISBN: 978-0-9915942-1-4

Cover and Formatting: Streetlight Graphics

DEDICATION:

My special thanks go to Chuck Steinberg and Catherine Ann Jones, for believing in me enough to take the time to read and critique this novel when it was a work in progress. Jan Lipkin has my deep gratitude for her steady support, time and common sense. I thank Catherine as well for her publishing advice.

I never would have been able to write this without the help of Zhao Ruan Jin and Stephen Denstman. I also wish to acknowledge Allen Kronstadt, who was my unwitting inspiration.

AUTHOR'S NOTE:

Drogan thoughts are shown in upper case, for clarity.

ONE

**35TH CENTURY
AFTHAR**

A SWIRLING COCOON OF light and energy pulsed rapidly through space in distorting waves. When it drew close to the dark side of the planet Afthar, it slowed, then wavered in place above the rotating surface, as if it was deciding its next action. Suddenly it dropped through the atmosphere toward the planet's surface. The turmoil of light seemed to lose cohesiveness along with speed. When it penetrated the jungle below, the remaining shards of energy broke up, silently disgorging the dark still form of a man into a thick cushion of vegetation. Then the last of the light was swallowed by the darkness.

For a while the man lay on the ground as if dead. Finally, his hand reached out and clutched at some leaves. He tried to lift himself but disorientation doomed the attempt. He fell back unconscious — tunic, pants and fine boots torn and dirty.

Finally, he awoke fully to the certainty there was something very, very wrong. Where was he? He could feel vegetation and damp ground but could see nothing — not a hint of color, not even a shadow of a shape in the dark. Nothing.

Dead silence. Silence quieter than the stillness in an unpowered, drifting ship in deep space. This was like nothing he had ever known. Whenever he had really listened, even in the quietest place, there was always an ever-present background buzz. Always. But now there was no buzz. That too was gone.

He shifted his jaw but it didn't seem to move. His hands fumbled over his face. His eyes and ears were gone. Of his mouth and nose, only holes remained on the flat plain of what was left of his face.

Aghhh… No! This can't be. Patushah!

The shock was replaced by an inexpressible anguish. But soon his misery was pierced by an intruding disquiet. A close up image of a green and gold bird with sharp teeth danced through his head.

Strange thoughts intruded with the image and made no sense.

WHAT IS THAT RACKET?

SEEMS TO BE AN ALIEN. HOW DID A SUFUNAAA COME HERE WITHOUT US KNOWING?

They didn't seem to be his own thoughts, since his own were also in his head.

A lost memory?

Maybe his mind was creating a hallucination to avoid dealing with what had happened.

Am I going crazy?

Was he sick or somehow drugged? Maybe all of it was just a bad dream.

But the pain from the scratches and bruises across his body felt real enough and he was sure he was awake. He pinched himself to make sure.

IT WILL NOT BE AMONG US LONG. I CRAVE ITS BLOOD.

Goosebumps prickled across his skin. The green and gold bird snapped its jaws. The ground under him began to quiver. These vibrations intensified into what seemed like the approach of pounding footfalls. Something heavy enough to shake the ground was after him.

Instinct replaced thought. He clawed away with his hands, feet and then knees, bumping into everything as he frantically tried to flee. He soon felt the crashing vibration of undergrowth. Whatever was after him was closing fast.

SUFUNAAA BE STILL. WAIT FOR ME.

He was now certain the voice in his head was not his own. Terror engulfed him. In his mind he now watched his own pathetic figure scurry through the undergrowth as if from other eyes.

WHY ARE YOU NOT STILL?

The man slid down a rock face.

Hide, must hide.

He could feel a brush of cool air raking him from below while an intruding scream of frustration filled his mind.

YOU CAN'T HIDE ALIEN. BE STILL AND FULFILL YOUR PURPOSE.

Death breathed down his back. He pushed himself off the boulder and tumbled down further. His foot slipped into a hole. The rest of him quickly slid through the narrow opening into a cave. The threat and the fearsome voice in his brain disappeared. The man collapsed in relief.

When his strength returned, he fought rising panic.

There's got to be some sense to all of this. Got to be. One step at a time. Aye. Start at the beginning.

He clearly remembered being on the bridge of his ship, the *Farbagan,* with a hold full of muon compressors. The cargo was destined for the Jurgalian aqua farms. It was just another routine trading run through the Betelguese Parse. But ship sensors picked up some sort of turbulence.

Then what?

That was it. That is, until he remembered being thrown around as he fell to the ground.

Wait. What about the Farbagan? What happened to it?

The trader was sure it didn't collide with anything. If his ship disintegrated in some sort of catastrophe, the wreckage should have fallen with him. He hadn't stumbled across any on the ground. And how could anyone even survive a fall from space, without any protection, onto dry land?

Habitable land at that.

Where could he be? The *Farbagan* had been more than ten light years from any star system, and a lot more from anywhere with a breathable satellite.

The man desperately felt for his face again. There were no wounds, just the horrible holes and flat skin.

None of this makes any sense. None of it.

He slumped in overwhelming despair.

TWO

MINING COLONY, PLANET ADDEHUT

DOWN ON HER knees, Maranth-sa-Veddi nimbly pushed a slimy bio-relay in place inside an open cavity in her medibot named Doc. He was not as sleek as most other types of workbots, a general term encompassing the various free roaming cybernetic units that provided the heavy labor and other support functions in the workaday world. Actually, Doc most resembled a soft, velvety blue canister mounted on two fully motile feet.

The living skin that covered his form was creased with access panels and apertures, a few of which were now open for Maranth's inspection. The notation 'J6 Medibot — Various Earth Divisions and Directorates Inc.' was tattooed in black around his midsection. On his top, several visual scanners, auditory nodes, and sensory implements blinked and moved in a manner reminiscent of a lobster, observing what Maranth was doing.

Maranth sat back on the floor and stretched her small frame. Boredom shadowed her delicate Eurasian features and large, light brown eyes. She tucked back a strand that escaped the rest of her sleek, dark hair bound in a fine web of black cord. "You only needed a standard DS3-3 component, Doc. You're fine."

Doc quickly closed his apertures and declared, "That's a relief. It's so hard to get spare parts this far out."

9

Maranth nodded. She had chosen Doc's name, an archaic term for healer, because it was a linguistic relative of her own title of meddoc. Doc functioned as her medical assistant and mobile treatment center, all in one. She would have been lost without him, as the clinic did not have much more than waist-high cabinets lining the walls.

Like all modern workbots, Doc was a synthesis of manufactured inorganic components and cultured living tissue. Workbots varied in size, shape and intelligence, depending upon their function. Those that did basic labor had limited intelligence and were, effectively, mobile tools. Others that hauled material might be massively big and strong.

Many, like Doc, were high functioning personal assistants of different shapes and capacities, depending on their owner's needs. These 'bots were also highly intelligent, with sophisticated programming that could learn from experience, and they could even speak with personality, usually with a distinct male or female voice. But they were actually gender neutral.

The supply ships didn't carry much of Doc's specialized J6 medibot gear. Fortunately, bio-relays were locally available, being a standard component in all workbots.

The medicine and medical chemicals the supply ships brought were packaged in Number 13 size containers, not standard medibot issue. So Doc recycled his original containers until they wore out. Then Maranth improvised replacements.

Maranth first noticed their new patient when her medibot turned an inquiring sensor toward the door. She rose and bowed slightly, with her palms together, offering the traditional Veddian greeting to the unfamiliar miner timidly peering through the portal.

"I'm the meddoc here. My name is Maranth-sa-Veddi-Dimore. Please come in."

The thin, slope-shouldered man with drab hair and eyes silently slipped into the clean treatment room. The door slid closed behind him. Maranth had observed similar unease from most of the other Addehut miners who visited the clinic.

She knew the Huts, as they call themselves, regarded Veddians like herself in awe. The one in front of her had probably been surprised to see her on her knees. To the outerworlders here, she was a delicate aristocrat from the oldest and most cultured of the innerworlds.

The miner approached reluctantly and stretched out his arms, revealing reddened, blotchy skin. "I be Soddi. You can fix this?"

"Doc…"

"Preparing…"

As a bat might unfold its wing, Doc silently stretched out supple skin and supporting struts from a horizontal body seam to create a cot. Tough-looking, hollow arterial material hydraulically inflated along the side struts down to the floor to support the cot's bed and root it firmly in place. Doc then waited motionlessly for their patient.

Maranth beckoned the man. "Just lie down on the couch and we'll take a look."

The man gingerly lay down and watched anxiously as Doc swept him with an eyelike, blinking device, bathing him in blue light. The diagnostic light was silently accompanied by a highly sensitive ultrasound scan and, most importantly, an extremely sensitive sniffing intake that let Doc detect a myriad of illnesses by sampling the molecules coming off the patient.

"What's your name again?" Maranth asked as she studied the data on Doc's view screen. She could have displayed the data on her wrist comm. But it would then appear holographically in the air, which tended to distract patients.

"I be Soddi, Soddi-ad-Addehut. Veddi don't work in slag-busting outerworld shitholes like Addehut. So, you bein' punished, or what?"

"I'm doing my first Medservice here. When the supply ship arrives with my replacement, I go back."

Maranth didn't mention that it had seemed like punishment.

After she arrived, it was several months before any of the Huts would come in for treatment. Though everyone in their early centuries had the vigor and looks of someone in their early twenties, Maranth actually was young, only twenty-four.

The Hut administration knew Medservice was her first career as mostly first-career meddocs wound up in places like this mining settlement. Apparently she was their first female meddoc. They would tell her she was too pretty or too young to be a meddoc, or she needed to learn a thing or two. Maranth had been briefed she might encounter such attitudes and just let the fears work themselves out over time. To reduce the Huts awe of her, she always wore the rough tunics of the miners, not the flowing, shimmery robes from her home world.

She wondered if any other meddocs from her class were enduring conditions as primitive as this in their cross-planetary service. Besides the social backwardness, the clinic was unequipped, the colony grimy and ugly, the food poor and the quarters cramped and dirty. Even the air was slightly poisonous.

Since the planet was little more than a frozen ammonia snowball, the entire mining colony was environmentally sealed under the planet's surface. There was nothing topside except lethal ice and poisonous wind. As the planet was located on the fringes of galactic commerce, there was little from the outside to break the monotony. Worse, none of the miners seemed to have any interests beyond the local beer, each other's mates and other vices. It had been a struggle not to lapse into depression.

"How long have you had this rash?"

"More'n two tours. And now I be itching like a hoddog scratch-miner's ass."

Maranth pushed up the man's loose pants and examined his legs, which also showed signs of the rash.

"I don't wonder." She turned to Doc. "For his raddad mobie let's give him the bella light treatment and SK438 pills, standard dosage."

Doc's blinking device again passed over Soddi, this time emitting a high whine and a yellow-green beam.

Maranth eyed the numbers flitting across Doc's screen and was satisfied.

She patted Soddi's arm. "You'll be better soon."

"Why you be carrying no heft?"

For a moment Maranth was puzzled, then realized this man expected her to be heavier, coming as she did from a planet where you could eat all you wanted. Few in Addehut carried any fat.

"It's natural for me to be this size. Please roll over so we can treat your back side."

Soddi flipped over and the treatment was repeated.

Maranth turned to Doc. "Remind me to ask the Miners' Council, again, to fumigate the dorms. By Veddi-hut, if they won't do it this time, I will!"

"The Council has not fumigated in the past. Perhaps they don't regard raddad mobie with any priority around here."

Maranth nodded. Every attempt to improve hygiene had been met by ignorant indifference. Thus the close quarters promised a rapid spread of contagions such as the fungus she was treating now.

A small aperture in Doc opened iris-fashion, revealing a transparent vial of pills. Maranth handed them to her patient.

Soddi was relieved. "No more itching now. I be done?"

"Aye. You take these three times a day until you've taken them all."

Soddi happily pocketed the pills and hopped to his feet.

"Remember, take all the pills or it will come back. And tell your friends who have it to come see me."

There was suddenly a loud commotion outside. As Maranth and Soddi reached the doorway they heard cries, scuffles and the sounds of people running by.

When the door slid open, a frightened miner, his clothes torn, face blackened and bloody, raced by.

Maranth called back to Doc, "There's been some sort of accident. Gather the emergency supplies."

In the sealed environment of the colony, a serious accident like a fire or leak could be devastating.

Doc retracted his cot. Padding along on clubby feet, he quickly reached the supply cabinet, where he stretched out a translucent siphon, inserted it into a port and began to suck out various small stock items into his bulk. All the while two of his retractable limbs picked up and stored medicines and equipment from shelves and counters.

Soddi pointed down the hall. "You see that one move? Looks like a fat wartcow bein' chased by harewolves."

Maranth was too busy overseeing Doc's preparations to look. Then two miners staggered up to the clinic. A blinding blast of light hit them and they both fell just outside.

She ran out to help the stricken men and noticed a lone figure at the end of the narrow hall. He was swathed from head to toe in orange clothes and matching helmet with an attached scarf-like cloth wrapped around his lower face so that only his dark eyes were visible.

He leisurely reset and leveled his blaster at the meddoc.

Maranth froze.

Soddi managed to yank her back into the clinic a split second before the blaster discharged. Wailing, Soddi frantically shut the door and set the auto-lock.

"Raiders! We be lost now!"

"Ridiculous. This is the 35th century, not the dark ages."

Reflexively, Maranth had expressed centuries of innerworld cultural conditioning. Thoroughly educated and intelligent, nothing in her experience had prepared her for armed aggression.

Doc pulled up to the two and pushed out his small siphon whose end now formed a shallow cup. In the cup were two small green pills.

"Calm-aid for stress?"

Just then a light blast seared a small hole in the door, melting and twisting the edges of the alumaskin to red hot around the opening, the tinny smell of burning metal filled their nostrils.

Soddi howled and both of them fell back. A second blast enlarged the hole enough to admit a man.

In a low voice hidden under Soddi's wailing, Maranth spoke to Doc. "Hypo of Was-Curare, standard dosage." She took the hypo and fell to the floor near the door, lying there as if she had been hit.

She watched the raider step over the fallen miners and duck through the hole into the clinic. When he saw Soddi he laughed under his head cloth and aimed his blaster. That's when Maranth hypoed his ankle.

With a flicker of surprise he aimed down, but could only manage to collapse without a sound or shot.

Soddi screeched in relief. "You killed him! You killed him!"

The man had fallen on top of Maranth so that her face was buried under his bulk. She worked herself free enough to squeak out, "I didn't kill him. He's just paralyzed. Get me up."

Soddi and Doc grabbed his legs and pulled the dead weight of the man off the meddoc. His scarf worked loose, revealing their attacker's face. Maranth was surprised to see that he was hardly more than a boy. Doc stretched out an appendage to help her up. She grabbed it and hopped to her feet. She smoothed her tunic and regained her composure.

Doc poked the fallen raider. "If there are others like him, I suggest we hide."

Not only was Doc's programming wide-ranging medically; it was also extensive regarding human social responses and emotional states.

Soddi brightened. "The deep mines! Even a Fargo miner'd need a whole blastin' tour to find us down there."

Sudden scraping noises in the hall drew their attention. Two black, all-purpose workbots were dragging off the stunned miners from outside the door. Maranth and Soddi exchanged frightened glances. For the first time Maranth experienced the searing stab of real, adrenaline fear.

None of the workbots on Addehut were black. No doubt these belonged to the attackers. Maranth could no longer deny what she was witnessing.

She tapped Soddi's arm with a look of apology. "Aye. It's the deep mines then."

She carefully peered down the now silent hall. "No one is here. Let's go."

Soddi followed Maranth out of the blast hole. As Doc trailed after them, one of his arms stretched to grab a last bit of equipment while the rest of his bulk slid through the opening. He swayed side to side as he stuffed this last item into a now bulging torso and sought to catch up to the fast retreating duo.

They quickly navigated several corridors of the shabby administrative section without encountering anyone, just empty offices in disarray. Several of these rooms had clearly been ransacked and some of the walls displayed the typical sunburst scars of blaster fire that missed someone.

Unless specifically set to kill, weapons blasters only disrupted the nervous system when hitting flesh. They had intelligent feedback systems, a safety feature since they were originally used as cutting tools. These weapons still seared anything inanimate.

The administrative sections, including the medical clinic, were located mid-level. The mines were below. Housing and docking facilities were in the levels near the surface. It was obvious to Maranth the attackers had moved on.

But above or below?

Soddi led them down a wide, down-sloping tunnel whose sides and ceiling were reinforced by ceramaplast ribs. When they were halfway to the bottom they could again hear sounds of conflict, and it seemed to be heading their way. They ducked into a narrow portal to a wide metal door, which remained closed. Soddi hurriedly tapped a code into the touch-sensitive security panel. Its status light signaled its acceptance of the code, but the security program wouldn't release the door.

Blaster fire spat across the corridor with a whiff of ozone. A ragged miner with hollow eyes streaked past. There was another blast and they heard him drop. Maranth and Soddi exchanged horrified glances as measured footsteps approached. With sweaty hands Soddi frantically renewed his attack on the panel.

Maranth knew they were running out of time. But she couldn't think of any more tricks. She eyed Doc and motioned toward the door. The medibot inserted a ribbon probe between the frame and wall.

"Hurry." Her voice was reduced to a tight whisper. She didn't like this sweaty fear that crawled up her back.

Soddi angrily kicked the door but it wouldn't budge. He fumed, then irrationally bolted down the hall. Another blast followed after him and Maranth heard him fall.

There was nothing she could do for her patient now. The door finally slid open and she nearly fell through. Doc quickly followed her in. She then hit autolock on the inside panel. The door slipped shut just as the orange robes of a raider reached the portal.

The cavernous storeroom was stocked with large foam crates, spare parts and supplies. A very wide door gaped open directly across the expanse.

Maranth could hear the raider outside shouting something to his comrades. She wondered about the second door.

"It probably leads down into the mines." She ran, Doc following close on her heels. They heard blaster fire sizzling through the door behind.

When they neared the opposite door, Maranth glimpsed another black workbot, partly hidden behind a crate to her left. She skidded to a stop, then heard the terrifying click of a blaster being set.

She whirled around to face three orange-robed raiders. One of them leveled a blaster at her. Then her world erupted in orange light.

THREE

RAVINE, PLANET AFTHAR

A FOOT LONG, WORM-LIKE creature clung to the back of the maimed trader, who slept curled up among the rocks in the cave. The creature arched upward and waved some of its cilia into a narrow stream of daylight that found its way down through the gloom.

Still mostly asleep, the man stirred. He reached behind for what he could feel was moving on his back. His hand found the huge worm and he realized it was alive. With a start he pushed it away and scrambled up the rocks as fast as he could. When he felt the warmth of sun on his skin, he knew he'd breached the mouth of his cave.

The warm sensation gave him only a fleeting feeling of security as his mind was quickly engulfed by countless thoughts not his own.

He ducked back down and the voices in his brain faded away. He raised his head and they returned. So he ducked back down again. His rock lair seemed to block the assault on his mind.

Yet whatever had crawled on his back was still below, and he was now very thirsty. He decided to ignore the voices. He again slid his head up and tried to adjust to the mental bombardment. None of the voices above seemed threatening. His initial panic subsided and he hoisted himself the rest of the way. He deliberately focused his attention on his own body's sensations and movement, to separate himself from the foreign intrusions in his brain.

The air was damp on his skin and his hands found dew on the rich vegetation. His fingers brought what they could of the liquid to his mouth hole, but it wasn't enough to quench his thirst.

There might be a stream at the bottom of the hill. But how will I find my way back?

His hands fumbled into a tangle of vine-like plants snaking across the rock. He pulled several of thick strands loose and began to twist and knot them together into a makeshift rope. After testing its strength, he tied one end of his improvisation to the base of a sturdy bush near the mouth of his cave and let down the remainder. He used the rope to steady himself down through the tangle of plants and rock. When the trader ran out of line, he went back up and found more vines and added them on, all the while taking frequent rests back inside his cave. When he could find no more of the vines, he gathered the long grass-like plants that grew further down and wove them in. In this manner he slowly made his way down the ravine until he stumbled onto a small stream.

As he drank his fill, a strong image filled his brain, overwhelming the many voices. A feathered, bird-like creature soared like a red and white kite overhead in lazy loops high above a ravine. Its long, thin tail stabilized its flight and its narrow jaws were filled with needle-sharp teeth. A pair of claws arched out of the first strut of each of its wings.

A flyer.

How did he know this? Even stranger, he seemed to be seeing this flyer from the eyes of another just like it. It was as if he could feel the push of air through his feathers as he banked and turned over the jungle. He could feel the small exertion that came from beating his wings and the warmth of bright sun on his face.

It was as if he, himself, was scanning the rocks and vegetation for food or anything out of the ordinary, occasionally flapping wings to catch an updraft in the bright sun. As he passed low over a small stream, he caught sight of a man's arm.

His flyer shrieked and its mind cried out. *ALIEN... ALIEN... ALIEN...*

Then another strong image filled his head. Something like a giant bird rose up and glared at him, but in place of a beak and wings were the jaws and claws of a terrestrial animal. It stood on two thick legs, its forward body balanced by a stiff tapering tail that whipped to the side in a cascade of gold plumage tipped in black and white chevrons. Its head and neck plumage was similar, though the balance of its body was feathered in iridescent green down.

THIS SUFUNAAA IS MINE.

That thought didn't come from this creature, who sat down with a rattle of plumage. Then his mind found the other one, much like the first, except its plumage was less striking.

Bantaaa!

She was the one who chased him before. How did he know that?

All of this is impossible.

He sensed Bantaaa shake her plumage and accelerate her footfalls as she worked into a gallop. Now her mind was boring into his head. It seemed like she somehow recognized him. He also sensed she intended to hunt him quickly before others like her reached him first.

I THIRST FOR YOU. SUFUNAAA, BE STILL.

Her command chilled his being.

He forced his will to resist and quickly scurried up using his woven vines. In a few seconds he reached the cave and threw in his line. An annoyed scream filled his mind.

HIS KIND HAS PRIMITIVE MINDS. SO WHY IS THIS ONE ABLE TO RESIST ME?

He jumped down inside and the feathered predator's thoughts died in the safe cocoon of rock. Only a slight vibration hinted at the danger above.

The trader again curled himself up inside the rocks. The alien voices were now only a faint, harmless hum.

How can this all be happening? Why can't I wake up from this nightmare?

He carefully felt his featureless face and then slumped against the damp rock.

No point dwelling on what happened to me. What's done is done. Now how can I get out of this fix?

He thought about it all, going over everything he had learned since he reached the planet.

Who am I kidding? Even if these monsters weren't hunting me, how could I survive in this wilderness without sight, sound and smell?

He slowly ran his hands across the rock and tried to visualize the space around him. But he could only visualize its general shape in gray and black. The man sagged further into depression.

What am I struggling for? Even if I manage to get out of this mess, what's left for me?

My life is over.

He had struggled in a primitive, animal reflex to survive. Now it was time to let go. Death came to all eventually. Sooner or later these alien predators would end it quickly, albeit messily, when he left his cave. His worry and fear lifted off.

I hope I make them sick.

The little joke brought him a brief pulse of pleasure. Ironically, the only thing left to him in this lush place was his choice of death.

He leaned back and thought about his life. He began by recalling his childhood on the *Piliar*, then the raucous times he had on the *Zanitos,* serving under his uncle, the master trader Garth. From studying the teachings of Patus, he matured and learned his place in the great cosmos. And then he recalled his life and the best trades he had made on his own since then.

The life of a trader was always hazardous: an accident in

space, some natural calamity on an alien world — even murder. He'd had a good run.

Aye. My accounts balance. Now it's my time.

He climbed up to the entrance and slipped out. Instead of the expected mental din, he was now engulfed in a soaring chorus. The minds of the fierce creatures that'd hunted him were now joined in one exalted voice, like a chant or great song. As it went on and on it took him over and he lost himself in its beauty and power.

Then new images, smells and unfamiliar sounds began to fill his brain. It was as if he was actually seeing, smelling, and hearing more of this world, even as he sat by his cave.

As it had with the flyer, his new vision swept across the forest of the blue-green, exotic tree-like vegetation that formed the checkered canopy above the shrubs and vines of his world. Now with it all was the smell of damp, sweet decay, something like overripe melon. There were unfamiliar, indescribable colors in the shadowy areas that should have been dark. He watched strange insect-like creatures, some as large as swamp boars, skitter and slither through the undergrowth, sometimes grunting or clicking as they moved. And all of this he saw with a wider horizontal field of vision. He suspected this vision came through the eyes of the birdlike creatures that hunted him. They called themselves the Kin.

All this is part of the Kin Song!

This is when his perceptions were drawn upward on the wings of the flyers to a much higher altitude.

Aye. These flyers are part of it too!

He saw details in the vegetation that should have been impossible at this distance, such as the antennae of a small creature scampering along a branch. And he smelled its acrid scent separate from the background smells. From this height, it was clear his jungle was actually confined to a gorge walled in by the weathered rock embankments of a high plateau.

He could feel the push of wind and hear it rush through the beating wings that carried his vision toward the high ground.

Soon he passed over empty, rocky terrain. In the distance it formed a dusty edge to the violet-colored sky.

The magnificence and immensity of it all overwhelmed and frightened him. His fear finally broke the connection. When he regained himself, he quickly slipped back into the cave and slept.

When he awoke sometime later, the warmth from the beam of sunlight was gone. His hand brushed another of the cave worms. This time he gingerly probed it with his fingers. It was dry and a bit squishy. He seized the creature and lifted it to his face, hidden in the gloom, and squeezed its juice into the hole that was now his mouth, neither able to taste or smell what he had ingested. But the liquid killed the burn of hunger in his stomach.

I can always die tomorrow.

The next day, the sun again returned to parts of the cave. A thin beam of it had caressed his arm, awakening him. He thought about the bird creatures that hunted him. From almost the beginning he sensed he somehow could read their minds.

And what minds they have!

Now he was sure he was reading not only the sensory perceptions of these beings, but also those of their pets, the flyers. From the sky, he had seen, heard and smelled a wondrous world through their alien senses.

The Kin had to be intelligent, though in a way different from men. Whatever sentience and intelligence they possessed seemed to be enhanced, maybe increased through the telepathy. He had no trouble understanding them because their thought communication was direct, below the overlay of any language. Didn't the creature that hunted him try to control his mind with her own?

He was certain she was named Bantaaa and their kind called themselves the Kin. So they must have some recognizable language, at least some verbalized names for each other.

But how can I read their thoughts? That is the question.

There were people who had a reputation for clairvoyance

and other psychic talents, particularly the Baradian clones. But no human he'd heard of had ever possessed the Kin's telepathic ability. And he had no such talent — until now.

He wondered if the creatures themselves, or some other condition specific to this planet, had somehow induced his ability to mind-read. Yet Bantaaa seemed surprised when he responded to her thoughts. She clearly had hunted non-telepathic humans before.

Aye. So I am different. Why?

His face had been destroyed, too. Could it be that whatever destroyed his face also left him telepathic?

Could it all have been deliberate?

He knew this line of speculation would go nowhere. So, instead, he focused on the radiance of the Kin joining. All the loneliness, fear and weakness had dropped away.

The visions!

The extraordinary beauty of it all had awed and frightened him. No doubt he had telepathically seen this world through the Kin's eyes. If he could do it once, could he do it again?

By practicing?

He wondered if it would be possible to use their eyes and ears to get around and find proper food. The Kin were very intent on eating him — that was clear. It also was clear, since he could read their thoughts, they could probably read his. And they had a lot more practice at it. Bantaaa had even tried to command his mind and was surprised when she hadn't. There was a whole planet full of Bantaaas to hunt him down. And they used their flyers as extra eyes.

Ironic. They are my salvation and also my death.

They had unwittingly provided their perceptions and collective soul to comfort him, to nourish a will to live. Yet they were likely to devour him without a thought. He was only safe underground.

It seemed hopeless. Nothing he had learned in the last few days really made any difference. He had allowed unrealistic hope to cloud his judgment. Death was inevitable. He began to climb out of the cave. When he reached the entrance he stopped.

Can I remain open to their thoughts, yet not broadcast my own?

It was worth exploring. He had nothing to lose.

Nothing to lose but a quick death.

So he squeezed the juice from another cave worm and practiced not thinking. At first he could only manage to blank his mind a few seconds at a time. Not to think about what he was doing was the hardest. At least he recognized when stray thoughts pushed through so he could practice in the cave without risking his neck outside.

Try not to think about thinking... Right.

When he got more skilled he ventured above ground for short periods. He would try to pick up bits and pieces of information from Kin communication. Eventually one of his own thoughts would slip out, breaking his receptivity. Then he would blank his mind and try again. If he were quick, the Kin would not notice him.

As he got used to them he began to recognize the nearby thoughts of Bantaaa and her mate Hosaaa, from those of the more distantly located Kin. And it was these two who always picked up his stray thoughts first and hunted him if he remained above ground too long. He also noticed their mental emanations seemed stronger when they drew closer.

Does telepathy diminish with distance?

Because Bantaaa and Hosaaa made no effort to conceal what was on their minds, he always knew when they tuned into him. That gave him time to scurry back to the protection of his cave. With practice he gradually got better at controlling his own thoughts, safely remaining outside for longer periods.

FOUR

RAIDER SHIP, UNKNOWN LOCATION

MARANTH WOKE UP in total darkness to chattering and cursing Huts all around her. The Hut style of cursing was all too familiar and unmistakable. Really fine curses ran on and on in almost a musical tempo. She could hear them stepping and falling on one another as they tried to navigate blindly in the dark. She was jostled and pushed. The general consensus was that they were locked in a hold of a space ship. The floor was smooth and, from the acoustics, Maranth guessed the cramped space was made of alumaskin.

Like workbots, spacecraft were engineered through evolutionary modeling and were part biologic and part industrial. There was a faint hum and vibration underneath and all around. The hum no doubt meant the induction ring of the ship was engaged. The negative energy such rings generated warped space into a sort of bubble around a craft. Effectively, gravity was reduced on one side of the ship to produce rapid acceleration. Induction rings were normally engaged outside planetary systems. So the ship had to be in deep space. Around planets, spacefaring ships were required to use their less disruptive, though slower, antigrav engines. Such travel was very quiet.

Everyone was angry and frightened, and the smell was very

ripe. One of the men hit the wall and wailed. "They locked us up tighter than phoboclams in hibernation."

Then panic seemed to spread, others started to holler and cry.

A deep-voiced Hut shouted them down. "There be no chance if we don't pull together. So each who can, call out your name."

Maranth thought he sounded like Saddad-suul. She remembered him as a rather large, gregarious man with a tendency to bronchial infections and bad jokes. He was not joking now.

Among the many commiserations of comrades and kinsmen, she counted 23 captives. Soddi wasn't among them, and neither was Doc.

"Where be the meddoc?" A reedy-voiced woman called out.

"I'm over here." Maranth reached out her hand and it found the arm of a well-developed man.

"This Hut's not movin', can you help?"

"I doubt there's much I can do."

The man next to her ignored her doubt. "Up you go."

With that he hoisted her overhead and set her down half on top of another Hut who yelped. Maranth apologized and negotiated as best she could toward the woman's voice.

"He be here, meddoc." A hand grabbed her arm and guided Maranth down to a prone man's form. She quickly felt for the man's face and leaned close. There was good, regular breath. She felt along his body and didn't detect any obvious wounds. There was some swelling in his leg. His right tibia might be broken, and maybe the fibula as well. At least the bones seemed aligned properly and the skin was unbroken.

There's nothing to work with!

She let that spasm of panic pass and calmed herself.

"He's alive but unconscious. He seems stable for the moment, but his leg is probably broken. He needs anything you have that is rigid enough to be used for splinting. He also needs a few belts or sashes to hold it in place."

There was a general murmur, some grumbling, and a bit of

rustling and elbowing as Huts fumbled in the dark for the items Maranth had asked for.

"Geez, what matter? We all be dead soon enough."

That voice sounded like the tall, black haired woman she'd treated a couple of weeks ago.

What did it matter now?

"I'm sorry there's nothing more I can do in these circumstances."

A hand inadvertently poked her in the eye as several items made their way to her. Of course she could see nothing, even before her eye was poked. But her fingers quickly identified a couple of sashes and a belt. There was also something that felt a lot like a hard truss.

Not ideal, very makeshift... It will just have to do.

"Thanks everyone."

She positioned the girdle firmly around the break and tied it securely with the two sashes.

Probably the increased pain from her efforts stirred the poor man enough to moan a bit. He shrieked when he fully awoke. There was a lot of explaining and calming by their neighbors. The man wordlessly settled back to moans.

Maranth suddenly remembered an esoteric practice from medical history. She doubted it actually reduced pain. A lot of early medicine worked via the placebo effect, which was really just a psychological trick. If a patient believed in the treatment, they felt better, even if the treatment had no medical value.

"I might be able to ease your pain."

The man croaked out what seemed to be "do it."

She positioned herself as comfortably as she could. Her hands again found the makeshift splint. She gently laid her right hand just above the splint, and rested her left hand just below it. She relaxed and imagined her energy flowing from her right hand through his leg, to her left. She remained still for some time.

The man spoke in a clear, strong voice. "Meddoc, the pain be most gone. Thanks."

She removed her hand in surprise.

It actually worked?

There was a bit of mild congratulating from some Huts nearby and the mood lifted a bit.

The realization that, even in these appalling conditions, she could help a patient stunned her.

The Huts settled down, but soon the atmosphere of misery and fear seeped back like a dark fog.

"Thievin' filthy raiders."

There was a murmur of desolate agreement, then bitter silence.

"Why would they go to all the trouble of capturing us alive if they wished to kill us? No, they probably expect to ransom us back." Maranth hoped that her comment would lift the pervading gloom.

"No one be payin' two galact of script for poor slag-bustin' Huts, not even our own." Again it sounded like the voice of Saddad-suul.

"Meddoc, you be right these raiders on purpose grabbed us. But for what? I be guessing slavery. Low-life slave raider scum."

The others murmured in agreement.

Maranth was stunned. Though her home world was now largely a planet of scholars, scientists and artists, she knew that slavery existed in ancient times, when slaves were forced to do the backbreaking labor. Even among the most lawless, poorest elements in the outerworlds, modern slavery couldn't possibly be economical. Relatively cheap workbots did the real work everywhere.

Several generations before the modern era, at the end of the 21st century, before the Biotic War, man had traveled to the stars and began colonizing other planets. During this period, the biologic revolution spawned increasing mental and emotional breakdown, social instability and violence at home, on Old Earth. Such problems were commonly attributed to the effects of economic and cultural dislocation brought about by the introduction of workbots, which greatly increased leisure time. Genetic enhancements, implants, and every possible social pathology metastasized through society, eventually spreading to the new worlds. Mankind was fully compromised by genetic modifications and implants.

A core of self-replicating workbots almost took over Old Earth. It was difficult to distinguish the two sides in the conflict, as many born humans no longer desired a separate, biological existence.

That war nearly caused humanity's demise, but in the end workbots were redesigned so they could never be fully alive or reproductively independent. All non-medical implants and genetic modifications were banned.

At the same time, the Humanity Movement took hold and mankind found its way, rescuing not only itself from cybernetic oblivion but creating the social utopias of the innerworlds.

The Humanity Movement actually began long before the war and had its roots in ancient Eastern traditions. Its adherents believed the real root of social pathology lay in the human mind's imperfect, neurotic adjustment to stress. They developed a focused training and series of therapies, used first on themselves, and then others, to balance the psyche. After the war, their techniques were refined and incorporated in early childhood training, first on Old Earth, renamed Veddi, and then on the other settled worlds. Humanity entered a new era of enlightened rationality. Now only a scattering of remote outposts like Addehut still suffered the old evils.

Maranth tried to think of some other explanation than slavery. There were political and social rivalries to consider, and territorial conflicts still occasionally flared up in the outerworlds.

But the Huts had no interest in politics or in anyone else, and there would be no reason for anyone to have much interest in them. Their planet was virtually uninhabitable. The minerals they extracted were easily obtained elsewhere and barely supported the miners. No one would have any reason to fear, hate, or envy them.

So why did these raiders take them? Why?

Before leaving Veddi she had been thoroughly briefed about the people and old dysfunctions they suffered. That included information on the depravities she'd encountered: adultery, addiction, thievery, gambling, even the violence of wife beating. There was nothing in her briefings about the barbarisms of kidnapping or slavery.

When she accepted her cross-planetary residency she knew there would be hardship. Many young people from the innerworlds served a standard year or so in the outerworlds before assuming their place in society. It was a civic duty to endure this service, even when there was some personal risk, to bring civilization bit by bit to the outerworld unfortunates.

And now, inexplicably, she and the others had been blasted unconscious, taken prisoner and were being transported somewhere.

Why?

SLAVE MARKET, TIGENNE

The next thing Maranth was aware of was an intense light through her closed eyelids. Then a voice pulled her up to full consciousness.

"Now miss, time to wake up. Don't worry about the headache. It will pass when you sit up."

She rolled her head to avoid the light. When that didn't work she protected her eyes with her forearm. That's when she became aware of the headache.

What happened? Where am I?

Maranth sat up and found she had been lying naked on a narrow bed covered by only a thin cloth. There were a few other such beds in the oval room whose walls were completely covered in colorful finery. She had no memory as to how she got there.

Was I drugged?

"Good. You're waking up fine. Just catch your breath and you'll feel a whole lot better."

In front of her was the most ridiculous workbot she had ever seen. It was hourglass shaped, in day-glo colors and dripped colorful shiny and sheer fabrics, wigs, false eyelashes and whatnot.

"I'm dresserbot Emma." With that Emma whirled a quarter turn to shine a narrow beam of light into the face of a second woman lying in the next bed, motionless, also tucked under a thin sheet.

Emma's finery rustled comically. "My sole function is to get you two awake and dressed."

The second woman stirred. Maranth recognized her as one of the chef mates in the kitchen. She was a pretty woman with reddish blond hair and rosy cheeks, a contract worker who got along well with everyone.

What was her name?

The second woman squirmed under the light as Maranth had done. Emma offered her the same platitudes. "Take it easy, now. Just open your eyes."

The third cot on the other side was empty. Maranth tied the thin sheet around her body and looked around the room. It had no discernible door or windows. In addition to the cots, there were several low-slung, rather eclectic chairs facing two low tables against a large mirror. The walls were festooned with women's finery similar to that draped over the dresserbot.

Where are the others? And why do the raiders want to decorate us? A knot of fear spread across her mid-section.

When the other woman finally woke, she jumped up and backed against the wall in terror, the sheet clutched to her neck.

"Where I be? Aiee. What be this place?"

Emma gestured and vocalized as soothingly as possible while slowly edging toward the frightened woman.

"Oooh now, don't be frightened, Miss. I'm dresserbot Emma and I'm here to serve."

The woman jumped away and raised a fist as if to strike. Emma stopped in her tracks.

"You won't hit me, will you? I'm programmed to not hurt you. Honest. You can relax."

The woman dropped her fist and Emma rested one of her appendages on the woman's arm reassuringly. It seemed to calm her.

Maranth bowed. "I'm the meddoc, Maranth-sa-Veddi. Perhaps you remember me?"

The woman nodded. "I be known as Belamae, Belamae-Lamat-Nor."

"Again, I'm your dresserbot, Emma. I am programmed to help you ladies dress." Emma busied herself examining the various costumes she carried and held some of them up against Belamae.

"Are you also programmed to explain things?" Maranth asked.

"That too." Emma waved a scanty number made from a rich red fabric that shimmered blue. "This one, I think. Put it on and you'll look ravishing."

Emma scooted over to a peg on the wall and pulled down an elaborate silvery blond wig. "And more so with this. Don't you think so?"

Maranth tapped Emma on her visual scanner. "Emma, where are we and where are our clothes?"

"Those awful rags? You'll thank me that I burned them when you were decontaminated and cleaned. Look at what you now have to choose from. Isn't this much better?"

Maranth ignored the clothes. "And my wrist comm?"

"You didn't have one when you arrived." Emma pirouetted, billowing the finery out all around. A curly wig flapped precariously. Belamae laughed.

"This here," the dresserbot pointed around the room, "is the finest women's attire. Nowhere. . . well nowhere in the outerworlds, is there a collection as fine as mine."

She tossed Belamae the selected costume and the wig.

Belamae dropped down on the bed with the items clutched on her lap. She fingered the red fabric speculatively.

"These sure be finer than any I seen, Addehut or anywhere."

She held up the skimpy costume and stretched it. "But there's not much to it."

In a soft, intense voice Maranth again addressed the dresserbot. "Where in the outerworlds are we?"

"Tigenne, Miss."

Belamae slumped over and began to quietly sob. Maranth turned Emma about and eyed her grimly. "Tell me. What about this place frightens her so?"

"I'll tell you what I know, if you two let me dress you. We don't have much time."

The dresserbot held out an intensely hued, skimpy red outfit with a heavy metallic belt. "Why don't you try on this Gambelli tunic and girdle?" She held it up against Maranth. "See, it would be lively against your skin and it's quite comfortable, too."

"So, you won't talk to me until we dress. And this is what we're expected to wear." Maranth dropped down on the bed next to Belamae and wrapped her arm comfortingly around her. "I'll try to speak to someone in a position of authority."

"I am only doing what I am programmed for, you understand. This really would look sensational on you, Miss. And the better you look the better it will go for you."

Belamae looked up through wet eyes and spoke in a bitter, resigned voice. "This be the slaver market of Tigenne and we be destined for the brothels."

Maranth had never heard the word. "What are brothels?"

"That be where the slavers sell us for sex." She anxiously turned to the dresserbot. "Where be the others we come with?"

Emma laid a sympathetic appendage on her arm. "You must be strong. Most in your group were men. They're in a separate market. The other three women in your group are there too."

"To wind up in the death games?"

"Some will. Some will be sold for special skills elsewhere. You are lucky to be here."

"Lucky? I heard about Tigenne's flesh houses."

The discussion left Maranth scandalized and appalled. Though she hadn't thought of it before, she could comprehend barbarians running slave brothels. There might be a profit from it among the uncivilized.

But death games?

"What possible reason could they have to deliberately kill people?"

Belamae answered quietly. "There's them that be paying to watch it and also them who gamble on the outcome."

The Veddian meddoc was flabbergasted into silence.

Emma dropped the clothing picked for Maranth onto her lap. "Do try it on."

Then Emma gently poked Belamae. "You too, Miss. Just step into it."

Belamae listlessly obeyed.

"Good. Better the bordellos than the gladiator sports. Besides, if you show well, you might just be bought by one of the nice private houses." She whipped one of her appendages around Belamae and fastened the garment in the back.

"There. With a little luck, you will have fine clothes and a life of ease, except for a bit of effort on your back now and then. Most humans would find such work pleasurable."

Emma took one of Belamae's roughened hands and held it up. "The life I speak of is certainly easier than the one you've known."

Maranth angrily stood up. "You're only telling her what you're programmed to say. If such a life were so desirable then women would be here by choice, not as slaves."

Belamae hung her head. "I heard there were some private pleasure houses."

A compartment in Emma opened, revealing an ample collection of cosmetics. Each was actually the tip end of a thin tentacle that Emma extended out to make over Belamae's face, emphasizing her eyes and giving her a glamorous look.

Meanwhile, the dresserbot's scanner swung around toward Maranth.

"You too, Miss. Please try on that tunic. My programming is infallible for choosing what will make the most of any woman's looks."

"Your programming is designed to serve this house, not us. No doubt they figure we'll bring higher prices decked out in this... this finery."

Maranth regretted her failure to comprehend the despair the other captives had felt. Now she finally understood. What seemed inexplicable in the dark hold of the raider ship was clear. It was also clear that, as well educated and intelligent as she was, she had just not been prepared to think like a savage. No doubt this was also why her briefing had been incomplete. No one on Veddi would have believed such things still happened.

She made her way to the clothing festooning the walls. "Since it seems practical to dress, I will. But I'll choose my own clothes."

Emma waved an appendage. "As you like. It's your fate."

Belamae joined Maranth and spoke quietly in her ear. "They be selling us anyway. Why not try for the best you might do?"

The chef mate sadly surveyed herself in the mirror. "Winshoe laborers like me never have much choice in life. So we have to shift for what little we get in all the hard diggin' fract dumps like Addehut."

She pulled Maranth around to face her. "Now you, bein' a Veddian meddoc, well, you had more and expect more. But now we both be in the same rough place, meddoc. You hear me?"

Maranth remained impassive so Belamae shook her gently. "They hold all the credits, weapons, and there be no law here for us. Else you be bendin' to survive, they be breakin' you or killin' you quick."

"Please understand. I won't make it easier for them." Maranth squeezed the other woman's hand and smiled grimly.

"What they do here is barbaric and immoral. If I cooperate, then this evil is stronger by my effort."

She began to pick clothes off the wall and dress as Belamae watched her in silence.

Maranth managed to find enough types of clothing to outfit herself in silver, green and purple modesty. Of course nothing she put on matched, so the effect was somewhat absurd.

Belamae giggled at the result. "Those Veddian principals, they'll be the ad-fricken death of you."

"Aye." Maranth smiled. Then she began to study the walls and ceiling very carefully. "I imagine some of the others who'd passed through here might have objected quite violently to this slavery. Emma?"

"Aye. Quite often I have required major repairs after being attacked. And the destruction." Emma waved her tentacles despairingly.

"Emma could certainly have dressed us when we were unconscious. And that would have avoided any damage to this dresserbot and all this expensive finery." Maranth's attention focused on the large mirror.

"So why do they risk us awake, without restraints, while they prepare us for sale? It wouldn't seem to be good economics. No, they wanted us awake for a purpose."

Belamae understood. "Maybe so they can watch us naked and see how we behave, without us knowin'."

"Aye."

Maranth picked up a cream jar and threw it into the mirror. It went through, breaking out some of the plastiglass. Behind, several men, including one of the orange-robed pirates, laughed outrageously as they picked the shards out of their clothes.

FIVE

RAVINE, PLANET AFTHAR

THROUGH THE KIN'S eyes, the trader had pieced together a visual map of his ravine. It was really a jagged canyon of blue-green cutting through the barren plateau, one of many such rifts that split the dusty high ground. The rocky outcroppings were ribs of tan stone that had fallen from the plateau walls. His cave was in one of these rock falls. Various Kin trails crisscrossed through the gorge. Where it bottomed out, several clear streams meandered along, forming still pools in the low spots. His instinct to climb down for water had been sound.

With this knowledge, he found it easier to get around. Although the Kin could have followed him inside his cave, they never did. He realized they could not endure being out of contact with one other. After experiencing the comfort, rapture and intelligence of that contact, he understood.

Yet even if his thoughts were under control, the flyers would betray him with their sharp eyes. So he learned to keep to the coolest spots, the places shaded by vegetation from the sun, and thus hidden from their sharp eyes overhead.

Outside his cave, the continuous mental effort was more draining than anything he had undertaken in the past. After each foray in the jungle he was exhausted and needed to sleep. Perhaps the alien bombardment somehow threatened his mind, which needed repair as well as rest. He couldn't be sure. Slowly he was rewarded, bit-by-bit, with some of the Kin's knowledge of their domain.

By reading the Kin while they hunted, he began to learn about the plants and the animals in the area. The Kin liked to eat brasiaas, a plated, low-to-the-ground grey creature. They would also hunt various kinds of yorbanaaa, dark insect-like animals that were plentiful in the undergrowth. The furry mottled-brown malaaas were a special treat. The Kin regarded them with almost spiritual reverence.

Neither they, nor their flyers, ate any of the vegetation, although the Kin spent a lot of time carefully cultivating and studying the native plant life for its ecological and medicinal value. Much of their communication was processing and sharing this environmental knowledge.

The trader quickly understood that they viewed their jungle as some sort of preserve with themselves as its caretakers. When they cultivated, they planted only a few plants in a spot to correct some perceived imbalance. They spent much of their time and intellectual energy in such pursuits.

They used their shared intelligence almost like a computer, storing and assembling the myriad details of their individual domains, available to all as needed.

I am only a tasty morsel in their garden, something that doesn't belong, something to be rooted out.

Their frequent, lofty songs were the only things that inspired him to stay alive. Though he could not hear them, these songs were vocal as well as mental. He could hear their song in his mind, as easily as he saw through their eyes. One or a few of the multitude would begin and others would join in until the entire Kin harmonized as one. The chorus would rise and fall, each time with different variations that would build for some time. Then it would abruptly recede and die away.

And when it was over, the maimed trader always sensed loss. For the songs moved him, took him over and expressed the profoundest truths. Yet if he ever had to explain what he had experienced, he would be unable to do so, as it was beyond his ability.

In time, he gained more experience outside the cave and began to discern the mental patterns of other life forms as well. All of these were unintelligent and disordered. He practiced trying to detect and identify various creatures by their patterns just as the Kin were able to.

By necessity, he practiced first on the cave worms. He had gotten over his repulsion of them and they kept him alive. At least he had no sense of taste to offend. When he began to have some consistent success finding the worms, he tackled the numerous, small bug-like creatures that populated the undergrowth around the mouth of his cave.

He would open his mind to the mental scrawls of instinct they gave off. When he got good at finding them, he tried to neutralize them by overwhelming their puny patterns with his own. Then they would remain still and he could catch them.

He ate these as well, crunching them up so he could pour them into his mouth hole. But he needed a lot more of these to equal one cave worm, which were fast disappearing because of his predations.

Time to tackle some real game.

It was risky. He had only managed full mental control for relatively short times. But if he didn't find something larger, he would starve.

He carefully willed his mind under control and left the cave. He searched through the babble of Kin chatter for the telltale mental activity of any prey animals.

At first he detected nothing and moved up the hill. At the top he detected the activity of an animal, and it was nearby. He focused on the creature.

Don't move. Stay...

He began to push through the overgrowth.

That's it. Stay where you are. Stay...

That thought repeating in his head, he moved in. As he drew closer, the creature remained frozen in place, mesmerized. The man's hands hunted around for it. When he felt it he grabbed it without resistance. It was a plump spiked creature, a wasavaaa.

SUFUNAAA!

He jerked up at his name and his prey suddenly squirmed away, squawking and squealing.

SUFUNAAA, BE STILL. THIS TIME I WILL HAVE YOU.

Terror gripped him. Bantaaa was closing in!

Quiet mind. Don't think…

He fumbled, then bumped and clawed through the brush. He started slipping down the hill when he sensed her breaking through vegetation nearby.

BE STILL. I'M COMING FOR YOU.

Caught for a moment by her command, he tripped over a vine and sprawled across a fallen log.

Aghhh! No. Quiet mind…

Bantaaa screamed in his head and, before he could get back to his feet, she was on him.

BE STILL!

Her command cut through his brain as he tried to scoot away but she sunk her teeth into his leg. He struggled in a haze of pain but could not break her grip. His flesh tore terribly.

WHY DOES THIS SUFUNAAA RUN WHEN I'VE COMMANDED ITS MIND?

Her confusion ate through his animal fear. He fought to regain focus.

I have my own mind. Let me go.

Surprised by his unexpected answer, she broke her hold.

I IMAGINED THAT. THESE ALIENS CANNOT COMMUNICATE.

He squirmed away but she quickly recovered and grabbed him again.

NOW, TO EAT.

Agony tore through him as she pinned him down with her claws and ground her teeth into his leg. He could feel her sucking out his blood. He fought to stay conscious and probe into her mind.

Aghhh! Kill me and you'll still want my blood later. So let me recover. Then you can drink from me again and again.

She lifted her bloody jaws. He tried to pull away but she had pinned him in place with one of her powerful back legs. Doubt filled her.

THIS SUFUNAAA BARGAINS WITH ME? IMPOSSIBLE.

Aye. The unborn you carry will be stronger if you let me live.

His thoughts pierced her confusion and she realized he knew she carried unborn young. She could no longer deny he had intelligently communicated with her. The trader felt her purpose dissolve into uncertainty and worry.

I MUST COMMUNE WITH THE KIN. GO, SUFUNAAA.

He crawled off, dragging his badly mangled leg. Though in fiery misery from the slightest movement, he sensed Bantaaa joining the distant mental murmur of her kind.

He tore off some of his pants' fabric and fashioned a crude tourniquet. He tried to cushion his damaged leg as much as possible as he made his way down, but every movement sent more searing pain shooting through his body.

The bone must be broken.

When he reached his cave he tried to ease his way in headfirst. By the time he was all the way inside the agonizing pain and loss of blood left him woozy. He gently pulled his leg around as best he could and passed out.

It wasn't until sunlight again returned to the cave that he awoke. The pain reminded him of his ordeal, but it had lost most of its intensity.

His fingers found and removed the tourniquet. He gingerly probed his wounds to gain some sense of the damage. But the gashes were almost closed and seemed to improve even as his fingers touched the now smooth skin, not scab. And when he tried to move his leg, it moved comfortably, with little pain.

Impossible. It's almost healed in just hours. How can this be?

SIX

AFTHARI RAIDER COLONY

MARANTH COULD BARELY walk after being drugged again. The last thing she remembered was breaking the mirror and men laughing. A workbot pulled her into a room.

She quickly found herself pressed against the wall in terror, a knife at her throat. The blade was held by an intense, pinched man wearing brown drab, with a lot of metal buckles and a bronze collar around his sweaty neck.

"A good bit of fortune that we get this one. But why is she here? The Afthari do their whoring in Tigenne or Ramos."

Her tormentor's close-set eyes never left her skin as he conversed with his huge compatriot lounging on the nearby sofa. The second man was obviously Yurblun, a descendant of the bluish, genetically enhanced clones who settled that world. The exotic Yurblun hardly paid any attention as he slowly ate a soft fruit.

"Oobviously she's here because Saad Obbad didn't sell heer." His deep voice slowly shaped the elongated vowels peculiar to his people. With each word his belly bobbed in rhythm. He, too, wore brown drab robes and a bronze collar, but no buckles.

The thin man fondled some of Maranth's eclectic clothes. "She dresses strange. Maybe she's Oronian. I hear they like it rough, the Oronian women."

"Why didn't Obbad sell heer? 'Da raiders neever bring women back to Afthar. 'Dey're own women forbid it."

The wide sofa straining under the Yurblun's weight was the only piece of furniture in the small blue room, whose most distinguished feature was the metallic orange ceiling, curved and ribbed as it arched high to one side, as if the it were a section of a larger dome.

Maranth felt her tormentor press himself against her and slowly rub up and down, relishing the play of the knife tip along her side against her clothes and skin. He brought the blade up to her nose and she was breathing the backwash of his stale breath.

Panic-stricken, Maranth tried to shrink back, but there was nowhere to go. She had not thought about death when the raiders hunted her down. Now she sensed it from this madman.

He let the knife slip down her cheek to her straining neck. "Ah. Saad Obbad must have given us this little morsel here for our faithful service. You can take your turn with her later."

Just then a commanding raider strode into the room, flapping orange robes, and threw off his helmet, its scarf trailing behind, along the floor. "There will be no turns. Let her be."

Her persecutor jumped back and the Yurblun struggled to his feet. Both assumed a servile air as they faced the irritated man that Maranth soon learned was Saad Obbad. Thick and mature looking, he wore very large and ornate earrings.

He crossed his arms with imperious amusement. "So, I provide my slaves a slave of their own, yah? For good service?"

Obbad's broad face hardened. He strode over to the pinched-faced man who averted his eyes.

"Slave Gannet, you assume something like that again and I'll throw you to the drogans myself."

Frightened, Gannet shifted from one foot to the other. Obbad then turned his attention to Maranth, who was trying to regain her composure. He eyed her mismatched finery and stifled a smile. Maranth realized he was one of the faces behind the shattered mirror.

"Number Three, bring in the medibot."

Outside the doorway, a large black workbot wordlessly carried Doc into the room. Except for a slight vibration in his blue skin, Doc was devoid of other signs of life. Some of his components and bio-relays were missing. Maranth tried to examine him but Gannet pushed her aside and excitedly began to inspect the medibot himself.

"Yaow, a J6 medibot. Veddian, too. Haven't seen one of these since Troos."

Obbad poked him. "And you fix it good for our new meddoc here, by morning. Yah?"

Gannet seemed surprised at the mention of Maranth's station. "I'll fix it up like new, Saad Obbad."

Obbad turned back to Maranth. "What is your name?"

At least he doesn't hold a knife at my throat.

Maranth bowed in the Veddian manner. "I am Maranth, Maranth-sa-Veddi-Dimore. And you are Saad Obbad?"

Obbad ignored her question and turned back to Gannet. "You fix it for Slave Maranth, yah?"

Gannet servilely nodded.

"Now get out of my sight."

Gannet again nodded and dragged Doc out.

Obbad turned next to the Yurblun, who was standing back, as still as possible.

"Slave Jobbar, prepare one of the store rooms for her use and get her some proper clothes."

Jobbar bowed.

"You see that she fits in, yah?"

"As you wish, Saad Obbad." Jobbar waited still as stone, his face set like a mask. But Maranth noted something in the Yurblun's eyes that indicated he was going to be more careful with her now.

Obbad focused on Maranth. "For your looks alone I'd have gotten a good price for you." He fondled a bit of her blouse in a familiar way.

Maranth stiffened. *How far does he intend to go?*

"But a meddoc, a Veddian one, yah? You'd bring five times more. Yet I give up this great profit for a greater honor, the honor of bringing Afthar its first meddoc."

Obbad took her hands and rubbed them between his own and grinned proudly to himself.

"Now my House of Obbad is second only to that of Zedd himself."

Maranth softly took his hands into her own and implored him, "How can my slavery bring you honor? Can honor come from the pain and anguish you've caused me and other humans?"

His impassive mask returned. "So, you think you can talk me out of my prize?"

He squeezed her hands painfully hard. Maranth was forced to her knees but did not utter a sound. She would not give this barbarian the satisfaction.

"Remember, Slave Maranth, we Afthari can live, as we've always done, without a meddoc." He pulled her up and held her close in a half sexual, half-threatening way.

Maranth could feel his hot breath in her nose but was too frightened to turn away.

He shook her. "You cooperate, yah? Or you will be put outside."

He ran his hand along her body. "Yah. The drogans would find you a juicy bit of meat."

Obbad cuffed her to the floor and abruptly strode out. When he was gone Jobbar offered her a hand and pulled her to her feet.

"He can be naasty if you question whaat he does."

His voice was friendly and Maranth was surprised, as he was indifferent when the other slave attacked her. She felt the warm spot on her cheek where Obbad had hit her and realized she was tired, afraid, repulsed and most of all, angry.

I've allowed these mental defectives to drive me into psychic imbalance.

46

She closed her eyes a moment to let the anger dissipate before she spoke.

"So it seems. What are drogans?"

"Drogans? 'Dey are laarge, smart creatures with a raavenous appetite for human flesh. You do not waant to meet one."

"They don't sound any more dangerous than that sadopath who just had a knife at my throat."

Jobbar let himself smile and a slight rumble of humor rippled across his ample belly.

"'Dat is funny, meddoc. Coome."

He took her arm and led her through a large, clear-walled circular room with a six-sided, golden dome roof. An abundance of furnishings from all corners of the inhabited galaxy filled the space.

There was an elaborately inlaid Ebanite sitting couch in glass, black enamel and white fur with a pair of graceful Baredian gold filigree tables. A number of iridescent silklin rugs overlapped one another across the floor in colorful abandon. There were other, very plush white loungers across the room that Maranth couldn't identify. Sculptures, wall hangings and curiosities, including the freeze-dried remains of a Jobin harewolf (poised to attack) completed the decorations.

Aesthetically, such furnishings should have been offensive to Maranth's Veddian sensibilities. Veddians strove to achieve interior function with tasteful, graceful lines, harmonious, muted colors and minimalist structures. This was the heart of the distinctive and renowned Veddian style whose influence had spread through the outerworlds, though many places like Addehut were too rough and poor to aspire to any style at all.

But Maranth could see there was an artistic order to the layout. Dissimilar items were grouped by color, line and scale. Except for the harewolf, she was surprised that the effect, though a bit unsettling, was not unattractive.

Jobbar lead her through an arched corridor into a lush hanging garden. She stopped and a pleasing fragrance from the white flowers enveloped her as she reveled in the muted sunshine. But Jobbar proceeded on to a passage on the other side, rolling along like a great ocean-going ship. Maranth sighed and hurried after him. Halfway down the hall he stopped and a door slid open. He pressed his wrist comm to summon a workbot.

Maranth followed Jobbar into the room, labeled 'Storeroom Four,' and looked around. A few of the dusty crates were open, displaying preserved food, workbot parts and rolls of fabric in the bare plasticrete space.

"'Dis will be youur room, meddoc."

She eyed the preserved head and claws of a Buradian lizardcat hanging on the far wall.

Another dead animal. Disgusting.

"You can't tell me that some slave here hasn't stolen a weapon and taken his chances with the drogans?"

Jobbar chuckled, then intently pulled her a little closer to foil any prying eyes and ears.

"Weapons are useless. I've been heere twelve standard years. Sometimes a damaged raaider ship crashes outside. A ship of armed, traained Afthari fighters. And even when 'da rescuue ship is quick, 'da men are dead and part eaten. Alwaays. And if 'da rescuue party takes too long, 'da rescuuers are eaten, too."

A black workbot arrived and Jobbar waved it toward the crates. "Remoove 'dese provisions and put 'dem in Storeroom Six."

"And please remove that dead animal from the wall." Maranth pointed to the lizardcat trophy.

The workbot dipped an appendage in acknowledgement and set to work.

Jobbar returned when the sky was dark. The workbot removed the last load and brought back a sleeping cot.

Jobbar nodded to Maranth. "You reest now. I will return tomorrow."

He started down the pale orange hall with the workbot. Maranth called out after him, "Where's the hygienic facilities?"

Jobbar pointed to a nearby door. "Eliminaation facilities 'dere. You will have wash powdeers and fresh clothes in 'da morning."

She closed the door and sat on the small cot in the now empty storeroom. The impulse to panic welled up.

I must retain balance.

She crossed her legs, straightened her back and began a healing trance.

The next morning she woke up to the sound of one of the black workbots shuffling through her room. It ignored her and deposited a bundle by her cot. Then it scurried away.

She peered over to see what it had brought. No doubt the neatly folded brown fabric and bronze collar was to be worn. Along with a hairbrush were also several generic wash powders in plain white household containers. She examined the powders and tried to figure which one was for what purpose. Apparently Obbad had bought or stole these in bulk lots.

Wash powders were one of the early fruits of basic research in cellular function and genetics centuries earlier. Cultures of bacteria and microphages that cleaned human skin, hair and teeth were genetically engineered, cloned and sold in freeze-dried, powdered form. The user's own body moisture revived the live cultures to consume dead skin, harmful bacteria, body secretions, dirt and anything else that didn't belong. The cleansing effect was continuous, but the powders for different parts of the body needed to be reapplied every so often to freshen the culture.

Since the hygienic practice in ancient times had been to wash with water and fatty compounds, people called the powders 'wash powders' instead of the more appropriate 'cleansing' or 'hygienic' powders.

But her sidestep into history still gave no clue as to which powder was which. She decided to wait until Doc could scan the vials.

No sense mixing them up.

Before she finished dressing in the new clothes the workbot

returned with some unfamiliar, though spicy smelling food. Maranth hungrily devoured it and felt better.

Soon she was trailing through the compound behind Jobbar with his slow-rolling gait. This time he led her through another hall with arched skylights.

Maranth hoped they wouldn't run into that other slave, Gannet. She moved closer to Jobbar.

"Why do the Afthari want slaves? Cheap, docile workbots do everything these days."

"Slaaves mean status. Why settle for imitaation when you can afford 'da real thing?"

SEVEN

AFTHARI RAIDER COLONY

JOBBAR STOPPED AND Maranth nearly ran into him. He motioned for her to wait near a closed door. When it slid open, Maranth could hear sounds of mock battle inside, along with a woman's voice.

"Like that… Yah!"

There was a pause and then the voice added, "Enter."

The blue room was eclectically decorated much like the large room Maranth had passed through the day before. In the middle, a woman with piles of dark red hair lounged on a silver couch, smoking from a large baroque water pipe. Part of her voluminous mauve robes draped over the back of the sofa. Children's' toys littered the floor. The silvered, arched ceiling soared to meet a large skylight on one side.

"Saad Fromar." Jobbar bowed.

Maranth guessed she was Obbad's wife.

The woman's attention, however, was on her young, curly-haired son, who was intently working the controls to a holographic space battle game from a small box on his lap. Between him and the newcomers danced the holo images of brightly colored spacecraft dodging and firing weapons at one another. The battle was noisy and, at times, its holo smoke mixed in with the real smoke from Fromar's pipe. Maranth recalled that there was no sound in space. Perhaps the noise was added for the amusement of children.

Behind a small mauve couch near the wall, a lavender workbot was overseeing a chubby toddler playing with a furry green, biotic toy. Both children had the same dark eyes of their mother.

With a last blast of excitement, the boy's game died away. He squealed victoriously and Fromar gave the boy, no older than seven, a loving hug. "Vazeen, you are so clever."

Maranth saddened. Of course they are barbarians. They are raised to it.

Fromar reset the control box. "Now we start a new one, yah?"

The boy took the controls while Fromar coolly appraised Maranth. "I understand Veddian women are chaste until marriage, and then are always faithful?"

Maranth was surprised by the question.

"Aye. Sexual discipline is necessary in an ordered civilization. We Veddians…"

"…Yah. But do YOU hold to such chastity beliefs?"

She thought the question rude but answered. "Certainly."

"Good. Then we will get along. So you tell me if anyone takes sexual advantage — and I mean ANYONE, yah? I will not have it in my house."

Maranth didn't know what to think. Would Fromar really protect her against the sexual predations of her husband, Obbad, or another slave like Gannet? Or would the mistress of the house kill her if anything happened?

What am I thinking?

Fromar took another puff and her mood softened.

"Of course our Afthar, even being so far away in the outerworlds, can't match the cultural aspects of innerworlds like Veddi. But we are every bit as civilized, yah."

Maranth was flabbergasted at the assertion.

Fromar just rattled on. "Our children are brought up with a strong sense of honor, respect and virtue."

You mean pretense, ruthlessness and brutality.

Maranth struggled to conceal her feelings. She was perplexed that Jobbar remained calm and remote.

Fromar smiled. "That's more than some of the innerworlds can claim, I can tell you."

Fortunately for Maranth, a childish shriek drew the woman's attention. Her toddler was joyously banging the furry 'bot on the floor, its little antennae waved erratically. The lavender workbot shot one of her appendages in front of the baby's nose and waggled its tip.

"Now, now. You must play nicely with your toys."

The baby glanced up and dropped the toy uncertainly. It just up-righted itself and began to coo and sing, hopping up and down on its little feet to please the child. The youngster, again, happily grabbed it.

Vazeen impatiently tugged on Fromar's robe. She gave him the control box. "Now Vazeen, this time you set it yourself."

"Yaaah!"

When Vazeen was again happily absorbed in the game, she turned her attention once more to Maranth and studied her through the battle images dancing between them. Fromar turned down the sound.

"Slave Maranth, since you are the only meddoc on Afthar, you are responsible not only for the health of everyone in this house, the House of Obbad, but everyone else in the colony. So remember, you bring us nothing but honor or you will be put outside."

Along with Fromar's threat was a hint of respect. Maranth realized being a meddoc meant something, even here.

Fromar took another puff on her pipe and her gaze shifted to Jobbar.

"Slave Jobbar, is she adjusting?"

He nodded servilely. "She is adjuusting, Saad Fromar."

"Good. Now go." She waved them off and returned to her pipe and game.

When Jobbar and Maranth reached the far end of the hall, Maranth tapped Jobbar's arm. He patiently turned to her.

"Does any of this ever bother you?"

A tiny smile broke his face. "A slaave's best asset is being inviisible. 'Dat is what I do."

He headed on and Maranth trailed after him, wondering how this enormous man imagined himself invisible.

She followed the lumbering giant across a narrow courtyard to a small circular structure with a wide, open doorway. She caught sight of Gannet and tried to bolt but Jobbar grabbed her arm and pulled her in.

Gannet did not even look up, as he was watching Fromar undress on his repairbot's view screen. He made no effort to hide what he was up to and ignored them as they stepped inside.

"You risk muuch for so little," Jobbar sighed, then snapped at Gannet's repairbot, "Screen off."

Its screen promptly blanked out. Gannet chuckled and stretched his skinny frame. "Risk nothing, get nothing."

Maranth's fear dissipated in a puff of realization. This crack-brained twerp's peeping meant she now had leverage over him.

Assorted workbot parts, tools and diagnostic equipment hung high on the walls and covered the worktable in a jumble. Several bins of the stuff crowded the floor. There was hardly any room to move around.

Maranth found Doc crammed up against a wall, under a shelf. He looked clean and whole, but still non-animate except for breathing.

She knew the breathing was a good sign. His organics worked much like a super-efficient plant leaf, using light and carbon dioxide to make its own food. Like a plant, Doc inhaled carbon dioxide and exhaled oxygen. 'Bots and buildings everywhere in the inhabited cosmos used similar organics to create both oxygen and their own energy.

No doubt Doc will need more work, considering his unbalanced repairman.

"Doc, self test," she commanded. Various compartments

in his side opened and closed with a slight thrum. He silently moved out from his confined space and his assorted sensory stalks and appendages stretched and moved about. Maranth was relieved to see Doc come alive.

"I have full function, thanks doll."

"Doll?"

Gannet sidled close to Maranth, his eyes on her breasts. He smirked, "I do good work."

Maranth backed away in disgust. "Did you modify any of Doc's programming?"

But before he could respond, she whirled back to the medibot. "Did he change your programming?"

"Not that I'm aware of. Nice seeing you again, Maranth-sa-Veddi-Dimore." Doc dipped a telescoping siphon in greeting with a slight woosh. She bowed back uncertainly.

She turned to Gannet. "I must have a wrist comm to communicate and read data from my medibot."

Gannet smirked. "I'll have one ready for you by evening."

Jobbar harumphed. "Since no one from 'dis House needs you, Maranth, you will treaat the beggars today. Come."

"Beggars?" The too familiar feeling of dread laced with fear returned. Since the raid on Addehut, every time she seemed to face the worst, there was some new brutality. For a brief moment she watched herself wallow in anxiety, as if she were outside herself, dispassionately observing someone else.

Indulging fear is nonproductive.

She shrugged the feeling off and grimaced. "Slaves and beggars. Of course."

And she could not help feel there were more barbarities yet to come. Resigned, she followed Jobbar out, but at least Doc was at her side now.

As they passed through the house, Fromar's lavender workbot sidled up to Doc and dipped an antenna. "You must be the new medibot. Greetings. I'll happily orient you, if you like."

Doc stopped and politely dipped his antenna back in greeting. "Aye, and thanks. You are?"

"A WZA 240-M housebot. Call me Wiza." She slipped an

appendage into Doc's receptor port and it secured with a slight click. She began to transmit.

Maranth fought the impulse to object. Since the housebot transmitted via line, it must be too primitive to broadcast without affecting other workbots in the area. No doubt it was an earlier vintage and was not capable of overwriting any of Doc's core algorithms. But clearly Doc's personality matrix had been tampered with.

What else?

She followed Jobbar through the impressive entry arch, an iridescent mating of spirals in elastifoam and permaplast. When Doc did not quickly follow she stopped and turned back. "Doc."

"Gorgeous, I've got to motor now."

Wiza understood and retracted her appendage. "Then modem me this evening, after 1800. We can share more data."

"Love to. Tonight." Doc called back as he hurried to catch up to the humans.

He trailed Maranth as she stepped out from the arch into a narrow, unpaved lane that wound between other residential compounds, most of which were smaller than the House of Obbad. These stood shoulder to shoulder, topped by soaring, ribbed domes and arched skylights in various hues of orange, gold and blue. The muted, violet-blue sky was nearly cloudless.

The Afthari certainly weren't poor like the Hut miners. She found the jumbled architecture, like the house furnishings, unnervingly eclectic. And again, the effect was surprisingly agreeable.

Maranth's confidence revived and she considered the possibility of escape. The planet was hospitable enough that the Afthari built their dwellings above ground, open to natural atmosphere and weather. Maranth took a deep breath. Perhaps this openness would work in her favor. But she realized she didn't know enough about the colony to seriously plan an escape just yet.

When Doc caught up she whispered, "Stop."

He obligingly halted. Maranth bent down and began to

fiddle with one of his openings. As Jobbar had continued on his way he did not notice. Doc expanded his auditory aperture and whispered back, "Is this a ruse?"

"Aye. We must escape this maladapted, barbaric sinkhole. So, find out everything you can about this place. Check out their spaceport security if possible. Look for any weaknesses we can use."

Doc shook his antennae. "They'll have detection systems. I'm just not built for that sort of thing."

Out of the corner of her eye Maranth saw Jobbar hesitate before he rounded a turn and look back for her.

He patiently called back, "Slave Maranth. Is 'dere a problem?"

Maranth looked up. "Just a moment to fix this."

She turned back, speaking under her breath as she pretended to examine Doc's innards.

"Any Veddian medibot working with an intelligent, civilized person such as myself can outwit savages. Just take your time and be very careful. And let no one notice you."

"Well, Wiza just related something that..."

Maranth grabbed one of his antennas and, her voice barely audible, whispered. "Later."

Jobbar impatiently broke in. "Maranth?"

Maranth winked at Doc and looked up with an obedient smile. "Coming."

They had gone only a short distance when several laughing children in short, colorful tunics and leggings darted in from another path that emerged between two compounds on their right.

A harried pink housebot, much like Wiza, chased after them, calling out. "No! Very naughty. No, no, no."

It grabbed for the round-faced blonde girl, who easily dodged out of reach and danced ahead, giggling. The two boys circled behind Jobbar, using him as a shield.

There was a sudden buzzing in the sky. The children immediately ran into a narrow passage and cowered under an overhang. The frazzled housebot joined them.

The sky seemed ever more muted, almost electrical. As the sound increased, a growing dark mass hurtled down toward them.

Jobbar remained rooted in place. But he shut his eyes and involuntarily stiffened as the object approached. Maranth pushed up against a recessed doorway. Doc didn't know what to do so he circled, antennae askew, then finally pinned himself against Jobbar.

A blackened remnant dropped through in a shower of sparks and cinders, landing near Jobbar with a 'thunk' and a puff of dust. He composed himself and resumed his rocking gait as if nothing had happened.

A shaky Maranth caught up. "You must get these meteors often to need a full-dome force field."

"'Dat was no meteor." He turned to her with a sardonic smile.

"'Da drogans sent one of 'dere birdies to test the field. 'Dey drop down and fry. If ever a birdie lives, 'den 'da drogans know 'da field faailed. 'Den 'dey will come and eat us all."

The children ambled out of hiding and gathered around the blackened remains. The older black-haired boy, with thin legs and a hard expression, poked it with a stick. The two others joined in, poking and worrying the charcoal feathers and flesh that smelt like burnt dinner.

Doc approached the corpse. He turned an antenna toward Maranth. "Should I get a tissue sample and structural assay?"

"Aye. And check for parasites."

The children raggedly gave way as Doc pushed through them to the blackened mess. He buried a thin probe through the charcoal and retreated with a small hunk of uncooked flesh. Then he irradiated the mass with various intensities and colors of light.

Maranth wondered why Jobbar believed the drogan creatures controlled these birds. Perhaps the raiders had made this up to frighten the slaves. But then Jobbar had related that the drogans always defeated armed humans outside the force field. Could any animal really be so formidable?

EIGHT

RAVINE, PLANET AFTHAR

A FLYER CIRCLED LAZILY overhead in the last light of day. It called out once with a rasping cry, then glided into a nearby gorge. The deep blue-greens of the vegetation had turned violet with streaks of gold in the last rays of daylight. Afthar's two small moons, the one nearer the horizon twice the size of the other, ushered in the night sky.

Bantaaa shook her feathers. She thought she caught a wisp of the Sufunaaa's thoughts. But then it was gone. This worried her. In fact, everything about this alien worried her. She settled herself near her mate, Hosaaa, and began to preen with her teeth and claws, straightening and ordering her plumage.

She noticed he grew restless from her mood. She had been distressed ever since the sufunaaa had appeared in their gorge. Now nothing was as it should be. Hosaaa would have finished the alien himself, but the offspring growing in her belly gave her the first right to its flesh. She, more than he, needed the special nutrients in the alien's blood. Because of the life she was nurturing, he would not nip at her for disturbing his rest. Instead, she felt him directing soothing thoughts to calm her.

YOUR FUSSING UNSETTLES THE SERENITY OF THE NIGHT. TRY TO THINK OF SOMETHING PLEASANT.

Bantaaa ignored him. Hosaaa just didn't want to understand. Of course, she wasn't sure she fathomed all of it herself. One thing she was certain. The alien in their ravine was intelligent. But how could he be intelligent while the others of his kind were not?

Hosaaa flicked his tail gently in her face. She turned her head away and caught sight of her nest sister, Vabaaa, stepping out from among the trees. Vabaaa ambled into their glade and stretched her neck and waggled her head in greeting. As the custom of the males of his kind, Hosaaa stood, spread his red neck feathers and cawed his acknowledgment. Then he slipped back down. The newcomer settled her feathers and dropped to the ground between the mated pair.

BANTAAA, YOU CLEVERLY MILK THE SUFUNAAA A LITTLE AT A TIME FOR HIS BLOOD. BUT TODAY YOU ARE AS THIRSTY AS THE REST OF US.

Bantaaa could not deny the truth of her communication.

HIS MIND IS NOW SO DISCIPLINED I CANNOT FIND HIM.

That was too much for her mate. He screamed out in annoyance and his jaws raked air.

IT'S YOUR MIND THAT'S GROWN WEAK.

He settled down in a sulk. *WHEN THE SUN RETURNS I WILL FINISH THIS SUFUNAAA MYSELF.*

Bantaaa nipped him.

SO, I'M WEAK? THIS ALIEN BARGAINED WITH ME! AND WHAT ABOUT THE SHIELDED HIVE HIS KIND BUILT ON THE PLATEAU?

Earlier in the day, the chanting Kin had fogged the mind of an old, dying flyer and sent it straight down into the alien hive to test it. As before, the flyer crackled and burned. The Kin mind could not penetrate their hive structure any more that it could pierce the ground under their feet.

Bantaaa felt calming thoughts emanate from Vabaaa as her nest sister preened. When the anger in the air subsided Vabaaa asserted her own view.

THE KIN EXAMINED THE ALIENS THOROUGHLY. THEIR HIVE AND THE PODS THEY SEND ZIPPING THROUGH THE SKY ARE THE RESULT OF HIGHLY EVOLVED SOCIAL INSTINCTS, NOTHING MORE.

Bantaaa took to her feet in a screeching rage.

I TELL YOU BOTH, THIS SUFUNAAA BARGAINS!

Again, Vabaaa struggled to emanate waves of calm. But her impulsive thoughts leaked through — that Hosaaa was right and Bantaaa too touchy. Vabaaa had always felt Bantaaa was the first to nip in anger when they were nestlings.

Now Vabaaa mulled whether the stress of carrying new life or something poisonous in the alien's blood had addled Bantaaa's brain. But Bantaaa broadcast a rebuke to her nest sister, pointing out that only hours ago Bantaaa joined voices with the Kin in harmony, and there was nothing wrong with her then. Vabaaa tried a different tack.

THE ALIENS ARE WEAK-MINDED AND CAN'T PROPERLY COMMUNICATE. YOU KNOW THAT. SO HOW CAN THIS ONE BARGAIN? AND EVEN IF HE POSSESSED SOME UNUSUAL INTELLIGENCE, HIS KIND BROUGHT THE PLAGUE THAT IS KILLING OUR MALAAAS. AS THEY DIE OFF, WE THIRST FOR THEIR BLOOD. YOU KNOW OUR THIRST GROWS WORSE ALL THE TIME. UNLESS WE GET SOME RED BLOOD FROM THE ALIENS, WE ARE AT RISK. ISN'T THIS SO?

Bantaaa and every one of the Kin knew this was true. When the first of Kin inhabited this world, back in the dawn of time, they brought the malaaas with them so they and their descendants would never starve. Even though the native life sated much of the Kin's hunger, it lacked a necessary nutrient only their non-native, red-blooded malaaas could provide.

Bantaaa felt Hosaaa's thoughts join with those of Vabaaa. *IS IT NOT JUST, THEN, THAT THESE RED-BLOODED ALIENS FULFILL OUR NEED NOW?*

Bantaaa acknowledged the logic of their argument.

CERTAINLY WE SHOULD DRINK FROM THEM TO LIVE.

Her head arched and her yellow eyes burned down ferociously on the other two.

BUT WHAT IF WE UNDERESTIMATE THEM?

Bantaaa knew the other two thought this unreasonable. But she was resolute. Whether the sufunaaa could truly bargain or not, she had witnessed him learning to control his mind. Of that she was sure. A feeling of trepidation passed through her. She shook her feathers and regained her resolve.

I FEEL THE NEED TO HUNT.

With a flick of her stiff tail she was gone.

PLATEAU, PLANET AFTHAR

The maimed trader, the void of his face in shadow, emerged from the lush gorge onto the dry plateau. A gusty breeze rippled his clothes and cooled his skin that was no longer warmed by the sun's rays. He had grown thin and weak and now he needed to rest from the effort of the climb. He rested until the soft murmur of the sleeping Kin filled his head. Now he did not need to control his thoughts.

When he'd marshaled his reserves he began to pick his way across the plain. He knew the going would be slow. The map that he had painstakingly gleaned from the mental images that he culled from the Kin and their flyers did not include the smaller features of the plateau. So he stumbled and tripped blindly over little boulders and depressions, and scratched himself in the thorns of the nomadic ochaaa plants.

He first learned about the ochaaa from a flyer when his mind soared with it over the plateau. At first he thought the plants nothing more than balls of nondescript, tan fluff, the remains of dead and dried shrubbery, drifting and rolling across the rocky ground. Some were nearly as big across as a man was tall. Then later, again through the flyer's eyes, he watched one of these seemingly dead plants drift over a shallow puddle.

The wisps of fluff that brushed the water suddenly swelled and weighed the ochaaa down, slowing it. More fluff was dragged into the water and swelled so that the now blue-grey plant became firmly anchored. Then the rest of it metamorphosed into a thorny, spike-leafed bush. The transformation was rapid and quite amazing. Some days later, when the water was gone, the plant shriveled back to dry brush and drifted away again.

The trader slowly made his way from one large rock formation to another. He felt and used these landmarks like steppingstones across the terrain.

It was almost dawn when he reached the colony's force field. As he drew close in, the hair on the back of his arms stood up and he could feel the vibration the field gave off.

SUFUNAAA, WHERE ARE YOU?

Fear coursed through his innards. He knew Bantaaa was somehow nearby, patiently waiting for him, her mind seeking the errant thoughts he gave off.

Mind, quiet. Empty of thought… Quiet. No thoughts.

But he knew Bantaaa had already felt his fear. She had jumped to her feet and was triumphantly racing to his position, though more slowly than usual due to her heavy belly.

The trader slipped behind a jumble of boulders, took a slow breath and willed himself still, his mind now focused on her thoughts, her mind.

He felt her nearby on the other side of the rock pile. She had sniffed his presence. Now she circled around, her mind keenly seeking any betrayal of his thoughts, her eyes and ears raking the terrain for him.

As the trader focused on her mental images of the terrain, he was able to fix her position relative to his own, and automatically shift out of her sight. Now it was her mental activity that betrayed her, rather than the other way around.

After a short time of fruitlessly pacing back and forth, she screeched and headed off across the plateau, away from the colony.

He was elated though exhausted. *Bantaaa, you cannot take me now. Go back to the Kin.*

His mind saw Bantaaa angrily turn and worry the air with a long cry. He could sense her belly slow her movements, even as it increased her need. Suddenly she stopped, ruffled her feathers and relaxed.

SUFUNAAA, YOU CAN ESCAPE TO THE ALIEN HIVE, BUT YOU WILL COME BACK TO ME.

A fluster of dread passed through the maimed trader. He could not help but let it escape to his enemy.

But she made no move. *IT IS SO, SUFUNAAA, YOU WILL COME BACK TO ME.*

His mind raced with the possibilities. *What does she mean? It must be a trick.*

Through her eyes he knew the Afthari sun had begun to lighten the horizon. Day was about to arrive and with it, the flyers, who would easily find him on the plateau. But Bantaaa did not care. She sent him an image of his blank face regenerating: eyes, nose and features restored as they once were.

At first the maimed trader was puzzled. When the realization of her message hit him he was stunned.

Bantaaa could feel the jolt and knew he understood.

SO, YOU WILL COME TO ME, SUFUNAAA, BECAUSE I AM THE ONLY ONE WHO CAN PROVIDE WHAT YOU MOST NEED.

NINE

AFTHARI RAIDER COLONY

LIKE EACH DAY in the last several, her patient load was light. The beggars' clinic took only a few Af-hours. Seeing to the medical needs of the other Afthari took about as much time.

Maranth sadly watched an elderly man, missing most of the fingers on his left hand, drop his dish into the garbage bin across the plaza. It incinerated in a soft puff. Then he wiped his hands on tattered robes and sauntered past several other beggars still in line for the lunch being provided by three cookbots: specialized workbots who functioned as food preparers and servers.

They were rather large for domestic units, wider than a man is tall. Well-insulated, manufactured compartments protected their biotics from the heat and cold of food preparation and storage. Though equipped with all the needed appliances and tools, their particular model was not known for its culinary inspiration. But the food they made was free, nutritional and plentiful. The beggars of Afthar never went hungry.

As was the custom, the cookbots worked their kitchen at the south end of the main plaza, an open park centrally accessible from the narrow, twisting pathways that threaded through the colony. Paved lightstone paths crisscrossed the plaza. Extensive plantings of low-growing vegetation broke up the open space into smaller areas for the Afthari to meet and pass the time.

When the last in line, a small one-armed fellow finished his lunch, the cookbots packed up and went dormant. The one-armed beggar meandered back to where Maranth and Doc were holding their clinic in the middle of the park.

Jobbar had related the Afthari believed in tossing a credit now and then to beggars for good luck. So these sad people, mostly old and infirm former raiders too poor to be self-sufficient, worked the square for spare credits and got by. A few in foreign garb were former slaves or mercenaries, now no longer useful.

The one-armed beggar moved past Doc and circled behind Maranth, who was examining a florid-faced beggar named Kojji, sitting on Doc's stretched out cot. Maranth was relaxed in her work. They'd encountered nothing but routine, minor complaints from their patients, including this one. Maranth consulted Doc's readouts. "Aye, already improved, I see."

She patted Kojji's shoulder and asked, "Feeling better?"

He happily looked up and nodded, then angrily motioned to the beggar behind her. Maranth turned to see the latecomer eyeing her backside. He looked up, mumbled, then ambled away.

Kojji beamed.

She chuckled. "Aye, you're better. But you'll need another treatment in a week."

He nodded and rose to his feet. "In grace, meddoc. Thanks."

Maranth acknowledged his politeness by bowing in the Veddian fashion. Kojji grinned and headed off.

Doc pointed a baleful antenna at the retreating Kojji. "That's the last one today."

Doc folded his examining cot back into his side and retracted his diagnostic appendages.

Maranth stretched. The day was only half over and they had nothing more to do.

The workday is short here. Except workday is the wrong word.

No Afthari did any work in the colony. That was left to workbots and the handful of especially skilled slaves such as herself. Raiding was the only 'work' any of them knew.

Her first regular patient had been an elderly man from the Umstrat House, which was one of the smaller compounds near the main square. A frantic workbot had fetched Maranth right after dinner her second day in the colony. But the man's case turned out to be simple. When Maranth was about to leave, Saad Umstrat dropped a few credits into her hand. Embarrassed, she had tried to give them back. But Umstrat reacted angrily and was not placated until she accepted with feigned grace.

The Afthari oppress their slaves yet give them money.

Doc assured her tipping was the Afthari custom, something he had learned from Fromar's lavender housebot. The Afthari tipped the slaves for services when the slave was not a member of their own household.

In one week she'd collected a small pile of credits. But there didn't seem to be much to trade for them, as there were no stores. At least she had a good deal of time to figure some way out of the mess they were in. In fact, it seemed this was a good day to work on it.

"Let's go for a walk."

Doc dipped an antenna in agreement.

They began to pick their way through a throng of beggars lounging off their lunch in the center of the plaza.

"You know, we've been enslaved nearly a standard week in this barbaric pit." Maranth tucked back a wisp of hair as she stepped over a sprawled leg.

"Actually, six days and four hours, standard time." Maranth smiled. No doubt Doc viewed it as his job to be more precise.

"Well, it seems longer."

A hairy-armed beggar tried to lift her robe. Maranth deftly swept her skirt from his hand without missing a step.

"And for them, too long. By the way, you made any progress on our private project?"

Doc drew very close so that his speech organ was practically in Maranth's ear.

"One item that the workbot Wiza told me: Afthari custom allows slaves to buy their freedom, if they get enough credits..."

Maranth broke in excitedly. "Just how much is enough?"

"Take it easy, doll. I already asked Wiza to find out."

Maranth sagged a little, but still it was the first real hope she'd had since that grim last day in Addehut. She flicked Doc's antenna happily.

A few steps beyond they crossed the paths of Fromar and another woman who Maranth knew as Rozia, the wife of Mier Zedd, head of all the Houses of Afthar. She was an attractive matron lavishly dressed in shimmery form fitting blue tunic and heavy golden jewelry, some of it on her thick dark hair. Maranth bowed as the two women chatted and continued by without acknowledging her greeting, their personal housebots trailing closely behind.

The panhandlers now sat up straight and begged with new vigor. The women obliged and dropped a credit or two into most of the outstretched palms and bowls.

A few paces beyond, Rozia snagged her hem on what appeared to be a pile of rags. The woman's color-coordinated blue housebot quickly scurried around to free the hem, shifting the rags a little, revealing the fabric was snagged on a flaccid hand.

"Beggar!" Rozia snapped. When there wasn't any response she turned to her housebot. "Wake him up."

Rozia indignantly surveyed the open square.

"Where are the enforcebots? There are laws against public sleeping."

The man's hand remained lifeless as the housebot freed Rozia's hem, then shook the rag-covered body. It stirred.

The housebot turned an inquiring antenna to Rozia. "It may be diseased."

With that, the two matrons shrank back and nearby beggars crowded in to see.

Maranth quickly pushed through the gathering crowd, Doc at her heels. The beggars respectfully gave way.

Her hands expertly turned the body and the rags fell back, revealing a man's arm, shoulder and blonde hair.

But what a face! Blank, smooth and pale except for holes where a nose and mouth would be. There was no hint of ears, eyes or eye sockets.

Maranth involuntarily shuddered with the others. Then the unfortunate reached up with his hand. Maranth didn't hesitate. She gently took the hand and then began to examine the poor wretch.

Fromar first noticed the Head of the Afthari across the crowd. She called to him and Mier Zedd strode up with two raiders, a teen-ager and several workbots in tow. He was a big man with a sour expression, and earrings even longer and heavier than those worn by Obbad.

The murmuring group quickly gave way as he strode into the crowd. His entourage closed in around him.

Rozia pushed through to his side.

"My husband, this alien with no face has appeared out of nowhere."

Fromar added, "There were no alarms, no warnings."

Rozia waved her off.

"He's in rags among the beggars. I practically tripped over him before anyone even noticed!"

Mier Zed eyed her skeptically. "Couldn't he be one of our beggars who'd been injured?"

Rozia grimaced. "He really has NO FACE."

The teenager awkward and lanky with the first hormones of puberty, wiggled through to see for himself. He gasped and fought to collect himself.

"He seems too tall and pale to be one of us." His voice cracked.

Maranth guessed the youth was Mier Zedd's son.

69

Mier Zedd looked down for himself. Maranth noted that only the tightened muscles of his jaw betrayed any reaction. No doubt he was just as disturbed by the alien's face as everyone else had been.

Mier Zedd said nothing. His eyes just swept back and forth over the gathering. Maranth guessed that, like most leaders, when he wasn't sure what to do he would buy time until he was forced to make a decision.

She was not surprised when his gaze finally came to rest on her, tending the man on the ground.

He barked, "You must be Obbad's new meddoc slave. He was smart to keep you."

Maranth knew she'd brought prestige to Obbad's House, maybe enough so he might rival his leader? Fear crept into her belly.

What am I thinking?

"Meddoc, everyone else says much but tells me little. So what can you add about this, this… alien?" The others fell silent. His heavy, ornate earrings swayed slightly as the colony's leader hard eyes assessed her.

She carefully weighed her words. "Except for his head he's a structurally normal human. Of course he's completely blind, deaf and mute. And he's weak from malnutrition and loss of blood."

"Will he live?"

"Aye, with proper care."

Zedd mulled over what she had told him. Only a thin bead of sweat on her forehead betrayed her disquiet. She prayed she had said the right thing. The fate of this man hung in the balance. Maybe her own did as well. Hopefully, the Afthari might let him live if he were seen as no threat. On the other hand, they might kill him to get rid of a useless nuisance. She fought down a rising panic. She just wasn't designed to think in such barbaric terms.

Obbad, along with two other Heads of Houses, broke through the throng to view the alien. News in the colony traveled fast.

Obbad quickly spoke next to show his status. "Perhaps this outsider comes from some alien race, a race that naturally have no faces?"

Fromar embellished the idea. "Yah. Maybe he's a scout with other alien senses we know nothing about."

A murmur passed through the crowd.

Maranth quickly jumped in. "This man is no alien. His deformities are not genetic, but are the result of some accident or disease. He's really quite helpless."

She actually wasn't very convinced of her assessment. True, the man's genetic map was normal. But along with his other deformities, there was some sort of functioning gland or nodule in his brain. It looked like no injury or tumor she had ever seen. But she knew if she mentioned it, the Afthari might kill him. And her first duty was to her patient.

Mier Zedd eyed her sternly. "You seem so sure, yah? You've seen such injuries before?"

She gulped and decided it served no purpose to lie.

"No, I haven't."

The crowd fell still for a moment. Then the group began to mutter. Someone called out, "Witchdoc!"

Rozia echoed his words. "Yah. A witchdoc."

Now frightened chatter swept among the observers.

Fromar fearfully pulled on Obbad's sleeve. "Husband, who else could drop him in our laps, through our force field, yah?"

A raider added, "Without our knowing."

"It's a sign," Fromar concluded.

Obbad nodded gravely. "Or perhaps a warning."

Mier Zedd impatiently motioned everyone quiet.

"So, if we were sent this wretch by some witchdoc as a warning, what are we being warned about?"

Obbad was stumped. So were the others.

Maranth turned to Fromar. "What is a witchdoc?"

But Obadd's wife just ignored her without answering. The teenager now addressed Mier Zedd, his voice cracking.

"Poppa, could it be that a witchdoc took vengeance on the

alien and just dumped what was left of him here, only because it was convenient?"

Mier Zedd beamed approvingly at his son. Then he asked the others, "Any one else?"

A murmur crossed the crowd but no one spoke up.

Zedd crossed his arms over his chest. It was the stance of a leader who was about to render a decision.

The others respectfully fell silent.

"Alien plots? Witchdoc warnings? Vengeance? Perhaps something else, yah?"

He looked down at Maranth. "You say this alien's weak, deaf and blind?"

Maranth nodded.

Zedd turned back to the others. "Then he's unsalable and useless for work. Until we know more, we do nothing. For now let him live with the beggars."

The maimed trader remained where he was until everyone was asleep. Only then the mental chaos, disorder and jumble that had assaulted him ever since he'd burrowed under the force field was gone. The steady torrent of memories, desires and schemes that engulfed his being was now just wisps of dreams.

When he entered the colony, he was at first surprised, then overwhelmed. Strangely, human mental patterns weren't much different from those of the malaaas, the Kin's revered prey. No wonder they thought humans were unintelligent.

Would he ever adjust to the racket? He grimly realized that if he didn't, he was finished. Eventually, exhaustion had taken over. There had been no place to hide except in sleep.

Then wonderful, cool fingers took his hand, and lightly touched his forehead, neck and wrists. He focused on the being that controlled them, absorbing her femaleness. For the first time since he'd arrived on the planet he felt a connection with one of his own kind.

TEN

AFTHARI RAIDER COLONY

AS THE SHADOWS grew long across the ground, the domes, spires and arches of the Afthari skyline metastasized into bizarre, stretched-out dark shapes behind the open areas.

The waning light through the force field created a slight shimmer in the shapes, almost as if they were alive. The formerly busy place now had a lonely, surrealistic air. Only a few beggars remained in the square, partially clad in shadows, wrapped in cloaks against the evening chill. The unfortunate man with the maimed face was one of them, sitting still as stone, off by himself at the far end.

The telltale structures of the spaceport rose beyond the eclectic compounds surrounding the plaza. Bunched around the hidden spacecraft, impassive blue warehouses and maintenance scaffolds silently shimmered a bit of gold in the last light.

Maranth watched the encroaching anonymity of darkness from her hidden lair, a shadow-draped alley off the main plaza. Doc was at Maranth's side. She knew he purposely stayed close, unless she sent him on an errand. The stress of their situation had sapped her health.

Since the raid that brought them here, her body endured chronic stress, to the point where it could not maintain itself properly. No doubt Doc recognized her irritability and anger as symptoms of decline, since Veddian dispositions were normally serene and balanced. Regardless of his new leering personality, as a core construct, her health was Doc's first priority. He would monitor and try to reverse her deterioration.

Who else was more qualified to treat a meddoc than the meddoc's right hand?

The only problem was neither of them was sure of what to do. Maranth refused to take calm-aid or other stress reducing potions, fearing the drugs would eliminate the 'edge' she needed to survive this place. Meditation did not seem fully effective against the constant psychic assault. Doc could suggest nothing else. Much of the Afthari behavior was as beyond his programming as it was beyond her experience.

So, as Doc quietly perused his data for further insights during downtime, Maranth deliberately relaxed into the shadows and enjoyed the last of the dinner smells that washed into their tiny domain. She playfully whipsawed one of Doc's sensory antennae and yawned. But then she remembered the maimed man among the beggars on the square and tucked back a stand of her hair.

"That man who has no mouth needs a liquid diet. I better program the cookbots before I go back for dinner."

"Take a load off. I'll do it. I've been meaning to connect with those boxy beauties anyway."

No doubt Doc's reference to the "beauty" of the limited cookbots was a ruse to lift some of her burden. Maranth tapped her assistant.

"You don't have a love life. And I may be tired but I'm still quite able. Just remember who made who."

Even if his personality was altered his basic algorithms seemed intact, and those required he defer to her instructions. Yet his programming enabled him to determine patient treatment every bit as well as she could. He could often do this better than his mistress. His superior memory and recall prevented errors that she, as a biologic, was prone to make from time to time.

Yet Maranth had certain abilities that transcended Doc's programming. Doc could never have hypoed was-curare into the raider back at Addehut. There were nuances of the human psyche that were beyond her assistant. Often patient outcomes and general health were affected by the patient's moods and beliefs. Some patients even acted in ways harmful to their health. Thus, her uniquely human insights combined with Doc's biotronic memory and equipment forged them into a powerful medical unit.

Maranth knew Doc would accept her lead because, to him, it would bolster her confidence and thus improve her function. Getting humans to function well was, after all, his prime directive. Regardless of Gannet's tampering, Doc would naturally protect and improve his human creators as long as a spark of power remained in his biotronics.

Humans are so fragile and erratic. It's a wonder we reached the stars at all.

Doc took another tack. "The cookbots will take orders from me easier than from you."

Maranth decided there was no point in pushing the matter. "Aye, you take care of it. Just be sure that he can get the food down and that it's a YIH 32 diet. Oh, and get him some wash powders."

"No problem." He punctuated his response with a gentle poke in Maranth's belly as he turned and headed into the park toward the cookbots.

Without the cloning facilities of an innerworld hospital, there was little they could do for the man's severe deformities. At least they could fix his anemia and improve his nutrition, as he was clearly malnourished. And he would no longer smell.

Maranth stood up and softly called after him. "Also get more assays of that nodule, or whatever it is, inside his skull. It's certainly an unusual deformity."

"Yo." Doc dipped an antenna in response without breaking his stubby paddle stride.

The disfigured trader had struggled for hours to make sense of the myriad disjointed thoughts and images that flooded his mind. He alternately practiced and rested.

It was clear that even if he could learn to pick through the mental bombardment, he had no real future as he was, in the colony or outside. Bantaaa was right. He must return to her. Though she ate skin, muscle and sinews of his leg, it healed perfectly. The missing parts were restored and his skin renewed unscarred, all in just hours. She probably could restore his face. But the price would be steep.

At least the meddoc here could replace his blood that did not seen to regenerate fast enough.

A rising vibration broke the trader's concentration. Someone approached but he could read nothing mental.

A workbot?

There was a soft tap on his shoulder. Instinctively he looked up. His arms were gently grasped and he was slowly pulled to his feet and, steadied by a second hold on his collar, led toward the cookbots. He knew the direction because he had formed a mental map of the area from bits and pieces gleaned from the people in the square earlier in the day.

He hands quickly confirmed that a workbot, not a person, was leading him along. Soon he bumped to a stop, no doubt against one of the cookbots, and a tube was inserted into his mouth hole. Warm liquid coursed down his throat. He grabbed the tube and experimented with squeezing the flow so he wouldn't choke. His belly warmed as it welcomed the nutrition.

He eagerly drank though it bothered him that he couldn't use the senses of the workbots. With them, he was truly blind. When he had enough he pulled out the tube and sat down to digest the bounty.

The background flood of thoughts was now more distant, muted, almost tolerable. Images of children and smells of food passed through him that were not there before. But none of these were of the immediate surroundings to refresh his mental map. And of course nothing emanated from the nearby workbots.

Can I survive here?

He felt warmth on his head. Instinctively his hand stole up to seek its source.

The gentle woman from before?

But his hand glanced off the workbot's appendage and dropped in disappointment.

Probably the workbot who'd led him to the cookbots. Her assistant?

Soon it left him alone with the cookbots. There was so little here. He had allowed a flicker of hope to capture his imagination and risked his life to reach this place. At least outside the force field he could get around.

Patushah. Think like that and end up meat.

He had learned about the Afthari force field and the natural tunnel from the Kin. There was a dip in the ground at a point under the force field. With a little excavation of their own they could have breached the colony long ago. But they never ventured underground because the earth blocked their telepathic union. Now, for the first time, he understood how vulnerable they felt without it.

He supposed the Kin had allowed the colony to be built in the first place because they considered the barren plateau of no consequence and rarely ventured there. The Kin could never have anticipated the force field.

Why does the force field block our telepathy?

Aye, our telepathy...

His thoughts drifted, as they had so many times before, to the how and the why he acquired the Kin's telepathic sense. It was a subject that, no matter how hard he tried, yielded no answer. But now he had an additional bit of information. He was sure no other human here was telepathic. Anyone telepathic would need a disciplined mind to survive among the chaotic swamp of mental activity inside the colony. Since entering, all the human minds he encountered were erratic and undisciplined, and the force field clearly blocked all Kin telepathic intrusion.

He guessed the field to be outerworld standard. Most outerworld weapons were relatively low tech. Only the innerworlds could afford the really sophisticated weapons, and they jealously guarded whatever they had. Besides, it didn't take much firepower to blockade or destroy many of the outerworld colonies. Most of them were synthetic bio systems dependent on some artificial life support. Here, the situation was different. The planet was naturally compatible with human life.

So this force field was probably average. Generally, such fields allowed the lighter gasses of the natural atmosphere to pass through, incinerated smaller items and deflected most everything else, including energy beams. It protected against biological contamination, invasion from the sky and space debris.

But without more sophisticated and expensive shielding, particularly where the field ended at the ground, determined invaders could easily breach the field at its base. All they would need is heavy blaster fire below the area where the field would be corrupted by the heavier elements in the soil. It wouldn't take very long to dig and reinforce a tunnel below the interface layer. Effectively, the shield could at most slow down, but not stop an invasion by land.

Probably why the colonists chose this planet.

Their force field protected them from any attack from the sky and the formidable Kin protected them from attack on the ground.

Could a force field also prevent what would be a natural development of telepathy among the colonists? He alone among the humans had the Kin's power and he alone had lived outside the field. Could any sentient being, including humans, develop this power naturally by just living on Afthar where there was no field interference?

Not likely.

There'd been no natural, gradual development of his telepathic sense. He was fully telepathic the moment he fell to the planet. The struggle was always to control his mind and use what he had. If telepathy were some immediate condition of the planet at least some of the other humans would also be telepathic upon their arrival.

And what happened to my face? Nothing about this cursed place makes any sense.

Eventually the surrounding mental noise thinned to shreds of surreal dreams amid wisps of sexual imagery as the colony slept the deep part of the night.

The Man With No Face slept too, dreamless and still.

ELEVEN

AFTHARI RAIDER COLONY

AFTER DOC LEFT, Maranth returned to the Obbad compound and slipped silently into her room. Its baseboards emitted enough light to provide dim illumination. She spilled her cloak onto the floor, then dropped heavily on the couch-like bed, kicked off her shoes and got out of her clothes. Other than apparel and toiletries, there was nothing of her among the cast-offs that furnished the space. That's the way she wanted it.

Nothing to attach to.

She tiredly unpinned her thick, dark hair and shook it out so it cascaded down her shoulders onto her back. She massaged the back of her neck and idly wondered if Doc stopped off to visit that lavender workbot to exchange some files.

She smiled at the thought and flopped down. But Maranth wished he was around to massage the tension out of her back before she fell asleep.

In the outerworlds most women slept with a man or fell asleep wanting one. But this was not so with Maranth. Like the others of her kind, Maranth's years of enlightened Veddian training, supported by suppression hormones, enabled her, with minimal effort, to channel and dissipate her natural sexual energy.

Veddians long understood that raw sexual energy squan-

80

dered mental and emotional resources in the instinctual need to mate. Further, potential mates usually expended as much energy dealing, one way or another, with the sexual seeker. Thus unchanneled sexual energy invariably led to neurotic patterns of behavior and social friction.

Veddians knew true personal fulfillment required good health, personal clarity and a supportive social environment. They sought various methods to balance the psyche and promote such social harmony. This included methods to free the unmarried from the psychic stress of sexual instinct, reserving its pleasure and procreative aspects to marriage.

The resulting approach refined ancient Hindu tantric and Buddhist meditative practices in the crucible of modern Veddian science in the 22st and 23rd centuries. Though the ancestral forms of such practices required years of repetitious mental visualization, breathing and other exercises, the modern forms were easy enough for even children to master. By adulthood, it took Veddians normally only a few moments a week to maintain the effects via codes that triggered thoughts and images, each recreating an entire meditative practice.

After the methodology was incorporated into the educational curriculum in Veddi it spread quickly throughout the innerworlds, but never gained any strong following in the hardscrabble, remote outerworlds.

Given her training and present circumstances, Maranth laid down and naturally dropped into a meditative state. Her mind repeated the series of codes, one by one, that balanced her physical state and tempered her emotional balance.

Her training also enabled her to direct her dreams. Since ancient times people knew dreams offered windows into the psyche, sometimes revealing unthought-of solutions to all kinds of problems. Directed dreaming just made the process and outcome more certain. So when she began to slip into sleep Maranth ran a simple mental chant that coded for directed dreaming. Thus, she drifted off to mental images of her sun washed fingers dismantling a security panel.

Sometime later, Maranth groggily awoke from some noise in her room. A silent dark form blocked the light from the hall.

Must be Doc.

But it was Saad Obbad who strode over and dropped on top of the still half-asleep woman. Maranth cried out. But Obbad squeezed her face with a powerful hand and laughed as he tugged at his clothes with the other hand, radiating a heavy perfume laced with lust. "Yah. My sweet prize."

Maranth was shocked. He certainly must know unmarried Veddians were essentially asexual. Yet he seemed very sure of himself. Maybe he thought, after a bit of grab and tussle, she would loose her Veddian training. Could he actually fool himself into believing she would become lively, if not passionate, between the sheets? Maranth decided to try reason.

"But you have a wife!"

He angrily cut her off. "If you tell Fromar…"

Then he brought his face down to within a centimeter of her nose. "…She will put you outside. And if you refuse me I will put you outside. Your choice."

Doc burst into the room and circled by the bed in frustration repeating "no" over and over in a staccato chant. Maranth concentrated on his activity as a way to keep her wits and not give way to panic. No doubt Doc remotely monitored her health, and raced back when he detected her distress. All he could do was circle. Workbots were core programmed to never use force on anyone, even an obvious aggressor.

Maranth knew Doc normally regarded the restriction a blessing, one that safeguarded him from infection from his human parent's innate tendency to violence.

How does he feel about that now?

Obbad slowly slid his hands up and down her torso.

What could she do? *What? What?*

Maranth struggled without success to slide out from under the much heavier and stronger man.

When he straightened to pull off his robe she tried to rise. "I am bound…"

He repinned her with relish. "So you are. It will go much easier if you relax, yah?"

"Once you have a taste of this you will want more." He kissed her possessively.

He stroked her neck provocatively. She turned her face away.

"I'm betrothed. When I return…"

"You will never return." He jerked off her covers and held her down with his massive hands. His eyes celebrated her warm skin, the arc of her struggling belly, her young breasts and hips. He pressed his belly down, freeing his hands so they could slowly fondle what his eyes already owned.

Maranth felt what must have been his penis, warm and stiff, pushing down her belly, probing for her vaginal opening. Maranth concentrated on detaching her mind from emotion and sensory experience. She was so practiced that in just a second or two her body ceased to struggle, becoming slack and unresponsive. Her mind emptied and her consciousness altered to a state more like sleep than wakefulness.

She was distantly aware that Obbad's jaw hardened and his hand groped more roughly for a response. He pulled off what remained of the bedcovers and nuzzled her left ear.

Doc furtively slipped something into Maranth's hand. There was just enough consciousness in her to register Doc's action and she roused. Obbad kissed her hungrily, his mouth wet on her neck, as Maranth fingered the granular substance. She guessed it must be something to cool Obbad's ardor, as Doc would not harm anyone. Obbad sought to push her legs apart. She used his shift in position to work her hand below his belly.

"Arugggh!" Obbad jerked away and tried to shield his genitals from the pain.

Maranth fiercely followed him up, her determined face centimeters from his own. "By Veddi-Aut, I serve you because, on my oath I must serve humanity, even in this corrupt, depraved pit. But you violate me, you will never know if the next medicine I give you, or one of your family, will cure or kill. I can do it so easily, so slowly, you'd never even guess..."

The horror sputtering from Obbad's eyes stopped Maranth's furious tirade. She drew back as Obbad raised a fist to smash her face.

Maranth met his gaze resolutely. "Aye, you can put me outside. But you'll have to explain it to the others here who need my services."

Furor etched his face, but he eased his fist.

"Or you and I can decide this never happened. I will continue to heal your people, on my oath as a Veddian Meddoc."

She covered herself without taking her eyes from his face. "So what will it be?"

He pushed her down and sullenly rearranged his clothes. "Your round, slave, but it's not finished between us."

A hard glint passed across his dark eyes.

"Yah, not finished." He grimaced and stalked out.

Maranth shakily dressed and, as soon as her legs steadied, she, too, escaped the room.

Doc followed her, of course. No doubt he was more worried than ever. This latest attack had driven her to actually threaten to kill someone, though she knew she'd never do so. But Doc must think she would, something that was difficult for his programming to even contemplate. Would she actually do it? Would she actually use her Meddoc skills to kill someone?

I've finally cracked, no doubt about it...

The thought sent a shiver up her spine.

Get a grip.

She stormed through the compounds. Doc followed as best he could.

She was muttering "crack-brained, egotistic, pervert degenerate brute" when she entered the main plaza. The stillness of the night began to seep into her consciousness. Was she angrier at Obbad or herself? Her mood softened and she slowed.

Doc caught up and extended one of his telescoping

appendages, offering her a pill. "Take a soothing mellowmint. There are no contraindications."

"Aye. Soon. But not now. I must think this through."

Doc retracted the pill and purred, "How soon? Maranth, you're just not handling the stress you're feeling."

She was again overwhelmed with terror, loathing and anger, notwithstanding Doc's purring attempt to calm her down. Anger wasn't strong enough. Fury was a better word for it — fury at Obbad, fury at her own failure, her vulnerability.

Just raw fury.

Psychological norms foretold that her body, in defense, would eventually transmute such chronic, stress-induced emotions into apathy and depression. And she would, in time, become like the miserable, neurotic savages inhabiting Afthar. That prospect scared her more than not getting home.

"We must escape. But how? How?"

Doc lightly tapped her arm. She turned and his screen appeared and flashed several charts showing her physical condition. All showed declines to the right.

"See? You QET level had dropped nearly 21%. Your Ruuges Index is down over four points. And those threats you made to Obbad? Healthy Veddians don't behave that way. Babe, you're way over the edge."

She sighed. "As bad as that."

After a brief pause she continued walking. "Let me stroll the park once again, then I'm in your hands. I promise to take your meds, meditate more and eat my vegetables. Pleased?"

Doc opened and shut a couple of compartments, whirred and flashing some lights in an improvisation of sarcasm.

Maranth stopped short. "I only threatened him to protect myself."

By Veddi-Aut, what am I saying?

"Even in self-defense, no Veddian meddoc would sink so low. You're right, Doc, I'm losing myself."

She sank to her knees in utter despair.

Scanning his psych data for the best bedside response, he

draped a tentacle reassuringly on her shoulder. "Doll, give me a wet one and I'll fix everything."

Maranth went rigid.

Doc despondently dropped his tentacle. "I'm not myself, either."

"I know Gannet tampered with your personality code. I don't know how to fix it. But at least we can ban words like 'babe' and 'doll.'"

Savage animals.

The Man With No Face woke in a sweat. Intense anger, fear and loathing wrenched his gut. Yet his psyche was calm. He realized the emotion that roiled through him was not his own. He probed for its source and found her nearby. From her angry memories he saw a man forcing her down, ripping away her clothes, her loathing. The man's hot sexual stink burned his own face and it revolted him.

The woman's anger scoured him dry and he wanted to tune her out. But there was something familiar about her. He picked through the motley tangles of her experience and feelings. Recognizing the sweet creature that had helped him earlier, the outrage gripping him was now his own, outrage against the one who forced her.

In adolescence he envied women. It seemed they could have sex whenever they wanted, as much as they wanted. At that time he was apprenticed on his uncle's family ship, which supported both family and a crew. As with most males at that time of life, sexual desire seemed to rule everything. The crew women enjoyed his attentions, as well as those of other men. But few women wanted to indulge the appetite as he did.

Not that females were indifferent, just different. They were hot enough, but slower to engage. Most women were slower to peak. They also were coyer, and rationed their pleasure for other things. Once he got his own small ship with no crew, he learned they preferred the older traders with a bigger ships.

So he adapted, improvised. Eventually he learned the exquisite eroticism of seduction and the building heat of foreplay. Thus his sensuality, conditioned by experience, ripened. Like most men, as he matured he integrated his sexual needs into a workable accommodation with life.

He managed a sex life with women where he found them planetside, given his constant space travel. Pairing with a woman was unlikely. Though he had his own ship, it was too small to support any crew. Patushah women preferred big ships with big crews, for companionship and for raising children. Which is why Patusian traders didn't have wives without a family-size ship or a big stake, something he had not yet achieved.

Of course he could have kept a sexbot. But he observed that traders who did so usually didn't amount to much and never seemed to gain families of their own. Shipboard sexbots were a trap, sapping a trader's drive to grow a stake. They ruined the odds for a real mate and family. They were certainly convenient and pleasurable, but a dead end.

So his sex life in recent years had been hit or miss, but he got by. He would have his large ship one day.

A dream from another life.

Of course he knew of men who had forced or brutalized woman for pleasure when they could get away with it. From time to time he'd had fantasies of overpowering reluctant nymphets. Sometimes with a lover he'd done so in play. But even in his most secret imaginings the women really wanted him.

Nature endowed men with the ingrained desire to sexually conquer, tempered by the need to please and be loved. From this poor woman, for the first time, he personally experienced one without the other.

No balance.

She had helped and comforted him with no thought to herself. She deserved comfort and protection. Then his outrage melted into despairing frustration. Helpless, impotent to act, he could do nothing.

Nearby, Doc's light beam probed the dark for the source of the low, painful grunt or cry that drifted across square. Maranth was too lost in herself to notice. When the cry repeated Doc tapped her on the shoulder. She dutifully rose and the two headed toward its source.

Maranth welcomed this diversion from her personal anguish and quickly regained her calm, professional demeanor. There was a certain inner peace in duty. Peace because one's focus and path were clear, the only concern lay in details.

Doc's beam found the Man With No Face squatting near the cookbots, a begging bowl in front like the other beggars. When they reached him he held a steady hand out in their direction.

"Diagnostics." Maranth slipped to her knees in front of the unfortunate.

With a familiar rhythm Doc set to work and scanned the now silent man. Throughout Doc's probing, the patient's hand remained outstretched. Maranth finally took the hand in her own. With her touch he covered her hand with his other one and squeezed reassurance.

She gently pulled back her hand. "Doc?"

Doc pulled in his probes. "Nothing physical explains his distress."

"Aye. It's as if he only wanted to reach out to me." *Irrational. How could he know what happened?*

Her patient threaded through her thoughts and learned she understood his gesture. Could he communicate directly by speaking into her mind?

Would it work?

He gently sent a simple message, careful not to press and overwhelm her.

I feel your anger, your pain. Sorry for what happened.

Maranth rose. "Well, there's nothing more we can do."

From her reaction he knew he failed. He tried again, this time with a firmer texture.

I feel your anger, your pain. Sorry for what happened.

"Did you hear that?"

"Hear what?"

By his reaction Maranth knew Doc had not heard it, and his senses were more acute than hers.

Am I so far gone I'm now imagining things?

Elated, the maimed trader knew he must again repeat the message or she would dismiss the experience.

I feel your anger, your pain. Sorry for what happened.

"Doc?"

Doc knew enough of her facial expressions to read she was serious.

"Tell me what you hear." He could offer nothing more without further data.

"He just spoke to me. Doc, he talks, he must also hear me."

"Impossible. I heard nothing and he has no speech or auditory organs. You might be more stressed that we thought." Doc spoke the last statement slowly, as he began to scan her with full diagnostics.

She knew why he was examining her. No doubt Doc viewed this unexpected development as ominous. Of course Maranth suffered neurotic adaptations, and of course she was agitated. But hearing imaginary voices was a symptom of severe psychosis. Now he was busily assessing if she now suffered such an illness as he checked for its physical symptoms.

Doc finished without a word and became very still. Maranth knew if she were psychotic he would immediately start some sort of treatment. So, she wasn't psychotic.

And she was sure she was not mistaken about the message, not twice. Yet the man clearly could not speak or hear.

What was that famous old dictum?

When you eliminate all reasonable possibilities, then whatever is left, no matter how improbable, is the truth.

But how can you be sure you've identified all the possibilities?

Whatever is left, no matter how improbable...

"This man spoke into my mind. My mind!"

She backed away in shock, then fled into the night.

"Maranth?" Doc did not to wait for a response and trailed after her.

When both were gone, the Man With No Face crossed his fisted hands, palms up, and slid them out in the Patusian sign of confirmation.

Then he dropped his head, exhausted. It wasn't much but it was a start.

TWELVE

AFTHARI RAIDER COLONY

CLAIMING ILLNESS, MARANTH minimized her work schedule and kept to her room as much as possible. Fortunately, the next days were uneventful — no barbarities, medical emergencies or attacks. She carefully avoided anything stressful and rigorously followed Doc's regimen of dietary supplements and meditation.

But now her meditations were much deeper than those she normally did as part of her daily routine. As odors are among the strongest memories the human mind retains, Maranth used aromas to master the deepest delta brain waves to calm her psyche and rebalance her endocrine and hormonal functions. She also prescribed herself a series of musical tones and colors that Doc provided with his sound module and lasers. These low-tech additions added resonating properties that enhanced her mental control.

In fact, maintaining her sexual hormonal balance might soon be a problem. Her sexual suppression contraceptive was nearly gone from her system. And none were available in the colony.

In fact, there was little of medical value among the colony's stores except a few basics. She had relied on what Doc brought from Addehut to treat the Afthari. No supply ships ever came here. The Afthari seemed to depend solely on what they could steal or barter off world. Apparently medical supplies had no priority.

And when everything runs out?

She had set a man's broken leg in that hellish slaver ship, in complete darkness, with no medical equipment or supplies.

Aye. Just my hands and common sense.

Doc took over the beggars' clinic so she could remain in her quarters to recover. That also meant she would not have any contact with the man without any face.

As for Obbad, at first he ignored her as if their confrontation never occurred. When she crossed the family compound to take a meal the second evening after his attack, she caught him eyeing her from the shadow of a portico. His mouth worked itself into a tight smile. The look wasn't reassuring.

Doc checked her several times a day and was pleased with her progress. Her diagnostics steadily improved so that, by the third day, her readings had more or less normalized. He happily pronounced her fit for duty that evening.

Good.

Maranth began early the next day by delivering a baby. At mid-afternoon, as usual, she headed for the main plaza for her beggars' clinic. Her fingers counted the morning's credits in her pocket as she strolled through the narrow alley with Doc.

"Fifteen more."

Doc dipped an antenna in acknowledgement. "That brings your average up a little, to twelve per day."

"Doc, have you learned how many credits we need?"

"To buy freedom?"

"Aye, what else is there to buy?"

"My time with Wiza wasn't all laughs. I downloaded all the Afthari data she had. It suggests very few slaves purchase their freedom. There are only four such records and the number of credits varied between 500 and 755. That would be just for a slave. Even though sales of high-level workbots are common, there is no fixed price. But it seems we sell for about half that amount."

"Presuming the maximum, for both of us that means 1,125. Assuming I continue to earn about twelve a day... Aye. It would take a little over three more standard months."

Can I survive here that long?

Now that she resumed a normal schedule, her top priority was clear.

Escape.

But how exactly does a slave go about buying freedom?

Toward that end she resolved to learn as much as she could about Afthari customs. Befriending Jobbar was a first step. He was certainly observant and had learned as much as he could in his years here. She considered including him somehow in her plans, but quickly dropped the idea, at least for the time being. Jobbar seemed too well adjusted within his slave persona. Maranth was not certain he was even emotionally capable of leaving, or even of wanting to leave. His freedom, and the freedom of the other slaves, would probably have to wait until she could summon a Veddian patrol.

As they entered the plaza, the smell of the greenery hit her and a stab of homesickness cut through as she recalled home. Dispassionately, she let the feeling drift off. Such indulgences accomplished nothing.

She led Doc through a group of young children noisily playing with a dancing ball whose color and melody changed with every kick. A nearby housebot discretely watched over them. Maranth suddenly realized she had missed the significance of the children. There were lots of children, everywhere, all over the colony.

Normally, there were few children in any human population, even in the outerworlds. In the 21st century, soon after the Biotic War, scientists unlocked the unique genetic characteristics of certain reptiles and fish that had no defined life spans.

These characteristics were incorporated into the human genome via an artificial, airborne virus. Thus, the disease of old age was vanquished in a moment. But humanity still was not immortal. Over time, the specialized cells of the human organism continued to accumulate damage from radiation, replication, injury and other factors. Medical intervention corrected a lot of the damage, but could not correct all of it.

As a result, the average lifespan now extended to more than 350 years and people remained youthful and vigorous all their lives. Even 'old' people looked like the young middle-aged of former times. The very old at the end of life might betray their extreme age with a slightly stiff or slow gait.

Yet a stable, long-lived population required a much smaller proportion of children to the adult population than in old times. As a necessity the innerworlds enforced a low birth rate. And marginal outerworlds such as Addehut prohibited children altogether.

Why so many here?

Maranth made a mental note to ask Jobbar about this.

An Afthari matron dropped a credit into a beggar's bowl and nodded pleasantly as Maranth passed. She reciprocated with her traditional Veddian bow. A few seconds later two Afthari raiders strode across her path, cutting her off. She ignored the rudeness and patiently waited until they passed, then threaded her way around them to the cluster of beggars waiting for her ministrations. She settled into her usual spot.

How many decades, even centuries, did some of these people live as beggars?

They came to the clinic, no doubt as much to relieve their endless boredom as to get treatment. A few, like Huffo at the head of the line, were former slaves.

What a waste.

Doc set up his cot and Huffo beamed as he sat on it.

"Meddoc, your potions stopped my pains here." He pointed to his right hip. Then he pulled up the fabric on his left arm, exposing the forearm to display a nasty swelling. "You can also clear this up, yah?"

Maranth looked closely at the swelling. "Another one of those bites. Well, I think we can soothe that away."

She looked at Doc. "Beta light and Cort-106 standard."

Doc obliged by beaming a focused light onto the sore. He extended one of his tube-like appendages to the wound and exuded an ointment.

Maranth tapped the beggar on the shoulder. "If you bring me some of these biting bugs that did this to you, I can make a better treatment."

There was a buzzing sound from above. Most of the beggars just looked up, though a few of them closed their eyes and gritted their teeth. As before, a dark, growing mass hurtled down into the force field. It hit the crackling field and sliced through in a shower of lights, the blackened corpse plunked down near the cookbots.

One of the beggars called out, "Meddoc, you got a remedy for that, yah?"

Several snickered, as much to break the tension as from the joke.

Maranth placed with her hands on her hips and giggled with them. "Do you have a sample I can work from?"

With that, the others roared, some even falling on their backs in hilarity. Maranth watched them, very pleased with herself. Laughter was, perhaps, the best medicine of all.

Then she noticed the still form of the maimed man at the back of the group, squatting behind the beggar Kojji. And like the other beggars, he had a begging bowl with him. The lower part of his head was now swathed in an Afthari-style face cloth. But it could not hide his missing eyes. The man tilted his blank face toward her as if he knew she was there. Maranth willed herself to remain calm.

On my oath, I must treat him as I would treat anyone.

As if on cue, he scooted over to her. Maranth gestured to the other beggars to be patient and patted him on the head.

Be calm. Remain professional.

"Doc, let's do a diagnostic update." Doc extended his diagnostic appendages and began several quick tests.

Maranth watched the results on Doc's embedded monitor.

"Last time it was stable, now it is down again. Why do you continue to lose blood?"

Even as the words escaped, she feared her patient would actually plant a response into her brain.

"Hemoflox?" Doc knew the treatments as well as Maranth.

"Aye. Same dosage as before."

Doc injected the medication and the man did not react, since he could not feel such a micro fine spray go through skin.

As Doc worked, Maranth tried to find anything out of the ordinary in her brain, anything in her thoughts not her own. She was relieved that she 'heard' nothing from him now.

Could I have been mistaken before? Maybe a bit crazy?

She sighed as her patient moved off. The remaining patients needed little attention. Most of those in attendance were just onlookers.

"That should do it for today. Let's get back."

As they negotiated their way between the various family compounds towards the Obbad household, Doc slid close to Maranth so he could relay more information without being overheard.

"Wiza told me there are 34 active slaves here, including you. Adding in the retired slaves…"

The Man With No Face suddenly sensed violent intent within the mental chatter around him. He jumped to his feet and hurried after the meddoc as fast as he could by feeling his way.

Doc was suddenly shoved aside and fell over. Big hands grabbed Maranth from behind. These hands roughly pulled her into a narrow, dark alley between two compounds. She screamed but one of the hands had already muffled her mouth. She twisted her head enough to make out Jobbar's bluish, massive fingers. Gannet emerged from the shadows and leisurely strolled up to her.

She bit hard into Jobbar's hand and it flinched. She was now able to squeak, "Stop it. Let me go."

Jobbar's hand shifted to her forehead and held her tighter.

Sensing opportunity, Gannet slowly rubbed his hands up and down her torso and sniffed her neck.

By then, Doc staggered into the alley but just rocked back and forth, repeating over and over his staccato "No, no, no…"

The maimed trader grabbed Gannet from behind and tried to pull him off. But Gannet easily beat the weakened man down. Maranth struggled to help but Jobbar's grip was implacable.

Gannet kicked the downed man. "Stupid move, lump face."

"Doc! Our patient!" Maranth's cry reset her medibot. He tottered over to the injured man.

But her voice drew Gannet's attention back to herself.

"Almost forgot." His hands easily found the credits in Maranth's pocket. He jingled them and then slipped them into his own tunic. As he'd done before, he squeezed her nipples painfully with a smirk.

"Don't worry. We'll put these to good use."

Maranth eyed him contemptuously. "You risk much for these credits. Fromar…"

"Fromar? Ah, my view screen. It's gone, at least for now. Too risky watching that one." He smirked again, then slowly licked her cheek, chin to eye.

Against Jobbar's bulk Maranth could not shrink away. The smell of Gannet's saliva was sickening. Though more furious than afraid, she was impotent to prevent his assault.

Pleased with himself, Gannet casually strolled off; humming as he rhythmically fondled the coins so they jingled in time with the melody.

Jobbar wordlessly released Maranth and heavily followed after his co-conspirator. Maranth's fury focused on the retreating Yurblun.

"I might expect something like this from that crack-brained pervert. But you?"

She angrily grabbed Jobbar's sleeve. She tried to hang on a moment or two, but she could not even slow the man. Jobbar ignored her and just continued his slow, rocking gait down the path.

"Ashamed, huh?"

Jobbar slowed, but never turned back. "I never do more 'dan I haave to. Never."

Maranth stopped dead in her tracks. "Obbad…?"

Jobbar's only response was a slow nod as he moved on.

She returned to her medibot and their patient.

Doc swiveled his view screen. "Contusions. Minor internal bleeding. Look at this."

Maranth peered closer at the highlighted data. "Aye. But rerun these diagnostics anyway."

"Always do." As Doc reran his tests, the injured man painfully tilted his blank face up and lifted a hand.

Maranth tried to comfort him. "Thanks for trying to help but you can't stop anyone in your condition. Anyway, they were ordered to just steal my credits. They wouldn't dare to really hurt me."

What am I doing? He can't hear me. She concentrated on thinking a simple communication.

Thank you.

He found her face with his other hand. *Please keep me alive.*

His message filled her brain and spooked her. He understood and dropped his hands.

Doc was too busy to notice the interplay. "I still get a lower reading. Hemoflox again?"

"Aye. Half dose."

Doc injected the remedy into their patient's arm.

The maimed trader decided to try again. *You have no reason to fear me.*

But Maranth was afraid and backed away. He reached for her but she was gone.

THIRTEEN

AFTHARI RAIDER COLONY

SHE RETURNED TO the Obbad compound drained and raw. The next morning she intended to resume her normal schedule. But Doc vehemently opposed her working so soon after this latest attack. So they compromised. She spent the morning in meditation and waited until mid afternoon to head to the main square for her regular beggars' clinic.

She felt it was necessary to maintain some air of normalcy, to show Obbad that she was not intimidated. Her prep work for Addehut included briefings on the personality maladaptations she would likely encounter, including bullying. This disorder reinforced itself through the victim's fear. Thus, she could not reward such behavior and decided to transmute her anger into resolve, a single-minded resolve to escape.

It was now clear she would not be able to buy her freedom. She figured that even if she could slip out of the colony and survive the drogans, there was no other way off the planet. The only way out was on one of the ships in the colony's spaceport. That meant stowing away on an Afthari ship. If she got caught, they'd kill her, or worse.

More than anything, she and Doc must learn everything about the spaceport and these space ships. To start, she would have Doc carefully mine security data from various workbots and other data sources. Then they both would discretely observe spaceport activity. She intended to observe and find any weakness that might lead to a way out. That included eventually gaining information about ship security systems. She knew all of this would be very dangerous and they must proceed very, very carefully.

Over the next several weeks, Doc easily got a fair amount of information about the spaceport from Obbad's nameless scheduling workbot. It was a slightly improved version of the generic simple, black workbots that did all the manual labor for the Afthari.

Maranth figured Gannet had done a nominal upgrade on it, which no doubt accounted for its poor security defenses and minimal reasoning algorithms. Somehow it was satisfying this pervert was actually helping them observe the port itself.

Though usually quiet, Afthar's spaceport was now bustling. Maranth watched it from a shadowy recess halfway up the crane of a deactivated portbot, well away from the activity. Her unnoticed perch was located at one end of the arc of ships and abutted one of the high compound walls that separated the spaceport from the rest of the colony.

She had scouted her roost during an earlier reconnaissance when the spaceport was deserted. In keeping with Doc's spaceport intel, there was no perimeter security. Carefully moving in among the perimeter crates and equipment, away from the ships, she avoided any unknown security that could still be in place. Then she cautiously climbed up to her position just below the compound's wall, invisible to both the Afthari around the ships as well as anyone from the adjacent compound.

Various crews of raiders in their orange robes checked gear and weapons. Some oversaw the tall, crane-topped portbots lifting large equipment and big plasticast crates into the topside hatches of four of the six space ships arrayed in a half circle. A few of the men were testing and verifying ship components and systems. The four active ships shimmered different colors and patterns with the various tests. They looked much like rounded grey squid without tentacles, resting in a dull reef among small fish and crustaceans.

The two dark ships in the semicircle seemed dead next to their active companions.

Low-toned, excited buzz from the raiders' voices were a constant under the noisy port activity. Meanwhile, black workbots steadily loaded the smaller packages and weapons into open side hatches.

From Maranth's vantage, the constantly changing colors from the active ships reflected off the spaceport's shiny structures. This created a subdued lightshow that even reached the housetops of some of the nearby compounds. A bit of gold shimmer from the afternoon sun through the force field added to the effect.

She first noted that all the ships here were relatively small vessels, too small to contain the slave hold on that ship from Addehut. This probably meant the Afthari had at least one larger vessel somewhere else, maybe in orbit.

The thought of that hold triggered the frightening smells and sounds in the dark after the Addehut raid. She mentally pushed this aside and concentrated on the task at hand.

A shiver of fear crawled up her back when one of the black workbots ambled in her direction. But it only thrust its built-in forks into the base of a small, nearby plasticast crate, then hoisted it up off the ground and headed back toward the bustle around the ships. Only then did she let out her breath. When the workbot was back among its brethren, Maranth pressed a button on her wrist comm to remotely access Doc's view.

Now Maranth's comm displayed a close up, ground-level holo of a workbot shutting a hatch. Her view was partly obscured by a crate draped with one of Doc's appendages, which then slipped out of sight as Doc shifted position slightly. From her distant vantage she looked out and recognized the same activity at the vessel second from the far end.

Doc had obviously managed to get close in behind some crates by that craft. He certainly was correct that spaceport security didn't check the workbots, probably because the raiders didn't care or didn't see the 'bots as a risk. Clearly its security protocol didn't distinguish Doc from the others. Maranth knew this was an important weakness. Of course a big question still remained. Could Doc slip in, unnoticed, when no other workbots were around?

The raiders began to coalesce into groups. They checked their blasters, then carefully placed them by the passenger ramp of their designated ships and paced about like hungry wolves.

The black workbots silently finished loading the last supplies and then followed the provisions into the hatches. The ships fell dark and the portbots moved away. The mood of the men grew tense.

Maranth could not recognize any faces at this distance. But she easily recognized the raiders' leader, Zedd, by his huge earrings and bearing.

He suddenly threw up his arms with a quick jerk. The raiders quickly formed large, loose circles around their leader, each placing his right hand on the shoulder of the one to his right and his left arm straight out in front.

They began to bob and chant in unison, low and rumbling. Then the chant suddenly died. After a short beat, they threw their fists in the air with an electric whoop.

When it was over they headed for their ships with a lot of swagger and backslapping. Each reclaimed his blaster as they gathered into tight knots by the gangway ramps. When each ship's leader strode up its ramp, the other raiders followed, eagerly jostling one another through the narrow opening.

Doc's view screen clearly revealed Obbad leading his crew into the nearby ship. Doc had really done better than Maranth expected. Obbad's ship was the best choice. By living in his household she had access to him, its 'bots and crew. That might give her a way in or an edge somehow.

Soon the gangways lifted and the last hatches closed. The four ships began to hum. As the hum grew into a low rumble, the dull gray skin of each vessel transformed into a dazzling bluish yellow.

Maranth knew just enough of space ship mechanics to know their biosynthetic hulls acted as huge capacitors and the brilliant yellow indicated each hull was storing energy from its engines. When the charge was complete it would discharge as a counter-gravitational force allowing the vessel to quickly rise and leave the planet. Space ship hulls were actually only semi rigid, comprised of a tough but pliable superconductive skin that was continually replenished by the living cells that formed it. Its plasticity enabled it to deflect, evade and distribute the impact of smaller objects without the power overhead that a rigid ship force field would require.

The ship furthest down the line whitened, then vertically shot up and hovered a moment. It then arced out of sight. There was only a muted crackle in the colony's force field to mark its passing. The other three vessels quickly followed suit.

The men and black workbots were gone. The portbots now sat in place, immobile. The spaceport was once again frozen and still, as if nothing had happened.

FOURTEEN

PLATEAU, PLANET AFTHAR

ON THE BARE ground of the plateau, the Man With No Face drifted within a twilight world barely above sleep. No ties anchored him now to his life, not desire, not hope, not even reason. Pain and physical need were merely a slight eddy somewhere nearby.

Suddenly, strong human thoughts flooded in and washed him into consciousness. He was now practiced enough with telepathy to flit from mind to mind. He focused his attention on what was obviously the bridge of a spacer with three Afthari men in their orange robes, plus two workbots.

"Primary and secondary systems check," a dull-witted man, Mazo, announced from a sunken control station. His eyes remained focused on the controls.

The imposing one replied, "Now run security. Let's see if we have any slave stowaways, yah?"

Probing deeper, the maimed trader recognized Zedd, the leader of the colony who had let him live. Zedd radiated the strong confidence and control of a leader certain of himself. No doubt he was the captain of this vessel. All of them exuded an expectant, charged energy.

Plugged into the panel on Zedd's left, a workbot produced a holo image of the interior of the ship. The positions of the crew were clearly marked with orange man-shapes. Threads of other colors, corresponding to sensor sweeps of the ship, crept through the schematics as the image rotated, the threads occasionally popping in tiny bursts.

Sitting at the weapons console, Facomitz smiled. "Nothing larger than an insect."

Zedd grinned, "Yah… Time to raid, and then we slave trade!"

The men settled into the respective stations while the workbots attached themselves to cabin panels.

They are slavers!

The Man With No Face had been so busy adjusting to human mental activity in the colony that he had not learned much about them. No wonder he hadn't sensed any real economic activity. They lived on the misery and efforts of others, creating no value.

Parasites and devils.

His attention was drawn back into their minds when Mazo droned, "Screens on."

Through Mazo's eyes the Man With No Face viewed the holos displaying everything around the ship. The colony below was now shriveling into a rusty stain on the plateau. The three men silently checked and rechecked their controls and views.

The Man With No Face suppressed a fleeting nostalgia. Being on the bridge of a ship was so familiar, so comfortable. It was the true home of a trader like himself.

A change in the ship's vibration indicated the vessel was beginning to power for space travel. Zedd crossed his arms. "Exit on my mark. Course on-line in slot three."

Facomitz called out, "Look at that!"

The view from the floor station quickly holoed up in size, displacing the other displays, with a zoom-in image of a small section of the sparsely vegetated plateau. This section of the image magnified to maximum size. The three could clearly see the blinking outline of a drogan covering what looked like part of a sprawled human, where only legs were visible.

Feet? Kin?

But his attention snapped back to the crew by their fear, the gut-grabbing, sweaty kind.

Zedd barked out, "Stop present course. Execute a slow pass over this location."

The realization roused him fully awake in a sharp wash of pain.

Bantaaa!

Her jaws released from his chest with a jolt. She had been communing with the Kin and did not notice these humans before his mental cry to her.

Through Zedd, the trader felt the spacer bank into a swift portside turn and slowly descend. The image on the ground grew larger. The colorful gold feathers of the green, two-meter female drogan clenched a man. Only ragged clothes and a pair of feet could clearly be seen from their top-down vantage.

His mind was assaulted by Zedd's command, "Destroy the beast! Forward blasters."

Bantaaa had tried to cloud the men's' minds. But she was too slow and too late.

Through Zedd, he watched Mazo direct the ship into a dive. Facomitz aimed the ship's blasters with a virtual arrow onto the image of Bantaaa's back, now clearly displayed on the main holo. The three men screamed their war cry as their ship attacked.

As the laser blasts burned into her body, the trader felt the searing pain as if it were his own. His mind filled with her agonizing shriek. His body felt her faint gasps of breath on his chest.

In his head, her agony was quickly supplanted by the raiders' roar of triumph. Through their eyes he watched the ground come up and the ship land with a whine and bump, confirmed by the thump he felt through his skin.

The men swiftly armed themselves and, with force of habit, masked their lower faces with their orange scarves. They quickly descended as the hellish glow of the ship's hull faded away.

Zedd and Mazo warily approached the dying Bantaaa, while Facomitz remained on guard by the vessel. She could only turn a malevolent eye toward them before her body stiffened, shuddered, and was released by death.

The Man With No Face felt the moment she was gone. Her presence just stopped, ended, and with it her pain ended too.

But he sensed a slight agitation from Bantaaa's lower belly. His mind probed and found a fuzzy desperation. It seemed weak, unfocused. How? He felt Bantaaa die.

Consciousness! Aye.

And there was clearly more than one. *Of course. Her unborn young… still alive!*

He struggled to regain his hands and push off Bantaaa's feathered bulk. But he was very weak from loss of blood and could barely move her corpse.

Then the raiders helped pull her off of him and for a moment he could only lay there. He sensed sweaty fear mixed in with their uncertainty as they gazed down on his bloody face. He managed to raise a hand. Their triumph over saving him morphed into shock when he opened his new, very blue eyes. His vision was still blurry but he could actually see them!

In the distance he sensed the Kin gather their anger and begin to move onto the plateau. The raiders seemed nervous. They did not dare stay long. Zedd growled and motioned the others back to the ship. Mazo grabbed the bloody trader and pulled him up to his feet and tried to tug him along.

But he angrily grabbed Mazo's knife and dropped to the ground, slick with blood. He crawled to Bantaaa's belly and gutted it, freeing three fully formed eggs, ready to be laid, from the gore.

Mazo watched him with disgust. Using a clean slicing motion from his blaster, Mazo severed Bantaaa's head and hoisted the bloody thing up with a whoop. He then ran to join his comrades in the ship.

The gangway had already receded. But when Mazo reached the still-open hatch, a hand from within grabbed the gory head, then another hand grabbed Mazo and quickly pulled him inside. The hatch sealed and the ship began to hum and glow. Then it arced up and was gone.

The Man With No Face sensed a flyer far overhead swooping in on him. He looked up and his eyes could actually track it, though its image was fuzzy. He entered its mind and saw himself watching from below. It was unsettling to see this creature's eyes watch him, and still see himself through those eyes at the same time.

The drogan young squirmed inside their shells. And like a gathering storm, the Kin began to notice him. He could feel furious probing into his consciousness. He pushed it out and let their chant fill his mind. With the eggs in his arms, he began to lope toward some outcroppings not far to the south.

There was a small cave there. He found it during one of his prior excursions while hiding from Bantaaa, before he had gained full control over his mind. He would only be safe underground.

But he was so weak. Could he make it at all? Could he get there before the Kin reached him first?

He felt at least eleven drogans on the plateau and they were closing in fast, racing from various points in towards Bantaaa's mutilated corpse. Their angry legs hit the ground in tandem, like a single galloping cavalry.

The trader focused all the energy he could muster on his own ragged legs. He struggled to match the pace set by the Kin's chant. Focusing on this rhythm helped him ignore his own weakness. With a few stumbles he finally neared his destination.

There was a blur of movement on the left. In panic he saw one of the Kin bearing down on him. He fought to get to the rocks before this female reached him. But his feet were very heavy.

He stumbled and she was nearly on him. He could feel her hot breath on his back. He closed his eyes and focused on the chant. To his surprise she passed him and ran on toward

Bantaaa's body. He reached the outcropping and quickly found the small grotto. He gently dropped the eggs inside and caught his breath.

He forced his mind to stretch out to the Kin converging on Bantaaa's remains. As they gathered in around her body, their chant broke off into shards of horror and grief. Then Kin became silent and still. After a moment, their ear-rending scream filled the sky.

FIFTEEN

AFTHARI RAIDER COLONY

WHEN SHE REACHED the edge of the main square, Maranth smoothed her robes and deftly made her way around the clusters of Afthari throughout the green park. As usual, few were in transit. Most conversed on benches or sprawled on the grass. She passed six raiders intently throwing and betting on dice. She also passed several who seemed to fill their time doing nothing at all.

Doc trailed closely behind. Since the last attack in the alley, he always stayed close to Maranth and never let her out of his sight. Though not much had happened since, there were no new attacks, no serious medical cases, and also no progress on Maranth's escape project.

Today just a few beggars waited in the usual spot for her afternoon clinic. She smiled down at Kojji who seemed to be first in line. He certainly was her most frequent patient. She bowed.

Kojji tugged her robe as he lifted his shirt and pointed to another nasty swelling on his side. "Meddoc, can you fix this up?"

Maranth smiled. "Aye, another of those bites? Well, I can soothe it some until it heals."

She turned to Doc. "Beta light and Court–106."

Doc whipped out a laser appendage and began treatment. Kojji closed his eyes and relaxed.

Maranth was pleased that everything seemed so calm and normal. But her satisfaction was quickly pierced by a splinter of humiliation and anxiety. She pushed it away.

No matter.

Maranth knew she must maintain her normal calm, clear Veddian state of mind. She would not let the pathologies, the evils of this debased society, corrupt the equilibrium that was her birthright.

When the treatment was finished, Doc cut off the light and applied a salve. Kojji opened his eyes and looked up.

She smiled. "Next time, bring me one of the little pests and I'll make you a better remedy."

"Yah. Almost forgot." He grinned and held up a big, grey wiggly bug.

Doc slipped over one of his telescoping tubes and sucked the bug inside with a vacuumy slurp.

Kojji stood and stretched. "Thanks, Meddoc."

He then sidled up to Maranth and whispered in her ear. "You heard Zedd's crew got a drogan?"

Maranth delicately pulled away and smiled. "It's all everyone has talked about for the last week."

A passing raider, a tall man with a minor limp and not much hair, joined them. "I heard that man without any face got back his eyes and ran off, all bloody. No one can figure it."

She frowned. *Eyes? Impossible.*

Kojji slightly jostled the other man backward and gave Maranth a wink. He then turned to the bald raider. "All of it sounds crazy. But Zedd's crew just got back and brought that drogan's head as proof."

He pointed over to a small crowd gathering around some swaggering raiders near the center of the square, about 50 feet from the cookbots. "It's over there."

The raider turned and mumbled as he ambled toward the excitement. "Never thought I'd get to see one and live."

The remaining beggars in her clinic also took off to join the growing crowd. With nothing more to do, Maranth trailed after them with Doc at her heels. She managed to slip between a few of the less boisterous Afthari to see a lanky, grizzled raider and several older children noisily worry what was left of the bloody drogan head. They poked, kicked and dragged it around for the benefit of the spectators.

Maranth pushed through the others, who raggedly made way for her and her medibot. She quickly assumed her most authoritative presence and pointed to the carcass.

"Don't touch it. It could be diseased."

Doc then probed through its flesh and took samples. He also drilled into the bone, then scanned the carcass with some of his sensors and irradiated it with several beams of light. When finished, he hobbled back to Maranth's side.

"It's safe. They may continue."

As the crowd surged forward, Maranth and Doc slipped back to the periphery and then headed to a quieter spot, away from the activity. Maranth settled on the grass while Doc quietly processed his samples and ran various tests.

Doc urgently tugged Maranth's sleeve. "What I'm about to say won't make any sense. Okay, I am off, but not when it comes to science. Honest."

Maranth sighed. "Honest?" She regretted she couldn't safely fix his personality matrix.

Doc wiggled an antenna excitedly. "I gene-mapped cell samples from that drogan head, and compared the results to the samples from the flyer that fried and fell through the force field. Okay, if my database was compromised, my results could be inaccurate. But I've self-tested twice and retested the samples."

"Doc, just out with it. Please."

"My analysis clearly shows the flyers and drogans are genetically related, but not to the other life on this planet. At least not the biting pests and microbes that I have samples of. I've tested and retested everything. There is no mistake."

Doc pushed out his screen and displayed the information so Maranth could see it from the ground.

She viewed the scrolling data carefully and then got to her feet. She considered Doc's conclusions thoughtfully.

"Two separate evolutionary lineages on one planet are highly unlikely."

"More than that." Doc wiggled the screen. "Take another look."

She re-examined the readouts. "Veddian-like? Highly unlikely. Your logic routines most likely need an overhaul. Did that pervert tamper...?"

"He didn't touch my logic or database storage. My self-tests include firmware and core dumps regarding all changes. I'm good."

She eyed him critically. "Your personality matrix is clearly not good."

"Aye. He did change that. Said I'd be more fun. Anyway, these creatures are more than Veddian-like. They genetically map to known Veddian fauna. See?"

Maranth looked again. "If correct, this means these drogans and flyers are related to birds in some ancient way, which should be totally impossible."

Loud arguing near the cookbots interrupted her train of thought. Several Afthari men surrounded something on the ground. Sensing trouble, she hurried over to this new disturbance, where her services might soon be needed.

One of the men was a beggar she recognized from her clinic. He caught Maranth's eye. "He's back. Look!"

"Who is back?"

"The Man With No Face. He's back."

The men surrounded the maimed wretch tucked into a fetal position on the ground. One of the raiders kicked him.

"Yah. He's back alright."

The man on the ground sat up. He clearly was the same faceless stranger, except now his brilliant blue eyes tracked the faces around him. He eyed the raider who kicked him and the raider shrank back a little. "Those eyes, whoa!"

The others just stared with mouths open.

Most everyone in Afthar had naturally brown eyes, though there were a few with grey, green or blue ones. However, his were such an intense blue they seemed almost artificial.

Kojji looked around at the other Afthari. "The rest of his face is still gone."

He turned back and scrutinized the wretched man's eyes. "So how did you get back in here? Anyone else would be dead. Dead and eaten by drogans."

He thumped the man with his knee. "So?"

Another raider then shoved the unfortunate hard enough to knock him over again. "Yah, how do you survive outside?"

The Man With No Face just shook his head weakly.

The raider poked him harder. "Yah. And how did you get your eyes?"

Maranth pushed her way between the raider and the injured man. Maranth suppressed her own disquiet and tried to project calm and reason to the volatile men around her.

"Eyes or not, he still cannot hear or answer your questions."

Does he know I'm here?

He had not yet looked in her direction. Then his words slipped into her head.

Thank you.

She was sure it was his words and decided she would not let them frighten her.

He took his head cloth and wrapped it, Afthari-style, around his still-deformed lower face so that only his eyes were visible. "Doc?"

Doc slipped between two of the onlookers and began his diagnostic of the unfortunate. "He's depleted again. Same problem, but worse this time. His new eyes are complete and functional… aye, with normal vision. The new injuries are superficial. Hemoflox?"

She nodded. "Please adjust the dosage as needed."

He keeps losing blood. Why, why? And those eyes!

He straightened and looked up at her so she could not help staring into them. Maranth knew of nothing besides some advanced facilities in the innerworlds that could regenerate eyes, or any other complex organ of human anatomy from scratch. This man had no eyes before, not even any proto eye tissue under his skin. Now, suddenly, he had a complete pair with normal sight and tear ducts. He even had eyelashes and brows.

Another mystery.

Strangely, a very ancient Veddian classic came to mind. She was Alice and this was just some savage Wonderland where nothing made sense. That thought seemed strangely relaxing.

The Man With No Face had felt Maranth nearby before she even realized he was there. In the chaotic jumble of mental disarray that filled the colony, hers was always the most controlled, the calmest. He had resisted looking directly at her because she still feared him. Only when she hovered directly overhead to examine him did he dare look straight into her face.

He was surprised she was so delicate looking. Somehow he'd expected hardier, more motherly features. He'd been careful not to do any real probing of the other Afthari, just light forays within the jumble of consciousness to get his bearings. His attempts to connect with this one woman had not been easy. Despite her nurturing nature and logical mind, she had been afraid of him. If the other Afthari even suspected his mental ability, they would kill him for sure.

He'd only caught a glimpse of her dark hair and honey skin through other eyes. But Maranth was actually exquisite looking. This realization rattled him and he looked down. He willed his mind still and let his treatment progress.

Returning to the colony was risky given all that had happened. But he needed this woman's treatments to recover his strength, to survive. She'd protect him if she could. His own reaction when he actually saw her was an unexpected complication.

The crowd gave way to Mier Zedd. Maranth bowed. He ignored her and towered over The Man With No Face, studying him.

Mier Zedd's eyes narrowed. "Before, did he have eyes under his skin?"

"No." Maranth willed herself calm as Zedd's tone bore into her.

His face hardened. "A drogan was eating him and then suddenly he has eyes. So, explain these eyes."

"I cannot. Many life forms can naturally regenerate body parts. Humans cannot. Perhaps the drogan somehow regenerated his eyes, or perhaps something else. I just don't know. But he remains helpless. He still has no nose, mouth or ears. And he is very weak, very depleted."

Mier Zedd scowled. "He's been living out there with the drogans. Why didn't they finish him off? They kill and eat the rest of us easy enough."

He yanked her patient's head back by his hair. "I don't like it."

Just as Zedd raised a fist, there was a buzzing sound from the sky. Most looked up, though a few just closed their eyes and gritted their teeth. As before, a mass hurdled down into the force field in a crackling shower of lights. The blackened remains fell among some nearby compounds.

Kojji tugged at Maranth's sleeve. "Meddoc, you got a remedy for that?"

Maranth grimly responded. "Only if you catch me one, first."

Some of the others laughed nervously. Not amused, Mier Zedd motioned for silence. Again he tugged the man's hair, this time yanking him to his feet. Maranth tried to intercede. Zedd roared and shoved her away.

A black workbot raced up. "After the flyer fried it dropped on Zella, your daughter…"

Zedd dropped his victim and began to run. Maranth and Doc raced after him.

The other Afthari began to drift off. The Man With No Face moved off to the periphery among some bushes. He set his begging bowl out and hunched over to hide his face, hoping to go unnoticed as just another beggar to be left alone.

Soon after, the cookbots rumbled to life. It was their time to prepare the beggars' supper.

He tried to sleep. But it was harder now that light seeped through his eyelids. He'd forgotten about that. But he could rest, maybe doze, and let his thoughts drift.

They first drifted to the Afthari who'd tormented him earlier. He had fought the impulse to take over their minds in self-defense. It would have been as easy as taking over any malaaa. But he didn't dare, there were too many. And they would know and kill him. Clearly their leader, Zedd, intended to finish him off later. What if Zedd hadn't been drawn away? Could he have influenced Zedd's thinking without him knowing?

Maybe. Maybe not.

What were his options? Nothing else came to mind.

His thoughts then drifted to his lovely meddoc. At one point he had had the impulse to just take her mind over, to make her understand. Even though he was sure he could do so, he knew he wouldn't.

Self-defense against force was one thing. But normal social interactions are just like trade. Energy flows from one person to another. Any Patusian trader knows such interactions must be voluntary or his accounts can't balance. The Afthari had fed and sheltered him. This woman had freely given him medical care and tried to protect him. No balance here.

He owed her the most, but he owed them all.

SIXTEEN

AFTHARI RAIDER COLONY

HOURS HAD PASSED since the confrontation on the main square. Maranth tiredly pushed back a strand of hair as she monitored the unconscious little girl in a bed too large for her small body. It was deep night and the room was nearly as dark as it was outside, only lit by some of the sensors and probes Doc had in the child's ears and nose. A small monitoring device and bandages covered part of her head and face.

Maranth gently cupped little Zella's cheek, then stroked her hand. "Let's run the ERG again."

Doc let out a thin tentacle with a small clamp at the tip that lifted the girl's eyelids one at a time while he beamed a bluish light into each eye.

As he was doing so, Maranth carefully monitored Doc's data screen. "The pressure's down. She will fully recover. By the way, tomorrow please Hemoflox the Man With No Face again. His anemia is worse than ever."

Doc retracted his instruments. "The Hemoflox is nearly gone. But I found an Edian blood cloner among this household's stores. Oh, there's something else, something that I didn't get a chance to tell you before. About that unusual nodule in that man's skull, the drogan head had one just like it."

Maranth slowly stood, stretched and grimaced. "Aye, so this

unknown feature is shared by this single maimed, but telepathic human, and a race of terrifying creatures that shouldn't exist."

She sighed, then smoothed her robes. "I'm going back to get some sleep."

"Good. I was just about to prescribe the same. No problem here. I'll stay the watch."

"Thanks, Doc." With that, Maranth slipped out into the dimly lit compound and wearily made her way to its entrance. She was met by a grim, white-faced Meir Zedd, and his overwrought wife, Rosia.

Maranth took Rosia's hand. "You know we almost lost her. But Zella's out of danger and will be fine. She's sleeping comfortably. Now I'm going to do the same."

The matron fearfully squeezed her hand. "You can't leave now."

Maranth gently pulled her hand away. "I must sleep to function. My medibot is monitoring her and will contact me if her condition changes in any way. I promise."

"Then when will you come back?"

"Morning. Sooner, if needed." Maranth bowed and turned for the path to her own compound. Mier Zedd stopped her. He hefted a large, heavy bag of credits and dumped it into both of Maranth's hands. She was too stunned to say anything.

"For your great service to my House of Zedd." He stiffly nodded. It was both an acknowledgment and a dismissal.

Maranth picked her way through the now empty and poorly lit main square. Only the dim light pavers that meandered through the vegetation indicated the way through the park. The bag in her hands was very heavy and she was exhausted. But she didn't care. Such a huge number of credits in her grasp, all at once, meant she could buy freedom, buy her way out.

Freedom, freedom, freedom!

She dropped the bag and flopped down on the grass, then rolled over and over like a child. She lay spread-eagled on her back for a few moments, then flipped over and deeply inhaled the greenness that so reminded her of Veddi. She started to relax and realized she was fading into sleep. So she hopped back up, grabbed the heavy bag and continued across the square.

She was nearly at the edge of the empty park when she noticed the maimed trader sitting cross-legged on the ground by his begging bowl. She went over to him and knelt down.

"Tomorrow, my medibot will give you an Edian blood cloner device and show you how to use it. It will grow all the blood you need. You won't have to come back here anytime soon."

He did not look up or respond. She tentatively put a questioning hand on his shoulder. He just leaned into it and closed his eyes.

She sighed. *Rest. You should rest now.*

It was then she caught a bit of movement behind her patient, just off the plaza. She realized it was Gannet fading back into shadow. She also noted the not quite concealed tip of a very large boot caught in a wisp of light along the path, a boot that could only belong to Jobbar.

Obbad knew what Zedd would give me and sent his two thieves.

Impotent anger and frustration washed through her. The Man With No Face sensed her alarm and looked up. He now could clearly see her frantic brown eyes. Suddenly she met his gaze with determination and shakily eased the bag of credits into his begging bowl.

Take care. And when you get back the rest of your face… remember me. I'm slave Maranth.

She bitterly rose and slipped off. He opened the bag and realized what she had done. Shocked, he looked up again, but she was gone.

His mind sought her out and witnessed her humiliation and pain at the hands of the same two men as before. He now understood why she had given him these credits. And he knew he could not stop their predation as he could barely move. The trader could only console himself that she wouldn't really be harmed.

I will never forget this debt, Maranth. Never.

SEVENTEEN

AFTHARI RAIDER COLONY

THOUGH HIS EYES could now navigate the darkness, out of habit the maimed trader made his way along the path by feeling the wall to his right. It was the following night. As usual, the late hour was filled with the background whisper of sleeping Afthari and a smattering of mental chatter from a few that were awake.

He shifted his shoulders a little, to square the makeshift backpack tied across his chest and neck. The featureless part of his face was swathed Afthari style. Though it was unlikely he would run into anyone this late, the less attention he brought to himself, the better.

He began to feel a low vibration in the wall under his hand. This meant the force field was not far off. The vibration grew stronger as he progressed. His wall ended and both his hands now traveled around and over a line of cargo crates on each side. Larger crates were jumbled together on his left.

The crates on both sides converged at the high perimeter wall. The vibration was strongest here, punctuated with strong spikes and missed beats. The colony's force field was very close, meeting the ground just beyond the wall. The intensity of the field seemed to dampen the mental noise from the colony to a low buzz.

He couldn't trust his new eyes because they didn't hold

the memory of the crate he needed. That memory was in his hands. He closed his eyes and carefully felt each crate for the right one. When his hands found it, he pushed it aside to reveal the narrow tunnel he'd dug out some time ago.

By now, his face cloth had fallen away. But it didn't matter. He took a quick look around and again reconsidered his options. None were good. If he stayed in the colony he wouldn't live long. Outside, his chances weren't much better. The Kin, except for Bantaaa, had mostly ignored him. He doubted he would be so lucky now that she'd been killed. They would certainly see him as the cause of her death. He thought of the stake in his backpack.

Even with this, the risk is so great.

But he had no real choice. He took a deep, centering breath. *Patushah… Maranth. Strengthen me!*

Maranth awoke with a start. She looked around her room, but nothing seemed amiss. She settled herself and drifted back to sleep.

PLATEAU, PLANET AFTHAR

The trader soon emerged from an outcrop of rocks and underbrush outside the colony, onto the plateau. Even here, the ground softly vibrated from the nearby force field. He shut his eyes and willed his mind quiet among the telepathic murmur of the sleeping Kin.

He adjusted the position of his backpack, re-fastened his head cloth, and set off across the empty plateau in a slow jog, accompanied only by a cold breeze. He had to stop now and then to catch his breath and regain strength. After some time had passed the sky to his left began to lighten. Clearly dawn wasn't far off.

Cold and exhausted, he squatted and doubled over, his head down between his knees. He must hide from the Kin in the distance as well as from the wind that cut to his bones. He cleared that thought from his mind and rested.

By the time he slid down from the plateau it was full light. Now it was a lot warmer. The wind had died among the outcroppings and the sunshine of the new day dusted the vegetation. He found a natural path that snaked between vine-wrapped boulders into the denser vegetation farther down. The air was thick with moisture. In the quiet dampness, one of the voices in his head grew angry and loud.

I'm getting careless. Quiet mind.

The voice, now nearer and much stronger, shrieked out. Its owner's face filled his brain.

Bantaaa's mate. He found me!

The Man With No Face closed his eyes to clear his mind again. Then he raced through the steamy vegetation, using his hands to push off and slip around tree trunks. He sensed the vibration of the drogan crashing after him from above and behind. Hosaaa's rage filled the trader's head. The man swerved down into a patch of fog and pulled himself inside a thicket of scratchy vegetation.

No fear. Be still.

A telepathic roar cut through his brain. His pursuer was closing in. The man's blue eyes searched the fog and found the dim outline of a nearby rock fall. He bolted for the outcropping. He found a crevice under two of the boulders just large enough for his torso. He belly-crawled through the mud until he found a space big enough to shift himself around. The telepathic cries faded and then were gone. He was safe in the quiet — for the moment.

Above, Hosaaa angrily crashed about in the fog. His mind bellowed out to the Kin.

I FELT IT. I FELT BANTAAA'S ALIEN.

He howled in frustration and the disquieted, distant mental murmur rose in intensity.

A nearby drogan broke in. *ANYTHING MORE FROM IT?*

Hosaaa nuzzled the outcropping. His claws delicately raked back nearby vegetation seeking the alien.

NO. I SMELL IT HERE. BUT THERE'S NO WIFF FROM ITS MIND.

BANTAAA WAS RIGHT ABOUT THIS SUFUNAAA. IT HIDES FROM ME.

Hosaaa pushed further on, back into the thickest part of the fog.

After some time passed, the Man With No Face slid out toward the entrance to sense if his pursuer was still around. The telepathic banter of the drogans was lighter now. There was nothing from the drogan who hunted him.

He emptied his mind and made his way down to the misty stream at the bottom of the ravine. After quickly rinsing off the mud, he made his way along the stream bank. A mantis-like creature the size of a chicken bolted from under his feet and crashed off to his right.

He quickly composed himself and blanked out his thoughts. He slipped into a familiar tangled thicket that was emitting a lot of disorganized mental grunts. Pushing aside leafy branches, he exposed his makeshift box trap half covered in ground litter. Inside were four plated creatures with snapping pincers.

Brasiaas.

Their hard shells were a mottled brown, a perfect camouflage for a creature that lived in the leaf litter of the forest floor.

It would hide them from Flyers above, but not from the Kin.

His trap had a funnel affair on top, made of upside-down thorn bark. The downward pointing thorns coated the interior. He dropped a handful of seeds into this funnel. It's bottom lip depressed with the pressure and the seeds slid into the woven branch and bark box that formed the rest of the trap.

The brasiaas attacked the seeds hungrily. One of them was accidentally pushed up by the others and tried to escape through the funnel, but the thorns forced it back down. The Man With No Face opened the side of the box away from the funnel area. He grabbed each of the creatures from behind and dropped it into his sack.

He sensed a Flyer soaring above, searching for him. He hurriedly covered the trap and hunkered down under the foliage while the Flyer swooped overhead. It cried out again before it disappeared down the ravine.

Good time to sleep. Wait for dark.

It was very dark when he finally awoke. There was only a docile somnolence from the Kin. That meant they were asleep.

Wriggling sack in hand, the trader felt his way in the dark to a set of low boulders. He went around them and climbed up a bit, then sidestepped between a narrow passage splitting two boulder piles. He pushed aside a handful of decaying vines to reveal his cave.

Glowing bits of fungus and glittery minerals dimly lit the way. His new eyes watched a couple of iridescent cave worms rhythmically wave their cilia as he passed. He had been surprised that his first food on Afthar was so pleasant looking. These worms would be safe from him, as he now caught larger and more filling prey like the creatures in his sack.

The faint hint of the Kin had disappeared in the rock. But it now was replaced by a faint, lively babble that grew louder as he progressed deeper into the cave. Soon the chatter turned into eager cries as he entered a larger chamber.

He set his wiggling sack down and carefully removed his backpack. He brought the bag over to a large pen he'd constructed to contain Bantaaa's three offspring. Much like very large bird chicks, they cried and clamored hungrily. Each was covered in a plain, downy coat. None of the promise of their parents' bright plumage yet showed.

The pen was a makeshift assemblage of branches and handmade rope. Its straw floor was littered with now-trampled eggshells, animal bones and plating. At one end was a natural rivulet running down from the top of the stone wall until it disappeared into a crack between the cave wall and its dusty floor.

Hush children. I've brought you your favorite, brasiaas.

He held up the squirming, grunting sack. The little drogans' cries become softer and shriller. He emptied the brasiaas into the pen. They tumbled out, snapping their pincers and running in all directions.

He sat down by his backpack to rest, ignoring the pouncing, grunting and crunching of the drogan chicks as they awkwardly captured and ate their prey. After a while, a new clamor in his head replaced their predatory cries.

MORE, MORE!

The exhausted trader looked at the pen and the little drogans returned his gaze in an intense, entreating manner. *MORE...*

He knew what they wanted.

ANYTHING ELSE? WHAT ABOUT JOLICKIES? GOOD AND JUICY THIS TIME OF YEAR. OR RABBITWORTS? YOU ALWAYS LOVED THEM BEFORE.

But Bantaaa's young would not be put off.

NO, IT'S THE THIRST. FEED... FEED US, FEED US. THE THIRST...

The trader reluctantly rose and approached the youngsters, who eagerly fixed on his every move. He opened the gate, the motion knocking aside a brasiaas shell stained with greenish gore. Then he crept in, carefully closing the gate behind him.

WE THIRST... THIRST, THIRST. FEED US, FEED US.

He squatted down and rolled up his sleeves. He thrust his bare arms out. The three youngsters each found a spot and sunk their teeth in deep. The Man With No Face's eyes closed and he seemingly slept as they fed on him.

He soon shook the torpor off and tried to find the strength to rise, pulling the youngsters off his mangled arms.

Enough.

They tumbled off him, blood-smeared faces satisfied. Weak and pale, he stepped back through the gate and carefully closed it behind. His wounds began to close almost immediately.

EIGHTEEN

RAVINE, PLANET AFTHAR

BANTAAA'S YOUNG NOW ignored him. They jostled each other as they drank water off the wall. In the process, they managed to wash the leftovers of their meal from their fuzzy faces. Then the chicks began to tumble and play together.

The maimed trader lay nearby, safe enough to relax and eventually slip into sleep. His thoughts drifted to Bantaaa. Strangely, as scary as she was, he missed her.

Why?

He was lucky she had mostly finished his eyes before she died. They continued to regenerate to the point where he had perfect vision, maybe better than in the past. Before he made the deal, he'd almost backed out, fearing eyes would dull his telepathic abilities. He knew his telepathy kept him alive. But the Kin had eyes and their telepathy was intact. So he set aside his fear. Only by regaining his face and senses would he ever be able to live among his own kind.

Aye. He had traded Bantaaa his blood, strength, and pain for these eyes. His accounts balanced with her. He missed her because she was the only being he had any real contact with for a long time.

He had needed to save what was left of her, those three eggs. It was lucky she was about to lay them when she died. So they were formed enough to survive outside her body.

Even so, he wasn't sure he could keep them alive. A bit of information he'd picked up from Bantaaa led him to bury them in rotting vegetation that received some sunlight, so they would stay warm. He also checked and turned them over several times. He knew the chicks inside were alive from the disordered shards of thoughts they gave off as they moved around with increasing energy.

Meanwhile, he prepared this particular cave because it had its own water supply and a narrow opening. He'd actually found it some time before and slept in it from time to time. He built the pen to nest the youngsters safely until they were bigger, and also protect him from their predations while he slept.

The afternoon of the second day after Bantaaa died, the chicks started to crack through their shells. As they hatched he gathered them into his arms and clothes to keep them warm. As soon as they were dry he moved them into the cave and settled them in a rough nest of leaves inside the pen. Eventually, the leaves were scattered everywhere by their boisterous play.

The Man With No Face smoothed his backpack to support his head, and soon dropped off to sleep. His wounded arms relaxed and slipped down his sides. The bloody gashes had already half healed.

Half a day passed. Muted, broken streaks of morning light now veined the walls of the cavern, carried by the reflective minerals in the rock. Even this far underground, they added enough to the glow produced by the fungus to light the space with a subdued, greenish cast.

The drogan chicks were friskily at play: nipping, pouncing and tumbling with one another. Their chirps began to rouse the sleeping man and he moved a little. A nearby cave worm crawled over to his head and one of its cilia touched his skin. He brushed it away without opening his eyes. It returned and he tried to brush it away again but instead awakened with a start. Realizing what it was, he relaxed and gently pushed it off.

He dreaded what he must do next. He emptied his mind

and entered the pen where he stripped down to his waist. The chicks stopped their play but he warned them off.

Back away.

They stayed where they were, but carefully watched him wash his face and drink from the water flowing down the wall. All the while he kept a wary eye on them as well. The wounds from the night were nearly gone.

Move away!

The chicks slipped back a little, still watching his every move. He backed out and closed its latch securely.

Soon he was fully dressed, backpack on, ready for what he dreaded. He undid the latch and the youngsters bounded out. He watched them attack and eat the cave worm in the open space of their lair. He closed his eyes.

Patushah! Strengthen me.

He strode up the passageway.

Come children…

The chicks excitedly bounded after him, leaving behind the half eaten worm oozing violet and green gore.

They soon tumbled out into the ravine with all its sights, smells and wonders. One of the chicks experimented with mud while the other two shyly tested some plant life nearby. An insect type of creature flew up from the leaves and the two adventurers sprang back and hid behind the maimed trader, who was squatting nearby. He waited, still as stone, his backpack open by his side. A flyer swooped over but the man made no effort to hide.

Peace. You of the Kin, come trade. Though your malaaas die, I can quench your thirst for red blood. For all of the Kin. Everyone. For all time, forever.

The flyer returned and circled lazily overhead.

ALIEN, ALIEN, ALIEN…

The youngsters soon heard drogans crashing toward their clearing. They also sensed rage from the Kin and huddled up against the trader in fear.

THE SUFUNAAA DARES RETURN. I WILL DRINK HIS BLOOD TODAY.

In his head, the maimed trader saw Bantaaa's angry mate Hosaaa through the eyes of another drogan.

TOO EASY. HE TRICKED BANTAAA TO HER DEATH.

When Hosaaa responded, the trader saw the first drogan through Hosaaa's eyes. Its plumage was less flamboyant, like Bantaaa. Its green and gold plumage was a bit shorter and contained no black and white chevrons. He understood Hosaaa knew her as Vabaaa, Bantaaa's sister. Amazingly, neither drogan seemed to notice his mental intrusions.

Vabaaa ruffled her plumage angrily.

THEN WE WILL GIVE HIM GREAT PAIN FOR DAYS WHILE WE SLOWLY DRINK HIM DRY.

They were closing in. The Man With No Face fought down the terror rising from his gut. He willed his mind empty, stood up and tried again to communicate.

If you kill me your thirst will still return.

Hosaaa broke into the clearing with a shriek and scatter of feathers.

SUFFER AND DIE SLOW, ALIEN.

Then he noticed the drogan chicks.

WHAT'S THIS?

Three more drogans poured into the clearing from various directions. Vabaaa was the first of this group.

A second female called to the youngsters. *BABIES! COME.*

The chicks shrank away from her, trying to hide behind the human. The trader realized her name was Fawasaaa. And her iridescent green down was darker than the down of the other females.

He spoke into her mind.

Bantaaa's young. I saved them when she died, nurtured them…

He gently picked one up and held for the Kin to see.

…For Bantaaa, for the Kin.

Hosaaa plucked the drogan chick from his hands. Fawasaaa

grabbed another while the third still clung to the man's leg in terror. Three more mature drogans crashed through the vegetation to join the confrontation.

The maimed trader took a bulky device from his open pack.

With this device you'll never thirst again. Is your vengeance on me worth that? You know I did not kill Bantaaa, though others of my kind did so.

Fawasaaa tried to sooth the frightened youngster. She cocked her head thoughtfully.

I FEEL NO DECEPTION FROM THE ALIEN. HEAR HIM OUT.

Hosaaa would have none of it. He dropped his chick and grabbed the human with his claws. The third drogan chick clung to the man's leg shrieked in terror as Hosaaa positioned his jaws to bite through the human's shoulder. But Vabaaa shoved him away with her body.

THIS ONE SCHEMES TO APPEASE US. IT GIVES US BANTAAA'S YOUNG AND OFFERS THE ONE THING WE CRAVE. CAN BANTAAA BE RIGHT? IS IT INTELLIGENT?

Fawasaaa gathered Hosaaa's dropped chick to join the one she already had.

AT LEAST IT'S AMUSING.

There was a lot of head bobbing and murmurs of assent. Another drogan gently took the last clinging chick off the trader. She passed it back to Fawasaaa behind her. The trader laid his device on the ground and opened its case.

I am a male human. Fill your bellies with all of the food animals of Afthar. Yet you and your flyers still must eat malaaas now and then. Only the malaaas and flyers are red blooded like you. Only they provide the key nutrient from red blood you need to survive here.

Hosaaa tossed his head venomously.

YOUR KIND ALSO PROVIDES IT.

Another wave of assent passed through the Kin.

The hairs on the back of his neck stood up. He quickly suppressed his surging fear.

Your malaaas have been dying off since my kind came here.

Your flyers are too small for your needs. The Kin can't breach the human 'hive' on the plateau. And the occasional shipwreck of my kind can't feed all of you.

He eyed each drogan around him.

Have you ever caught more than a dozen of my kind in an Af-year?

Vabaaa flicked her tail in annoyance, barely missing his head.

THE MALAAAS MAY COME BACK. CERTAINLY SOME HAVE GOTTEN SICK AND DIED, REDUCING THEIR NUMBERS. THE REAL PROBLEM IS WE EAT AS MANY OF THEM AS WE DID BEFORE. SO WE ARE EATING THEM FASTER THAN THEY CAN REPLENISH THEIR NUMBERS.

He eyed her.

Then they are dying off. How much longer for the thirsty Kin?

Fawasaaa settled herself on the ground with a quick rustle of feathers and inspected and preened her young charges with her talons.

IT DISQUIETS ME THAT THIS SUFUNAAA COMMUNICATES WITH US INTELLIGENTLY WHEN THE REST OF HIS KIND CANNOT.

The trader ignored her comment and picked up his device.

This machine makes as much red blood, every day, that you can drink from six of my kind.

A gasp of disbelief swept through the crowd. Hosaaa roared and moved in threateningly.

YOU DARE TOY WITH US!

His teeth bit deeply into the trader's arm and the machine dropped from his hands. Vabaaa tried to restrain her brother-in-law while Fawasaaa called out.

YOU'RE IN SUCH A HURRY TODAY. DID YOU NOT SLEEP WELL?

Hosaaa sheepishly let the alien go. Arm dripping blood, the trader shakily returned to the open machine and removed a large, transparent container of nearly clear fluid.

As you can see, the container holds a type of water made from fresh roots, leaves, and stems.

He shook it and showed it around.

Hosaaa snapped his teeth near the trader's neck.

A TRICK.

The human poured a small amount of the liquid onto Hosaaa's clawed hand.

You can make this liquid from living plants.

The man squatted down on the ground and pulled the entire mechanism apart.

There is no red blood here yet. See?

He then put the parts back together and closed up the device. He held a pipette up to the wound on his arm and the pipette carried a thin line of his blood into the device.

The sight of the tiny stream of blood entering the device excited the drogans. They eagerly crowded in closer.

The Man With No Face set the controls.

Now we must wait for the machine.

A bit later, a soft noise from the device alerted the crowd. Their minds focused on the thin, clear hose that the maimed trader held out.

Who'll be first to drink?

Hosaaa stepped up belligerently.

The trader stood up to face him but otherwise did not react.

You must open your mouth.

The drogan opened his jaws close to his head. Ignoring the implied threat, he aimed the hose into Hosaaa's gullet. The maimed man activated the machine and a stream of blood flowed into Hosaaa's mouth.

A tremor of excitement passed through the others.

After Hosaaa had a deep swallow, the trader offered the hose to Fawasaaa, who also drank deeply.

Hosaaa knocked the tube away.

IT TASTES REAL BECAUSE HE HAD RED BLOOD HIDDEN INSIDE.

Fawasaaa kicked her compatriot and knocked him over.

There is no room to conceal that much blood. The trader picked up the tube.

A large male drogan grabbed the machine to examine it.

The trader realized the others recognized him as Fawasaaa's mate, Giraaa. Using his talons, Giraaa pried it open. The large container was now nearly full of fresh, red blood.

The trader could feel this drogan was well respected from the feelings of the others. He directed his thoughts to him.

Blood is made up of small cells of life. The liquid feeds these blood cells to multiply fast until they grow to fill the container. As your saliva nurtures the regrowth of my flesh around a wound, this machine nurtures the growth of blood.

Fawasaaa stood, shook her plumage and nodded.

IT TASTES JUST LIKE THE ALIEN'S BLOOD, SLIGHTLY SWEETER THAN OUR MALAAAS.

The other drogans clamored to quench their thirsts as well. Giraaa closed the machine and grabbed the tube. He drank a portion, then passed the machine on. He eyed the human for a long moment.

WHAT DO YOU WANT FROM US, SUFUNAAA?

Fawasaaa broke in.

THIS ONE WANTS THE SAME THING HE WANTED FROM BANTAAA, THAT WE RESTORE HIS FACE AS IT SHOULD BE.

The Man With No Face slowly nodded.

Giraaa shook out his plumage to its maximum effect as he rose to his full height.

IF WE LIVE ON THESE DEVICES FROM THE SUFUNAAA, THEY CONTROL US.

Fawasaaa sidled up to her mate and nuzzled his neck.

SOON THERE WON'T BE ANY KIN LEFT TO CONTROL. HOW CAN WE BE STRONG IF WE'RE ALL DEAD?

The Kin murmured in acknowledgement.

Hosaaa flicked his tail in disapproval.

IS THIS LIFE IF WE DEPEND ON SUCH ALIENS FOR OUR SURVIVAL?

Fawasaaa bucked her head in agreement.

TRUE. WE MUST USE THIS DEVICE FOR A LIMITED TIME ONLY. JUST LONG ENOUGH TO LET OUR MALAAAS REPLENISH.

Hosaaa's eyes bored into the trader.

HIS DEVICE CAN FEED ONLY A FEW OF US. IT MEANS NOTHING. LET ME DRINK HIM DRY.

The trader jerked back as Hosaaa snapped at his head. The drogan's breath washed his face.

Vabaaa again knocked her brother-in-law from the human.

ONCE YOU REGAIN YOUR FACE, WHY WOULD YOU RETURN TO US?

The trader squatted down.

My people will give me several machines for each human you return alive, plus something more to me for my trouble. I'll return because I also gain with each trade.

He paused a moment, then continued.

You must restore my face so I can communicate with my kind to get many machines like this. In time, enough machines for all the Kin. Enough for the flyers, too. Eventually your malaaas may replenish themselves and you will not need these anymore.

Fawasaaa stepped up to him on his right side. Her face dropped down to where it was just inches from his own.

WHY CAN YOU, SUFUNAAA, COMMUNICATE WITH US INTELLIGENTLY WHEN THE REST OF YOUR KIND CANNOT? EXPLAIN THIS.

I don't know why I am the only human on this world that is telepathic.

Fawasaaa nudged his head.

OUR FLYERS ARE TELEPATHIC, BUT NOT INTELLIGENT.

The trader knew he had to tell them the truth, but the truth would change everything.

My kind has a complex language using many variations of sounds to communicate. We talk to each other. As a result, our intelligence and culture work differently.

The Kin heatedly mulled over what he'd told him.

Finally, Giraaa spoke for them all.

SIX MACHINES AS GOOD AS THIS, NOT ONE LESS, FOR EACH ALIEN WE SAVE FOR YOU. BEFORE YOU LEAVE US, YOU MUST SHOW US HOW TO MAKE THE CLEAR LIQUID THAT GROWS BLOOD.

Giraaa ruffled his feathers and shook his neck. *YOU GET YOUR MOUTH BACK WHEN YOU BRING US THESE MACHINES.*

What about the rest of my face?

Fawasaaa poked him. *WHEN YOU BRING ENOUGH MACHINES FOR ALL THE KIN.*

It was a bad deal. But if he didn't agree, they would eat him. He crossed his hands, palms up, and slid them out in the Patusian sign of confirmation.

Giraaa shook his feathers and hung his head down.

BE VERY, VERY FRIGHTENED, MY KIN. DANGEROUS ALIEN CREATURES NOW RULE OUR SURVIVAL WITH DEVICES.

The minds of the Kin joined together in a melancholy dirge.

NINETEEN

AFTHARI RAIDER COLONY

A FEW DAYS AFTER he made his deal with the Kin, the Man With No Face returned to the colony. He had hidden Maranth's credits in one of his caves and now carried only a few on him. His face cloth wrapped Afthari-style, he wandered between the compounds that were the farthest from Zedd's House. Sometimes he hid among the crates and debris near the force field. He only visited the main square in the early morning, when few people were around, then left right after the cookbots fed him.

On one of his forays among the compounds, several children passed him by and one of the boys dropped his school tablet. These tough, common devices provided school lessons according to a student's age and progress. A child could also write on it by rubbing a finger across the screen. When the boy stopped to retrieve his tablet, the trader held out a credit. He motioned to the tablet and then to the credit in his hand. The boy almost immediately understood and gave him the tablet for the credit.

The maimed man was elated. This inexpensive, simple device meant he could now communicate by writing. The first thing he intended to do was negotiate a ride off the planet!

As before, most of the time he stayed in the shadows. But now he experimented with his telepathy. He had learned

Maranth had only become aware of him in her mind when he was trying to send her a message. So he gently picked through the thoughts of various men who passed by.

It was soon clear his telepathy was never noticed when he read another man's thoughts while the man was talking. Now, when he found an honest raider, he'd use the tablet to try to make a deal. Of course, if any of the raiders thought about it at all, he would assume the trader was lip-reading his words, not mind-reading his thoughts. And the trader had the advantage of reading the man's true intentions, not just his words.

It took him five days to find the right raider, a portly man with long, reddish hair tied in a ponytail. Reading his mind, the trader knew this easygoing man, Jax, could be trusted. Jax agreed to hide the maimed trader on his ship to the nearest spacer port, Tigenne. But the trip would cost the Man With No Face most of Maranth's credits.

Jax was a raider on the ship owned by Saad Donley, Head of one of the less prominent Houses. Late night, before the ship was due to leave, Jax hid the trader in a back compartment. The next day during the pre-flight check-off, Donley routinely asked Jax to scan the ship for stowaways. Jax replied there were none.

TIGENNE

When the ship landed in Tigenne, the Man With No Face stayed hidden even after everyone else left. Hours later, Jax returned to the ship and made his way to the small storage space that concealed his stowaway.

Jax opened its hatch and smiled. "Time to pay up."

The trader climbed out and stretched his cramped body. Then he reached into the compartment and pulled out the large bag of credits and gave them to the raider.

Jax grinned as he hefted the bag amiably. "Nice doing business with you."

He happily led the maimed trader through the ship and out

its main hatch. Under the cover of night, the two headed to the edge where the spaceport met the settlement. In front of them lay the commercial district of Tigenne in all its raucous glory.

Jax patted the maimed trader on his shoulder. "This is where we part, yah?"

His former stowaway nodded. Jax took off towards a gaudily lit casino about 100 yards away. It had a big sign flashing 'We Got It All.' He disappeared around the building.

Actually the whole district was a jumble of bright flashing signs and holos that mesmerized the eyes. Everything else was obscured by the flash and brilliance that promised excitement and vice. The trader headed into the closest street with his face cloth wrapped securely Afthari-style. He stayed in the shadows as he made his way over to the darkened section of the settlement. He looked for a place he could sleep and hide until morning.

His spirits had risen as soon as he had seen Tigenne. He understood spacer ports. Even with his deformities, his telepathy would give him the edge to make it here.

That is, if I survive.

He found a comfortable spot hidden by vegetation and large debris and slept comfortably until the sun rose. Tigenne looked a lot shabbier in daylight. The colony was hemmed in by steamy jungle. He noted there were no structures beyond an obvious boundary fence around the settlement and spaceport. That probably meant there were some really nasty things living out in the wild.

His first priority was finding a restaurant where he could eat privately. He noted he had only fifteen credits left. After walking through most of the commercial district, quiet at this early hour, he found the right place. The small eatery had curtained tables along one wall and was open for breakfast. There were only a few early risers eating at the bar when he entered. When a serverbot greeted him, the maimed trader showed his tablet with the words, 'I am deaf.'

The serverbot then holoed, 'May I serve you?'

The trader nodded, then indicated the curtained tables. The 'bot led him to the one in the far corner. The trader sat down and rewrote his tablet. 'I cannot chew and must drink with a straw. Pulverize my food in some water.'

The serverbot dipped an appendage in acknowledgment. It then holoed a brief menu.

The Man With No Face pointed to the first item and the serverbot left. It soon returned with a large beaker topped with an ample straw. The serverbot left it on the table, backed out and the curtains closed.

The maimed man removed his face cloth and sampled breakfast. Of course he couldn't taste it, but the drink seemed to go down well. So he drank until the container was empty. The fluid was warm and filled his belly. He replaced his face cloth and waited.

The serverbot soon parted the curtains and the trader dropped a credit on the table and wrote, 'could I open an account here? If I eat here every day, two meals per day — 20% off?'

The serverbot picked up the beaker and holoed the words, 'Our restaurant doesn't do that because we never know how long our customers stay. But eat five meals here and your sixth, non-breakfast meal is free. Breakfast is one credit, but your other meal is two or three credits, depending on what you order.'

The man replied by writing one word, 'Deal.'

Back outside, he could feel the steamy air already heating up. He hung out in the shade until early afternoon. By then, the Afthari ship had left and had been replaced by a couple of small freighters and a cruiser. There were a lot more people on the streets and the town shook off its sleepy feeling. All the stores and clubs were now open for business.

The maimed trader watched a couple of local wannabes set up some sort of street game down the block from two casinos across from each other. They installed an elaborate box on a four legs. It was completely open on one side, revealing various wheels, slides, chutes, mirrors, and rebounding surfaces. The top of the box held a small, movable chute. The bottom contained three narrow, covered exit chutes that were fixed in place. When the game was assembled, the heavy-set man slipped back under a nearby shaded overhang. Meanwhile, the other man with the greasy smile and skinny neck began inviting onlookers to play.

He would roll a small red ball into the top chute. The ball would roll and bounce through the labyrinth until it fell into one of the three bottom chutes. The object of the game was to guess where the ball landed. The player could manipulate various knobs and springs to work the ball into his chosen chute, implying skill would determine the outcome.

The trader moved in closer to see better. He watched the man tending the game fast-talk a visitor into playing. He won the first two rounds with small bets. Then the stocky man came out from the shade and stirred up the growing crowd.

He convinced the man to bet a lot more than he'd won. Finally the man put a bunch of credits down. The crowd cheered him on as he worked the knobs and jostled the box for the desired result. He was sure the ball had fallen into the middle chute. But it was not there and he lost.

The fast-talker now suddenly invited the maimed trader to play. He was quite a sight to the crowd in his ragged, dirty clothes and face cloth. He shook his head and wrote on his tablet that he was deaf.

"I'm not going to hold that against you. But you better not have anything to cheat with under that rag over your face." His stocky partner pulled off the trader's face cloth. The crowd roiled back in repulsion and the maimed man rewrapped his lower face.

The man running the game motioned him up to the box. "Sorry. I'm going to make it up to you. Instead of paying three-to-one, I'll pay you four-to-one if you win."

The trader shook his head dubiously. The accomplice

rummaged in the trader's pocket and pulled out a couple of credits. The trader grabbed them away angrily.

The first man grinned. "You put down two credits and win, I'll give you eight back."

The trader hesitated, then finally put the two credits down. The man gave him the red ball. He dropped the ball into the top chute and watched it carefully flit down the obstacle course. He didn't bother with the knobs and springs. And of course he couldn't hear it drop into any of the bottom chutes. But he read the man running the game and knew it was in the chute on the left. So he opened that one and pulled out the ball. The crowd was ecstatic. When he was paid eight credits he tried to leave.

The heavy-set crony grabbed his arm and worked the crowd some more, pushing the point that the maimed man couldn't leave with such good luck. With now everyone egging him on, the trader put down another two credits. The man running the game pushed them away.

"Come on, play at least four. You'll still be ahead if you loose. But the extra payout last time was one time only. If you win, you get three-to-one. So play four, win and get twelve back."

Again, the trader hesitated, but finally gave into the pressure and pulled out two more credits. Again, he won and was handed twelve credits. The even larger crowd was jubilant. The trader nodded to everyone and tried to walk away with his winnings.

Now it was the crowd that wouldn't let him leave. He finally put down four credits, but the second shill pulled out the remaining twenty-four from the trader's pocket and added them to the four he already put down.

Before he could snatch them back the fast-talking man grabbed them and gave him the red ball. He now was forced to play the ball for everything he had. While the ball worked its way through the box, the crowd hushed. When the ball was no longer in play, the trader carefully bent down and eyed each of the bottom chutes as if looking for a clue.

Finally he wrote something on his tablet and tossed it back as he simultaneously pulled open the left and right chutes, revealing both were empty. The man who caught his tablet read it out loud. 'Not in right or left chutes. Must be in middle one.'

The crowd went into an uproar. Of course the man running the game, as well as the trader, knew the ball fell into a hidden chamber, made invisible by the mirrors and other construction in the box. Thus, none of the bottom chutes actually held the ball. But the con men couldn't challenge the trader without exposing themselves.

The trader retrieved his tablet and wrote '84' on it. The smaller man silently paid him. Since the two were nearly cleaned out, they packed up and left.

As they were doing so, the maimed trader noted a tall man with a shaved head and dark beard laughing his head off just outside a store with a simple holo reading 'Rx & Sundries.' He followed the bearded man into his store.

"Watching you con those bums was the most fun I've had in a week." The bearded man smiled.

"My name is Towles."

He hesitated a moment before continuing in a softer tone. "I don't have anything that can fix your problems. Sorry."

The trader nodded and wrote on his tablet. 'You carry any blood cloning devices?'

Towles was surprised. "I can get you one. Take a week or two and it'll cost you 164 credits."

The trader again wrote on his tablet, 'I need 36 of them, for 120 apiece.'

The shopkeeper was even more surprised. "I'd need at least 145 credits each. And where would you get the money to pay me?"

The Man With No Face wrote his reply. 'I am a good gambler.'

Towles looked the unfortunate man up and down. He noted the dirt, the rags and deformities. He also remembered how this stranger had cleaned out the two con men in fifteen minutes.

"Probably take me about as long to find that many devices

as it will take you to get the money to pay me for them. I'll have to get them a few at a time."

He held out a small personal hygiene kit. "Consider this your welcome to Tigenne."

The trader took the gift gratefully and nodded his thanks. He recalled the venomous looks from the departing con artists. He wrote on his tablet, 'Is there an honest bank here?'

Towles understood and grinned. "Either casino down the block. Every business here has a direct tie-in. So you can go anywhere without cash. Good for the repeat trade."

The trader's eyes crinkled in amusement. Not only had he made a small stake in the last hour, but he'd also met the second human who treated him as a person.

He ate his next meal around four, when his restaurant was mostly empty. He located a spa where servicebots cleaned him up and gave him a haircut. Next door he purchased a simple shirt, pants and sandals suitable for the heat. The clothes were ordinary, perfect for a gambler in a hot climate, though his new face cloth would certainly make him stand out.

When it got dark he began checking out the casinos and back rooms of the smaller clubs. Eventually he found what he was looking for, drunken spacers playing a small stakes game of hold'em. It was an old-fashioned card game that relied on strategy and bluffing as much as luck. The House took five percent of the winnings.

When he was much younger, he had gambled regularly for more than a decade. Among his people, gambling was not subject to the laws of exchange. It was considered an amusement where anyone playing should expect to lose. Any edge was fair as long as it was sanctioned by the game's rules. Some gamblers had a superior ability to read emotional responses from the slightest body variations. Others were statistical geniuses. A few relied on perfect memory. Given his years of experience, the trader knew his telepathic sense would give him a decisive edge.

So he gambled night after night. Nobody forgot him with his deformities and face cloth. He pretended not to understand anyone out of his visual range who spoke to him. Everyone assumed he read lips.

He knew when to lose some hands and when to fold others, all the while steadily winning without angering anyone too much. Soon the local gamblers knew to avoid him. But there was always a steady stream of spacers who wanted to play.

In four months he had acquired the blood cloning devices. He also had made enough to buy good clothes and some items that would improve his life on Afthar. It took him more than another month to acquire sufficient credits to bribe the master of a small cruiser to drop him and his small cargo onto the drogan planet. Its reputation meant no spacer, other than the Afthari raiders, would go there.

TWENTY

AFTHARI RAIDER COLONY

IN THE MONTHS after Maranth supplied the maimed trader the blood cloning device and bag of credits, she never saw him in her beggars' clinic. Nothing much else changed.

Maranth was actually relieved her patient hadn't returned – given the likelihood that Zedd or somebody else would kill him. She assumed he could get all the blood he needed from the machine. But she had half-hoped he would somehow try to free her. She also knew this was wishful thinking, given his precarious situation.

She continued on as before, with the help of Doc, gathering information on the workings of Afthar's spaceport and the ships that came and went. Though they had gathered some useful information, none of it pointed to a safe escape.

At least not yet.

As she usually did when she had no more patients, Maranth retired to her quarters while it was still light. Thus she avoided any run-ins with Obbad, Gannet or any other perverts that might be lurking in the dark. Of course she meditated, but she also passed the time using Doc's extensive database to improve her medical knowledge. Sometimes she would amuse herself with music or watch a holo vid from his large recreational library.

Maranth was glad she had Doc load up all kinds of Veddian entertainment before they left for Addehut. Her wrist comm stored only a limited amount of data. As it turned out, the raiders stole her comm when they captured her. But anyone wanting her services knew she needed her medibot. Thus, the raiders left Doc with her. Inadvertently, by putting her entertainment into Doc she'd saved it from being lost.

Maranth was watching a holo vid and Doc was deep in data research when they heard a distant chanting somewhere outside.

"Doc, please finish the work you are doing. I'm going to find out what is going on."

He nodded an antenna.

She made her way through a now silent, empty compound onto the path to the main square. Late day had already morphed into a solid night. The chanting grew louder as she approached the park. Others now jammed the path, heading the same way. By the time they reached the square, it looked as if all of Afthar were gathered there, completely filling the expanse.

Everyone was rocking side-to-side in time with the dirge-like chant that sounded something like "We mourn, we mourn…"

Several Afthari, their faces lit from below by burning torches, stood well above the others. Maranth figured they must be standing on a raised platform. The shifting light and shadow from the flames under their features distorted them so much that Maranth did not recognize any of them. The effect was ghoulish.

Hoping to see better, she moved in closer and soon was able to recognize the big earrings. The men on the platform were the Heads of the Afthari Houses. Somberly lined up, they each held one of the torches that lit their faces. Solely by his huge earrings, she recognized Mier Zedd in the middle.

Zedd raised his arms and took a step back. When the crowd quieted, Zedd dropped his arms and bowed his head. The man next to him addressed the crowd.

"No one has done more for our welfare than the House of Zedd, Yah?"

Maranth had no doubt the voice belonged to Obbad.

Meanwhile the crowd chanted back, "Yah... Zedd! Yah... Zedd!" over and over.

She looked around for someone she recognized. She caught sight of Kojji a short distance away and skirted along the edge of the assembly to reach him. Meanwhile, Obbad raised his arms and the crowd again fell silent.

"We mourn their loss as our own."

With that the crowd let out another droning wail.

Maranth lightly tugged Kojji's sleeve. "What's going on?"

"Funeral for Mier Zedd's son, Pagg, and his crew. Pagg's ship went down in the jungle. Drogans got all five."

Obbad was again addressing the assembly. "The great young Pagg. And four of our best."

The crowd now droned Pagg's name over and over. Maranth again slipped back from the crush of people and disappeared down one of the pathways. She could hear Obbad continue with, "Our brother Douy..." followed by the crowd chanting raider Douy's name over and over.

As she made her way down the deserted path, the volume of sound from the chanting began to fade.

Everyone's at the funeral. This might be my chance! At least it's a good time look around the spaceport.

As she turned a corner, she thought there was someone hugging the shadows behind, following her. Elation turned to dread, even as the spaceport loomed up ahead and the chanting had faded. There was a short scurry of movement behind, to the right.

She stopped dead, torn by turning back to confront or confuse her possible follower, yet afraid of what he had in store for her.

Could it be Doc?

Hands from behind grabbed her arms, pinning them behind her back. Then she was pulled back against her captor. By his breath and scrawny stature she recognized Gannet. The pervert slowly rubbed himself against her as she struggled futilely.

His voice was low in her ear. "Spaceport, huh? And not a patient in sight. Planning escape, maybe?"

He drank in the scent of her hair and neck.

"You disgusting animal." Maranth managed to free an arm and jabbed her elbow hard into his ribs. She nearly succeeded in pulling away.

He managed to jerk her back by the other arm, then tightened his hold by pulling both her arms up behind her back. She was again helpless, pinned by one hand. With his other, he searched her pockets for money, lingering to explore her body.

"Sorry our fellow slave, Jobbar, couldn't make it. Now let's see. No money here…"

He fished out her purse and hefted it. "Ah, here it is… a bit light. But we've got lots of time. You and me."

As he pocketed the purse she was able to turn slightly and tried to bite his shoulder. He fended her off but the purse dropped.

Gannet angrily grabbed her by her hair and pulled her head back. "You're going to pay for that. If you think…"

At that moment a strong arm clamped Gannet around his neck from behind. The other hand nuzzled a blaster against his head. Maranth's tormenter let her go and his arm that held her relaxed. Sadistic bravado had puddled to raw fear by the time Gannet turned to see who had bested him.

The Man With No Face, his lower features wrapped Afthari-style, met his gaze with menace. Sweat beaded Gannet's forehead and arms. The maimed trader waved the blaster under Gannet's nose. He took the hint and ran off. Maranth's purse remained on the ground where it fell.

The trader looked her over for injuries as she rearranged her clothes and tried to regain composure.

"I'm all right." She then bowed in the Veddian way. "Thank you."

She took a breath, held it a moment, and relaxed. She looked her patient over. "Aye, you are much stronger and have good color. And you've put on some weight. Very good."

She also noted that he was now cleanly dressed in fine clothes and boots, including an elaborately embroidered shirt and coordinating face cloth, his dark hair neatly trimmed.

He nodded.

"Again, thank you." She turned to go.

"I've come to pay my debt."

She froze, not sure she really heard him speak. But the voice was low pitched and slightly hoarse, different from how she remembered his thoughts in her head.

She swiveled around. "You can talk?"

"Aye, I can speak. I've come to pay my debt, Maranth-sa-Veddi Dimore."

She reached for his face cloth.

He stopped her hand. "The drogans gave me enough of my mouth to talk and eat, to function better. Nothing more."

Maranth smiled. "They also gave you eyes somehow. How did you get them to do it? Everyone here says they eat humans whenever they can. There's a funeral going on now for men that were eaten."

"It's complicated. I traded them your blood-cloning device. Your money bought me smuggled passage to Tigenne, plus some extra credits that I turned into a stake. When you gave me that money, everything you had, you asked only that I remember you when I was free."

Maranth was caught off guard. "That money would have been stolen from me anyway."

"But you gave it to me, a hopeless, deformed stranger."

"Not so hopeless, you'd already gotten back your eyes."

He nodded. "Aye. I've come back to finish my business here. And I intend to settle our accounts."

His took her hands and eyed her intently. "There's no time for a lot of explanations. Go back to your quarters and gather what you have, to take with you. Try and get some sleep. Someone will come for you. Go with him or her."

"Go? Where?"

"To me. I intend to buy you from these slavers and take you where you want to go. I owe you that."

Before she could object, he cut her off. "I'm a Patusian trader. Trading is what I know how to do."

She just stood there, torn between the freedom dangling in front of her, and the risk she faced by placing herself in this man's power. He was no longer the unfortunate fragment of humanity she had cared for. No doubt he was afflicted by the primitive pathologies endemic to the outerworlds. And he knew everything she was thinking. Though he hadn't tried to control her with his mind, she figured he could do so.

How can I possibly trust him?

She must find her own way out. "Thank you. But no."

Unnerved and uncertain about the choice she just made, Maranth pulled away and shakily took off.

He let her disappear around the bend, then picked up her purse and tucked it away.

You will learn you can trust me, Maranth-sa-Veddi-Dimore.

She didn't know what to think when she returned to her room. She tried to sleep after a short meditation, but was too agitated to do so. So she meditated some more. She asked Doc pack a few of her things into one of his compartments, just in case. Finally, she fell into a fitful sleep.

As large and slow moving as he was, Jobbar managed to silently enter Maranth's dark room several hours later. Only a flick of Doc's antenna noted his approach. Doc tapped Maranth as her fellow slave called out to her.

"Wake up Slaave Maranth. Saad Obbad waants you to come — now."

Jobbar didn't wait for her to rise and just pulled her up and out of bed.

Maranth did not resist. "Did he say anything else?"

"No. You muust come. Now." With that, he dragged her to the door, barefoot and in her sleeping gown. Her hair hung thick and loose down her back.

"Doc. Bring my things."

Doc padded around the room and gathered a few more items: some wash powders, her hairbrush, and a pair of sandals. These he stuffed into various compartments as he followed after his mistress.

Jobbar stopped in the shadows at the edge of the now lit garden and tugged Maranth close in to his side. His bluish color helped him fade into the dark. The Head of the Afthari, Mier Zedd, with his wife Rosia and a couple of raiders strode through the compound gate. Obbad and Fromar rose from a low settee and greeted them with solemn nods. Obbad held up a hand in formal greeting.

"My House is honored by your presence. Please take this couch for your comfort." He motioned to the vacant settee nearby.

Zedd nodded curtly and mumbled something under his breath. But he settled into the soft seating. Rosia joined him and the other men stood behind.

Maranth noted the couches were arranged facing away, toward the shadows at the opposite side of the garden.

"Well?" Zedd spat out.

With that, the Man With No Face slipped from the dark, with one of Obbad's raiders and a black workbot at his back. His lower face still swathed Afthari-style, he squatted in front of the assembly. The trader opened the top of his shirt to reveal an elaborate round tattoo on his chest, mostly in gold, with iridescent blue and red. Zedd and Obbad eyed each other in surprise. They both recognized the mark of a Patusian master trader.

Zedd scowled at Obbad. "You have the meddoc slave here, yah?"

As if on cue, Jobbar dragged Maranth forward. "She is heere, Saad Obbad." No one, other than the trader, bothered to look in her direction. Ever the good servant, Jobbar then motioned a nearby workbot to serve drinks.

Finally, the Patusian spoke to Zedd in a voice just above a

whisper. "The *Acacia Glyn* for Pagg, who will be eaten alive without my help."

"He now speaks?" Zedd roared at Obbad, who just nodded back meekly.

Then Zedd turned back to the trader and crossed his arms. "That's my newest cruiser. You go too far. Take the *Privelium*."

"Does the wealthiest, most powerful House in Afthar expect to trade an old tub like the *Privelium* for the life of their future Head? Is it that your son, Pagg, is only worth the *Privelium*? Or is it that the House of Zedd is not as rich as it seems?" The trader held up his hands and cocked his head as if in surprise.

The other men eyed Zedd speculatively.

Rosia spat out a quick retort. "Our son is great and everyone knows our House is the richest House of the Afthari."

Zedd broke in. "You may have the *Acacia Glyn*."

"Fully fueled and with all original and current fittings?"

Zedd put his hands on his knees and leaned forward. "That will cost you... Forlal."

The trader thought for a moment. "Agreed. Now we have only three hostages to bargain for."

He glanced at Maranth. "For these three I want the slave Maranth, and 40,000 credits."

Maranth now knew for certain she was going to be traded. She concentrated and tried to mentally broadcast as clearly as she could.

You must buy my medibot, too.

Obbad can barely contain his glee as he addressed Zedd. "So that's why you do this business in my House. A Veddian Meddoc? Worth at least 15,000..."

Fromar broke in. "...20,000 credits at least."

Zedd scowled at Obbad. "I negotiate with the Patusian. Then we settle up later."

Through the interchange Maranth was unwavering.

...Buy my medibot. Buy my medibot...

Zedd now addressed the trader. "She is the only meddoc in forty sectors or more, and she's Veddian, yah? I will trade her for these three men. I will even throw in 1,000 credits as good will."

The trader shut his eyes for a moment. Then he looked up. "Is this ONE slave worth more than a Afthari warrior like your Second, Douy, plus two other tested men?"

Maranth held her breath and concentrated.

Please, my medibot!

Zedd stood with a roar. "The slave and her medibot and 1,000 credits. You have the *Acacia Glyn.* Do not try my patience!"

The Man With No Face mulled over the offer.

He crossed his wrists, hands up, and slid them out in Patusian confirmation.

"Agreed."

TWENTY-ONE

AFTHARI RAIDER COLONY

A GRIM-FACED MIER ZEDD, Obbad, and three raiders threaded their way through the spaceport in the dim light of the breaking dawn. Jobbar followed a few feet behind the Afthari with Maranth in tow, and Doc followed close behind her. She was still barefoot, in her sleeping gown. No one said a word.

Zedd nodded to two of his raiders and they discreetly faded into the shadows of cargo containers scattered about. The assemblage skirted a scout vessel and approached the *Acacia Glyn*. Though the ship was dark, it clearly outclassed the others in the spaceport by being larger and newer looking. There was a gangway from its hatch to the ground, but the hatch was closed.

The Patusian squatted next to the ramp waiting for the others. Another raider stood nearby, but when the Afthari approached, this man joined Zedd and handed him the security key. "I did as you asked. I let him in and he checked the ship."

Meanwhile, Jobbar held Maranth in place and Doc bumped into her.

"Doc?"

Jobbar sternly motioned her quiet.

The maimed trader stood up and nodded. "The *Acacia Glyn* checked out."

Zedd put his fists on his hips. "Yah. My best ship. Now your part of the deal. Where's my son and the others?"

"Nearby. But first send over the meddoc, with the ship security key, 1,000 credits and her medibot."

Maranth watched the two missing raiders sneak behind a cargo container to the left of the trader, not far from the ship. She thought about trying to alert him, but was she really on his side?

He already knows.

Zedd's eyes hardened. "You try my patience. Show me my son."

The trader stood and raised his arms wide. Then he turned in a circle. "You have me in your sights, Mier Zedd."

He pointed to the hatch. "Send the meddoc, the key, the credits and the medibot to me. Then they go to the top."

Zedd nodded to Obbad, who then nodded to Jobbar. Jobbar softly shoved Maranth forward. At first a little unsteady, she headed for the ship, Doc dogging her heels. When she reached the raiders, Zedd put the security key in her hand, and then a hefty bag of credits. She managed the load with both hands against her torso as she continued forward. When she reached the trader he took the key.

"Go to the top." He spoke to her without taking his eyes off the Afthari.

As she climbed up the ramp she could now see the two missing raiders each prop a blaster against the cargo container and level their aim at the trader. Maranth didn't know what to do. She stopped at the still-closed hatch and waited with Doc, terrified of what would happen.

The maimed trader squatted down again. "Now get rid of the two slavers behind my back and I will release your men."

Mier Zedd and Obbad exchanged a quick angry glance, then Zedd motioned to the men behind the container. The two emerged and joined the other Afthari.

Zedd crossed his arms. "They were just insurance, trader. I pay my debts. Now give me my men or prepare to die."

"As we agreed." He got to his feet and eyed each of them.

"You fed me. I still owe for that." He crossed his wrists, hands up, and slid them out in confirmation.

He shouted out. "Come out — now."

Then he immediately tapped the security key to release the main hatch. Though the hatch opened, everyone's eyes were on the cargo container to his left. Its side slowly creaked away from the rest of the container. Pagg, Douy and the other missing three, dazed and confused, tottered out. Though dehydrated, thin and dirty, they were otherwise unbloodied and whole.

The survivors were quickly surrounded by their comrades with whoops and yells. Meanwhile the trader quickly sprinted up the gangway and pulled Maranth and Doc inside.

Soon the ship began to glow yellow and flash color. The Afthari fell back. Zedd's jaw hardened. He turned away from his lost ship. The Afthari followed as he led them back the way they had come.

But Jobbar lingered. He watched longingly as the *Acacia Glyn* lifted up and hovered a moment. Then it arched through the force field and out of sight.

As soon as the ship was in high orbit, Maranth unstrapped from the webbing and stood up. She silently leaned against one of the consoles on the cruiser's bridge. She had never been in such a space before. Most of the walls and its three consoles were covered in controls. There were no hard angles or surfaces anywhere. Every seat and surface was padded in metallic red and silver, while the floor and ceiling were black. Even in the dim light, the metallic surfaces defined everything in the room clearly.

The Man With No Face dropped under the central console to fix something. Only his lower torso and legs were visible. He was assisted by a shipbot, who looked much like a metallic soft grey version of Doc's basic blue canister design. It was also topped with various specialized appendages. 'JONA' was embossed on its side. The trader's face cloth and shirt were in a rumpled pile nearby.

Maybe fabric will catch on something under there.

She didn't know what to think or how to feel about what had happened. The only thing she did know was that she was tired, her feet were dirty and scraped, and she was still in her bed gown.

The shipbot, Jona, plugged one of its appendages into the console. Various readings flashed across his top screen as well as the console holo itself. Then it passed one of its stalks with a small viewer under the console to the trader.

The 'bot spoke in a male voice. "Still off three-oh-four-six."

After a few minutes the trader replied. "Repeat the test."

Maranth wondered why the 'bot spoke since the trader must have told Jona he was deaf.

Maybe Jona thinks I am part of the bridge crew.

The shipbot ran more diagnostics and spoke once more. "Now the system checks out."

The man pulled himself out and glanced up at Maranth. He put his shirt back on and picked up his face cloth, hesitated, then dropped it. He slipped into the captain's chair and began to test other ship systems.

This was the first time Maranth had seen his face since he'd begun to talk. He was right; the drogans had not completed his face. He had a mouth with a workable jaw, teeth and tongue (because he could speak). But only vague finished lips and still no nose or ears.

Maranth realized the only way he could have responded to the Afthari during the negotiations was by reading their minds. As with the shipbot, he could not possibly hear them.

He moved to another seat on the left and flipped on navigation.

She walked over to his console. "Am I now your slave?"

He never looked up as he replied. "No. You're free. I will take you anywhere you want. I certainly owe you that."

"You really mean that? Anywhere?"

"Even Veddi."

She studied him for a moment. "You just read my mind."

"Of course. You know I can't hear you."

"Some time ago, in the colony, you inserted your thoughts into my head. Did you MAKE them trade you this ship? Me?"

The trader looked up into her eyes. "No. And this is not the time. We're about to leave orbit. You need to sit and web in. Jona, strap up her medibot, he's named Doc."

As she took a seat, two holographic hemispheres formed in front. The upper one displayed a dome of the stars and the lower one showed the curve of the planet Afthar hanging in space.

He slid a card into a slot. "Course to Dullarea on-line in slot three."

He threw a small lever and the ship heaved upward to the left, the stars blurred slightly. Afthar shrank to nothing in the right lower quadrant of the lower holo. In a few moments the apparent motion stabilized. Stars now filled both holo hemispheres. Jona unhooked himself from the wall. Doc watched Jona and did the same.

The Patusian was going to offer Maranth a quick tour but recognized she was exhausted and still afraid.

"I will take you to your private room. As the ship's master, I sleep in the captain's cabin." He motioned her up.

She wordlessly rose and followed him down a corridor, into a narrow room with three bunk beds against one wall. Everything here was also padded in the same metallic material. The beds were secured by safety webbing and there were obvious drawers and cabinets flush into the opposite wall.

"The only sleeping spaces in this ship are the captain's stateroom and these crew quarters. Facilities are there." He pointed to a door at the end.

She still said nothing.

"Do you have any other clothes?"

"Doc brought some, and sandals."

The trader nodded. "Good. Get some sleep."

Hours later, Maranth woke up in total dark. It took her a few moments to realize where she was. She quickly sat up and the room lit automatically.

Now what?

She felt a lot better after what was probably a long sleep. Doc was right there, quietly by her side.

She reviewed what had just happened. This man, the one the Afthari named the Man With No Face, had bought her from her slave owner, even after she'd told him not to. Yet he had always treated her with respect and twice risked himself to stop Gannet. He'd stated several times he was indebted to her. But what did that mean to a primitive, one who was also telepathic? For all she knew, he was reading her mind now. Her situation was uncertain at best.

Then for some reason, the ancient classic *Alice in Wonderland* again came to mind. She was now somewhere else in Wonderland, and just behind her hovered the Cheshire Cat, invisible at the moment but the cat would not stay that way for long.

Putting herself in that old story somehow comforted her. She relaxed and fell into a short meditation that soon pushed away all emotion and cleared her head. It was time to dress and face her purchaser.

When she reached her cabin door it automatically slid open. She headed down the hall toward the bridge. A much larger door slid open on her left, revealing a wider cabin colorfully eclectic in the Afthari style. But here everything hanging on the walls was made of soft materials and the table in the center was just a low padded platform surrounded by flamboyant bolsters and cushions for seating.

Her maimed patient was comfortably settled in, drinking from a large bowl that gave off the smell of a hearty soup.

He looked up. "Hungry?"

TWENTY-TWO

ACACIA GLYN, DEEP SPACE

THE PATUSIAN WAS relaxed and happy. He was on his own ship, no longer bombarded by the mental chaos of the Afthari. And he didn't have to fend off any blows or bites. He knew this time was only a short reprieve. The cosmos clearly had other plans for his existence.

Patushah. Strengthen me for what will come.

Of course Maranth had entered his consciousness as soon as she awoke. Now she faced him calmly, her mental clarity renewed. No matter her looks, her company would have been welcome. His gaze slipped from her dark eyes to the soft curve of her neck and her breasts…

He looked down and quickly willed these thoughts away. His recovery of health had brought a natural renewal of sexual energy.

A big distraction.

Mutual sex was for the healthy and normal. He was neither. His deformities closed that door.

"Please sit."

He pointed over to a small serverbot.

"Order what you want. I can't vouch for the flavor, but the Afthari no doubt stocked food they liked."

She asked for a dish he'd never heard of and then took

her place across the length of the table from him, though her medibot remained where he was.

Her mind and face were not friendly.

"I am a trader, not a raider nor a slaver. I don't take women."
Maranth turned red.

"You sold other humans to buy this ship and buy me. Were they drugged? You're taking me someplace I haven't heard of. What should I think?"

"Aye, they were drugged. By doing so, I saved those men from death and restored them to their community. And by doing this, also freed you. Dullarea? After trading for the ship, you, and your medibot..." He thumped Doc.

Doc flashed a holo in front of the trader's face. It read, 'Please don't. I'm delicate.'

The trader withdrew his hand back to the table.

"We're broke and can't afford fuel for any long trips. Those thousand credits I got in the deal will only buy the right to land at some minor port."

He leaned forward. "I would have done better if you hadn't filled my head with 'buy my medibot, buy my medibot.' Don't you know I was just as focused on you as those slavers?"

"Sorry."

As she thought about the negotiation she recalled it was Zedd who first mentioned her medibot, not this trader.

Without waiting for Maranth to voice her suspicion he broke in.

"I didn't MAKE Zedd include your medibot in the deal. On my oath, my transactions are by mutual agreement, freely given. Otherwise my accounts can't balance."

He eyed her speculatively. "But you were blasting the idea, could he have somehow picked it up from you?"

She was instinctively about to blurt "impossible," but quickly remembered the man across the table read every thought she had.

The serverbot put the sweet pudding on the table in front of her. With a click, the plate stuck to the table surface, no doubt a safety feature. She liked the smell of the confection, but couldn't eat.

"Maranth, I have no quick way to raise a stake in any port we could reach, to pay for enough fuel to Veddi. That's why Dullarea. It's a Diam mine and it's close by.

"I have some playpacs and can trade them for a few crystals. With the crystals I can then raise a stake a lot quicker. But Dullarea is dangerous. Most traders won't risk the trip.

"You can say no. It will take some time, but I will find another way to get you home. On my oath."

His mind followed her thoughts and, as expected, she would not wait for anything, not even danger.

"Dullarea then."

For Maranth, it was unsettling he didn't even wait for her to say what she wanted. But given the circumstances, she needed to get used to this. For him, speech had to be slow and cumbersome.

"You're not eating. You need to keep up your strength."

"I just can't eat now."

She found herself smiling. She was the meddoc, and yet he was giving her medical advice.

Then a darker thought intruded. *I must be worth a lot more to the Dullareans than playpacs.*

His neck reddened as he rose to his feet and rounded the table toward her, Doc at his heels this time.

"Maranth, I'm no slaver and I pay my debts."

"Take me to Veddi?"

He offered her his hand and sighed.

"For now, I'll take you to your cabin."

Hours later her cabin door slid open to reveal the little serverbot.

"The captain requests you come to dinner."

She was really hungry now. And there was no reason not to go. So she tied back her hair and followed the little 'bot to the main cabin. Of course, Doc followed as well. Maranth realized that Doc had hardly spoken since Afthar. She would have to ask him about that, later.

The trader nodded a greeting when she entered. She took the same seat as before, across the long end of the table from where he sat.

Experience told him they would be together for some time. They had to become more comfortable with each other or bad feelings would fester into trouble. They both needed to learn more about the other.

He knew at least some of the Afthari had laid hands on her. It was common knowledge women who suffered such trauma either avoided and distrusted men, or acted seductive, even hypersexual. Both were survival mechanisms. Maranth was clearly distrusting. Yet she was intelligent and logical, her spirit unbroken. If he could reach her, he felt she would meet him halfway. He remembered a bit of a thought about her past she revealed in the square the night the slaver, Obbad, attacked her.

Something about being betrothed. Was she promised in marriage?

"Tell me about the man in your thoughts, the one who waits for you."

He reclined back so that his face fell in shadow.

Though surprised by the question, she saw no reason to not answer. "There's not much to tell. Jomri and I were betrothed when I entered meddoc training. Of course we're very compatible."

"Compatible? What does that mean?"

"Our psychological and social profiles match to the 96th percentile."

Her response baffled him.

"What is he like? I get no feeling of him from you."

"I've never met him."

The trader sat up in surprise.

She felt she should explain. Outerworlders did not know of Veddian social advancements.

"On Veddi, computers identify our mates. Rational choices, based on compatibility, ensure marital success and harmony in childrearing."

He again leaned back, his face returning to shadow.

"Maranth, why would Jomri think you're still alive? And why should he wait for a woman he's not even met? By now your computer has probably found him another perfect mate."

"Perhaps. But there's no rush. We were not expected to marry for at least thirty years."

He said nothing. She ordered a hearty meal and began to eat as soon as the serverbot brought food.

Finally, when she'd consumed most everything she'd ordered, the trader spoke again.

"Veddians take lovers then, until they marry?"

Maranth was appalled. But she realized he could only see such matters from his limited perspective.

"I will try to explain, but my answer may be hard to grasp. You must agree that outerworlders are unhappy, cruel, vicious, ignorant, drawn to vice, and wallow in violence and depravity.

"These neurotic adaptations flow from psychic stress. One of the sources of such stress is sexual desire, which is, if you think about it, just another primitive drive like hunger or thirst. We all now live centuries with the sexual hyper-desire of youth. Yet we only need to make one child per person to perpetuate ourselves.

"Veddians from early childhood are taught to control and channel emotions and optimize personal wellbeing. So, as Veddians mature sexually, we take medications that significantly reduce sexual need and we also meditate to rechannel the rest. Thus, much of Veddian society happily lives asexually, except when making and rearing children. We marry only for that purpose."

He was stunned. But the trader in him had a practiced, open mind. And he just learned more about the innerworlds from her response than from anything he'd heard before.

He had no idea the innerworlds had asexually adapted to

long lifespans. And more important, the insular innerworlds didn't mix with outerworlders because of snobbery. They simply shunned the vice and brutality.

Who could blame them?

He stood. "Maranth, the *Acacia Glyn* will reach Dullarea in a less than a day. I need to prepare. But first, how about a tour of the ship?"

"What's your name?"

He just stood there and said nothing.

She got up. "What should I call you?"

His eyes remained blank.

"Who were you before?"

He headed out the door and she followed him into the corridor.

Finally he stopped and turned back to her. "I'm not who I was before. Afthar remade me. So I must take a new name. From now on I am the Man With No Face."

"That's not a real name. You can't mean it."

He smiled. "I do."

Then it hit her. "A bit theatrical?"

He nodded. "The first thing a trader learns is how to turn a weakness into an advantage. Now when I negotiate, the other side will be a bit off balance, distracted by wondering what's under my face cloth."

He tapped the cloth hanging across his shoulders. "And they won't forget me."

Maranth laughed and he was pleased.

"Now for a quick tour. Then I have a lot to do."

Much later, near the end of his sleep shift, the Man With No Face awoke to terror. He quickly realized it wasn't his own.

Maranth!

He bolted for her quarters. When her door slid open she was still asleep, sweaty and sobbing. Doc was trying to rouse her with taps and repeating her name over and over.

The trader pushed the medibot back and retracted the webbing.

"Traumatic stress?"

Doc's holo displayed, 'She's never done this before.'

Peering into her mind, the trader saw himself motionless, crumpled on top of a pile of diams filling a large, square bin sunk into a floor.

Pushing the image away, he sat on the bed and pulled her up and held her against his shoulder.

"Maranth… Maranth! Wake up."

Doc telescoped out a syringe-tipped appendage.

"Not yet." The trader pushed it away.

He rocked her back and forth. *Just a bad dream. I'm here. See?*

She stirred and finally opened her eyes. He gently let her go.

"A bad dream. I'll come back in a few hours. Try to get more sleep."

Maranth was sleeping quietly when he returned. From the doorway, the trader watched her wake up in the light that now flooded the cabin.

Fully dressed with his head cloth tied over his lower face, he also wore a blaster strapped to his side.

"You'll have the ship to yourself for a while. I'll return at 14:20."

He hesitated before he spoke again. "I've transferred ship title to you. If I don't come back, Jona is programmed to transport you to Tigenne. You can then sell this vessel and buy passage to Veddi."

"I could be useful here."

He shook his head and remembered her dream. "Dullarea's too dangerous. I can't protect you and trade."

"Don't you think someone there might need a meddoc's services?"

He nodded. "Aye. And they'll pay a lot more for your skills than my goods. But very bad people run this place."

"I believe you. It's still better if I help."

He chose her resolve over his own doubts.

"Aye." The Man With No Face crossed his wrists Patusian

style in confirmation. He pulled her old clothes from the cabinet near the door and tossed them over.

"While you dress, I'll set things up. No reason for you to wear a slave collar any more. If Doc can't remove it, I will."

TWENTY-THREE

DULLAREA

THE PATUSIAN, MARANTH and Doc stepped through the hatch and faced four rapacious looking characters waiting at the foot of the ramp. The *Acacia Glyn* automatically sealed the hatch behind them.

The Man With No Face quickly glanced up at the dome and then around the spaceport. This port was smaller than the Afthari version. Only one other, rather seedy vessel was parked here. The space was completely sealed from the atmosphere and it smelled like sandy dirt. There were no structures in sight except a large portal, no doubt leading to the Dullarean mine and colony.

He put his mouth against Maranth's ear. "Please let me communicate directly into your mind. It will give us an edge."

She hesitated, then nodded affirmatively. They headed down the ramp. Doc seemed to read the situation. He drew up close to Maranth, practically on her heels.

Maranth's head filled with the trader's words. *Just follow my lead and stay in sight.*

This intrusion was just another thing she must get used to. Though it was a little unsettling, she knew he was right about both his instruction and his method of communication.

She thought two words. *That bad?*

One word filled her head in reply. *Worse.*

At the bottom of the ramp, The Man With No Face was the first to speak. "This is my Veddian meddoc slave."

Maranth was shocked by his words but remained silent as the two men in front appraised her closely. The other two stayed back, blasters at the ready.

Probably guards.

The trader put his hand around her waist and pulled her back a little, nearly toppling Doc.

"I call her Maranth. My medibot will assist her."

Doc wiggled an antenna. "I am a J6 model. You can call me Doc."

The trader ignored everything except the two men fixed on Maranth.

"Since this slave is very valuable, and mine, anyone who touches her…" At that point he pulled out his blaster and waved it around.

The tall, oily looking man on the left held out his hands in deference. He shrugged in a "can't win" fashion and grinned.

"Mothar." He tapped his chest. Then he pointed to his companion. "Loba-Zuda. We agreed to trade diams for her Meddoc skills, no?"

His partner, a short balding man with thick jowls and pebbled skin, nodded but said nothing.

The Patusian put his blaster back in its holster and the Dullareans led them through the portal onto a wide empty passage hewn from rock.

Maranth concentrated on a single angry thought.

So, now I'm free only aboard ship when no one's around.

His reply filled her head.

A woman who's not seen as property is fair game in a place like this.

Maranth blurted out. "You have no right…"

Loba-Zuda broke in with a hard grin. "You have some problem with your slave, Man With No Face?"

Maranth stopped speaking and dropped her gaze down. The trader said nothing.

Finally the group passed onto a long ribbed bridge near the top of the huge, centrally vaulted area of the mine.

There were a number of thin, dusty men grouped around large, truck-sized minerbots. These giant 'bots transported and processed rock in the tunnels that radiated out at different levels and directions from the center.

The air was tinged in mineral dust and awash with the noise of machines and breaking rock. Every surface in the mine was coated in powder. The mineral smell was very strong here.

Maranth recognized slave collars on every one of these miners. They worked without supervision, almost robotically, using industrial blasters to roughly separate diams from the rock matrix. The minerbots' multiple side appendages scooped up the pieces as they fell, sometimes catching them in mid-air, sometimes scooping them off the rock floor.

Loba-Zuda waved his arms proudly over the operation. "We have a little cocktail that makes slaves most cooperative. You can try it on her."

The trader sent her a message. *Maranth, I'm playing a part.*

Then he replied to the slaver. "There are times when real spirit is enjoyable."

Maranth held her temper while the slavers laughed knowingly, and the guards grinned.

Mothar moved closer to her and his eyes swept over her body. "True enough. Perhaps we pay you for her pleasures, aii?"

The Man With No Face ignored Maranth's alarmed look and replied smoothly. "Those I reserve for myself, Mothar. You spoke before about an epidemic."

Loba-Zuda pointed out a miner as they passed him. "You see in this one."

The slave ignored them as they circled around him. He continued to run some sort of check on a control panel set in the rock. Loba-Zuda pointed to a greenish area on the sick man's pale arm. Parts of the man's face and hand also showed the same cast. All the while, the miner ignored the visitors.

By his pallor, Maranth was certain this man had not

experienced a healthy light spectrum in a long time. And he looked malnourished, even dehydrated.

She pointed to a patch of the greenish skin. "Doc, let's get a reading on this. And a full workup."

Doc took a scraping of the area. As he ran various scans and tests, Maranth consulted the readouts on his view screen. Meanwhile the unfortunate man mindlessly continued his tasks as if the others weren't there.

He's clearly drugged, no doubt the 'cocktail' Loba-Zuda bragged about.

Loba-Zuda vaguely waved over the complex. "Of seventy-five slaves still alive, most have it. When bad enough they stop work, die. We must control it soon or close down." His last words were almost wistful.

The trader spoke stiffly. "My meddoc slave is very skilled."

Maranth turned to Loba-Zuda. "Do you have a dispensary?"

"Aii. You cure the slaves?"

She nodded to both slavers. "If you have the right medical supplies."

Mothar grinned, even though his eyes remained hard. "Come. You tell us."

The group then made their way down into one of the lower tunnels.

It was easy for the trader to read Mothar's thoughts as the walked.

We wait until AFTER woman treats slaves. If we upset her, she may not work. Then we take them. She will be so tasty. The slaver's thoughts devolved into explicit images of Maranth being violated.

The trader did the best he could to push these from his own mind.

Soon they were led into a fair-sized room hewn out of the rock. Diams were visible in its walls. The dusty, sparsely equipped space had some crates and tables lining the sides. Three large, clear vats dominated the far end of the space. Each was open to the air and about half full of some an amber-colored liquid that smelled medicinal. A light coat of dust floated on its surface.

Maranth grimly nodded to Doc. "Let's do an inventory."

Doc waived an antenna affirmatively.

As they checked the cabinets and crates, the others stood by, watching silently.

All the while, Maranth mumbled to herself under her breath. "Filthy, debased, disease ridden… It's a wonder anyone survives a day here."

Doc blew the dust off a beaker, causing Mothar to cough. The action revealed some brownish dregs at the bottom, which Doc quickly analyzed.

Using a hand-held analyzer, Maranth took a sample from one of the large vats with the clear liquid.

Mothar quickly grabbed her arm and pulled her back. "You stay away from our cocktail."

The Man With No Face knocked Mothar's hand away from her arm. "I will see that she does. But only I touch her, understand?"

She then searched through some crates. "Do you have azadoxol?"

Mothar and Loba-Zuda shrugged.

A few minutes later, Doc called out. "Here's some."

One of Doc's appendages pointed to a large, dusty container of liquid sitting under a table. He extended an appendage out and wiped off an area near the top. "The seal is unbroken."

Maranth knew this was the key that could end the pain and misery of this place.

She crossed her arms and turned toward Mothar and Loba-Zuda. "Your slaves are suffering from Rubazza. It spreads in filthy quarters and thrives in bodies weakened by drugs."

The men eyed her suspiciously.

At this point, the Man With No Face broke in and put a hand around her upper arm and gently pulled her close and spoke almost seductively. "The conditions here are none of your business. You're here to treat the sick."

Maranth was a bit unsettled by the way he'd just addressed her.

He said he was playing a part.

"After I treat the active cases, everyone else must be vaccinated or it will come back."

The trader now stood in front of her, facing the slavers. "So, I will rid you of this plague, at the terms we agreed."

Mothar responded with a nod and cold grin. "Aii."

Maranth joined Doc. "Task schedule?"

She viewed his readout and made some changes by tapping items on the screen.

"We need five hours to prepare. Then please send the infected ones in first. Then send in everyone else, including yourselves, for vaccination. Otherwise, the infection will return."

Mothar suspiciously squinted. "How we know you not lying about cure?"

Maranth thought a moment. "The green cast on the skin will begin to reduce within minutes, then totally disappear within an hour. As for vaccination, how can I possibly prove that someone will not get sick some time in the future? But you have my oath, as a Veddian meddoc." She bowed.

The Man With No Face undid the top of his shirt and exposed his tattoo. "On my oath as a Patusian trader."

Loba-Zuda was impressed by the trader's tattoo. "Good enough."

Mothar nodded. "You work now. We return in five hours."

Then Mothar and Loba-Zuda strode off, leaving the guards. These two wordlessly took positions inside the room, one on each side of the entry. They hungrily watched Maranth while she and Doc cleaned the outside of the azadoxol container.

Maranth thought as clearly as she could, so she could communicate with The Man With No Face.

These people are half-starved and drugged to a stupor. They won't hang on long after the fungus is gone. Isn't there something more we can do?

Then his words filled her head.

We're outnumbered and outgunned. Difficult enough for us get out in one piece. Maranth, I can't read their thoughts through this rock and I'm deaf. I can't read you if you are out of my sight. Understand?

Doc tapped the now clean container with his tubular appendage and pointed over to a crate.

Maranth nodded. "Aye. We'll next clean up the saline tubs and sterilize everything. Can you begin synthesizing?"

"Everything checked out. I'm already growing the vaccine."

She and Doc began their new tasks, working silently for some time. Then the Man With No Face flooded her mind.

They intend to take us later, after we finish here. So stay sharp. Our edge is that they're greedy. They will try to take our ship rather than destroy her. The Acacia Glyn's weapons will cover us, since they can't break her security.

Her anger spilled out. "Afthar seems civilized compared to this hell."

Noticing the guards' displeasure at her outburst, the trader roughly grabbed her arm, shook her and spoke harshly.

"Quiet slave or be punished." Even as he spoke his eyes remained gentle and he winked.

Exactly five hours after Maranth and Doc began their work, enslaved miners spiritlessly began to queue up at the door. Maranth poked her head out and saw a long line of them, one behind the other, out the door and down the corridor into the central staging area.

One of the guards strode back to where the vats were. When he nodded, the other guard began waving the men into the dispensary, two at a time along the right side of the room. Each miner obediently headed to the vats where the guard pressure-injected him from a unit connected by a thin hose to the vat on the right.

"Hurry." Maranth motioned to Doc. He lined up next to her along the left wall. As each miner headed out, Doc stopped him and beamed a full light treatment from four different light tipped appendages. When the treatment was done, Maranth then vaccinated him with a hand-held pressure injector while Doc counted off each slave treated.

"Forty-five…"

Again, Maranth mumbled angrily under her breath so only Doc and the miner in front of her could hear.

"They pay us to inject a cure, but first they inject the destruction. This evil is beyond…" She sighed.

I'm just Alice, someone who fell into this Wonderland chasing a stupid rabbit.

At least the Cheshire Cat was nearby.

Doc sidled up a little closer and whispered. "These particular humans baffle me, too. I thought it was some flaw in my programming."

Maranth chuckled. She stopped to smooth back her hair and noticed the miner now in front of her looked familiar. With a start she looked closer. Though he looked terrible, she was sure it was Bollin.

"I treated you on Addehut. Bollin? Bollin? I'm meddoc Maranth. From Addehut. Remember?"

He only returned a vacant stare and Maranth let it go.

No doubt he was sold in Tigenne to these slavers.

She fought back tears. "Doc, you sure there was enough azadaxol in the vaccine, enough for everyone?"

When the guards looked her way, she continued in a bare whisper. "Remember where we are."

The closest guard was now watching her suspiciously. Maranth innocently vaccinated Bollin and Doc replied as he treated the next miner in line.

"Aye. There was enough for a full strength dose for everyone here."

As Bollin moved off, Doc added him to the count. "Forty-six."

Nearly an hour later, Doc reached the end of his count. "Seventy-five."

Maranth looked up and the Man With No Face met her eyes. He spoke out loud. "No more miners?"

Doc dipped an antenna in confirmation.

Maranth bowed with an exaggerated bob. "Man With No Face, Saad Owner, all the enslaved miners are treated. It's your turn to be vaccinated, then the guards and masters of this place."

She injected the trader, then herself.

Meanwhile Doc began retracting various distended parts back into himself. "A shame you humans are prey to all these diseases."

Maranth managed a weak smile. "Aye. Just remember who created who."

"Snippy." Doc gave her a quick scan. "I thought so. You're fatigued. Have a Pep-aid?"

One of Doc's little pills presented itself. She toasted Doc with it before she downed it.

"Modern medicine. May EVERY slave have his day."

"A joke for me. It was funny. Thank you."

The guards just ignored their banter.

The Man With No Face now stretched like a cat. "It's time to settle our accounts."

TWENTY-FOUR

DULLAREA

THE MAN WITH No Face, Maranth and Doc were led back into the main staging area of the mine by their ever-present guards. Only now they crossed another section of the expanse. Here fitted ramps covered square diam sorting bins sunk into the chamber floor. Maranth and the trader exchanged frightened glances.

Maranth, your dream. Patushah, give us strength!

Mothar and Loba-Zuda strode from the far side to a raised swivel cockpit that no doubt controlled the mine. A third man, who they called Haraq, sat in the cockpit's seat. A smallish, lizard-like animal squatted silently in a cage hanging from a pole attached to the console.

The trader could read the two at a distance through their thoughts, though he was not sure which one was saying what.

Why let her go? Take his ship and she stays.

A prize she is. She's even a meddoc.

Aii. This trader's nothing. We make him take cocktail, then he works like the others.

The Man With No Face watched Haraq's attention switch to one of the holographic displays. Reading his mind, the trader saw the now empty dispensary among the images. Then Haraq shifted a small lever as he spoke into a small mike that hung from his earphone in front of his mouth. The trader telepathically read what Haraq spoke.

Not so much power. Cut to 765 and move in slower.

The image from the display clarified into a minerbot that seemed stuck. Finally, the minerbot began to move again. Then he shifted the lever again and the *Acacia Glyn* came into full view. Two other guards were carefully laying out sensing devices at various points around the ship.

Haraq's attention returned to track the two visitors as they headed to his control station.

We take him, his lovely slave AND his ship. The trader read this from Haraq's mind, and realized this man was also the boss.

Loba-Zuda now spoke into his comm. He was too far away to be overheard. But the Man With No Face read his thoughts.

All trader ships have auto-defense. This ship new model, even better security.

Loba-Zuda abruptly stopped talking when Maranth and the trader came into hearing distance.

The trader was the first to speak. "The slaves are treated. The only remaining vaccinations left are for you and your guards."

Doc padded over to Mothar and vaccinated him, then Loba-Zuda. But Haraq waived Doc off.

The trader put his left hand in his pocket. "Give me the crystals and our account is closed."

Haraq just picked up a device from his counter and studied it as the trader spoke again.

"If I don't signal, my ship will blast this place. You'll loose this mine."

Haraq ignored him and addressed his cronies. "Aii. This device I just bought in Tigenne jams all security. So we take his, or any ship."

The Man With No Face hit a button on the security lock tucked in his pocket and gripped Maranth's hand.

Loba-Zuda asked the question before the trader could ask it himself.

"Why you sure-sure this works?"

Haraq grinned. "Outerworld ships use many security codes and patterns, but all depend on B wave encryption. This thing invades all B waves with its own. I try it out on many ships in Tigenne. It work on them all."

The trader slipped the security lock from his pocket. The indicator light told him it had failed.

Haraq laughed. "You see things too simple, trader."

With that, Mothar fanned out to his left, Loba-Zuda to his right.

The Man With No Face pulled Maranth close and invaded the slavers' minds. He blanked out their thoughts and began to work on the guards behind him. In the meantime, he grasped the handle of the blaster strapped to his leg.

Mothar and Loba-Zuda stopped moving. But Haraq broke the mental grip. He then tried to stop the guards moving in. But he hadn't controlled more than the mind of an animal before. And it wasn't working.

Mothar broke his hold and grabbed Maranth, who tried to fight him off with several kicks and bites. The Man With No Face aimed his blaster at Mothar but Loba-Zuda managed to inject him from behind. The trader felt like liquid sludge flow through him. Loba-Zuda took his blaster while Mothar injected a still struggling Maranth, who soon became still. Doc silently circled in frustrated impotency.

The trader tried to say, "My ship will attack..." But the words came out slow and slurred.

Mothar thumped him hard with the back of his hand. "What ship? You already know we broke your B wave encryption."

Haraq tapped his own chest and grinned. "Now you my slave. So is your woman."

From his console, Haraq opened a bag, flashing a handful of diams. "Why we fight so hard for this."

He rolled some of the stones in the dim light. "Just some glitter among a lot of dirt. Why then?"

He grinned again. "Why not?"

Loba-Zuda shook the Man With No Face. "You like cocktail, no? You now work in mines like others."

Mothar turned Maranth around to face him. He examined her with relish. "This one really very nice."

The Man With No Face tried to grab her but Mothar easily threw him down and kicked him several times.

Behind them Haraq issued a command. "Open bay 36Y."

Maranth watched the ramp under the trader rise up and then slide sideways from underneath him. He tumbled into a lifeless heap on the pile of diams below.

Just like my dream! She still could think but could barely move.

The ramp continued leftward until it rested on the ramp over the next bin. She then heard Haraq. "Put her in there for now."

She was shoved from behind and landed on the trader. He moaned and tried to rise.

He's alive.

The ramp slipped back in place and Loba-Zuda strode on top, standing right above them.

"Now you have plenty crystals."

The slavers chuckled and backslapped each other as they moved off.

Maranth slowly and clumsily moved to one side and tried to examine her companion for injuries. But she too felt the effects of the 'cocktail.' She felt like she was moving in honey.

The Man With No Face moaned in despair. "I've been away too long. Patushah, they broke the B waves."

Maranth fought to send her words into his mind. *Why didn't you control their minds, force them to let us go?*

There were too many and I'd never tried it on men before.

"The B waves! We're living dead."

Again, she tried to communicate with her mind. *There's something you don't know…*

But his own thoughts washed in over her own.

Better I left you in Afthar. I'm sorry.

He took her outstretched hand but couldn't look her in the face.

I'm so sorry. I didn't know. If I realized sooner...

She gently shook him but he didn't look up.

"Stop wallowing and listen."

That reached him and he looked up.

Doc and I added a drug antidote to the vaccine. The azadoxol contains a small peptide that just happens to break up a key protein in their 'cocktail.'

His eyes grew wide. *What?*

It was necessary for their health. The miners will start shaking off the drugs very soon now.

His next question skipped through her brain quickly.

And the drug won't affect us?

Not for very long.

He shook off his despair and joyfully took her hands in his own, then awkwardly let them go.

He laughed. "Never expected that. No."

You're good, Meddoc.

She smiled. *Aye. But I figured we'd be gone by the time the drug wore off.*

He stretched to test his muscles. The drugged feeling was not as strong as before.

The miners are probably getting free of the drug just about now.

He began to test the ramp that covered their imprisoning bay.

The slavers will figure out what's happened pretty quick and come for us. We must get out of here, to the ship.

Electronically locked, the ramp was beyond his strength. He rattled it in frustration.

Maranth. Your medibot, can you contact him?

Aye. I'll try. But they may have deactivated him.

She initiated the silent call on her wrist comm.

He's active but not responding. Probably waiting until he can get away.

She softly whispered instructions directly into the device while the trader began to fill his pockets with diams.

Store as many diams as you can. One way or another I'll settle this account yet.

Maranth began to fill her pockets too. She noticed his face cloth had fallen away and his facial deformities were outlined in the shimmer glow from the diams below them.

"What happened to you? You never told me."

"Use this." He threw her his face cloth.

She wrapped some of the crystals in several tied twists of the loose fabric.

"The Afthari think a witchdoc is responsible. What's a witchdoc?"

"Anything odd that happens in the outerworlds is blamed on witchdocs. But no one I know has ever seen one."

She put a hand on his arm. "What happened to you?"

"Why do you care?"

"I care. And any meddoc would ask, to increase our medical knowledge."

He searched her feelings. "Is that all, Maranth?"

Then the ramp above them released with a click, lifted up and began to slide away. One of Doc's sensory appendages peeked over the edge.

TWENTY-FIVE

DULLAREA

THE MAN WITH No Face led Maranth and Doc slowly up a rough bridge. The area below and around them was deserted. But sounds of strife echoed out from several nearby shafts.

Doc's antennas whipped around trying to make sense of it. "Disturbances everywhere. That's why the slavers forgot me and left for the tunnels."

As they neared the entrance to the first of the passageways off the bridge, loud shouts and sounds of fighting poured through.

Wild-eyed and wailing, Loba-Zuda charged out, nearly knocking Maranth off her feet and banging himself against Doc. His blaster swung wildly as he regained his footing. Then he tried to aim at the trader as he ran off.

The Man With No Face reached for his own blaster. But the weapon was, of course, gone. He dove as the slaver fired. The blast missed and hit the rock face quite a distance away.

Loba-Zuda cursed in some unintelligible dialect as he ran off.

Now a crazed band of miners poured out of the tunnel looking for blood. They immediately attacked the Man With No Face. Maranth shoved several aside.

"Let him be. Stop. Stop it! We're the ones who freed you. Remember?"

A tall miner, who was about to bash the trader's head in with metal rod, hesitated. He stared at Maranth.

Doc pointed his antenna at the fleeing Loba-Zuda.

"He's the one you want."

There were no more mobs of miners until they reached the spaceport portal. Here a bunch of them were unloading diams out of a still minerbot that blocked most of the space. The miners didn't seen to notice or care about the trader, Maranth, or her medibot. So the three quietly circled around them onto the spaceport itself.

Against one wall of the dome someone was holed up behind a bunch of crates. Scattered around the port, behind odd crates and machinery were other miners. The *Acacia Glyn* sat wide open nearby, her gangway down. The other, smaller ship was gone.

Whenever the man against the wall tried to move, these miners pelted him with diams. The miners by the minerbot resupplied those under the spaceport dome by rolling diams out to them. When the man under attack rose up to aim his blaster, the trader recognized Haraq. Fortunately, the miners managed to scramble to safety before he fired.

Meanwhile, a couple of miners tried to maneuver along the perimeter to get closer. Haraq noticed and blasted at them, forcing them back. Both sides were locked in a standoff.

The Man With No Face pulled Maranth over against the wall, out of the line of fire.

Please drop down and stay put. I may be able to fix this.

She looked at him skeptically.

Trust me.

His message flowing through her exuded a quiet confidence that calmed her. She did as he asked.

There was a miner that seemed to be directing the others at the minerbot. The trader approached this very large man with a dusty beard and tapped his shoulder.

"I think we can end this if you turn on the floodlights, the ones over there."

He pointed to a particular bank of the lights that lined the entire perimeter of the port. The man eyed him threateningly. Then his mood sort of faded into a 'show me' attitude.

"I'm called the Man With No Face. You are?"

"Quasama. I see where your name comes from." He glanced over at Maranth. There was a hint of gratefulness.

The trader was sure Quasama knew they had freed him.

"Aye. Do you want my help, or continue as you are?"

Quasama said nothing. He just walked over to a control panel mounted on the rock wall and tapped in commands.

The floodlights came on and the diams scattered around gave off a blistering display.

The Man With No Face sprinted to the lights across from Haraq and angled them onto the diams above and around Haraq's lair. When Haraq stood to take a shot, he was blinded by their brilliance.

The miners charged in and beat their tormentor down.

Maranth started toward the beaten man, but the Man With No Face stopped her.

It's a just death for his crimes. Let's go.

The three quickly headed for the *Acacia Glyn*.

Several miners closed ranks, blocking them at the foot of the ramp. A short man with a lot of bushy hair spoke for the group.

"This ship's ours. Leave and you live."

The very hairy man next to him grabbed Maranth's arm. "The woman can stay."

Maranth tried to wiggle free. "Let me go, you ungrateful half-wit."

The trader crossed his arms and his eyes bored into the two.

"We freed you and saved your miserable carcasses from a living death. So you repay her with rape and me by stealing my ship. We should have left you to rot."

A rumble of acknowledgement passed through the men.

The miners from the entry area joined the bunch gathering by the ship.

The bushy haired man nodded to his companion, who then let Maranth go.

"Look, trader. If we don't take your ship we'll be marooned here. There's only room for some of us anyway. You live here with the rest until we return. See?"

A murmur of assent ran through the men.

The hairy man again spoke. "Our need gives us the right, trader."

Maranth angrily piped in. "And what of our need?"

Quasama pushed through the crowd and they made way, as he was a head taller and a lot broader than any of them. He took the spot directly in front of the trader.

"We'll make you rich for your troubles."

"The cargo holds have no life support. Even if you left us here, you'd only have room for, say, three more of your own. There just isn't the cabin space for all of you, whether you leave us, or not. And which one of you hotshots will get through the pirates waiting out there?"

An angry murmur passed among the miners. The trader's eyes swept over them.

"Which one of you will bet his life he can get through without me?"

Confusion replaced the general consternation.

A rather non-descript miner standing next to Quasama locked eyes with the trader.

"I might, trader. Used to make the Junnata run myself before I was shanghaied here."

The crowd was now jubilant. The bushy haired miner hugged the newcomer but was waived off.

"But I won't. That is I won't if this trader here gives some of us a ride to the nearest colony. I'm a trader myself, not no thief."

The crowd was stunned to silence. The newcomer nodded

to the trader. "I'm Koban. The guy who hugged me is Dex. The big guy is Quasama."

Quasama nodded. The Patusian tapped his chest. "I'm the Man With No Face."

He squatted down and opened his shirt to reveal his golden tattoo. "So we do business."

Koban also squatted down. "Don't push it, Patusian."

The trader smiled. "Let's see. We've freed all 75 of you from a living hell." He waived at Koban's bandaged arm. "And healed you. In the process you've all become rich. Rich enough to stay and grow richer, or live in comfort anywhere."

The miners muttered in agreement.

"And we'll also ferry as many of you as we can safely transport to Tigenne. It's only fair we receive value back for all we've done and all we will do."

The Patusian pointed to the minerbot sitting at the portal. "Fair value? That would be a minerbot's full load of cleaned, top grade diams. A token, considering the trouble, the risk we've taken, and freedom and great wealth you've gained from our efforts."

Koban grinned. "Half a bin, cleaned, of the same grade mix that this mine produces, plus all the diams you're wearing."

The trader paused and thought for several moments. "Not less than 75% of a full minerbot's bin, standard weight. Plus what we are wearing. Plus Haraq's pet, alive, in its cage."

Koban was surprised. "The lizard?"

The Man With No Face nodded. "And a weapons-grade blaster. These slavers took mine."

He paused a moment. "I can take twenty of you. There's only crew bunks for six. The rest will have to sleep where you can. No one lays a hand on my meddoc, Maranth, or her medibot. And you miners will load my diams in the ship's cargo holds.

"But, as an added incentive, I will also transport all your diams that you can fit in the crew lockers and wherever we can store them in the cabins safely, other than my personal quarters. That should be enough to buy you allies and safe transport back here."

Koban stood and looked around at all the miners. "Fair?"

The men hollered happily and Quasama backslapped Koban approvingly.

Koban again squatted. "We have a deal, Patusian."

The Man With No Face crossed his wrists Patusian style and slid them out in confirmation. "Then done."

He now set his mind on Maranth.

Get Doc to gather your things and bring them to my cabin. I will sleep on the floor.

She considered the options and understood.

TWENTY-SIX

ACACIA GLYN

IT WAS ALL bustle, miners everywhere stowing away their diams, setting up extra strapping and webbing to secure themselves for the trip, and so on. Quasama and the small, bushy haired miner, Dex, seemed to be managing it all. The ship stank of rank body odor and beige dust covered everything. Maranth had Doc pass out all of the remaining wash powders. It didn't help. The men needed a real water bath to wash off the dust and grime, plus clean clothes. The ship was just not equipped to handle water hygiene for so many.

Maranth had a light headache and her belly hurt, probably a leftover from being drugged. The miners no doubt had much worse symptoms, given the length of time the poison had been in their bodies. Yet none of them complained. They were all happy and upbeat. She decided the smell and the mess were worth that.

Maranth's meager belongings, Haraq's "lizard," and the diams she and the Patusian had personally collected were stowed in the captain's cabin. But he was nowhere in sight. Maranth could somehow sense he was outside the ship near the cargo holds.

She slipped around a couple of miners in the passageway leading into the bridge. The shanghaied trader from the mines, Koban, sat in one of the console seats reviewing ship controls and testing ship systems with the grey shipbot, Jona. Several other miners were just sprawled about with their personal bags of diams.

Before she could say anything Koban grinned up at her.

"I have his okay. Someone's got to second chair this tug to Tigenne."

He pointed to the next seat. "Take a load off."

She bowed in the Veddian manner. "I am Maranth, Maranth-sa-Veddi-Dimore."

She then slipped into the seat and relaxed, grateful to be off her feet.

He continued to work at the screen for some moments, then swiveled his seat to face her. Dust drifted off his clothes.

"What kind of name is Man With No Face?"

Maranth felt he said it with kind eyes. "The Afthari called him that."

"I've heard of the Afthari. Slavers."

"Aye."

"Everyone here knows what you did for us, what you risked to do it. If anyone even looks at you funny, just tell me or Quasama, the big guy."

Maranth smiled. "It's really nice to be protected. Thank you."

His face flushed and he fell silent. Then he went back to work on the console.

Maranth rose to leave.

He looked up. "A fancy innerworld meddoc hooked up with a very ugly Patusian trader, in the most god-forsaken region of the known galaxy. You two must have some crazy story."

She smiled, but dared not reveal more to this stranger. "Aye. But maybe no crazier than yours?"

"You got me there."

The Man With No Face walked in carrying Haraq's pet in its cage. The funny thing was, Maranth knew he was coming. It was as if she could feel exactly where he was in and around the ship.

Maybe because he reads my mind?

His eyes told her she had actually caught him off guard. A new face cloth covered his lower features.

She smiled. "I seem to be in the way. I was just going to your cabin to meditate."

"Please stay and meditate here. You'll soon be needed."

She nodded, took the seat at the far console and closed her eyes.

The Patusian noted Koban was studying the both of them with great curiosity.

After placing the cage into its newly installed rig on the wall, the maimed trader joined the other man. "Status?"

The shipbot turned his holo projection to the Patusian. It displayed 'Power systems, Bridge Controls, Life Support, Navigation tested, adjusted and rechecked. Weapons... check. Security — odd configuration. Working... Security checks to your parameters.'

The Man With No Face eyed Koban. "No reflection on you, but I'd like a recheck. Pirates are out there."

Koban nodded. "Understood. I'd do the same in your place."

"Jona, retest everything."

The two men closely followed the readouts as Jona again collected and processed data on the ship systems. Without waiting for instructions, the shipbot extended two of his appendages under the left console to adjust something.

Just as Jona was finishing the adjustment, Quasama strode in and seemed to take up the whole room. Even after starvation and the conditions in the mines, his build was strong, his hands massive. He locked his gaze on Maranth but spoke to the trader.

"Everything's secured. Everyone aft is strapped in. And if they're not, it's their own stupidity."

The trader's voice was measured. "Please make sure the spaceport is cleared so your men can open the dome. It's liable to be a rough ride. You and Dex should do a quick recheck aft and then strap in. We lift off in, say, fifteen minutes."

Quasama's eyes shifted to the trader. "No problem."

He hesitated a moment. "We're all sorry for how we treated you two. We'd just been like animals too long."

The trader nodded toward Maranth. "Maranth is really the one who set you free."

The mention of her name brought her out of her trance. She opened her eyes and smiled up at the big miner, then bowed to him.

"Maranth-sa-Veddi-Dimore. If you know a man here named Bollin, would you relay a message from me?"

Quasama cocked his head. "I know him."

"Tell him the only other person from Addehut that I saw, after we were taken, was Belamae from the kitchen. She told me she would be sold to a brothel. Please also tell him I'm sorry."

Quasama just stood there awkwardly, not quite knowing what to say. Finally he just nodded and headed out.

Maranth stepped over to where the men were testing systems. "We encountered no pirates before. Why now?"

Koban answered. "They'd only hit the ship on the way out, when she carries diams. For a cargo like this, they'd kill their own mothers."

The Patusian's eyes confirmed what Koban said.

Maranth tied back a loose strand of hair. "Raiders, slavers, now pirates. Doc and I will prepare for casualties."

Her companion laid a restraining hand on her arm. *Please stay here. Doc will take care of the others.*

She gently pushed his hand away. *On my oath as a meddoc, I must go where I'm most needed.*

When the ship was fully energized and pulsing yellow, it lifted off, through the open dome, leaving Dullarea as a shrinking sore on the face of the hazy planet. The holo that danced between the front consoles displayed their ascent as a yellow ship icon pulling away from the small, grayish ball representing the planet below.

The Man With No Face monitored the main navigation and power controls from the right console seat, while Koban manned weapons to his left. The shipbot strapped in at the ship systems console.

The Patusian checked his own straps while he spoke his instructions directly into the console. "We head toward Homoth, execute course on-line in slot three."

The yellow holo image of the ship slid up and off to their right.

Koban was surprised. "Why that way? Tigenne's in the opposite direction."

"Aye. But a direct route is not always best."

PIRATE SHIP *WIREWOLF*

Its captain, Yrazz, watched a similar holo in front of his console. His holo also showed another planet in the Dullarean system concealing the red images of his three pirate craft from view of the blue ship icon rising from the mining planet. The blue icon was clearly heading toward a nearby star system. The image of a fourth red pirate ship lay in wait behind an outer planet in that direction.

His Second, Rogar, scratched his left side though his eyes never waivered from the holo. The two were scruffy and unkempt, not much to look at. Both wore nose rings but Yrazz sported a thick, black mustache.

His mustache bobbed when he spoke. "Hah. Her belly full of diams, she runs for Homoth."

Rogar stopped scratching. "We tell Sobad?"

"Naw. Sobad will see her come and meet her like this."

Yrazz switched the holo into simulation mode. Now the three red pirate icons chased the blue icon into the clutches of the fourth red pirate. "Yah! See?"

He was answered by an eager whoop.

ACACIA GLYN

"Here they come." The Patusian pointed out the three

blinking red pirate icons bearing down on the *Acacia Glyn* in the holo in front of his console.

He spoke into his controls. "Maximum speed within vector four — now."

The ship surged forward. A brilliant light flashed in the left viewports and the ship rocked.

Koban spat. "Roguelasers!"

"Jona, monitor their fire and evade."

Jona had already plugged himself into several of the console ports and began adjusting the trajectory to evade their pursuers.

The ship rocked again but the flashes were more distant. The holo icons of the pirate craft fell back.

Koban grinned. "Your ship's fast, Patusian. They're standing in our engine wash!"

"Aye. Zedd had to have the fastest hop-jock spacer in the region."

Koban was about to ask what he meant, but the red blinking icon of a fourth pirate swung out and raced in to meet their yellow icon. A small dot of light appeared in the front viewport and grew bigger as it approached.

"Shit." Koban spat out.

The trader responded. "Brace yourself!"

A brilliant burst rocked the Acacia Glyn and the bridge was badly shaken. Jona and Koban frantically tried to access and staunch the damage.

Koban was the first to speak. "Damage is containable, but the ship won't take another hit like this."

The Patusian activated the comm that gave him live feed of the ship internals.

Maranth and Doc were busy treating injured miners in the main cabin. Everyone looked alive. Cargo and engineering sections seemed okay.

Maranth, how bad?

She looked up at him on the wall comm. Before she could reply his attention jerked away.

The fourth pirate hurtled toward the *Acacia Glyn* as the three others pressed in and began to fire from behind.

"Koban, fire both forward guns — now."

Koban quickly complied.

The pirate in front slowed as the first burst hit, and then tried to dodge the next blasts.

Koban kept firing. "It's no good. He'll just slow us until the others catch up."

The Patusian placed a course disk in slot one. "We're going to move. Stop firing."

He again addressed his console. "Execute course on-line in slot one."

The ship started to move off when a blast from behind again lit up the left viewports. The *Acacia Glyn* shook hard. The Man With No Face thumped the console. "Patushah! NOW."

The ship now swung violently aside and shot away, directly at a Saturn-like planet.

Koban squinted at the holo. "What tha..?"

The planet seemed to rush in at them. The *Acacia Glyn* raced directly at the ringed giant, dodging blasts from the fourth pirate, now leading the pack.

Sweat shone on his forehead as the Man With No Face reprogrammed controls.

Koban's voice was tight. "They're gaining on us."

The planet's expanse filled the bridge holo as well as the front viewport. Everyone held on as best he could.

"Here we go." The Patusian tapped commands into two console screens and the ship subtly shifted and began to accelerate.

The *Acacia Glyn* veered from a collision course into a close orbit of the planet, slipping under its rings. The pirate ship icons pressed in, but their fire was now useless, absorbed by the ring debris.

The *Acacia Glyn* shot around the planet, then whipped back at incredible speed, speed gained from the massive planet's mass and rotation.

The pirate ships' icons overshot and quickly swung back and also accelerated around the planet. But the yellow icon had gained so much distance that it was decisively ahead.

Koban laughed. "Great move. You whipped her like she was a tail!"

The *Acacia Glyn* raced away from the Dullarean system. The pirate ships could only follow at a distance further and further behind.

TWENTY-SEVEN

ACACIA GLYN

HOURS HAD PASSED. The miners were mostly asleep. All was quiet except for the faint hum and vibration from the induction ring, as the ship sped through deep space.

The Patusian suddenly rose from his console. "Koban, take the helm."

He strode off to his cabin. Its door slid open, revealing Maranth on the floor in a corner. Some of the nearby miners tried to see what was going on, but the door slid closed behind him.

Maranth's arms were wrapped around her bent up legs, her face against her knees. She was shaking. *I've lost it. Lost it.*

He slipped down next to her. He knew two miners outside had their ears to the door.

I've been there, when I couldn't see and hear. Drogans intent on eating me alive. I know that fear. You know what brought me back?

She looked up, her face wet from tears.

His eyes were soft. *Kin Song. And cool fingers on my forehead. Yours.*

She finally spoke. "You're taking us to Tigenne. I was in that slave market. And that's where they hold death games."

"Maranth, that place must be somewhere else on the planet. We're headed to a regular spacer port. I know because

I've been there before. Only ship services, stores and clubs. I promise."

Let me return the favor you did for me, back in Afthar.

With that he just held her, and rocked her back and forth as if he were comforting a child. When he finally let go, his hand brushed the floor between them. His fingers came away wet and sticky.

Blood!

She pulled away and slumped down. Then he knew. He marveled at the contradiction. She had defeated a band of slavers, fought crazed miners, then nursed the same miners through a pirate attack. Now facing her own fertility, she fell apart.

It's more than that. She's so vulnerable.

"Maranth, there is nothing to fear in having a monthly. The serverbot will clean up. Doc will fix up something to soak up the new blood."

She spoke through gritted teeth. "I certainly know what this is. I'm not supposed to have a monthly. And I have no other clothes."

"Spacers are always getting into fights or accidents, so removing blood from clothes is no big deal for a serverbot on a ship. Meanwhile, you have a sleeping gown. You were wearing it when we left Afthar."

"So I do." She managed a small smile.

"There's nothing for you to do, except relax and take care of yourself. Tigenne will have contraceptives that will block your monthlies and fertility. This is nothing, really. Call Doc and I'll get the serverbot."

He waited at the door for the two 'bots, intending to shield Maranth from view of the miners he knew were gathering outside. When the door slipped open, he ushered the 'bots in.

The waiting men caught sight of blood on his pants. Quasama grabbed his shirt, and with one hand, pulled him into the hall and off his feet as the door slid closed behind the 'bots.

"No one saw either of you bleeding before. You do something to her?" His grip was iron and his words venomous.

"She's bleeding from inside."

Quasama dropped him. "Must have got injured when we were thrown around. She's such a little thing."

His eyes were suddenly wet. And he wasn't the only one.

The trader didn't know what else to say. He just hoped Doc would come out soon to reassure everyone.

TIGENNE

The *Acacia Glyn* swung in toward the red, green and grey of Tigenne's mass. As the planet filled the viewport, the ship slowed and began to course across its surface. The maneuver was replicated in the holo images flashing before the bridge consoles.

Koban grinned and swiveled toward the trader. He raised his forearm with his hand up, flat and wide. The Patusian swiveled around and did the same. Then the two men slapped hands.

As soon as the ship set down, the hatch opened to the large, garish colony steaming in the hot sun. Several armed men casually approached below. Others with weapons at the ready watched from further off.

A thickset hairy man, wearing not much besides a small arsenal and a large blaster in his right hand, looked over the now war-weary *Acacia Glyn*.

He loudly repeated what was clearly a well-rehearsed speech. "Payment 'fer landin' an' berth is 1,200 innerworld credits. No funny money. Payable 'n advance."

He shaded his eyes as he dubiously appraised the dusty, ragged miners crowding the portal. "So. You goin' to keep my bravo bustin' hump saggin' in the wind, or what?"

His armed men took aim. A cannon at the far side of the open port was now trained on the ship.

Lower features wrapped Afthari-style, the Man With No

Face pushed through the miners. "This ship is mine." He tossed the hairy man one of the diams.

The man inspected the gem, grinned, then nodded.

He didn't seem to recognize the trader when he thumped his chest. "Portmaster Kleigel here."

His armed men relaxed.

The Patusian in truth did not recognize Kleigel either. "Don't let the look of her give you the wrong idea. The *Acacia Glyn* is fully armed and capable of defending herself, me and mine."

Kleigel grinned greasily. "Welcome 'ta Tigenne. We satisfy every need, provide every pleasure. An' here your business is your business. Jus' don't cause trouble for any of us an' we don't cause you no trouble. So you just come down an' enjoy."

The miners whooped and cheered as they poured down the gangway with their bags of diams. Koban was the last of them to leave the ship.

Koban shielded his eyes and his nostrils flared as he inhaled the heavy, fetid air. "Now I remember why I hated this place."

From the mouth of the hatch Maranth and the trader watched the men disappear into the streets and gaudy shops.

She shuddered. *The Dullarean slavers cracked the ship's security. How can it stand up here?*

No more B waves. I unlock security by telepathy.

Maranth at first didn't understand. *Ah, Haraq's pet. You control the lizard's mind?*

His eyes twinkled. *Aye. I can connect to its mind and make it release the new lock with a few pecks of its snout. Once we leave the ship, it's tight. And if someone tries to pry it open, it will actively defend itself with blast cannons.*

Maranth shook her head and laughed. "Then I better get Doc to analyze the poor creature and see it is properly fed and very healthy, before we leave."

About a half hour later the two slipped into the steamy town. Revelry and the scent of vice poured out from a glittery club guarded by two oiled Husians dressed only in red loincloths. The trader had avoided the place before. It was a slave brothel.

Three drunken miners pushed past the two and entered the place.

The trader pulled her close as they walked past. *Tigenne is rough and raw. Stay near.*

They passed several clubs, then turned down a quieter street filled with various shops. The first shop was marked by a plain sign that simply said 'Drugs.'

Maranth turned to go in, but the trader stopped her. "It's not what you think."

He led her to another door further along, across the lane. It was marked by a revolving 'Rx & Sundries' holo.

He took her gently by her arm. "In here. Wash powders, potions, lotions, personal supplies and medicines."

She understood. "May I also replenish my med supplies before we leave?"

Maranth, we have a small fortune in the cargo holds, never mind the diams in our clothes. Buy anything you want.

She eyed him quizzically. *These are your diams?*

He winked. *And it's your ship.*

They burst into laughter so hard that Maranth nearly fell over.

The trader entered the shop first. Towles, the tall bearded proprietor, smiled and came out from behind the counter. "You couldn't stay away."

Maranth followed the Patusian inside and Towles' attention turned to her and noted her slave clothing. "Welcome."

"She's with me." The trader nodded to his friend.

Towles grabbed his shoulders. "You can speak!"

"Aye. But my face is still a work in progress." He turned to Maranth. "This meddoc is the reason I'm even alive."

Towles nodded to her with new respect. "I'm Towles."

Maranth bowed and introduced herself with a smile. "I understand I can buy medical supplies here."

Towles eyed her a moment, then shook his head no. "I won't sell you anything."

Then he grinned. "But, I will trade what you need for your medical services. Tigenne has no clinic."

Maranth sighed. "Of course. But unless there's an emergency, can you give me a day or two first?"

After she acquired what she needed right away, the pair continued down the street.

At the corner they skirted two flamboyant women who looked Maranth up and down and smirked. The trader recognized them as independents, freelance sex workers.

He calmly took Maranth's hand and pulled her onto the cross street. "Your clothes have to go. I think I know the place."

Maranth jerked away in alarm.

The Man With No Face quickly dropped his hand. *Maranth? I will never hurt you. Never.*

His reassuring thoughts calmed her.

He slipped back to her side. "A lot of the miners think you are my slave, given your clothes. You're very popular with them, you know? They'll probably kill me if you continue to wear these rags."

"You want to buy me clothes?"

"Aye. Over there." He pointed down the street to a revolving holo of a woman who, with every turn, was wearing a different outfit.

Maranth looked down. "I'm sorry I reacted so badly. I'm just not myself."

You don't need to apologize.

He knew the Patushah remedy was not possible here, so he called upon her own tradition.

"Shouldn't a meddoc be able to diagnose her own hyper-vigilance, given what she's faced for so long?"

"Aye. And thank you for taking me shopping."

He took her hand again. "Besides, what would your people think of me if I brought you back in rags?"

She smiled. *They will be just as flabbergasted when I appear in outerworld clothes.*

They walked through the holo into the store and were

greeted by a shopbot that looked a lot like the dresserbot Emma from the slave market. This 'bot also dripped colorful outfits and accessories from every appendage. The trader tightened his grip on her hand.

It's safe. And I'm here.

The shopbot dipped an appendage in greeting. "I'm Vera, programmed to provide all your couture needs."

Vera scanned Maranth up and down. "And you need everything. You've come to the right place."

Vera then pirouetted, billowing out her finery. "Have you ever seen such gorgeous fabrics anywhere?"

She stopped and sidled conspiratorially over to them.

"You want the works, right?"

The Patusian tapped Vera. "I'm deaf. Show me a holo."

The shopbot obliged and repeated her question in text.

The trader laughed under his face cloth. "Aye. The works."

Maranth jumped in. "An outfit or two, not too flashy."

With those words, Vera used her appendages to scan Maranth from head to toe from all sides. The 'bot then gently but firmly nudged Maranth over to a rack at the back of the store overflowing with garments. "Why don't you take a look at these and see what you'd like? I think I also have something in the window you will love."

With Maranth's back turned, Vera sidled back to the trader and holoed, 'The works?'

He replied in a whisper. "Dress her in clothes fit for a rich trader's wife. Three shipboard and two street outfits, plus one dress garment. And something nice for the hot weather here. Everything she needs, from the skin out. All accessories. Oh, add in three sexy sleep gowns, comfortable but not too skimpy. Don't show them to her as they are a surprise. You do shoes and boots?"

Vera dipped an antenna and displayed, 'Aye, from a catalog. Everything we do is custom made, top quality. You won't be disappointed.'

Maranth held up a silver tunic. Emma projected a Maranth

holo wearing the garment. Her holo image then turned in a circle so Maranth could see her choice from every side, and watch how the cloth draped against her moving form. She suddenly realized that all the clothes in the store were samples. She marveled that she could see how the fitted garments would actually look on her without having to try them on. Whatever she chose would then be fabricated to fit perfectly.

As advanced as Veddi was, clothes shopping there was not so interesting. Everyone of the same sex wore similar garments, with some variation of color and fabric. Most people chose a robe from a store rack, put it on and a 'bot would shorten it to the right length. There were special shops where people who were unusually broad, narrow or tall could find clothes that fit. Anyone could order from a catalog and any housebot could shorten the garment.

Vera now holoed 'Come back at 1730' towards the trader.

He shook his head. "I'll wait. Is there a secure, women-only spa around here, one that really pampers its clients?"

TWENTY-EIGHT

TIGENNE

IT WAS DARK when they entered the trader's usual restaurant. Maranth was now richly dressed in form-fitting, colorful clothes, with makeup that made her eyes seem even larger. Long, loose ringlets of her dark hair trailed down the left side of her face, shoulder and back. The trader nodded to the serverbot and the two were immediately taken to a private booth. As soon as they were seated, the serverbot filled two glasses on the table from its hose appendage and removed the two others.

"I eat regular food now. Please show us what you have tonight." The serverbot dipped an antenna in acknowledgement. Then it left and the curtains closed automatically behind it.

The trader held up his glass. "This is what everyone in Tigenne drinks with food. It may take a little getting used to, but I've never gotten sick on it."

She sniffed it and took a sip. "Not bad." In fact it was pleasant and somehow relaxing.

The trader smiled and removed his face cloth. "Content? Even a bit happy?"

"I am." *But you would know that since you read my mind.*

Maranth returned his smile. "You lifted me from Afthar. Thank you is not enough." She raised her glass to him. "Better days." Then she drank a bit more.

He raised his glass. "I would not have survived without your help."

The serverbot brought in several platters of food, all of them foreign to Maranth. "What would you like, honored guests?" It also holoed the same words.

The trader answered for both of them. "We'll try them all." The 'bot then filled their plates with food from each platter and left. Maranth found the aroma fabulous. The two ate with gusto.

Soon after they were done the serverbot silently removed their plates and again disappeared.

The trader began to reach for Maranth's hand but stopped. *Maranth. I'd like to ask you something. The business with Zedd adding your medibot to the deal in Afthar. Then later, your dream that exactly predicted what happened in Dullarea. You seem to sense where I am. Have you had other such experiences in the past?*

Maranth slumped a bit. *No. Sometimes I seem to sense, to connect… beyond what I should know. It's as if some sort of door opened, maybe because I'm with you most of the time. I'm not sure. I guess I'm not making sense.*

He was pensive. *Nothing that happened to me makes sense either. Yet I was remade on Afthar. I think maybe in some way you were, too.*

She bent forward. *What happened to you?*

I will tell you, if you promise not to tell anyone else, including the Veddi.

"Why?"

Do you remember how afraid of me you were when I first reached out to you telepathically?

She remembered.

He took her hand. *That's why no one can know.*

She understood and thought for a moment. "On my oath as a meddoc, your medical records are confidential unless you agree to release them. If anything you tell me is medically related in ANY way, then I may not reveal it. You were and are my patient."

Does your confidentiality oath include that I am telepathic?

Aye, it does. But everyone entering Veddi must go through a physical scan and complete medical workup. The authorities will learn of your brain nodule, but not know its function.

He closed his eyes in pain. *I was on my ship, just a trader on a routine run. Then suddenly I was on Afthar without my face AND fully telepathic. I don't remember anything else.*

He dropped her hand. *I've fought with every fiber of my being to keep what I was and to find peace with what I've become. I believe what happened to me cannot be an accident. And this frightens me to my core.*

Maranth considered the implications of what he just told her.

He shook his head. "Without your compassion, your strength, Patushah..."

Their curtain was suddenly thrown open by a couple of drunken miners.

The taller of the two spoke. "Koban is looking for you two."

The shorter one unsteadily pointed out the front door. Across the street there was a holo display of a woman seductively throwing dice over and over in the entrance to a large club festooned with bright lights. It had an even flashier sign, 'Lucky Club & Casino.'

The Man With No Face, his face cloth back in place, stepped through the holo into the darkened, noisy club. Maranth was at his heels. Music blared and a lot of people were crowded inside.

He spoke directly into her ear to be heard. "I'd like you to consider delaying your return to Veddi, beyond your medical clinic here."

Hardened characters from all over were smoking, drinking, or shooting themselves up at a bar that was tended by a lone serverbot. A bald man in red reached for a neuro stimulator off the bar's conveyer and gave himself a charge.

Maranth looked away. "I don't belong in the outerworlds. If you won't take me back I'll find another way."

They passed several human waiters of both sexes wearing revealing, erotic costumes. Three more were coming on to three eager men in soft pastel robes, flashing credits.

Maranth gasped. "They're Veddian. I could return with them."

The trader led her away but she twisted back.

One of the men pulled a male waiter onto his lap as another gulped down an inflammatory liquid that seemed to pour from the nipple of a female waiter, her body now sensuously rubbing his torso.

Maranth's eyes grew wide. "I might expect that from barbarians. But Veddi?"

The trader firmly pulled her back and held her face in both his hands so they were eye to eye.

"The only center of balance in this great and terrible life lies inside — here." He lightly tapped her chest.

He then quickly led her to the back of the room, which opened into an even noisier space. Several groups, mostly men, were loudly partying. Some were betting and cheering favorites in various games. The trader had gambled here himself and it was very familiar.

Nearby, a large brawny man howled, upended the table, then grabbed up a tough looking woman. He carried her off over his shoulder to the cheers and catcalls of onlookers.

Maranth barely dodged the woman's kicking foot.

The trader stopped. "Look. If you return to Veddi, the Innerworlds Council will learn about the Afthari raiding."

"Of course they will."

His voice was grim. "Then Veddi or the Council will wipe the Afthari out. Understand I also owe the Afthari, for feeding me."

Maranth spat back. "And what do the Afthari owe me, and all the other lives they have ruined? Their raiding must be stopped."

She composed herself. "The innerworld authorities will handle it humanely. We are civilized, after all."

He sighed. "You are in the right. I will find another way to balance this account."

She eyed him intently. "Will you honor your pledge to me, or not?"

Of course. I owe you most of all.

A holo of a spaceship wove around them and attacked a similar image hiding behind two men comparing hand blasters.

The Patusian caught sight of Koban, now clean and well dressed, along with another man with a nose ring, working the controls to the dueling spaceship game. The room and its patrons were the battle arena. Quasama, some miners and other men wearing nose rings looked on, drinking and doping heavily. The miners were now clean, their hair trimmed. Some of the beards were gone. A miner, stripped to the waist, arm-wrestled with a burly man in striped baggy pants.

The Man With No Face slipped into the seat next to Koban. Soon the ship image he controlled destroyed the other holo ship in a dazzling light display. His opponent rolled a diam from his pile over to Koban's.

The trader silently eyed the miners around the table. He nodded to the two he knew best. "Koban. Quasama."

His eyes then found Maranth standing just behind, to his left. He rose up.

Koban burped. "Hah. Stay. You bring me luck."

The trader dropped back into the seat.

Koban turned to his game partner. "Meet the man who ran his ship past your nose at Dullarea."

The man laughed heartily. "So, this is the faceless Patusian trader."

Koban continued. "It was Yrazz and his rum-guzzling pirates here that attacked us."

He glanced at the pirate captain. "No hard feelings."

Then he tapped the Patusian's arm. "Join us hooch-moochers. Yrazz actually thinks he can beat me."

The pirate grinned and his moustache bobbed. "What's there to beat?"

Quasama laughed and leaned across the table so he could be heard. "Seems pirating just isn't as lucrative as you might expect, fuel and labor costs what they are. So Yrazz here has decided to go straight. You could say we've struck a deal."

The pirate captain laughed and pounded the flat of his hand on the table. The others drunkenly did the same.

Maranth shook her head.

So the miners have thrown in with the pirates. Just when I think nothing more out here could possibly surprise me, something does.

At the other table, one of the arm wrestlers finally prevailed. There was renewed cheering, drinking and doping all around.

Koban drunkenly lurched back around to the Patusian. "His people will provide us protection and handle some of the cargo. 'Course if he beats me here, he might get the tourism concession, too."

Koban and the pirate broke out in mutual spasms of backslapping and good-natured cursing.

The Man With No Face again stood up. "Our accounts balance, Koban. Take care of yourself." He squeezed Koban's shoulder.

Koban swung his chair back around and seemed to sober for a moment. "None of us from Dullarea will forget what you did for us. Never."

Then he noticed Maranth and grinned. "So you finally got her some decent clothes."

He looked her up and down with admiration tinged with lust. "You look sooo good, really, really good... Oh, almost forgot. We miners got you a present, to say thanks and so you'll always remember us."

He pulled out a gold and talline ring. In the center was a brilliant diam. The colors from the room danced through the stone in luminous spasms.

Maranth loved it even though it was so flashy. She didn't know what to say.

Koban slipped it onto her middle finger. Her eyes grew moist. She took his face in her hands and kissed him on his forehead.

"Please thank them all for me. It's so beautiful. I'm so happy that I could do for you, what this man did for me." She put her hand on the trader's arm for all to see. Then she bowed in the Veddian fashion to all the men at the table.

As they walked away, Quasama came over and took Maranth's hand. The Man With No Face was about to interfere when the big man waved him off and kissed her hand. He winked at the Patusian. "I might forget you, but I'll never forget this little one."

TWENTY-NINE

TIGENNE & DEEP SPACE

THE *ACACIA GLYN* rose above the night-shrouded colony. As the ship climbed toward orbital altitude, a ray of light from the impending dawn cut across and lit her hull.

The trader turned to Maranth seated at the second bridge console. "Next stop, Veddi."

She was lost watching the single new ray of sunlight morph into a brilliant dawn pouring through the viewports.

Doc and the shipbot, Jona, were both strapped in at the third console. Doc was self-testing. "The mine dust still coats my insides. Yuk. At least on Veddi I will get a good overhaul and proper supplies."

Maranth mused. "I almost lost all hope of returning home."

These were the last words anyone spoke for awhile. Eventually, the induction rings were engaged for deep space.

Maranth meditated, then settled on cushions in the main cabin for a meal. Doc had her on a severe meditation schedule again. Of course he was right. She was so out of balance she just put herself in his hands.

Well, his appendages. Maranth grinned at her silent little joke.

The serverbot had done a credible job cleaning all the dust, sweat and blood from the cabins. Except for a few minor rips in some of the pillows, she would never have known there had been 20 really dirty miners sprawled about everywhere two days before. Now she missed them. The ship felt empty.

She sensed the trader leave the bridge and head down the hall to join her.

He smiled and settled nearby. The serverbot brought over full plates that smelled more of Tigenne than Afthar. Then the little 'bot poured them that wonderful drink from the restaurant.

After they ate, Maranth was the first to speak. "What is your home planet Patushah like?"

He smiled and leaned forward. "Patushah is not a planet. It is our name for my people. We have a common belief in the nature of things, a way of life, named for the first, Patushah of Aughnah Four. Outsiders call us Patusians."

"Is that where you are from, Aughnah Four?"

He found her question amusing. "The Patushah mostly live and die on our large trading freighters — family ships. We live everywhere, and nowhere."

He slid closer to her and then leaned back, so his face was in shadow.

"For us, trade is a flow of human energy, balancing dynamic systems within natural laws. We strive for balance and harmony as we seek the greater. We try to surf and heal the energy flows that we access. As traders, we are the part of nature that confronts human social chaos and destruction. Do Veddians have such beliefs?"

She thought a moment. "We strive to maximize what we are, what we know, within the bonds of social harmony. I can't say we look beyond that. For us, its not about belief, its about truth."

His reply was simple. "Maybe we hold different ends of the same beast."

Neither said anything for a few moments.

Maranth stretched. "You know 'Man With No Face' is kind of cumbersome. Is there any other, simpler name I can call you? Maybe your name from before?"

He laughed. "For those who knew me before, I was Yor. So, when we are alone, you can call me Yor... I'd like that."

Maranth blurted out. "I already miss you. I'm just not sure if its because you're always in my head or because of us depending on each other so much."

He leaned forward and his eyes locked with hers. "We Patusians call it 'bro-sou-fire,' brothers forged by fire. This tie is usually between soldiers who survived heavy combat together. It is a lifetime bond stronger than any other, save that between parent and child. This tie between us was forged on Afthar and Dullarea."

He settled back and sighed. "Aye. It will be hard for us to separate. And even when we do, the bond will always be there. You know that. Even a hundred years from now I will come if you need me."

She understood. "And I'd find the way to you if you needed me. Could your telepathy reach through space to let me know?"

He shook his head. "But you might be able to find me, with practice. Your abilities... surprise me."

In the weeks that followed, they shared what each knew about the Afthari. She told him a lot about her life on Veddi. Yor told her that he left his family ship for the *Farbagan*, to earn enough to create his own family ship. But he would not tell her about his childhood or life before. He said it was strictly forbidden for the Patushah to discuss family matters with outsiders.

They also shared what each had learned about the drogans. But since most of what Yor knew involved his telepathy, Maranth promised she would not reveal anything that would expose his ability.

Finally, the Acacia Glyn drew near the blue and white world of Veddi. The ship became part of a growing stream of spacecraft, satellites, orbiting stations, etc.

Both of them were again seated at the consoles on the bridge, taking it all in.

Maranth took off the diam ring the miners had given her. *Too flashy here.*

She stowed it in a secure inner pocket of her vest. "I suppose it's time I transferred back your title to your own ship."

He grinned. "No, I don't think so. Not now, anyway."

She didn't understand, but she knew him well enough that he had a good reason not to.

Soon they crossed from the day side to the dark night side. The ship passed over a megalopolis of lights that seemed to stretch on and on endlessly in all directions.

They watched the endless lights pass below through the viewports in silence.

Finally the trader spoke. "I never understood what millions of people meant, not until now."

Maranth replied. "Billions, billions of people."

A mechanical message appeared on the viewer. "Unknown outerworld vessel. You are in Veddian space. Leave immediately."

He got on the comm. "This vessel, the *Acacia Glyn*, though of outerworld construction, is owned and occupied by Veddian citizen Maranth-sa-Veddi-Dimore, from…?"

She blurted out "Selebeza."

"…Selebeza. She wishes to land her craft and return to her people. Transmitting ship papers and ship owner information… now."

After he transmitted the data he cut the comm. Maranth now understood why he didn't want title to the ship. They both laughed.

After several minutes they received another viewer message with docking coordinates to a nearby orbiting space station, with the added instruction to cut power.

The ship was pulled by tractor beam inside a huge hanger. There were a number of small craft tethered on its walls. The *Acacia Glyn* automatically moored amongst them.

Maranth, the Patusian and Doc waited at the main hatch.

The trader whispered in her ear. "When we enter the station, know that its walls probably have eyes and ears."

There was a knock and then he released the hatch door. Four officials in white isolation suits poured in from a sealed tube, followed by several workbots. Each official's function was printed on the suit: 'HEALTH,' 'PEST CONTROL,' 'DRY DOCK,' and 'CUSTOMS.'

The trader nodded to them. Maranth bowed and the officials returned the gesture as best they could in their clumsy suits.

The person in the CUSTOMS suit spoke with a man's voice. "Welcome, travelers."

He consulted a workbot's screen. "Please, which one of you is the ship's master?"

The Patusian pointed to himself. "I am."

The official looked him up and down. "Unfortunately I have no record of entry permits for this vessel. If that is so, you've violated various airspace and landing regulations. Do you have a Ship Master's License?"

The Man With No Face pulled out a couple of diams and flashed them quietly in front of the officials. "Perhaps this will cover your time and trouble?"

The officials were aghast. The one wearing PEST CONTROL sputtered. "A bribe!"

At this point Maranth tried to salvage the situation. "Please, I am Maranth-sa-Veddi-Dimore. I was enslaved in the outerworlds. This outerworlder rescued me and brought me here, at great risk and expense to himself, from a region where licenses and permits don't exist. So he believed you were asking for a... a landing fee."

The CUSTOMS official carefully looked her over and hrumphed. "Enslaved? Really."

He sighed. "As a matter of law all your claims will be investigated. Meanwhile, you and the ship and any cargo will be inspected, sterilized and impounded."

The CUSTOMS and DRY DOCK officials brushed between them into the ship. PEST CONTROL followed.

Maranth grabbed the arm of PEST CONTROL and pointed

to Doc. "My medibot contains extremely valuable biological samples. They must get to the Ministry of Exobiology."

Doc bobbed an antenna. "Aye. The samples are precious. From the planet Afthar."

The trader broke in. "My small pet is in a cage on the bridge. It is harmless and precious to me. Please do not harm or kill it."

The official nodded. "Very well. I'll see the biological samples are quarantined and transmitted. As for the pet, it will be harmlessly disinfected but not allowed to leave this vessel. Understood?"

Both Maranth and the trader replied in unison. "Aye."

Now it was the HEALTH official's turn. "Please, you people come with me."

The two found themselves in separate decontamination tunnels, completely naked. As instructed, each felt their way through via a handrail with eyes closed, to protect their eyes from the decontamination light that bathed them from all directions.

Soon they were in different cubicles, each a medical station staffed by a single medibot. The medibots thoroughly examined and inoculated each of them, then returned their clothes.

A short time later Maranth and the trader were reunited in front of a wide arch. A large sign over it read:

WELCOME TO VEDDI
VARIOUS EARTH DIVISIONS & DIRECTORATES, INC.
BELAIRE SPACE STATION

Workbots then led them to separate transparent cubicles, each manned by a Veddian official.

Maranth's official was a brown haired man in a soft grey robe with green piping, the uniform of Customs officials. His experience broach contained two gems. That meant he already had two 30-year careers before this one, suggesting he was between 80 and 110 years old.

Since everyone looked the same age until they were very

old, the broaches were a quick marker for age and experience, both highly valued on Veddi. Of course Maranth was too young to even have a broach.

Maranth's official bowed. "Welcome traveler. I am Customs Agent 3013. You are?"

Maranth bowed back. "Maranth-sa-Veddi-Dimore."

He waved to a single free chair as he consulted a screen that was part of his workbot desk station.

"Please sit… Let's see. No visa, no papers. Really, slavery?" He eyed her with amusement.

Maranth was tired and out of patience. She responded icily. "I am a Veddian meddoc, assigned to the mining colony Addehut by the Medical Ministry. Surely someone on Veddi should have noticed by now that the mining colony at Addehut was attacked and its inhabitants missing or dead.

"As I was officially one of those inhabitants, then someone in the Ministry should have noticed I was missing, particularly since I was due back a year ago."

The amusement drained from the agent's face and he reached for his comm.

The trader's delight flooded her head. *I hope you enjoyed your speech as much as I did.*

She laughed so hard she nearly slipped off her chair.

When she settled down she turned around so she could see him. *How's is it going with you?*

He met her gaze and grinned. *Not saying anything. This guy thinks I can't understand him and I'm retarded. Never thought my deformities would work so well for me.*

She tried to smother a smile.

His eyes grew serious. *Pretty soon higher ups are going to debrief you for real. When you need to, play ill or upset. That should buy you some rest and food. Don't let them bully you. You're the victim here.*

THIRTY

VEDDI

THE PATUSIAN WAS correct. Several military and ministry officials soon arrived, mostly to debrief Maranth. One of them was some sort of psychologist or social worker who hovered, offering pills, which Maranth refused. But Maranth was grateful the woman limited the debriefing sessions and made sure Maranth had rest breaks and food.

When they asked Maranth about the trader, she explained what they had gone through, and what he had done to return her to Veddi. But she never revealed any information about his telepathy, deformities or medical treatments. She explained that any questions that might veer in that direction were covered by medical confidentiality.

She never mentioned her own budding abilities. She had removed all such references from Doc's database when she encrypted the medical records of the outerworlders. She felt a bit guilty about doing it. But the meddoc in her knew her extrasensory experiences would be perceived as delusional thinking from psychic trauma.

The two were held on the station for more than three standard days. Most of that time they were separated. A couple of military intelligence types also interviewed the trader for a few hours.

Yor quickly realized they really didn't believe anything he

said, partly because he was an outerworlder, and partly because they saw him as mentally deficient because he was maimed and deaf. He found it astounding that their preconceptions overrode the reality staring them in the face. Their mental blinders, more than anything, explained why Veddi had failed Maranth.

Because he was left alone much of the time, he could monitor most of Maranth's debriefing and offer suggestions and encouragement directly into her mind, to smooth the process along.

Eventually they were shuttled off the station to the top of a tall tower in the city below. The large space was mostly plastiglass that revealed the city in every direction. The trader squatted by one of its expansive walls. He watched small personal vessels take off and land from vertical stacks of berths attached on the sides of the tall structures, much like the one they were in now. Maranth joined him and sat on the floor.

He shook his head. "So many people. So many."

She smiled. "After we visit my family and friends, I'll show you many wonderful things. And with the facilities here I can restore your face, something I couldn't do on Afthar."

He took her hand. "I can't stay long. There are accounts to settle with the Afthari and the drogans."

Besides, your people intend to deport me. I think the only reason they haven't already done so is that the Acacia Glyn is yours.

They both grinned.

Maranth squeezed his hand. *I won't let them. I owe you that.*

He gently squeezed her hand back. *Maybe you do.*

Her face reddened and she pulled back her hand.

He suddenly fixed his face cloth in place and stood. Maranth rose in sync with him.

The door slid open. A uniformed military intelligence officer wearing a broach with five gems, and a large-boned woman wearing a broach with six gems, entered from the lift.

The military officer bowed. "Greetings and good morning.

I'm Hreem-sa-Veddi-Rauch, Second Counsel, Ministry of Defense. My colleague is Orandar-sa-Veddi-Blukan, Head of Research, Ministry of Exobiology."

With her introduction, the tall woman stiffly bowed. Maranth smiled and bowed back at both of them.

The trader nodded. "Greetings and good morning."

Orandar turned to him. "First, let me thank you on behalf of Veddi for returning our meddoc, Maranth, and her valuable biological samples."

The Man With No Face squatted down and opened his shirt to reveal his gold tattoo. Unsettled by his foreign manner, the officials exchanged nervous glances.

The trader waved his hand in a hospitable gesture. "Your appreciation is welcome. But I did it for her. So we have no accounts open here. What do you want of me?"

Orandar cocked her head. "Direct. Well, we would like you to take myself and four others, plus some sciencebots and equipment back to Afthar, to study these drogans. Then bring us back to Veddi. They are an extraordinary find. This discovery upends so much of paleohistory, biology. The scientific repercussions are… are enormous."

The trader turned his eyes on Hreem. "What about the Afthari?"

"A Veddian cruiser will soon be on its way. I assure you they'll never raid or enslave anyone again."

Maranth remembered what the trader said before. "What will you do to them?"

"They'll be evaluated. The slavers will be scattered to agra and mining colonies throughout the outerworlds and taught to work for a living. Their victims will be returned to anywhere they wish."

The Patusian directed his reply to Maranth. "The Afthari will be little more than slaves."

Hreem crossed his arms over his chest. "Nonsense. They will learn to be productive, perhaps even socially responsible."

The trader knew it was time to deal. "What you ask of me is very dangerous."

Orandar awkwardly bent down to face him. "I'm authorized by the Veddian Government to compensate you very well. For one, we'll see that you have the necessary licenses and permits to sell your diams here. I understand this doubles what you'd get for them anywhere else. Further, we'll refit your ship, at our expense, to like-new condition.

"The ship belongs to Maranth, one of your own citizens. I am only its Captain. She wishes all the licenses, permits and whatever that her ship, and myself, need to return and trade in Veddi at will."

Hreem's eyes hardened. "Impossible. Her ship may come and go, but not with an outerworlder at her helm. CAPTAIN."

Orandar pulled Hreem aside and they conferred among themselves.

She spoke next. "If an exception could be arranged for, say, one 20 standard day trade visit, per standard year, would you agree then?"

He thought a moment. "Aye. If that includes all the licenses, permits, and so on, without taxes or any other charges, that allow me and another crew member of my designation to operate and berth the *Acacia Glyn* here. This includes transporting cargo to and from Veddi, buying and selling cargo on Veddi, and transferring funds to and from the Trader's Exchange Bank in Ursa Prime. A few more conditions. You throw in 1200 blood cloning devices for me to give to the drogans."

She smiled, "No problem. We will also refurbish your ship at our expense, not only to repair the damage, but also upgrade your systems to innerworld standards. And most important, refit your cargo bays to full life support.

"We wish to use these bays for laboratory and research work, and to transport small prey animals. In quarantine of course. We intend to solve the drogan food issue naturally, if possible."

He searched her eyes. "Humans probably brought the

disease to Afthar that caused the problem. How can you be sure that you and your animals won't make things worse?"

"Good question. We intend to do a lot of research before any animals are released. And we can quickly correct for anything unexpected via engineered airborne microbes. We really are very advanced with this sort of thing."

He looked at the floor. "How long do you want me and the *Acacia Glyn* at Afthar?"

"Forty five days. We will pay you for any extension." She straightened up. "It's settled then."

He shook his head. "Not quite. We use my existing ship security system. And I oversee and must agree to all refitting. You provide the fuel to Afthar and pay me in advance for sufficient fuel to return here. Regarding the existing cargo, your government will transfer the credits I earn from selling it here, as well as my service to you, to the Trader's Exchange Bank in Ursa Prime. You will do this at my direction, at no cost to me, with proper recording, documentation and receipts provided to me. All this with the full faith backing and credit of the Veddian government.

"Further, I accompany Maranth to her home and see she is comfortably settled in before I return to oversee her ship refit and my affairs here. Before I leave for Selebeza, I will return to the Belaire Space Station so I can inspect the *Acacia Glyn*. Then I intend to secure it until I return.

"However, I will work remotely with your engineers to plan the refit while I'm away. So no refit time will be lost. By the way, this ship has active defense systems for anyone who tries to break in."

Hreem smiled. "You think we will steal your cargo."

Orandar eyed her compatriot in annoyance. "We agree."

The Patusian slid out his arms in the Patusian affirmation. "Done." Then he stood up.

Orandar turned to Maranth. "Your father has arrived and your mother will meet you at his home in Selebeza. When you get there, a professional has been assigned to evaluate your health and aid your recovery. We very much regret what you endured and want to restore you to well-being."

Maranth's nostrils flared. "You regret? I may not yet wear a broach with experience gems. But given what happened to me I believe I have earned the right to say this. Those responsible for sending me to Addehut were completely ignorant of conditions out there, or they just didn't care what would happen."

Hreem cleared his throat. "If it's any consolation, we are very concerned. I really cannot say more."

Both officials bowed and left the way they came.

The trader shook his head. *Maranth, it is Hreem's job to monitor that sector. And he doesn't have a clue.*

His eyes crinkled in amusement. *This scientist Orandar views me as ignorant and dull-witted. Should be an interesting trip.*

Maranth bit her lip. *Thanks for seeing me back to Selebeza.*

He lifted her chin so their eyes met. *Do you know why you are afraid?*

She nodded. *Everything might be different. I'm different.*

He nodded. "Maybe you should wear that ring. It's your experience gem."

She put it on with a grin. Then they headed for the lift.

While they were riding down, Maranth grew pensive. "Yor, you never asked that your face be part of this deal."

No point. I have to go back to the Kin. Either they'll finish my face, or kill me.

He realized he'd frightened her. He took her hands and tried to communicate reassurance. *Odds are in my favor.*

She was pale and her fingers dug into his palms. "Why take the risk? Let me fix your face here."

His eyes were sad. *I owe them. And I still owe the Afthari.*

THIRTY-ONE

VEDDI

THE ELEVATOR DOOR slid open, revealing a tallish man with an oriental cast. His eyes misted when he saw Maranth. They both bowed, then embraced so that Maranth's face was buried in his soft white robe. His broach had three gems.

High above the ground, the open area of this floor spanned the whole side of the building. The air was warm with a light breeze. Benches and planters with lush vegetation divided the space into more human proportions, while the long balcony where the vehicles attached was completely open. Holo signs designated the berths of different types of craft.

Several shuttles clamped onto the side, taking in and disgorging passengers. They came from and joined lines of vehicles flowing in different directions at various altitudes around the soaring, graceful structures.

The vessels zipping around the buildings reminded Yor of flying insects in the tall grass of Aughnah Four.

Maranth's father finally looked up and locked eyes with the trader. Chen was shocked by the man's blue eyes, foreign dress and face cloth.

His demeanor was not friendly when he politely bowed. "I am Chen-sa-Veddi-Dimore. I understand you brought Maranth home. We thank you."

The trader simply nodded. Then he caught Maranth's eye. "I must check and lock down the *Acacia Glyn*. I'll rejoin you tonight."

He got back in the lift and left her alone with her father. The two then headed for the 'Outlying Locales' shuttle location halfway down the line.

While they waited, Chen took her hand. "The authorities told us you died in a mining accident. A year ago we held a memorial service and mourned your loss."

Maranth fought down rising fury. She finally responded, but her voice dripped sarcasm. "The authorities should have noticed my body was missing, along with the bodies of most everyone else in Addehut. And they certainly should have noticed the blaster marks all over the walls. I must conclude the authorities either lied, or they never really bothered to investigate."

Her father was shocked by her outburst and didn't understand what she was talking about. "Maranth, we were told only that you endured great difficulties. I want you to tell me everything, but your social worker asked us to refrain from questions until we get home."

They silently watched an air taxi that was flowing along in a level line of air shuttles break off and head toward their building. It clamped behind the other taxis lined up along the side.

Soon another shuttle berthed where they waited. It was three times larger than the city taxis, half full with a dozen Veddians occupying other seats. When they entered, the Veddians stared at Maranth's outerworld dress.

Soon they were soaring over hilly green fields and trees punctuated by low-rise structures. The weather was perfect. A little further along, the buildings got denser as they reached the coastline. Now the shuttle dropped altitude and began to disgorge passengers onto several medium-rise buildings. Maranth and her father were the last passengers on board. The shuttle finally reached an elegant white structure next to the beach and clamped onto a balcony at a high floor overlooking the water.

Maranth jumped out and swept ahead of her father into the lovely but minimally furnished apartment. She was about to run over and hug her mother, but stopped when she saw the uniformed man next to her.

"I am Captain Beal-sa-Veddi-Moar, of the Military Medical Service. You are Maranth-sa-Veddi-Dimore?"

Maranth nodded and bowed.

He bowed in return. "I am your social worker for your transition."

She then bowed to her mother and embraced her. There clearly was a resemblance in stature and coloring. She had her mother's large light brown eyes but her other features were a blend of both parents. Masima hugged her daughter back with teary eyes but said nothing.

Chen also bowed to her mother. "Welcome Masima."

Chen turned to the military man. "Why are you here, Captain? Maranth is a civilian."

The man bowed to Chen. "Greetings, Chen-sa-Veddi-Dimore. As you point out, the Medical Ministry would normally handle her deeper evaluation and treatment. I was sent here to help Maranth because she suffers from what is essentially battle fatigue, the result of all she has endured."

Her parents exchanged shocked looks.

The Captain then focused on Maranth who returned his stare silently. She noted his three experience gems.

He smiled and spread his hands in an open, friendly gesture. "Maranth, won't you tell your parents what happened, how you got back here?"

She had done enough explaining. "Why not just give them the report holos from my interviews on Belaire Station?"

He nodded. "Of course. You must be fatigued. Why not refresh yourself and change into Veddian clothes while I talk with your parents."

Maranth headed for her room before he finished what he way saying.

Masima was surprised at her manner. "She seems... abrupt."

The Captain pursed his lips. "Maranth has survived unthinkable, unspeakable experiences that will shock you. This has left deep scars on her psyche. She is in what the military recognizes as a hyper-vigilant state. She instinctively evaluates every discussion, every circumstance as it were a risky situation."

He eyed each of them in turn. "There's more. The only person Maranth trusts is the deformed outerworlder who brought her back to Veddi. I reviewed the holo of their behavior at the space station and realized they reflexively act in concert. No doubt this is how they managed to escape and get here. But it also means it will be very difficult for Maranth to separate from this man.

"However, the outerworlder intends to remain in Selebeza only for a short time, then he has business elsewhere."

Masima was about to ask a question but the Captain waived her off. "Maranth is on inferior outerworld contraceptives. Thus, she experiences sexual feelings. The proper contraceptives cannot be introduced until the current time-released dosage fades from her system, in about three months.

"Please do not try to stop her contact with the outerworlder. No doubt you must be uncomfortable with this relationship. But Maranth will not submit to your guidance in this. In fact, she will have difficulty trusting or submitting to any authority."

Chen's voice was now clipped, with an edge of bitterness. "Given how the Medical Ministry and the military failed her, her attitude seems logical."

The Captain did not respond and looked away.

Masima's jaw tightened. But her voice displayed no emotion. "With time and patience, can Maranth return to a normal Veddian life?"

The Captain was grateful for the question. "In our experience, it is possible, given years of therapy and calm environment. No doubt she will work again as a meddoc. More likely, she will have permanent psychological scars from this. The military has the facilities and staff to best help her now."

Chen's eyebrow rose. "Are you suggesting we give her over to you?"

The Captain shook his head and pressed a summoning button on his wrist comm. "Only for treatment. And no decisions need to be made right away. Spend some time with her and then we will talk again."

His small, military shuttle arrived and clamped onto the balcony. The Captain bowed and headed toward his ride.

Masima placed her hand on his arm. "Will Maranth be able to bond with a male companion in time? Have her own children?"

He stopped and nodded. "Aye. But a compatible mate will be a different sort of man, someone who has also faced such hardships, maybe a man from the military."

He addressed both of them. "Look, at least she is alive and will recover. In time she may know peace and well-being. But she has changed. The path of her life will likely be different."

He again bowed and left.

Masima turned to Chen. "What a strange circumstance brings us together again. Our marriage officially ended last year."

Maranth's father nodded and smiled. "You look well. Thank you for coming. Will you stay long?"

She shook her head. "No. Both of us have other commitments. Yet we must adjust our lives to Maranth being alive… and her problems. Perhaps we can alternate on her care until this sorts out? If you would take the first week, as you still live here, I will return to see to her next week."

He dipped his head. "Agreed." But he knew she probably would not return so soon. Masima had never bonded well with her daughter, or him, for that matter.

"Before you arrived, the Captain gave me a pill to ensure Maranth sleeps deeply tonight."

Masima waited until Maranth was asleep before she left. Chen then began to review the holo of her space station interviews. He could not, as a matter of any personal experience, understand or believe the events she relayed. He also knew she could not possibly have made any of this up. That the military showed up at his door was official confirmation it was all real.

Though he had served in its ranks in his former career, his military work had involved technology. He knew nothing of the outerworlds. The universe of his existence had suddenly shifted to include an ugly, very ugly reality.

As he watched his daughter and the outerworlder interact on the holo, he saw what the social worker had noted. The two acted as a unit. Most likely they were also lovers. The thought revolted him.

It was after 2100 when another shuttle delivered the Man With No Face to Maranth's family apartment.

Her father met the stranger outside on the balcony. He bowed and announced that Maranth was asleep.

The trader read the man's repugnance and reached his mind out to find her. But her father had been honest. She was in a deep sleep.

Chen again spoke in a clipped tone. "You cannot stay here. I'm sorry."

"Didn't expect to." The Patusian then summoned a taxi with his new, Veddian wrist comm. "May I speak with you before I go?"

Surprised, Chen nodded and waved him over to several chairs around a table at the far end of the balcony.

When they were seated, the Patusian's unusual blue eyes bore through her father's gaze. "I've never put hands on Maranth. I tried to stop some of it. But I was too... too impaired then."

He looked down. "I'm sorry about that. She's wanted only to come home, live the life that made her happy and safe. I owed her that."

His eyes now returned to the older man. "But you must

understand she and I will always be connected, as brothers forged by fire."

Chen didn't understand what he meant. But he realized the strange being in front of him was not a sub-human as he'd imagined. He deserved respect.

The trader closed his eyes a moment to choose his next words. "From Maranth I've learned something of Veddian customs and lifestyle. Now I'm here, I find it very pleasant that everyone's thinking seems more ordered. Nearly everybody I've encountered is content or happy. This is an extraordinary accomplishment in a place with billions of people. I would like to learn more. Are there any meditation training holos suitable for adults? I would ask Maranth for this, but I do not want to burden her."

Her father was amazed and smiled. "I believe the Rehabilitation Agency has something suitable. I will be pleased to help you with this."

The trader nodded. "Maranth knows how to reach me. There's one more thing. I understand most Veddians take a contraceptive that cools sexual desire. Is there a short acting version I could try? I think it would provide… relief. And experiencing life the Veddian way would help me understand your people."

"That also can be arranged." Her father was again surprised and now curious about this man. Clearly he read lips very well. Chen knew the man was deformed and deaf under that face cloth and brash clothes. Maranth would certainly want to repair his disabilities. Yet he did not intend to stay.

A taxi arrived at the balcony. The trader stood and grasped her father's shoulder. "Maranth was also remade on Afthar."

He thought a moment before continuing. "More than you can imagine."

THIRTY-TWO

SELEBEZA, VEDDI

MARANTH MET WITH Yor the following morning, wearing the slightly flowing iridescent robe worn by all Veddian women. They spoke briefly under the watchful eyes of her father and said little. She cried when he left, but not just for the loss of her companion. She also felt really alone. She had lost her anchor.

In the days that followed, Maranth tried to pick up the threads of her former life. Word of her return had already spread to friends and colleagues at the nearby medical college. A short time after the trader left, her best friend and neighbor, Vaneza, entered from the lift with Veddian treats in a small plain box. She was taller than Maranth, with light skin and hair.

Vaneza bowed, Maranth bowed back and laughed as she embraced her old friend. She knew her father was again watching the holos of her interviews. So she quickly took Vaneza to her room.

Maranth's outerworld clothes hung outside her closet, and they were the most colorful items in her space. As soon as Vaneza saw them, she dropped the treats on Maranth's deskbot and fingered the exotic fabrics in awe. "You actually wore this. It's so… garish, and revealing."

The reality of the foreign dress hit Vaneza. Her friend had really come out of an actual other place. In their universe of

Veddi, the outerworlds never seemed real. They were something on a school exam, of little importance. Nothing about them was newsworthy or fashionable. Maranth was the first person she knew who had ever been there.

"Maranth, please tell me everything."

Maranth dreaded this moment. How could she possibly explain? If she told the truth, her friend would not be capable of believing her. Before Addehut, Maranth would not have believed it herself.

"Vaneza, terrible things happened. There were also some good things, though I doubt you would see them as such. It's better for both of us that I don't tell you. Really."

Vaneza did not know what to say. She had never seen her friend like this. It was as if she were looking at the ghost of the person she knew.

But they both tried to renew their bonds. Over the next several days, after work hours, the two went to the beach. Maranth always loved that, and Vaneza made sure others in their circle joined them there. She missed her friend and wanted her back.

Maranth loved the open, tropical weather after the mines, the force field and the space ships she'd lived in for so long. She tried to join in the fun, but there was a wall she just could not scale. Everyone was very nice and polite, but they also knew the wall was there as well.

A few days later, the Medical Ministry recalled her to light duty at the hospital. At least she got Doc back on her first day of work.

She was assigned to a senior meddoc on rounds in the hospital's physiotherapy wing, seeing routine patients. She soon found herself among a group of new meddocs monitoring routine medical issues with the guidance of their medibots. Maranth pulled back a strand of hair and yawned. It was clear by the second day she would have no real responsibility. Her duties were make-work.

At the midday meal she joined a couple of other meddocs in the cafeteria who were two years behind her in school.

Loren was a lanky man majoring in nanosurgery. Compact, dark haired Karia was much like Maranth — a generalist. Everyone at the hospital knew Maranth had come back from the dead, from her outerworld residency. Though nobody seemed to know the details, Maranth could sense she was the center of gossip.

Loren spoke as soon as she sat down. "No one seems to know what happened to you. At least you have light duty in the hospital. From what I heard they regard you more as a patient than meddoc."

Maranth smiled. "You certainly are right."

Karia joined in. "Aye. Lots of meditation, not much medication. She gets to loaf."

Loren tapped Karia's arm. "She needs to recover. Don't tease her."

Then he turned back to Maranth. "Will the Ministry credit you for your outerworld medservice?"

Maranth thought for a moment. "Don't know. I didn't finish the last month on Addehut."

A small smile crept across her face. *Does slave service on Afthar and Dullarea count?*

Doc had been refurbished and his base personality restored. But all his supplies, most of which Maranth bought in Tigenne, were gone. The encrypted patient files were still encrypted. She ran several diagnostics and his learning algorithms seemed intact. Doc clearly possessed what he'd learned in the outerworlds. Presumably, someone from the Medical Ministry, or even the hospital, had accessed his non-encrypted experiences. But no one spoke to her about any of it. She didn't know if it was from embarrassment, or that she was now deemed a military problem.

At least she now had Doc to manage her diet and meditation. She found it really bothered her that he had no supplies. It felt a bit like she was walking around naked.

She did a lot of meditation under his guidance in her now ample free time. At the end of most sessions, she let her mind reach out to find her trader. She could still feel him, where he was on Veddi or on the Space Station. But she got no mental communication from him now. Perhaps he was just too far away to reach her mind. She decided not to call him. Their separation was hard enough. It would be harder with direct contact.

After watching the report holos, her father resumed work from the apartment, though he left for several hours each day as well. She could sense his anger, but it was not aimed at her. He said nothing about what she had reported. But she expected he would, eventually.

Maranth may have looked more like her mother, but she and her father had always been closer. They just seemed to see things the same way. No doubt that was why they got along so well. She and her mother just did not connect, even when Maranth was very young. Housebots and her father made up for Masima's distance.

She didn't know exactly what her father did. He formerly had standard 30-year careers in management, engineering and the military. An experience gem in his broach marked each of these careers. Now he worked in the Budget Ministry, in the Office Of Quality Assurance. Her mother, after a career in small business, was now a kinetic sculptress.

Maranth was his second child and her mother's first. Like careers, Veddian marriages were 30-year commitments. Generally, married people had two children. And most Veddians married only once. But somehow the second child did not happen in her father's first marriage. His second marriage to her mother was unusual. Maranth had never met her much older half brother. She only knew him from an old holo.

At the end of the week, that night, she went with Loren, Vaneza and some others to a new art exhibit in a large open-air gallery. They joined a number of other Veddians to watch the light and sound performance. Delicate lights and shadows flitted in harmony and chaos to a sedate music score. It was a lot like the dances she used to do in school. Maranth realized it seemed pale somehow. Though everyone else watched with interest, she found her attention drift off.

She had returned home, but nothing was the same. The truth was that she was not the same. Could she ever fit in again?

Her mother did not return the second week. Instead, Masima called Maranth and explained that given what had happened, she and her father agreed he was better equipped to guide her rehabilitation. But he still did not speak with her about what she had experienced, though he did tell her what her social worker told him. Maranth was beginning to think that he just didn't know what to say. She couldn't blame him. What could anyone say other than "I'm sorry this happened to you?"

The third night in her second week home, Maranth woke in a sweat. Her father was shaking her. She had been screaming as fire rained down onto the Afthari colony. Parts of buildings were falling into compounds and lanes, breaking the bodies of Afthari raiders and family alike. She could smell the burning, feel the ash and heat.

Her fingers dug into her fathers arm. "I know something terrible that will happen soon. And I have some responsibility for it. I must leave. Immediately."

He soothed her forehead. "You've just had a bad dream."

Maranth gently pushed his hand away and got out of bed. "You can't possibly understand, but I know what I know. I'm sorry. I must go."

She went over to Doc. "We need all the supplies that were taken from you. Do you know where they are?"

Doc nodded an appendage. "Meddoc Maintenance And Decontamination on the space station took everything."

Maranth threw on her Veddian robe right over her long nightshirt. "Then before we leave they will have to return what they took. Otherwise, I will get what we need from a hospital."

She turned to her father. "Those medical supplies that Doc brought back did not come from Veddi. My Veddian supplies were used up. Some of these supplies were given to me in Afthar. Most I got in Tigenne. It seems some part of the government owes me personally for what they took. Do you know who I should contact about this?"

Her father took her hands to calm her. "Those supplies were probably destroyed as subpar or contaminated."

"Then the Medical Ministry can collect the value of what I take from my back pay."

Her father was frightened. Was Maranth in some sort of psychotic break? "What do you need these supplies for?"

"People are soon going to be injured and die on Afthar. There are children, slaves and others there who have committed no crime. On my oath as a meddoc, I must go where I'm needed."

Chen decided, since she had set the military into action to clean out the slavers, she felt some guilt they would injure or kill others there. She incorporated all this into her dream and believed it real. Maybe she needed to go to Afthar with the military to put her demons to rest.

Then he realized she would go to the maimed outerworlder. She was an adult and he could not stop her.

He decided to get her supplies through his contacts, so there would be no problems later. But Maranth would not travel alone with this man, and she would return to Veddi.

THIRTY-THREE

BELAIRE SPACE STATION

THE EXOBIOLOGIST ORANDAR, who negotiated the drogan expedition, watched the Veddian portbot load her cargo into the now repaired and refurbished *Acacia Glyn*. She was a plain-faced woman who, like Maranth and most Veddian women, wore her hair tied back in a net. Her eyes carefully tracked the one of more than a dozen small ships loading or unloading on the vast hanger floor. The Man With No Face was barely visible inside the open cargo bay. He logged and inspected each item as it was brought to him. When the cargo was approved, the portbot's strong limbs placed it into its final position somewhere behind him.

Maranth, trailed by Doc, smiled as she approached the exobiologist. "Greetings, Orandar-sa-Veddi-Blukan."

When the woman turned to her, Maranth bowed and Doc dipped an appendage.

Orandar returned the bow. "Greetings. Are you seeing us off?"

"No. I'm going with you."

Orandar was a bit amused. "Not possible. You're no exobiologist."

The trader strode to the edge of the cargo hatch and his eyes took Maranth in. *I'm really glad you're here.*

She simply thought her response. *I've set a lot in motion. I just couldn't walk away.*

Understood. He put his hands on his hips.

"Welcome, Maranth-sa-Veddi-Dimore."

Orandar broke in. "She cannot come. She's not been chosen for this mission."

His eyes twinkled. "I work for her. It's her ship. You have clear authority over the members of your expedition. But she does not board in that capacity. She is a part of the crew."

Orandar frowned. "She is much too young to make such decisions. And she's been through a terrible ordeal that requires rehabilitation."

He shook his head. "Events are in motion where a meddoc will be needed. She knows that."

The portbot dropped a large, plastiwrapped bundle the onto the cargo deck. The trader speculatively cut the wrap open with a long slice. Heavy netting pushed through the opening. He grabbed onto one of the portbot's limbs and it set him down on the station floor.

He angrily strode over to Orandar. "Your ambition and narrowness leave you blind. You've never bothered to ask what I know about the drogans because you only see me as some inferior, someone without PROPER credentials to add anything to YOUR scientific breakthrough. Yet I am the only human who has interacted with them and survived."

She gathered herself. "You do not have the right…"

He broke in, pointing to the net in the hold. "You expect to net and tranquilize big birds. Maybe take their blood, confine some to pens for your experiments?"

By now his face was inches from her nose. "If you try any of that you will die, and so will every other human on the planet."

Her eyes widened.

He calmed down and backed off a step. "The Kin control Afthar. They safely kill and eat heavily armed slavers at will. They are not patient and they don't think much of humans, other than as food. They have their own culture and are as smart as you are."

Orandar was dumbfounded and just stood there with her mouth open.

The trader saw Maranth trying to stifle a grin. He also caught sight of the same official that had been dogging him at a distance since he returned from Selebeza.

The man had watched this exchange carefully and now he was speaking into his wrist comm.

The trader again focused on Orandar. "If you really want to make contact, then bring something that would interest them, like holos that prove Veddi is our common birthplace. They have a long memory, but 65 million years is just too long, even for them."

He took Maranth's luggage from Doc. "Maranth comes. Deal with it."

The anonymous official now strolled over to join them.

The trader expected he would, sooner or later. He'd picked up bits and pieces of thoughts and questions flitting through the man's mind. His questions were always about the outerworlder. This was the first Veddian besides Maranth that showed any interest in him. Of course the man was dogging the trader for a reason. Now maybe they would find out why.

When the man reached the trio, he nodded and bowed. "I am Hari-sa-Veddi-Haifan." He was slightly taller than the Patusian, with medium features and hair. He wore no experience broach. He was the sort of man you wouldn't notice unless he wanted you to. But Yor's practiced eye noted the man was fit and muscular under his soft grey customs robe.

Hari addressed Orandar. "Greetings, Orandar. I'm afraid your Ministry has made some last minute modifications to your expedition roster. Please check your mail."

She consulted her wrist comm and looked up in surprise.

"Aye. I will be joining your expedition to Afthar, as an observer. It seems your budget has been cut back a bit. Probably some issue of priorities. In any case, the other exobiologists have been cut from your roster. In their place, besides me, you've been assigned another 'bot that is specialized in linguistics. And you've also been issued a medibot."

It took Orandar only a moment to recover. "May I ask your qualifications?"

Hari smiled. "I am not a scientist."

He nodded to Maranth but next addressed the Patusian.

"Man With No Face, do you have any problem with this last minute change of personnel?"

"None. You are welcome." The trader then glanced at Maranth.

He is here for some other reason. Please see what you can learn about him, when you have time.

She nodded.

Their silent exchange was not missed by the newest member of their expedition.

The weeks spent in transit to Afthar were strained. Orandar and Maranth shared the crew cabin. Orandar was distant. She mostly ignored Maranth. When she wasn't meditating, she spent time checking supplies and equipment. This included working with her research 'bots. She rarely spoke to anyone.

She gave the extra medibot to Maranth, who promptly turned it over to Doc. He quickly brought it up to speed regarding the outerworlds. Maranth was relieved it came fully equipped and brimming with medical supplies. It was unnamed, so she decided to call it Eng, as it had a speech quirk of ending sentences with something that sounded like 'eng.' Maranth put a large silver chevron on Eng's blue front so she could distinguish the two.

As for Hari, he was more a shadow than a person. He slept in the main cabin but stowed his gear with the women. Though the ship was small, he never seemed to be around. And he politely ignored Maranth when she encountered him.

Maranth's extended time in meditation enabled her to decompress and regenerate. She often meditated with Yor. He was not very practiced, but he clearly desired to learn. She spent a lot of her downtime with the trader as he and the grey shipbot, Jona, checked and maintained the ship systems.

Even before they boarded, Yor had telepathically reminded her the ship might have eyes and ears, given its refitting by the Veddi. So she used her mind to describe her dream in Selebeza. They both knew he'd foreseen this.

Yor no longer wore his face cloth. The others would just have to get used to his deformed face.

When they were alone, she openly told him about what had transpired when she was away. Her father couldn't seem to talk to her now, even though they always talked before.

The trader took her hand. "Chen is angry, and for some reason blames himself for what happened to you."

She openly relayed that she had been reported killed in an accident. Someone had lied about Addehut. She didn't trust anyone from the Ministries. So she felt even more lost.

They both were used to being careful. So it was second nature to telepathically communicate anything sensitive.

The only time the four people came together was during meals in the main cabin.

At their first meal, the serverbot laid out healthy Veddian fare, perfectly proportioned to each person's size. Maranth found this so Veddian she almost smiled.

She turned to Hari. "Is the food to your liking?"

He smiled and nodded.

Maranth continued. "You don't wear an experience broach. Are you as young as I am?"

He only smiled again and she knew the answer was no.

Yor picked up the conversation. "I'm a bit confused. Everyone I met in some official capacity on Veddi always identified their office, their ministry. You wear the clothes of a customs official. Are you one?"

Orandar was suddenly very interested in the conversation.

Hari shook his head. "I actually am on loan from a ministry, to another ministry, to Customs and so on. It's my job to find ways to improve efficiency in government operations."

He glanced at Maranth for a reaction. But she was as mystified by what he'd said as everyone else.

But the trader picked up an image of Chen from the man's mind. *Maranth, he works for your father.*

Maranth reflexively glanced at the trader in surprise, then turned her gaze back to Hari.

Hari saw the interaction and was now certain his hypothesis was true. Maranth knew nothing until the Patusian had read his mind and told her telepathically. No doubt the trader was reading his mind now.

Hari smiled at the other man. "At least some on Veddi have paid close attention to what you and Maranth have told us. That's why I'm here."

But they both knew what he said was only partly true.

THIRTY-FOUR

AFTHAR

THE *ACACIA GLYN* approached Afthar and began to slip across its sunlit, slightly hazy face. The planet's tan surface was cut by a maze of green gashes. The ship soon passed around to the dark side where a large Veddian war cruiser hung in a low, synchronous orbit, its dark bulk roughly outlined by light from its various view ports.

All four travelers were seated on the bridge. Through the *Acacia Glyn's* viewports, they watched the warship occasionally fire a blast into the colony. When the beam made contact, it lit up the area below to reveal damaged structures and a bit of the surrounding plateau.

The trader's mind reached out to Maranth. *You saw this in Selebeza?*

She closed her eyes. *Aye. But from inside the colony. It felt so real, like my dream about you, before Dullarea.*

Now she spoke out so Hari and Orandar could hear. "We're so smugly sure of ourselves. Yet innocents, children are dying down there."

Orandar was the one to reply. "Our military only attacks as a last resort. You know that."

"Stop them. If not for the colony, do it to protect your mission. How will the drogans react to all of this?"

Before Orandar replied, a holo of a military officer appeared in front of the Patusian's console.

Unlike the military men on Veddi who wore soft black robes, this one wore a form-fitted black uniform with white piping. He spoke in a professional, even tone. "*Acacia Glyn*, this is the war cruiser *Kleig*. You are cleared to dock in our Bay Three. Cut power. We will bring you in. Acknowledge."

The *Acacia Glyn* was pulled inside and came to rest on the floor of the bay at the end of a row of smaller vessels. A clear, tubular passage arched out from the cruiser's internal port and covered the *Acacia Glyn*'s hatch.

The four made their way through the tube into the cruiser. The trader again wore his face cloth. They were met by a uniformed crewmember who silently led them through a maze of passageways and lifts.

Finally they reached the Commander's office. The uniformed man behind the extensive console gazed at them with clear grey eyes. There were no seats in the padded grey room, only a large viewport behind the commander and light panels covering much of the walls. His experience broach held four gems. It was surrounded by several bars that no doubt held military significance. The unnamed man who led them to this office stood by silently.

Orandar bowed. "Greetings Commander. I am Orandar-sa-Veddi-Blukan."

Maranth and Hari followed with similar greetings.

The Commander just nodded at the group. "I am Commander Woosan-sa-Veddi-York. Greetings and welcome. I look forward to your briefing me about this mission."

His eyes rested a moment on the Man With No Face who nodded back. Then he turned to Maranth. "We are investigating Addehut. Your patient files from there were encrypted per your obligation regarding confidentiality. However, could you provide us public information about the miners such as their names, planet of origin, physical description, face holo and so forth? This could help us find them."

Maranth smiled broadly. "Of course, Commander." She transmitted his message to Doc with her new, upgraded wrist comm.

Orandar spoke next. "Commander, your laser fire must disturb the native drogans I'm here to study. You must end it."

"Your drogans massacred the three crack troopers I sent down with warbots to take the colony. Massacred and, apparently, ate them. The warbots were useless. By Veddi-aut, what are we facing here?"

Fear crossed Orandar's face, but she quickly recovered. "Commander, you know this mission is high priority and top secret. Therefore, you must deal with the slavers without interfering with the drogans."

Woosan's grey eyes now turned to the Man With No Face. "You must be the trader who survived these creatures."

"Aye."

"What do you think of them?"

"They terrify me. But I've also missed them."

Hari noted that Maranth was the only one not surprised by this.

The Commander thought a moment. He clasped his hands behind his head and leaned back. "Tell me, how can we get my troops safely down to the colony?"

Orandar burst in. "He works for me, Commander. He's here to establish drogan contact for my study."

The trader squatted down and opened his shirt to display his golden tattoo. He eyed Orandar. "I agreed only to bring you here and take you back. Nothing was said about drogan contact."

She was dumbfounded into silence.

He then turned his attention to Commander Woosan who now had to stand to see him. "I won't help you attack the Afthari, Commander. So blast them and this planet to oblivion. Or wait and starve them out."

Hari suddenly realized with awe the trader had anticipated everything. He had skillfully set the terms of his deal with

Orandar so she couldn't control him on Afthar. He'd foreseen the military standoff. And he had Maranth.

Commander Woosan leaned forward and his hands came to rest on the console. He carefully studied this outerworlder: his face cloth, his demeanor and most of all, the round gold tattoo on his chest.

"Patusian. What do you want?"

THIRTY-FIVE

AFTHAR

AS SOON AS the first shards of dawn reached into the battered colony below, the *Acacia Glyn* separated from the cruiser and descended down to the planet in a lazy arc.

After the *Acacia Glyn* left the cruiser, Commander Woosan and Hari met alone in an empty charcoal grey lounge scattered with pale grey sofas and padded tables. The two stood together in front of the large viewport. Hari and the Commander silently watched the day side of Afthar. The planet looked very large and hazy this close in. There were no more laser bursts from the ship.

Woosan read Hari's orders in the holo projected by his wrist comm. "So you're our new civilian liaison? Chen's group?"

Hari nodded. "I hitched a ride with the drogan expedition to meet up with you here. There is concern about the quality of our military intelligence. What is your take?"

Woosan waved Hari over to a sofa. Then he sat down near him and leaned back. "Military Intelligence has its own network in the outerworlds. The regular military, like us, go where we are told to go. Mainly we put out fires like these slavers. We also cruise around to train and to show a presence in sectors where there have been problems."

Woosan hesitated a moment, then chose his words carefully.

"For the last several decades, we seem to have less and less assignments. Our cruisers have a lot of downtime these days."

Hari already knew this from the data. "And what have you learned about Addehut?"

Woosan frowned. "We found a working mine with miners. But we had no access to anyone except the manager who denied any problems. When we told him about their former meddoc, he claimed she was lying.

"I watched the man sweat when he said that. But we had no evidence to force the issue. Maranth's list of names should break this open. I've sent her information to another cruiser that's already on its way to the mine."

Woosan now asked a question. "Investigator Hari, how do you read this outerworld trader? You've spent some time with him."

Hari smiled ruefully. "Did you know when he showed up at customs, his intake officer decided he was retarded and didn't bother to question him?"

Both men laughed heartily.

He leaned in to share more. "The outerworlder insisted on keeping his own ship's security system through our retrofit. So when he was away, I tried to break in. Just to test what he had. Nothing we have broke it."

The Commander shook his head. "I reviewed the interview holos and his ship logs. His escape from the pirates was impressive."

Hari leaned back. "As for the man, clearly he is motivated by an alien world view, with its own rules. What do you know of Patusians? Military Intelligence seems to have no information on them, and neither do any of my other sources."

Woosan expected the question. "I've only heard of them. They are interplanetary traders, operating on the far side of the innerworlds past Ursa Prime. Some wear that distinctive gold tattoo. This maimed trader is the first Patusian I've met. I've requested more information from a source on Ursa Prime. But nothing has come in yet."

Hari again leaned toward the Commander. "Do you get the same feeling I have, that he's calling the shots here?"

Woosan frowned. "Perhaps. Especially given his limitations, how did he manage to survive? And he said he missed the drogans!"

"There's a lot we don't know… yet." Hari decided not to mention telepathy or Maranth. She would not be brought deeper into it unless necessary.

On the *Acacia Glyn*, only the trader and Maranth were on board, as Orandar had temporarily moved into the military cruiser. The two sat at adjoining consoles on the bridge.

Maranth's eyes never left the viewport as they descended. "You knew I'd have to come, for the injured."

"Aye. You're not to blame for their situation. Don't forget that. And don't forget you're no slave."

His face cloth was wrapped in place. She again wore an outerworld shipboard tunic, belt, pants and boots. The drapery of her Veddian robes would snag and get in the way here.

A holo of Obbad suddenly appeared on the bridge comm in front of the trader. Obbad's ear lobes were pulled down by the longer, heavier earrings that had once belonged to Zedd. A broken wall in the colony was visible behind his head. Maranth realized that he must now be the head of the Afthari. Her former owner's square face was harried and angry. "So, Man With No Face. Tell me why I shouldn't blast your ship right now, yah?"

The trader's voice remained even. "I figure I still owe you Afthari for feeding me and I've come to balance our accounts."

Obbad was now curious. "Then what do you bring us?"

The trader eyed him evenly. "A way out."

A small, wary band of armed raiders waited as the *Acacia Glyn* descended into the now shattered spaceport littered with the wreckage of destroyed ships and cargo.

The force field re-covered the colony as soon as the ship landed. But it now had weaknesses and gaps, marked by electrical discharges, patches of normal sky, and odd sputters and buzzing noises. Clearly it had not stood up under the fire from the Veddian military cruiser.

Nearby buildings were partially collapsed and the resulting debris was littered everywhere. As Maranth witnessed in her dream, the laser blasts had gotten through.

The slavers led the Man With No Face, Maranth and her two medibots through the damage. Weary Afthari cleared rubble and shored up ground defenses. An old woman forlornly sifted through some broken possessions and found a trinket in a pile of debris that once had been a room in one of the compounds. Tears filled her eyes.

Maranth covered the face of a corpse and Doc carefully lifted a crying toddler from the ground.

Maranth did not recognize the child. "Doc, treat this little one and bring it to where we used to hold the beggar's clinic. We'll triage from there. Eng will stay with me for now."

Doc nodded an antenna her way while some of his other appendages were already scanning his patient.

The trader stopped to wait for her, but one of the men gently tapped him with a blaster. "Mier Obbad is waiting. He's now head of all the Houses." A second slaver took Maranth's arm and led her along.

Soon they were entering Obbad's compound, one of the few without direct damage. Maranth was surprised she had mixed feelings about the place. It was still beautiful, though littered with debris. Of course she remembered what she had suffered there. Then she realized that mostly Obbad left her alone. After Dullarea, she really understood just how bad slavery could be. Her fear of the Afthari was gone, no doubt because of the Veddian cruiser over their heads. Besides, fear was now in the Afthari eyes.

Raiders, Heads of the Houses and workbots milled around the garden. Maranth bumped into her fellow slave, the massive Yurblun, Jobbar.

He looked down on her with surprise. "You've come baack. Why?"

Obbad peered around the Yurblun's bluish bulk and caught sight of Maranth, who saw him at the same time. Jobbar servilely retreated to one side.

"I came because I'm needed, MIER Obbad." She noted his confident manner seemed to be gone. He looked unkempt.

Then Obbad caught sight of the Patusian and roared angrily. "They won't take us. No one can reach us from the ground."

The trader squatted down and opened his shirt to expose his chest tattoo.

As he waited for Obbad to settle down, the others moved back, leaving a space around the two.

The trader spoke first. "The Veddi haven't blasted you to oblivion because of your families. But they must end it soon, one way or another."

There was a general murmur as everyone dispiritedly mulled the trader's words. Obbad motioned for quiet and grabbed a chair and sat facing the Patusian, legs wide, hands on his thighs.

He leaned forward. "So what is your way out, Man With No Face?"

The trader's hands waved over the gathering. "The Veddians say the families and the beggars may stay, to support a innerworld military and science station. They want one here for the drogans. Your people will be comfortable, and your children will go to a Veddian school."

The trader fell silent.

Obbad dreaded what he knew would come next. He wet his lips with his tongue. "Say it."

"As for you slavers, you've caused too much pain and loss. As far as they are concerned, you deserve to die. That probably would be the consensus of nearly everyone else in this sector as well."

Obbad realized the trader had not said they actually would die. He pursed his lips. "Spit out the rest."

The Man With No Face nodded. "Maranth and I testified that you acted with some civility in your own colony. As a result, the Veddians decided that you slavers might be redeemable.

Thus, they've agreed that you will be scattered to various work camps, serve only sixty years and then be freed. That means you will still have a life when you get out.

"If you don't take this offer, those of you that survive the coming attack will spend the rest of your lives in some sinkhole camp, if you're not executed or the drogans don't eat you. And, of course, that includes your families."

The crowd quietly discussed what he said.

Mier Obbad waved them silent. "He's bluffing and lying. The Veddi can't take us because of the drogans."

There was some uncomfortable whispering.

The trader eyed him angrily. "The military can't leave you here because of the damage you've done. And they don't need to take you from the ground. Believe it. They can blast you into oblivion whenever they want to. So far, they've only sent you a taste."

Obbad was unmoved. "Then you two die with us."

Maranth strode up to him angrily. "So your wife and son die for your pride?"

Obbad sputtered. "My son will forget me and my wife will find someone else. I lose them either way."

The trader broke in. "That's the point. You lose everything and get sixty years to think about it. But you will at least have a life, after."

Obbad shook his head venomously. The other Afthari looked down. Before another word was said, Jobbar suddenly beaned Obbad with a massive bluish fist. His master fell over without a word, unconscious.

Jobbar was momentarily elated. Then he quickly looked around to see if anyone would kill him. The other men just looked away and began to drift off.

Jobbar stretched to his full height and grinned down at the trader. "'Da Afthaari agree."

No one argued the point.

THIRTY-SIX

AFTHAR

WHEN THE FORCE field came down, the Man With No Face moved the *Acacia Glyn* to the edge of the plateau. It was time for him to join the Kin once more.

He fought down the terror that engorged his chest. He tried several Veddian meditations to calm himself, and they helped. As the rising mental hum of the drogan Kin infiltrated his head, he concentrated on riding it, as if he no longer existed as a separate being.

Finally, his mind reached out to them. *You of the Kin. Come. Fawasaaa, Hosaaa, Vabaaa, Giraaa, come. Come meet me. I have the rest of the promised blood devices.*

Hosaaa, Bantaaa's mate, was the first to appear, quickly followed by the two females, Vabaaa and Fawasaaa. He could sense the three were very angry and belligerent. Hosaaa shook his head and his feathers rattled with annoyance.

The trader's mind cried out. *I have done exactly as we agreed.*

But he braced himself for what he knew would happen. Hosaaa chomped down on his arm to the bone. Pain seared through him.

The devices are locked inside my ship. If you kill me you get nothing.

The darker green Fawasaaa nipped Hosaaa. *AGAIN YOU ARE*

HASTY. AT LEAST LET THE SUFUNAAA HAVE HIS SAY BEFORE WE EAT HIM.

Hosaaa let the trader go and nipped Fawasaaa back. The trader dropped to the ground and clutched his wounded arm.

Bantaaa's nest sister Vabaaa sniffed his blood seeping into the ground.

SMELLS GOOD.

Vabaaa raised her head and Fawasaaa's mate, Giraaa, knocked her face aside. He glowered at the man on the ground. *YOU BRING A DEATH MACHINE INTO OUR SKIES. WE SEE IT ATTACK THE PLATEAU.*

The trader shook his head. *It attacks the human colony, not you and yours.*

Giraaa now stepped down on his leg. *WHY?*

The trader worked to overcome his agony and terror. His mind reached out to the drogan pinning his leg.

You Kin are of one mind. My kind can only speak to each other. We are not of the same mind. The humans that live in the colony got their comforts by preying on other humans. They came here to hide from the rest of us. This is why the humans in the sky ship attacked the colony, to stop them.

The drogans were aghast. Giraaa finally unpinned the trader and Vabaaa sought the trader's mind. *DO THE SUFUNAAA ON THE SKY SHIP KNOW OF US?*

The Patusian tried to get on his feet. On the third try he managed to do so.

They do, since you killed some of them. But they decided not to harm you. They want peace with the Kin. They know this world is yours. They gave me the blood machines that I will trade you for finishing my face.

He steadied himself against a tree. *Three other humans from far away also came here with me. Like you, they think people from the colony brought something here that might have harmed your malaaas. If you let them study this ravine, they may be able to offer replacement prey that will stay healthy and multiply. The blood devices will not last forever.*

Fawasaaa linked with her compatriots. *NO MORE ALIEN INTRUSIONS. THE MALAAAS WILL MULTIPLY WITHOUT INTERFERENCE WHILE WE RELY ON THIS SUFUNAAA'S DEVICES.*

Her yellow eyes now bore into the trader. *LET US SEE THE REST OF YOUR DEVICES. IF THEY ARE WHAT YOU SAY, THEN WE WILL FIX YOUR FACE.*

He released the cargo hatch. The Kin gathered at the back of his vessel and tried to see inside. From the ground, they could see only the containers that lined the edge of the cargo bay. Most of the laboratory equipment, supplies, and prey animals were behind their line of view.

A flyer swooped down and flew through the cargo bay over the lab setup. It then landed on a nearby tree branch and waited.

The trader spoke into his comm, "Release the cargo."

A sciencebot pushed the containers out the hatch, one by one, until they were all on the ground. The maimed man opened the nearest one, revealing one hundred Veddian blood cloners.

He waved his good arm toward the other boxes that littered the dirt. *They are all the same. See for yourselves.*

He watched the drogans rip open the other containers and spread his hard-won goods across the ground. Vabaaa dipped a small straw into a bit of his blood that had pooled. She then added that blood to the liquid in one of the cloning containers. She closed the device with her claws. Now the drogans waited patiently. Meanwhile, his damaged arm felt a little better. He knew it was already healing.

The Kin communed and the Patusian gathered strength while they waited. When it was time, Vabaaa pried the container open. The drogans could see and smell the fresh blood that now filled it, and they were pleased.

He realized the split second they turned on him, intending to eat him anyway.

How could I just drop down on you from the sky, alive, my

face gone? Remember that? Remember I am the only human that communicates the way you do.

That stopped them cold.

What happened to me was no accident. You know it.

He waited but they made no response.

There is another, more powerful than my kind. More powerful than the Kin. This other remade me for a purpose. Do you really intend to eat me now?

The Kin now ignored him and communed with their brethren.

Giraaa now spoke for them all. *WE WILL FIX YOUR FACE, SUFUNAAA.*

He stomped and raised himself up to his full height. *DURING THE NEXT THIRTY ROTATIONS OF THE NIGHT MOONS, A FEW OF YOU MAY EXPLORE THIS RAVINE ONLY. YOUR KIND MUST STAY IN THE SKY OR THE HIVE ON THE PLATEAU AND NOT TROUBLE US.*

After the *Acacia Glyn* had left the colony for the edge of the plateau, military shuttles from the cruiser began to ferry down warbots, supplies and soldiers to ensure the transition. There was no resistance from the Afthari and most of the soldiers soon left.

Meanwhile, Maranth remained in the colony with the medibots, repairing broken bodies and overseeing the burying of the dead. Gannet, the slave that so tormented her, was among them. She felt a guilty pleasure he was gone. It would take the military time to sort out the living slavers, slaves, families and beggars. Maranth helped them with some of the identifications.

Mostly she worked with her medibots in the main square to stabilize and save the wounded. She even delivered a baby in the midst of it all. Her patients now lay in neat rows, on clean cots across the lawn. The cots had been supplied by the military cruiser, along with some extra supplies and another medibot.

On the second day of the military occupation, Maranth was gently washing off a gash on a boy's arm when Commander Woosan and a couple of his officers strolled over.

He nodded and bowed. "Greetings, Maranth."

She tiredly tucked a wayward strand of hair back and smiled. "Greetings, Commander."

He surveyed her open-air hospital approvingly. "You're doing good work here. Remarkable considering your youth and experience."

She smiled. "Commander, one either breaks or rises to the challenge."

He nodded. "What are your plans afterward?"

She answered while she sealed the cut with dermaglue. "Return to Veddi, I suppose."

His grey eyes were friendly. "You're too much of the outerworlds to stay there now."

She sent the child on his way and stood up. "Am I so changed?"

His eyes were now a bit sad. "All of us are, who stay out here too long."

Then he smiled. "The military lives on Veddi and in the outerworlds. You would find a home with us."

He nodded, then moved on with his inspection.

Three days later, the *Acacia Glyn* rose from Afthar and again berthed inside the military cruiser. When the smaller ship's hatch opened, Hari and Orandar were already waiting in the passage tube. They both bowed to the trader in greeting.

Orandar smiled. "Should we offer congratulations?"

Hari broke in. "Is Maranth with you?"

The Patusian wobbled. "I've arranged a truce with the Kin. Maranth is still in the colony."

His words were very slurred and he swayed before he collapsed forward onto Hari. Blood stained Hari's sleeve and oozed through the trader's face cloth.

Orandar and Hari exchanged frightened glances.

The Man With No Face shakily regained his feet and turned back towards his ship.

Hari propped him up. "Wait here. We'll get a medibot."

"No." The trader pulled away and slowly made his back into the *Acacia Glyn*.

THIRTY-SEVEN

AFTHAR

NO ONE SAW or heard from the trader for two more days. Finally, he contacted Orandar and invited her to begin her research. She quickly boarded the *Acacia Glyn* and the ship returned to Afthar.

When the hatch opened near one of the ravines, the trader, lower face again covered, slipped down the ramp. A flyer began lazy circles overhead. He did nothing to hide from it. Still at the hatch, Orandar watched him and was mystified that he fell to his knees on the ground, his eyes closed. He remained that way, not moving at all, for over five minutes. She wondered if he were still ill.

Finally he roused. "You can come down now."

She then descended the ramp, trailed by her two sciencebots. The linguistic 'bot had been left with the cargo.

The trader motioned her to the edge of the plateau. "We can get down here. But you must stay with me. Off by yourself, one of them might decide to eat you."

Her eyes grew wide. "You're not serious."

His eyes told her otherwise. As they traveled down through the vegetation, he left his mind open and simply monitored the chatter in his head. None of the Kin seemed to be nearby and they mostly ignored their presence.

He led her to one of the caves he'd lived in. It felt strange to crawl into it now after so much time had passed.

Once inside, Orandar looked around in awe. "Amazing that so much daylight carries down here. You can see everything. We must identify these rocks and sample the air."

Immediately one of the sciencebots began analyzing the glittering minerals. The other 'bot held up one of the exotic cave worms, its cilia waved languidly in the air.

The Patusian motioned toward it. "I lived on those for a long time. I'm glad they've recolonized this cave."

Orandar was shocked. She really hadn't thought about how he could have survived here. She said nothing and scraped some mold from a rock.

They spent the rest of the day sampling soil and air, analyzing the vegetation and exploring two more caves. Then they returned to the *Acacia Glyn*.

After they silently shared a meal, Orandar immediately headed for her lab. The Man With No Face left the ship for the plateau. He blanked his mind to let the Kin Song fill his head. It carried him along through the heights and depths of Afthar on the wings of flyers. Bits and pieces of the events now unfolding were woven into the telepathic chant that incorporated sound, memory and insight into whole. When it was over he felt empty. He knew that once he left Afthar, he would never experience its beauty and majesty again.

Then his mind sought out Maranth. He found her on the main square, asleep. He gently woke her.

I'm on the edge of the plateau with Orandar. She's still not talking to me.

Maranth roused and smiled. *I can feel where you are, sort of northwest. Everything going well?*

He already knew she was doing fine. *Aye. When do you want me to pick you up?*

She thought a moment. *Tomorrow evening.*

The next morning the trader led Orandar and her sciencebots back down the ravine. She scanned the trees and pointed to the top of one of them. "There's a flyer nest there. May I send my sciencebot into it?"

He shook his head. "No. The flyers belong to the Kin. They use them sort of the same way hunters in the past used dogs. But the flyers drop feathers everywhere. There's probably some around here."

They made their way quietly to the base of the tree. Orandar found several feathers. One of the sciencebots sniffed out the decomposing remains of a flyer chick in the leaf litter.

She excitedly examined the tiny corpse. "This is huge. We'll be able to get DNA and a lot of other information from it."

Two drogans silently appeared out of the foliage. One of them turned a penetrating yellow eye on the science team. Then, with a flick of their tails, they were gone.

Orandar watched in awe. "Drogans?"

The trader nodded.

Several hours later they found some bones by the stream at the bottom of the gorge. The sciencebots began to gather and catalog the find.

Orandar carefully began to brush dirt and mud from the largest bone that stuck out of the mud. "Can we go and sample other areas on the planet as well?"

The trader shook his head no.

Orandar sighed wistfully, but she was testing the trader. "They just seem like big birds. Where are their weapons? What makes them so dangerous?"

He eyed her with contempt. "You are the one who is dangerous. You remain blinded by your narrowness. And that could get us all killed."

They said nothing after that. At sunset they returned to the *Acacia Glyn*.

She broke the silence. "I really need to examine some of the other small creatures here, including the 'malaaas' that the drogans need to survive."

The trader thought for a moment. "I can trap these for you, but it's not safe to leave you alone in there while I'm doing it.

"We pick up Maranth tonight. When we come back here, you stay in the ship and study what you already have. I'll get you your creatures."

She nodded and climbed the ramp into the open hatch. The trader remained behind a moment. He let his mind search for Maranth. But she wasn't in the colony. When he contacted the *Kleig*, he learned she had already returned there. So he took the *Acacia Glyn* up to berth inside the much larger ship.

He felt something was wrong before he released the hatch. Maranth was already waiting for him in the tunnel.

She slipped inside and he lifted her chin to see her eyes. He knew some of it from her jumbled thoughts. And Maranth's mind was usually ordered. It would be better if she told him.

"Let's talk in my cabin. Orandar is around somewhere."

He sat on the floor next to his bed and left his face cloth on. Maranth simply flopped down on it, so her head was near his own.

"Commander Woosan requested I return to the cruiser. So I took one of the shuttles back. I met with him and Hari in front of a viewport in some lounge. Hari asked me if I'd seen any Veddians in Tigenne."

"So you told them about the three in the casino?"

She squinted in revulsion. "Aye. There was a little back and forth and then Hari had to leave. But the Commander asked me to stay for a moment."

Maranth sat up and faced him. *He grabbed me, held me against his body, and stuck his tongue down my throat. Then he let me go and said it was an instructional kiss. The military in harm's way do not suppress their sexuality because they need the edge, whatever that means. He told me I needed to understand how his men were reacting to me. Then he left.*

She radiated disgust and fear. And there was something more. The trader realized her body had instinctively registered a sexual reaction.

He said nothing.

"When I was down on Afthar, the Commander asked me

to join the military. And my social worker is from the Military Ministry."

The trader got to his feet. "You're upset and exhausted. So sleep here and no one will bother you. I have some business to take care of anyway."

He left her in his cabin. When he had entered the military ship he requested a meeting with the Commander.

He did not have to wait long before he was ushered into the Woosan's office. Woosan was alone, busy checking several status holos while he was drinking from a tall cup.

He glanced up when the trader entered. "How is the science mission going? Problems?"

The trader stood up against the console with his hands on its top. "The problem is you laid hands on Maranth, instructional or not."

He now had the Commander's attention. "What business is it of yours?"

"Maranth and I are, I believe you call it something like 'brothers forged in combat.' She has my back, I have hers."

A military man like Woosan understood. He realized he should have read more than the summary report on Maranth.

The trader waved his hand in a friendly manner. "As long as it does not happen again, there's no issue between us."

Woosan decided to test the trader. "What would you do to me if it did happen again?"

The Patusian's eyes radiated innocence. "Nothing, Commander. I'll just tell Hari and Orandar."

Woosan suppressed a smile. *Checkmate.*

But he wasn't finished with the outerworlder. "She responded to my kiss."

The trader nodded. "I know. Maranth keeps no secrets from me."

Woosan was surprised. He took another sip before he spoke. "Would you try to stop her if she wanted me?"

Now the Patusian's eyes twinkled. "I'd personally escort her to your quarters wearing nothing but her very soft skin, for HER pleasure."

Woosan put down his cup and completely missed the console, spilling its contents across the floor.

THIRTY-EIGHT

AFTHAR

THE PATUSIAN RETURNED to his cabin with a serverbot carrying enough dinner for two. Maranth woke up and her nostrils took in the smell of hot food. The smell was of Tigenne, not Veddi.

He sat down next to her. *There's something I want to show you first.*

He guided her hand to his face and she understood. Maranth slowly unwound and pulled off his face cloth, revealing perfectly formed features below his intense blue eyes.

She exalted in his joy. Maranth turned his head each way so she could see his ears as well. "The drogans did a really good job. You have a handsome face. You never told me how Bantaaa restored your eyes. How do the drogans regenerate missing organs?"

"I can finally hear your actual voice. Very nice. I feel and perceive everything normally."

She did not doubt it. She waited patiently for him to explain.

He hesitated before he replied. "They eat the damaged part. The wound heals quickly, then it comes back the way it should be."

Maranth's face froze and her hand dropped. "They eat you alive?"

"Aye."

"You felt everything?"

He nodded.

What torture you endured!

She suddenly thought back to his blood loss when he was a beggar in the colony. The loss was continuous, for months. *How many times did they...?*

"Please don't think about it. When you do, I know and remember."

He took his own advice and thought about the food. It smelled fantastic.

He beamed. "Let's eat."

They both slipped to the floor and ate directly off the serverbot. There was even some of the Tigenne drink to complete the meal.

When they were both done, he helped her to her feet. "Better?"

She smiled. "Much better."

"Good." He hesitated a moment. "Maranth, with what's happened, do you still want to go back to Veddi?"

She looked down dejectedly. "I'm not sure. I've changed so much. It seems I'm only fit for the military."

"Is that what you want?"

Her eyes told him otherwise.

He took her hands in his own. "You have a third option."

His intense eyes bore into her own. "Come with me, to live with the Patushah. My family."

He put his finger across her lips to keep her from speaking. "You don't have to decide for awhile. Meanwhile, I would like to give you a very special gift."

"A gift?"

"Aye. The gift of seduction."

Maranth was mystified. "What is that?"

His blue eyes sparkled. "It's easier to show you than explain. If you don't like it, it will stop."

She knew he'd never harm her and she was curious. "Alright, show me then."

He smiled. "We have a long day tomorrow." He led her to the cabin door, which slid open.

As she turned into the hall to leave he gently held her shoulders from behind and kissed her slowly on the right side of her neck.

Her breath caught. He slowly continued up her neck to her earlobe.

Maranth couldn't breathe. She felt a liquid heat spread throughout her body.

Yor sampled her passion through her mind and let it mingle in with his own desire. That was the price and pleasure of seduction, its slow, exquisite torture.

He pulled himself away. "Good night, Maranth." His voice was husky.

He left her there, outside his closed cabin door.

She returned to an empty crew cabin, as Orandar was not there. Maranth mechanically got ready for bed. But her nervous system had been reset and all she could think about was this man she was so tied to.

She was frightened she would lose what they had. He was her anchor. Now they had just crossed a very different threshold.

In truth, she was frightened by her own response. She had been overcome by what was just a biological instinct. She really desired a good meal when she was famished. This new hunger was so many orders of magnitude beyond that.

He was probably reading her mind now. She had no privacy even in her confusion. Maranth meditated, but she still didn't sleep much that night.

She awoke to the serverbot tapping her on her arm. "The ship will leave for the Afthari colony in fifteen minutes."

She soon joined Orandar and Yor on the bridge. His lower face was again covered. Orandar nodded to her but said nothing.

He glanced up at her as he tested the ship systems with Jona. *I'm hiding my face for a little longer.*

She nodded and took the free seat at another console.

Haraq's lizard seemed a bit fatter in its cage. The serverbot must be feeding it well.

They landed in the colony's spaceport to drop off Maranth. Only a couple of military shuttles still remained there. The wreckage of the slaver's ships and other debris had been cleared away.

As she left the open hatch, Yor spoke into her mind. *I'll pick you up before sunset.*

There was something else in his message that made her tingle. Of course she now understood seduction was sexual. Maranth got the feeling that it was something like a game, but she didn't know the rules.

When she arrived at the main square, the last of the cots were gone.

She contacted Doc. "Status please."

His voice seemed to display a hint of satisfaction. "I'm tending one of the six remaining patients in the new Afthar hospital. Everyone here is making satisfactory progress with no new complications. Of course most of them have traumatic amputations. We could really benefit from Veddi regeneration equipment."

Maranth sighed. "Understood. I'll check with the Commander but I doubt the *Kleig* has any. At least we have good prosthetics. Where are Eng and the other medibot?"

"Eng is doing rounds of the ambulatory patients and the military medibot has returned to the cruiser. Oh, and our new hospital is located in what is left of Zedd's compound."

As Maranth headed for Zedd's House, she realized that her work here was all but finished. In another week there would be no need for even a medibot.

Meanwhile, the *Acacia Glyn* landed in the same location as before, at the edge of the plateau. Only the trader left the ship this time, carrying inflatable cages. Hunting and trapping needed to be done. He would do it the way the Kin did, with his mind.

He didn't see any drogans. But he recognized Bantaaa's nest

sister, Vabaaa, stretching her mind into his own. She watched through his own eyes everything he did. It was the first time any drogan had done this. Even Bantaaa had never tried to reach into his mind this way. He made no attempt to block or conceal anything.

By late afternoon, he had caught seven different creatures, including a malaaa. He knew the furry malaaa was the key, as it also may have come from Veddi.

Orandar was really pleased by the animals the trader brought back. Her cargo bay lab was already cluttered with biological samples, mineral specimens, as well as all sorts of paraphernalia. The sciencebots were busy processing everything native.

She checked each animal carefully. "All alive, and in good condition. How did you do it?"

He answered offhandedly. "The drogan way. But now you must stow everything. We're returning to the colony in about ten minutes to get Maranth."

She looked away with a slight frown.

Yor knew it was her expression of disapproval of Maranth's attachment to him, as well as what she regarded as the younger woman's lack of proper deference.

Soon the Veddi must communicate directly with the Kin. He knew Orandar's inflexibility could doom the effort. She still did not regard him as anything more than subhuman. She could not get beyond her preconceptions to really see the drogans. It would be very dangerous, regardless. Though he wished it otherwise, Maranth had to be there. And Hari must also meet the Kin.

The sun was low on the red-orange horizon when the *Acacia Glyn* landed in the colony's spaceport.

The trader carried a clear tarp as he rode the gangway down to the spaceport ground. His lower face was again covered when he met Maranth. She had sensed his approach and was waiting for him. Meanwhile, Orandar released the cargo hatch so her lab could be open to the air in the safety of the colony.

Yor gently took Maranth's arm. "I've got something wonderful to show you. Please come."

A short time later she followed him through his tunnel under the colony's force field. Maranth looked up and saw wisps of yellow trail across the orange sky from the fading heat of Afthar's sun. She knew this star was hotter and whiter than the sun of Veddi. But Afthar was further out, so its sun on the horizon was slightly smaller than the sun she remembered from her home world.

He spread the tarp over the dusty ground not far from the edge of the colony. Then he dropped down and lay on his back.

"I've told you about the Kin Song. I'd like to try and share it with you, if you let me. I will relay what I experience into your mind so you can also experience it. I'm not sure this will work. Will you let me try?"

"Aye." She lay down next to him and waited.

Images, sounds and a very alien chant filled her brain. Then it stopped. In a moment it began again. She was soaring above the planet seeing it with an unnaturally wide view. She watched details from the plateau and ravines that should be impossible at this distance above the planet.

Maranth could see individual rocks on the plateau and the blue-green leaves on branches and shrubs. She watched a small plated animal skitter through the brownish leaf litter. She enjoyed the light reflections playing on the water in the streams that bisected most of the ravines. Soon the rise of the chant carried her somewhere beyond her senses and reason, beyond everything she knew.

After a while it all just stopped. Then she felt lost. She looked over at Yor and could see he was still with them. He took her hand and she once again soared with the Kin, lost in their chant.

When it was finally over they both lay there in silence, totally spent. The sun had just set, leaving behind a pink, purple and gold expanse of sky. When that was gone the stars took over.

There was a heavy swath of them running diagonally, the disk of the Milky Way across the night sky.

Yor pointed to what looked like two very bright stars. "That one. And the bigger one to its left. Those are the two small moons of Afthar. They move across the sky each night."

After resting awhile, they silently rose to return to the colony. Maranth had never really bothered to look at the Afthari night sky before. Though extraordinarily beautiful, she knew it was the Kin Song she would never forget.

When they passed under the open cargo bay, Orandar excitedly stepped to its edge. "You must come up. It's very important."

The trader summoned a portbot, who then lifted the two into the cargo lab.

Maranth bowed to Orandar, who forgot the formalities and just grabbed the meddoc. "Your theory has been confirmed. Confirmed!"

Maranth smiled. "Then the drogans are dinosaur cousins of our birds?"

Orandar was shaking with excitement. "Aye, and the Malaaa is also from Veddi. An extinct mammal. The implications are enormous, just enormous. How did they get here?"

"Maybe you should ask them." The Patusian carefully pried Maranth from the other woman's grasp.

Orandar just looked at him in blank surprise.

He went over to the cargo hold controls and closed its doors. "We're returning to the cruiser in about fifteen minutes. Orandar, would you please secure your lab?"

Orandar remained in the cargo bay for the short trip. Only the Patusian and Maranth were at the hatch when it opened to the tube leading into the *Kleig*.

Hari was waiting there. Chen's gifted inspector bowed. "So there is progress?"

Maranth bowed back.

The trader nodded his greeting. "Orandar is bursting with

news. So you might want to visit her in her lab. Then we must talk."

Hari nodded and headed for the lab.

When he was out of sight, Yor took off his face cloth and gently backed Maranth up to the wall. His voice was silky. "Would you let me share a kiss?"

He read a flash of the commander's unwanted kiss from her mind. He whispered near her left ear, "Maranth, it's me. No one else is here."

He thought for a moment. "Instead, why don't you kiss me?"

He stood back and watched her light brown eyes flash surprise. But then they dilated and it took great effort for him to remain still as she stood on her toes and draped her hands on his shoulders. She brushed her lips along his jaw. Then she rubbed her cheek across his own. Only then did she softly kiss his lips.

She was no longer afraid. Now he slowly pulled her up against his torso and kissed her, gently prying her lips apart enough so he could explore them without triggering any bad memories. She melted in pleasure and her knees buckled.

He caught her in a hug and held her tight. Then he spoke in a low voice. "Hari is finishing with Orandar. I must talk with him."

Maranth whispered into his ear. "This is part of seduction?"

Her breath in his ear sent a jolt through him that nearly knocked him off his feet. Maranth was surprised. For the first time she experienced her own sexual power.

It took a moment before he could respond. "We'll discuss that later."

The trader reluctantly broke from their embrace. He needed to convince Hari how dangerous the situation was since the *Kleig* attacked the colony.

Orandar stayed in her lab even after Hari finally left the *Acacia Glyn*. Yor found Maranth in the crew cabin meditating on her bunk. She looked up and smiled.

His eyes twinkled. He wanted to say, "It's later. And we have things to discuss, in private."

But he knew her seduction must be careful and slow. Sexually, Maranth was like a girl taking her first steps into womanhood. She needed time to be comfortable in her own sexuality and feel safe.

THIRTY-NINE

AFTHAR

ORANDAR WAS SURPRISED when the trader, his lower face still covered, arrived on the bridge with Hari and Maranth.

The Patusian nodded. "Good morning, Orandar. Hari has requested he join us today. He is very interested in drogan capabilities."

Orandar bowed to Hari. "I believe this outerworld trader has misled you by stating these creatures are intelligent. However, I've restrained the scope of my research out of caution until I demonstrate otherwise.

"Their brain/body size ratio is just too small for higher intelligence functions. They apparently make no tools nor have industry of any kind. There are other, more logical explanations for their fearsome behavior. In the unlikely event they are intelligent, then I will be happy to arrange a presentation for you."

Hari smiled. "I wasn't very busy anyway."

The trader took his seat at the main controls, then swiveled to face Orandar. "Do you have the dinosaur holos that I asked you to bring from Veddi?"

Orandar smiled condescendingly. "I'm sure I can put together something when and if there is a reason to do so."

He eyed Maranth now sitting at the fourth console.

Can Doc make a dinosaur/drogan holo comparison with the data he contains?

She smiled. *Aye. Give me about fifteen minutes in the colony. Eng can handle the clinic. Everyone is healing well.*

Soon, the *Acacia Glyn* left the cruiser's bay and slipped down to the colony below. Maranth departed as soon as the hatch opened.

Orandar impatiently turned to the trader. "Why aren't we leaving to study the drogans?"

He met her gaze. "We will leave when Maranth returns."

Orandar frowned. "There's no reason for her being here."

"We already had that discussion, on the Bellaire Space Station."

Orandar contained her annoyance and Hari said nothing.

Maranth finally returned with Doc, who immediately headed to the lab in the cargo hold. No one said a word. The ship soon took off and returned to the same location at the edge of the ravine.

When the hatch opened, all four left the ship for the plateau. Doc soon followed with a holo projection unit in tow.

He had completely set the unit up nearby before Orandar noticed.

"That's my equipment. You had no right..."

Hari intervened. "Orandar, what difference does it make? Do you really intend to bicker over a projection unit?"

She sighed. "Of course not."

She eyed the trader imperiously. "Seems to be your show, outerworlder."

He glanced at Maranth, then unwrapped his face cloth and let it drop to the ground. Both Hari and Orandar were speechless when they saw his normal face. The trader then opened his shirt, displaying his gold tattoo.

He now ignored the humans and concentrated on the rising mental hum of the Kin.

His mind reached out to them. *You of the Kin. Come.*

Fawasaaa, Vabaaa, Giraaa, come. Come meet me, meet others of my kind who have information for you.

Orandar nervously watched a flyer lazily circle them overhead. Hari noticed her discomfort and looked up. He marveled at how familiar, yet alien, it looked.

Doc moved close to Maranth. "They really eat humans? Would they eat workbots?"

The Patusian felt a disturbance in the growing mental babble.

His mind called out to them again. *Come. You of the Kin, come. We have information to share.*

Soon the first drogan appeared on the plateau some distance away. Then others began to emerge.

He recognized Vabaaa, Giraaa, Hosaaa and Fawasaaa among the other dozen or so drogans heading towards the humans. The drogans broadcast a mental jumble of anger, annoyance and curiosity.

Vabaaa again entered his mind to read him. He offered no resistance to Bantaaa's sister. Meanwhile, the voice of the distant Kin faded to a soft murmur. He supposed they were waiting for more information.

Hosaaa, Bantaaa's mate, was the first to step among them. Orandar cringed. Fawasaaa picked Doc up and examined him curiously.

Doc waggled his feet and antennae. "Put me down! I won't taste good."

She shook the medibot. *WHAT'S THIS? IT SQUAWKS AND MOVES BUT IS NOT FULLY ALIVE.*

Though terrified, Maranth grabbed Doc's midsection and tried to snatch him from her grasp.

The Patusian spoke into Fawasaaa's mind. *This device is hers. My kind makes these devices to serve us, as your flyers serve you.*

In awe, Fawasaaa let Maranth pull Doc away. The drogan rattled her darker green plumage to regain her composure.

The trader now spoke into Orandar's ear. "You want your

proof? Think what you want to tell them. They will read it in your mind. Let go of your negative feelings as you do in meditation. I'll guide you along if you let me."

Orandar nodded uncertainly.

"Control your thoughts or we could all be dinner."

Hosaaa swaggered over to Orandar and sniffed her fear. He was unimpressed.

The trader reached out to Hosaaa. *Open to her mind without probing.*

Hosaaa nudged her with his snout and Orandar went blank. The Patusian shook her but she remained immobile.

His gaze shifted back to Hosaaa. *Your probing has cut her off.*

Fawasaaa now rammed Hosaaa's side to get his attention. *THE KIN NEED YOUR PATIENCE.*

Hosaaa snapped his teeth at her but backed off.

The trader turned to Maranth and Hari. Maranth quickly jumped in. "Let me try."

He nodded. She gathered her courage and went over to the projection device. "Doc, run the presentation when I look your way."

"Understood." He plugged himself into the unit.

Maranth tried to clear her mind. She could feel light probing. It might have been Yor but she felt it was one or more of the drogans.

So she closed her eyes and concentrated on what she wanted to communicate.

By studying life forms, we've learned you, your flyers, and the furry creatures you call malaaas did not originate here.

She felt an annoyed murmur run through her mind. Then a voice that felt female responded.

WE KNOW THAT, ALIEN. IS THIS WHAT YOU'VE COME TO BOTHER US WITH?

Maranth gathered her courage. *We're sure you originated on our home world long ago.*

The drogans were dumbfounded and gathered in rapt attention.

She then began her next thoughts. *Your type of life forms died out on our world about 65 million years ago.*

Maranth looked at Doc. Holographic images of birds now soared and sung above them. Several drogans circled these images in awe, testing them with their claws.

Maranth emptied her mind and began again. *Our birds are the closest to your kind left on our world. Your flyers are much like them.*

Now a holo image of Archaeopteryx, much like the flyer circling over her, replaced two of the bird images.

We call your kind of life dinosaurs.

A holo image of a running Stenonychosaurus dinosaur replaced the birds.

This is the closest to you we know of, perhaps your ancestor or close relative. We suspected it was evolving to intelligence near the end.

Now a drogan's holo joined the Stenonychosaurus. Its feathers dissolved away to show the two were similar in structure, though the drogan was a bit larger.

There were others, too.

Now different kinds of dinosaurs appeared in the holos. When a viciously toothed Deinonychus joined them, the drogans shrieked out. The humans instinctively jumped back in terror.

With one voice the drogans on the plateau screamed "Kosaaan!"

Doc killed the presentation and the images dissolved away. The drogans uneasily settled down.

Hosaaa's thoughts flowed to the other drogans.

KOSAAAN. HOW CAN THESE INFERIORS KNOW OUR OLD ENEMY? IS ALL THIS TRUE?

Though a bit rocky, Maranth decided to continue. *Our kind arose much later, from a different line, the line of your malaaas. In a way, we are now what you once were on our home world.*

279

It's as if we are your younger cousins. Do you know how the Kin came here?

Fawasaaa dipped her head. *THERE'S MUCH TO CONSIDER.*

The mental voices of the nearby drogans cried out to the multitude. Others began to join their brethren. Soon all the Kin were part of the rising communion. The trader mentally rode their tide. Then the drogans on the plateau slipped back into the jungle below.

When they were gone, the *Acacia Glyn* left the plateau for the *Kleig*.

Hari led a still woozy Orandar back to the crew cabin and put her in bed. He then joined the other two on the bridge just as the ship entered the *Kleig*'s shuttle bay. Nothing was said.

The trader finally broke the silence. "Hari, why not take Orandar back to the *Kleig*, as proof of what happened?"

Hari replied with a 'you've got to be kidding' look.

The Patusian smiled tiredly. "I need to rejuvenate for awhile. After you leave, I'm setting ship's security to auto."

When Hari opened the hatch, several military crewmen met him in the waiting tunnel to the *Kleig*.

Hari was surprised. "Why the greeting committee?"

One of them answered with a big grin. "First contact is quite an occasion."

Hari nodded, then slipped around the crewmen and headed up the tunnel. He suddenly stopped and turned back. "Oh, don't try to pry anything open. This ship has active defenses. If you annoy it enough it will fire on you."

FORTY

AFTHAR

ORANDAR WOKE THE trader the next day, requesting he release the ship's main hatch. He did so without a word. He realized his mood was sour, probably because Maranth still did not share his bed. His mind reached out for her. She was also awake, getting dressed in the crew cabin. So he got himself up and prepared for the day.

When he entered her cabin she was putting on the belt he bought her in Tigenne. He liked that belt, but now he really wanted to take it off. He communicated the thought and she responded to his desire with the memory of their first kiss.

He obliged her with another kiss, this one very slow. "Maranth, stay with me in the captain's cabin. I'm a lot more fun than Orandar." He was serious, but he delivered the offer as a tease.

She laughed. "Aye. You ARE a lot more fun."

Her large eyes grew mischievous. "It would be scandalous. I'm already notorious, having been a slave and the constant companion of an outerworlder. Worse, I don't properly defer to my elders."

She turned to Doc. "What do you think?"

Doc noted Maranth seemed happy and her face was flushed with pleasure. Her wellbeing was his first priority so he was satisfied. He just whirred and nodded an antenna in response.

281

Meanwhile, on the cruiser, Hari, exobiologist Orandar and Commander Woosan were meeting over breakfast in the lounge.

Hari intended to speak through the meeting while he slowly drank his breakfast. "I've asked you here to review what I've learned and what I suspect."

He turned to Orandar. "What do you remember?"

She was visibly upset. "I only remember the drogans coming into our area, then waking up in the crew quarters. Perhaps I was somehow drugged."

Hari and Woosan exchanged glances.

Hari took another sip. "I'm sorry Orandar, I witnessed one of the drogans approach you. It nudged you and then you sort of blanked out. There were no drugs.

"However, Maranth made what appeared to be a telepathic presentation using the holo projector as a visual aid. Of course I can't be sure since she never said a word. But the drogans as a group clearly were interested and reacted to her, even before she displayed the holos. They got very upset when a dinosaur, which I learned is Deinonychus, appeared. They actually cried out something like 'Kosan.'

"Well before this, on Veddi and the *Acacia Glyn*, I can document that Maranth and the trader communicated telepathically. This probably explains why she connected with the Kin so easily, while you froze.

"Thus, the best hypothesis is that the drogans are telepathic, as is the Patusian trader, since he shares the drogans' brain nodule that you documented. We became aware of his version of it during his medical exam at Customs, where his missing ears and nose deformities were also noted.

"Maranth may have learned mental skills that are beyond the rest of us. Though I doubt she is truly telepathic, since she does not possess the brain anomaly."

Hari paused and took another sip. "Orandar, regardless of your drogan brain size analysis, telepathy means the drogans can quickly distribute knowledge and thinking throughout their entire population. Probably the information received by the few drogans on the plateau has, by now, been transmitted and analyzed through the entire population."

He now turned to Woosan. "Telepathy explains how they easily neutralized your troops and the slavers. The drogans probably just blanked them out, as they did Orandar yesterday."

The Commander somberly nodded.

Hari took another sip and again addressed Woosan. "This also means the Patusian trader probably reads our minds. We just assumed he knew what we said by reading our lips."

Woosan was clearly surprised and sat back.

Hari now directed his findings at both of them. "I've also learned from the Afthari that our trader suddenly showed up inside the colony missing his eyes, nose, ears and mouth. Can you imagine being left alive like that?

"The Afthari also said he came and went at will, later showing up with complete eyes, then eventually a workable mouth with speech. All of this is beyond the medical capability that Maranth had on Afthar.

"Yesterday, on the plateau, the trader dropped his face cloth to show us his restored face with perfectly formed features, including new ears, nose and completed mouth."

"We should ask him about it. But the drogans probably regenerated his face over time, finishing the job while we've been here. This, most likely, is why he never let Maranth repair his face on Veddi. And it means he can now hear."

Hari's able eyes bore into Orandar. "If the drogans fixed our trader, then they can regenerate complex body parts in various life forms. Logically, they should be able to do the same for themselves. Maybe they can live indefinitely."

Orandar gasped.

Hari frowned. "You should gasp. You were looking for brain size, tools and structures and missed everything important. If I'm correct, they don't need weapons, communications systems, computers, or medical technology. They have them all, built in. They need no structures to live in or clothes to wear in this climate. They don't need towns or meeting places to socialize. True predators, they hunt to eat, no doubt blanking out their prey as easily as they blanked you out. What you consider absence of technology is really the result of their innate physical and mental superiority."

Orandar looked down in shame. Woosan considered the military implications.

Hari's eyes now darted back and forth between the two. "We need to know a lot more about this Patusian, and respect him for what he's managed to achieve and what he's learned. So far, because of our Veddian insularity regarding outerworlders, we've marginalized his relevance and experience. We also shunned him personally. It's unbelievable that we don't even know his actual name!

"And it seems the only Veddian who actually knows what is going on is young Maranth."

His eyes again bored into Orandar. "You've been dismissive towards her because of her youth, ignoring her actual experience and abilities. Unforgivably, you have also ignored the trader, though he clearly is the key to understanding the drogans."

Hari's eyes first went to Woosan, then Orandar. "Afthar is not Veddi. Our reliance on our social prejudices and career status is leaving us blind, deaf and worse, incompetent."

Now his words were directed at the Commander. "The Patusian said the drogans are very upset about the attack on the colony and had only agreed to a temporary truce. We must be very, very careful not to do anything that appears hostile or out of place."

Chen's investigator finished his drink and once again turned to Orandar. "You must consult with both the trader and Maranth before you finalize your food animals' program. None of it goes forward without their approval. A misstep here could start a war. Do you understand?"

She silently nodded.

Hari opened his comm soon after he left the lounge. The trader finally answered after several attempts.

Hari was concerned. "Are you alright?"

"Aye. When do you want to meet?"

Hari smiled. "In a few minutes, your main cabin."

The trader hesitated. Then he closed his eyes and shook his head. "Make that ten minutes."

Hari actually entered the *Acacia Glyn* a few minutes early and found the main cabin empty. A minute after their scheduled time, he impatiently looked out down the hall both ways. Maranth's back was against the wall by the crew cabin door. The Patusian was reluctantly pulling away from what had obviously been an embrace. He took her hands and kissed them.

Please wait for me.

He then headed down the hall as Maranth smiled at Hari. Then she turned and went into the crew quarters.

Hari was speechless as the trader silently passed him into the main cabin. Chen had said the trader told him he never had taken sexual advantage of his daughter. Hari did not want to face Chen's wrath on this.

His first words to the Patusian barely contained his annoyance. "This…"

It suddenly dawned on Hari that the trader had wanted him to see them together. The man was probably reading his mind at this moment. Hari dropped down on some cushions.

"Why? Why now?"

The Patusian also dropped onto the cushions. "Please tell Chen what I told him on Veddi was true. Recently, Maranth has made it clear she is not sure she belongs on Veddi, or in your military."

He leaned forward and his startling eyes gazed into the other man. "I have offered her a third choice. She can come with me to the Padushah. I believe she will be happy with us. But if she doesn't like our life, I will return her to Veddi and her father. Or take her anywhere she wants to go. The *Acacia Glyn* will remain her property."

Hari sensed a hesitation. "Has she agreed?"

"She does not have to decide yet." The trader looked away.

His gaze quickly returned. "Both for her pleasure and mine, I offered her the gift of seduction, which she accepted."

Hari realized this development was inevitable. From the first it was obvious Maranth acted in lockstep with the Patusian. Hari was sure she would willingly go with him anywhere.

But there was too much at stake. These two could not just disappear to some unknown, remote Padushah. Besides, Chen would kill him if he let that happen.

The trader smiled. "Hari, I'm glad to know you. You think beyond the obvious. Your eyes are always open. And you were the only Veddian, besides Maranth, who looked past my deformities."

Hari was pleased by the complement. This also gave him the opening to ask the questions that brought him into the smaller ship. "You must have an easier name than Man With No Face. May I call you something simpler?"

"Maranth calls me Yor. You can too. But to others, I remain the Man With No Face."

Hari nodded. Perhaps it was a Patusian custom to have a familiar and a general name. "You and the drogans are telepathic?"

"Of course. You figured out most of it back on Veddi."

Hari laughed. "Aye. You knew what I was thinking. Were you always that way?"

Yor covered his eyes with the palms of his open hands. "No. I was only telepathic, without my face, when I arrived on Afthar."

Hari's voice grew very soft. "How did you arrive?"

Yor looked up in pain. "I was in a sector far from here in deep space, on the bridge of my own ship, the *Farbigan*. There was some sort of disturbance. Then I was falling into the jungle here."

He knew that Hari immediately grasped what this meant.

"Will you teach me to communicate with the drogans like Maranth does?"

Yor's mood soured. "I can but won't. I had high hopes when I brought Maranth back to the Veddi. But your Orandars and Hreems will blunder us into war with the Kin, and maybe a lot worse."

Hari nodded. "Chen also grasps the problems we create by our insularity. He has a long reach and there are already changes at home. I apologize for the way you've been treated by us."

Yor nodded. "What does Chen do in your society?"

"He is one of the three Directors of Quality Assurance. We relentlessly audit every ministry, department and agency for incompetence and wrongdoing. It may not seem that important, but we provide accountability. Otherwise our society would fall apart. A bad report from us means people lose their jobs and resources are transferred."

Hari just had one more question. "The drogans restored your face?"

Yor nodded. Hari stood up and smiled at the Patusian. "Thank you." As he headed for the door, his head was spinning with all the implications of what he'd just learned.

"There's something more you really need to understand." Yor's words stopped him and Hari turned back.

Yor now lay back with his eyes closed. "Your society will dream up diplomatic initiatives, trade, scientific and cultural missions and so on, focused on the Kin. This provides jobs for a lot of your people. It's the way many of you occupy your time."

Then he stood up and faced Hari squarely. "The Kin are not telepathic people with feathers. Outside of the food animals, you Veddi MUST leave them alone. That's the deal I made to get this truce.

"Though I'd rather forget, I think you will eventually need to know how I survived among them for you to understand why it must be this way.

"Your efforts should be to prevent other outerworlders, rogue scientists, and such from bothering them in their domain. Or there will be bloody war.

"This is also why I don't want to teach you to communicate with them. The whole weight of your society would be on you to do so. Believe it or not, I'm doing you a favor.

"We both know what happened to me was no accident. Something is coming. Possibly all the children of Veddi may face extinction. Maybe I was remade as a bridge between our two lines, from very different ages, so both can work together to stop it. Or maybe something else entirely. No matter what is coming, we don't need a war between the Kin and man."

Hari soon sent everything he learned to Chen. Then he conferred with Woosan about what the trader said. All three agreed to hold off any more drogan contact for a while.

This was fine with Yor. Except for ferrying Maranth back and forth to the colony to close up her clinic, and some discussions with a much-subdued Orandar, he had a lot of downtime to optimize the ship's systems, exercise, meditate, and spend pleasurable moments with Maranth.

Considering where he'd been, life was pure joy. But he knew it was just an interlude. He would face the drogans once more. Only after returning Orandar to Veddi could he finally go home.

An easy week had passed before Hari next contacted him. "Greetings. Things are stirring up. Chen and a top delegation are here to check out things for themselves."

The trader frowned. "How many vessels?"

"Just one more military cruiser."

"Why risk scaring the Kin? This second cruiser should stay out of sight from the ground."

"Understood."

Soon, an impersonal message holoed in on the bridge comm. 'Maranth-sa-Veddi-Dimore is requested immediately on the cruiser *Beltran*. Departure via military transport.'

Yor wordlessly accompanied Maranth to the hatch of their small ship. There were two crewmen already waiting in the tunnel that connected into the *Kleig*. He kissed her forehead. Maranth winked before she was led away.

The crewmen escorted her to another tunnel that led to one of the military shuttles. It was a fast vessel that soon berthed inside the *Beltran*'s equally ample bay. When the shuttle hatch opened, her father was waiting in the connecting tunnel. Both he and Maranth bowed, then hugged. Chen held her at arms length and shook his head at her diam ring, tunic, pants, boots and heavy, rich belt. "Again you wear outerworld clothes."

Maranth smiled sadly. "Our flowing robes, though beautiful, don't work well in the confines of a small ship. And the fabric catches on things when I'm triaging patients under attack by a military cruiser in orbit."

Chen smiled at the barb. "Your dream on Veddi."

He took her arm. "Let's go for a walk."

Chen asked Maranth to tell him all that had happened on Afthar. It took her a short while to realize that the questions her father asked had another purpose, as he already knew what happened. He was actually probing to see if she was herself, or if the outerworld trader now controlled her mind. Chen finally asked directly about the trader's telepathy, how it worked.

Maranth thought for a moment. "He can place his thinking and experiences into my head. It was frightening at first, but necessary or we wouldn't have survived. He can't help knowing what I think. So I have no privacy in my thoughts."

Chen became visibly angry.

Maranth placed a reassuring hand on her father's arm. "I'm used to it by now. I can't read his mind. His telepathy works only one way. But I always can tell the difference between his thinking and my own. And he's never forced me to do anything."

Chen sighed and said nothing as they silently passed one of the *Beltran*'s crew. They turned into a wider passage.

She remembered the Kin Song. "He's also shared experiences I would never had known otherwise."

They wound up in an empty lounge, similarly decorated like the one on the *Kleig*. When they were comfortably settled on a low sofa, a serverbot brought them Maranth's favorite Veddian tea. They both sipped the brew.

Chen put his drink down and smoothed his daughter's cheek. "I know this is not yet over. Please stay with me where it is safe. I worry so much for you."

Maranth shook her head sadly. "I am needed on Afthar so I can't stay."

She also put her cup down. "Father, I don't think I can leave him. We are tied by threads you cannot comprehend."

Chen frowned. "I do understand sexual heat. It rules us all when it flames. But that passion always burns out. It was never meant to last our long lifetimes."

Maranth nodded. "I am certain I no longer belong on Veddi. I've changed too much. And I don't want to join the military, live on grey ships and follow the orders of ignorant men. I had enough of that as a slave."

Chen was shocked by her words but said nothing.

She looked down. "I'm standing in front of an abyss and I'm terrified."

FORTY-ONE

AFTHAR

THE *ACACIA GLYN* left the *Kleig* once more for Afthar to deliver the prey animals. The ship lazily arced down to the planet and landed again at the same spot on the edge of the plateau. Now only Maranth, Orandar and the trader were on board, strapped into the console seats on the bridge. The military had installed a live feed from the *Acacia Glyn* to the war cruisers, so the Veddians could view the event.

While the other two began to unstrap themselves, Maranth remained still as stone, her eyes unfocused.

She soon regained herself and eyed Yor in anguish. "I watched a second cruiser join the *Kleig* in orbit. I think this is a drogan's memory."

She grabbed his arm. "They really fear we intend to attack them from the sky. They plan to take this ship, then the colony."

He could sense nothing from the Kin and immediately got on the ship's comm. "Cruiser *Kleig*."

"*Kleig* here."

"Please get me your Commander."

"Woosan."

"Commander, did the new cruiser appear in low orbit with your own cruiser *Kleig*?"

"Aye. Is there a problem?"

Fighting panic, the trader's voice was tight. "Did it ever

occur to you that the drogans might view this as a betrayal of the truce, a prelude to war?"

He held his head in anguish. "You've really done it now."

Then he cut the link. "Strap back in, Orandar. We're leaving."

He also strapped in as he started takeoff procedures. The ship began to pulse. Meanwhile, the trader stretched his mind out to the Kin. He now read surprise that their ambush had failed. Maranth had foreseen what he had not sensed. Somehow the Kin had deliberately blocked their intentions from him. She was right. They planned to take the ship as soon as he opened the hatch.

Now the Kin debated their next maneuver as the *Acacia Glyn* lifted off. They didn't seem to notice his mental presence. Maybe they didn't bother to block him now that their plan failed.

Yor contacted the *Kleig* again. "Cruiser *Kleig*. Tell your Commander to evacuate the Afthari colony. We are on the way there ourselves."

As soon as the *Acacia Glyn* set down, Maranth sent her two medibots outside to broadcast a loud warning through the colony to evacuate, that the drogans were on their way. Soon the lab, cabins, and hall were filled with Afthari. Surprisingly, Orandar helped move people throughout the small ship with calm efficiency. The *Acacia Glyn* soon took off as other shuttles began to arrive.

Yor figured the Kin must now be massing to overrun the colony. He again contacted the cruiser.

"Woosan." The response was immediate.

"Since they failed to capture us, they may try for your shuttles. They can easily disable your pilots. Once the Kin are on the plateau, lay down cannon fire with, say, a ten km gap around the colony. But do not, again, DO NOT kill any of them! Just scare them back. If you kill even one, there will never be any chance for peace."

Once the *Acacia Glyn* disgorged its refugees into the *Kleig*, it took off again. This time it flew reconnaissance. As Yor expected, the Kin were massing on the plateau. There seemed to be thousands of them coming in from all directions.

By now, both war cruisers were firing cannon blasters in a wide circle around the colony as the shuttles landed and took off. The weapon fire succeeded in keeping the Kin at bay. It also created a dark circle of burnt ground all the way around the settlement. From above, the colony looked like a messy bull's eye in its center.

The trader reached into Maranth's mind. *We almost died today. This time you saw the memories of a drogan, while awake!*

When the last of the inhabitants had left Afthar, the *Acacia Glyn* returned to the *Kleig* and berthed.

Maranth and Yor silently settled in the main cabin for a meal. Orandar soon joined them. The enormity of their failure weighed on them all. The serverbot set food in front of each, but no one had much appetite.

Tears welled up in Orandar's eyes. "Our carelessness has led to this disaster, nearly cost the lives of hundreds, and made us enemies of our only known equals in the cosmos. And there is nothing that can be done to fix any of it."

Yor nodded. "But you are not directly responsible for this war. As you point out, Veddian inbred carelessness and arrogance is. At least when you go back, tell others what you've learned here. Then maybe something good will come from this."

His eyes turned to Maranth. "No one yet knows how this will turn out. War always brings surprises."

A message holo appeared on Yor's personal comm. All three were requested to attend an emergency inquiry on the *Beltran*. They silently left their unfinished meals. Two waiting crewmen escorted them through the tube to a shuttle and then to the other cruiser. Now a single crewman escorted the three through the *Beltran,* to a room that looked like a small auditorium.

On a raised dais near the far wall sat several officials in both Veddian soft pastel robes and black military uniforms. Chen and Commander Woosan sat among them. Several others, including the ever-curious Hari, populated part of the first row. All the other seats in the auditorium were empty. This room, like the others, was decorated in shades of grey, broken only by the light panels in the light grey walls.

The crewman led the three to empty seats in the front row. Then he departed. A lightly built man in military black with a sharp face was the first to speak. "I am Commander Kellian of the *Beltran*."

He eyed the two women and noted Orandar's brooch with its experience gems. "You are Orandar?"

She nodded.

Kellian then focused on Maranth. "You must be Maranth."

She, too, nodded.

The Commander's eyes next swept the trader. "Are you the Patusian known as the Man With No Face?"

"Aye."

The Commander gazed into Yor's extraordinary eyes. "This has been a disaster from beginning to end. What do you have to say for yourself?"

Yor leaned forward and did his best to restrain his anger. "So now the Veddi want to hear from me. The Kin saw your second war cruiser and viewed it as a breach of the truce, an indication of YOUR intent to war. If your people weren't so narrow-minded and careless, you wouldn't have created this disaster."

The Commander thought for a moment and sighed. "You're right." His voice was sad.

His eyes briefly flitted from Orandar to Woosan. Then his focus returned to the Patusian. "Is there any way to salvage the situation?"

Yor thought a moment. "I intend to release Orandar's food animals, to close my accounts with the Kin. Perhaps, in time, they may settle down when they realize humans have solved their food problem permanently. I don't know. But that will only happen if they are not bothered by us or reminded of your military power. In other words, they are left alone."

His eyes swept the officials on the dais. "I barely survived the terrible things they did to me. They are not like us. They think differently and are tougher, stronger and mentally focused. They have little patience, even among themselves.

"You know by now I share the Kin's telepathy. You probably think I spend my time reading your minds. Actually, your mental babble is wearing, even painful to put up with. Mostly, I work to keep it at bay. This is how I react to you. Now try to imagine how THEY react to you."

He sat back and took a slow breath. "I see the Veddi and Kin as a lot alike. You both exist as masters of, and within, your own domain. Nothing is a threat to you. As a result, you both have grown complacent and narrow in the protective cocoon you've made for yourselves.

"Hari has, no doubt, told you about my faceless, telepathic transformation. This could not have happened naturally. Is there something more powerful coming? If so, that usually means the death of the established order. And the established order in this part of the cosmos is mankind and the drogans."

The trader fell silent and no one said anything.

Finally Chen addressed Maranth. "I watched very closely what happened on the bridge of the *Acacia Glyn* before your mission aborted. It seemed you were the one to realize the danger, not the outerworlder."

Yor responded for her. "Aye. The Kin hid their plans from me."

Chen remembered the trader's words on the deck of his apartment. "She also has been remade..."

He turned again to his daughter, almost afraid of what she would say. His voice was soft. "Maranth?"

"I sometimes see things, out of their time and place."

The weirdness of it all spooked the Commander. Kellian abruptly thanked Maranth and the trader. He called for an escort and they were taken back to the *Acacia Glyn*, even though the inquiry was not finished.

Just as they entered the hatch, Hari contacted Yor again.

"Guess what? Chen wants to check out his little girl's ship. Why don't you host the two of us to dinner, say in about forty minutes?"

Yor and Maranth exchanged surprised glances. Yor grinned. "It would be our pleasure."

While the serverbot made food and prepared the main cabin, the two straightened out the captain's quarters, bridge and crew cabin. They figured Orandar's lab in the cargo bay would have to stand on its own. Maranth managed to get into a Veddian robe at the last minute. She knew it would please her father.

Chen and Hari arrived exactly when they said they would. Everyone bowed, except the trader, who politely nodded.

Maranth smiled at her father. "Would you like a tour?"

Chen critically eyed the narrow corridor up and down. "Not now, perhaps later."

The trader led them into the main cabin and waived the newcomers to the colorful cushions on the floor around the central table. Then he dropped onto several at one end. Maranth had to grab the fabric of her robe to sit down across from him in a billow of shiny blue fabric. Hari dropped down into the cushions on the far side and Chen reluctantly did the same on the side by the door.

As the serverbot laid out cups, Chen addressed the trader. "These furnishings are Patusian?"

Yor shook his head. "Afthari."

Both Hari and Chen were surprised. This meant the ship had originally belonged to the slavers.

Yor replied to their thoughts. "I traded for the ship at the same time I traded for Maranth."

The serverbot now filled the cups with the last of the Tigenne ale.

Chen pulled out a holo pad. "Since we knew nothing of Patusians, we asked our sources on Ursa Prime about your people. I'd like to read to you what they sent, so you can correct any mistakes."

Yor nodded.

"Patusians are well known in the far sectors as nomadic traders and sources of rare minerals. They generally live on large ships and maintain no land-based settlements, except for a small enclave within the Outerworld Reservation here on Ursa Prime.

"Not much is known about them culturally, except they have their own religion. Master traders are marked with a large golden tattoo on their chests which they display when they are called to do a task."

Chen looked up. "You are a master trader?"

Yor nodded.

Chen continued. "Patusians do not socialize much with outsiders and are very clannish. There have been reports of large gatherings of their ships out in deep space, far from any star system. But they don't seem to stay in any place very long, and no one knows how many there are.

"Patusians are highly regarded by the way they do business. They don't cheat anyone and will fulfill a contract exactly. They do not indulge in drugs, heavy drinking or sex when they are on shore leave. Though some do like to gamble."

Chen looked up again, but Yor said nothing.

"Their enclave is the richest and best run in the reservation. They list their laws on its gates and enforce them diligently. As a result, their land hold is as safe as any place in the innerworlds.

"Patusians prefer to do business with their own. Thus, most of the enclave consists of their Traders Exchange Bank and Patusian warehouses. This bank is the largest in the reservation and seems to have a presence in the innerworlds as well.

"There is also a casino, and a brothel for outsiders. Both are considered high-end, clean and safe. As a result, both establishments are very popular.

"Patusian men always accompany their women when they are on land, even in their own enclave. Some of the women are active traders."

Chen hesitated a moment, then continued. "Though Patusian women dress conservatively, they are beautiful and seductive."

Chen's eyes bore into the trader. "Do you have any corrections?"

Yor shrugged. "No."

Chen didn't know what to say. Clearly Patusians conducted themselves with civility and honesty. Yet they were also members of some sort of extreme, odd cult.

The serverbot now displayed dishes of food that smelled a mix of Veddi, Afthar and Tigenne. Soon the multiple dishes were served and everyone ate, though no one seemed to have a hearty appetite.

Chen sat back into the cushions and smiled at his daughter.

She met his eyes. "What will happen to the Afthari refugees?"

Chen's gaze shifted to the Patusian. "Our military has a base in the Gentian System. The slaver families will relocate there and find comfortable work in ground support. Their children will attend the Veddian school. As we agreed, former slaves will go where they wish, at our expense."

Yor signaled no objection.

Chen turned back to his daughter. "Maranth, will you now show me around your ship?"

She smiled back and bowed slightly. "Of course." She had to juggle the shimmery fabric of her robe a bit, and nearly fell into the trailing edge as she got to her feet.

Chen sighed. "You're right. Veddian robes don't work here." He took her arm and the two left the main cabin.

Hari turned and raised his cup as if he were toasting Yor. "You have seen everything clearly."

He set the cup down and leaned forward. "I know you want to return to your people. But there's too much at stake for you to just disappear.

"The Veddian government wants you to join a three year expedition, on a civilian science ship provided by us, with a small unit of hand picked Veddians to survey what is going on in the outerworlds. Your vessel would have a shadow, a military cruiser to protect you and to clean out the slavers, pirates and such. Your mission will look for signs of any other drogans, and whatever it was that dumped you on Afthar.

"We must make peaceful contact and gather intelligence on any alien challenges that might be coming. You, effectively, would be our guide, and our ambassador."

Yor just looked at him for a moment, then closed his eyes and shook his head. "There's nothing that would entice me to live in one of your grey ships with a bunch of sex-starved men for three years."

Hari held up his hand. "You can take Maranth along."

Yor frowned. "How will she manage to be comfortable as the only woman? Look. None of this is healthy or pleasurable. A three-year ship is a home, not just short-term transport."

He thought carefully about what he needed to say. "Whatever transformed me might claim me again. I've already been through a hell you can't begin to imagine. All I want is to live with my people and Maranth, if she is willing, to be happy as long as I can.

"I am Patushah. I can't and won't pretend to be something else. And everyone in the outerworlds knows a Patushah master trader lives on a Patushah trading vessel, generally with other Patushah.

"Besides, who or what took me also managed to transport me across most of the inhabited galaxy without effort. So where I locate won't make any difference."

Hari thought about what Yor had said. The trader was not bargaining. He flat out refused to consider or even modify the Veddian offer. Hari knew he had to come up with a creative solution.

"Well, if you won't join a Veddian vessel, could you let some Veddians join a Patusian one? We'll even provide you a ship to your specifications. We'll live like you do. It will help us become more flexible to the challenges of other peoples. We'll blend in."

Yor laughed so hard he nearly fell over. Finally he recovered enough to speak. "What you propose is interesting. But there is a big obstacle."

Hari silently waited for him to continue.

The trader's tone now was serious. "You know we Patusians live by strict rules, among ourselves and regarding others. One of our rules is that no one may share information about our family life with outsiders. This is an airlock offense, no exceptions."

"What's an airlock offense?"

Yor was surprised. "An airlock offense means execution."

Now Hari was shocked.

Yor ignored his reaction. "Sometimes our ships take on crew members who are outsiders. These people know they are subject to this law their entire life, whether they eventually leave us or not. They also know we can reach them anywhere in the outerworlds. How could we be sure you Veddians won't break this law once you return to your world, out of our reach?"

Yor finished off his ale. "Even if you convince me, other Patusians must approve this venture. Your shadow ship going after pirates and slavers is very desirable to the Patushah. But we all live by the same laws that protect our own."

Hari knew he could not just let the trader return to his old life. Yor seemed in denial about his centrality, his importance. At this point the conversation died. But Hari knew he would have to find a way to solve this problem.

FORTY-TWO

AFTHAR

AFTER MARANTH AND her father returned from their tour, Chen and Hari left the ship. Orandar showed up about the same time and passed them in the tube.

Yor caught her eye and smiled. "With your help, we can at least finish the task we took on, delivering the prey animals to the drogans. Maybe we can drop them in cages, into the ravines of the planet. That means we'll need some sort of guided parachutes, or balloons. And an unlocking mechanism once the cages hit ground."

She thought a moment. "I have material that the 'bots can make into suitable parachutes. Guidance and a release system should be no problem to manufacture. I can be ready, say, by late tomorrow afternoon, if I can borrow Maranth's medibots."

Maranth agreed with a broad smile and nod. Yor took Orandar's hand and squeezed it softly. "At least we can have this success. It may be important in the future."

Orandar smiled for the first time. Though she had failed spectacularly as an exobiologist, at least this last task could be a win.

After she left for her lab, Yor told Maranth about his discussion with Hari. Then he just held her close. He was clearly troubled.

For the first time she slept with him in his bed. Neither was in the mood to explore seduction further. It was a time for simple comfort and rest.

Late the next day, as Yor was doing the final systems checks with the shipbot, he was hailed by Hari through the bridge comm. "What are you doing after you release the animals?"

"We're leaving immediately for Tigenne, on our route to return Orandar to Veddi."

Hari ignored what he said. "The brass here want to make amends for our poor behavior. They want to socialize with you on the *Beltran* before you leave. I think they have some sort of honor to present you. I promise, no strings attached. This will just delay you a few hours. Please come?"

"Maranth and Orandar also invited?"

Hari skipped a beat before he replied. "Of course."

"Then we'll berth in the *Beltran* after we finish."

Soon the *Acacia Glyn* left the *Kleig* for the last time. The small vessel slowly circled down and then swooped over the network of ravines that dissected the planet, occasionally dropping a padded cage hanging from a small gold or silver parachute. Then the ship faded into the darkness enveloping the night side of Afthar.

It was near midnight, ship-time, when the three from the *Acacia Glyn* were escorted through the *Beltran*. Yor looked exotically splendid in an elaborately embroidered blue, sleeveless coat with gold, black and orange detail. The decoration on the collar and cuffs of his gold shirt and black boots complemented and coordinated with his coat.

Maranth and Orandar both wore the multi-layered, iridescent flowing dress robes that were the hallmark of Veddian women. They both seemed to float through the grey passageways in a flutter of gossamer colors as they moved. Maranth also wore her diam ring. Its opulence complemented her gown.

Their two crew escorts threw open large, double doors to a long room. From Hari's description of the event, Yor expected a gathering of people standing about. Instead, the plastiglass domed room was dominated by a long table which sat at least twenty people on a side. The few robed officials stood out among the black fitted uniforms. When the three entered, the entire room stood and silently bowed.

Commander Woosan returned to his seat at the head of the near end of the table. Yor and Orandar were led by one of the escorts to the far end. As they walked the length of the table, the trader noted the men at Woosan's end of the table had few or no experience gems.

Yor was seated next to the *Beltran*'s Commander Killian, at the head of the opposite end of the table. Orandar was seated a few seats down. Chen and Hari sat nearby. Everyone else at this end seemed to have a lot of experience gems and military bars. Meanwhile, Maranth had been seated at the Woosan end of the table.

Serverbots now set the table with red, black and silver place settings. The 'bots then served fruited drinks to everyone. The men around the trader introduced themselves and engaged him in friendly conversation. Yor did his best to keep up with their small talk, while fending off their mental babble that filled his head. He noted Chen just watched him and said nothing. He mentally reached out to Maranth and found she was enchanting Woosan and the other men around her.

At least she's enjoying herself.

Hari noted Yor's discomfort and caught Killian's eye. The serverbots soon began to serve food and the room grew quieter as everyone ate.

When the last dishes were removed, Commander Killian stood up. "I believe everyone here has been briefed on the events of the last few days. This dinner is not a celebration because we have nothing to celebrate. But we are here to acknowledge, and honor, an outerworlder whose conduct, despite our failures, has been exemplary. We have learned hard lessons here. The cost would have been much worse without his help."

Killian motioned to the trader to stand up. When he did

so, the Commander attached a plain gray bar to his coat. "This badge will identify you and give you entry into any innerworld."

Killian now smiled broadly. "Effectively, you are an honorary Veddian citizen. Congratulations."

The trader acted surprised, then smiled. "Does this mean I have to pay all your taxes?"

Everyone laughed.

He nodded to the room. "Thank you very, very much. I know this is an extraordinary honor."

Yor knew he could say a few more nice words and just accept the valuable gift. Instead, he decided to do something more.

He waved over the men up and down the table. "From my time with you, I've learned about your experience gems. Among many of us in the outerworlds, we have something similar. You could call them accomplishment gems."

He walked down the row of sitting men until he reached Maranth. He held up her hand that wore the diam ring. "This ring, though perhaps gaudy by Veddian standards, contains such a gem. Maranth was given this ring by the more than seventy slaves she freed, at great personal risk, from the Dullarean mines."

He gently pulled her to her feet. He then took out a gold and talline necklace supporting an inlaid gold, female drogan straddling a diam globe. The diam flashed brilliant color across the room. "Without her special gifts, the *Acacia Glyn* would have been taken and we would be dead. The Afthari colony would have been overrun as well, most or all the people there dead."

He attached the necklace around her neck. "Maranth, I present your second outerworld accomplishment gem. You certainly earned it."

For a moment the room was still as a tomb. Then it erupted in applause. Yor noted Chen nodded at him in approval. It seemed the lesson he intended was not lost on Killian, Hari, and a number of the others as well.

The gathering soon broke up. The three from the *Acacia*

Glyn were escorted back to their ship. Orandar silently bowed to her two shipmates and headed to the crew cabin, the fabric of her robe swept the walls as she floated down the narrow hall. Yor took Maranth by her arm and gently pulled her into the captain's cabin.

"Would you do something for me?"

Maranth smiled. "What?"

He pulled out another necklace much like the one he'd given her. Its drogan had more colorful plumage. It was the male version of Maranth's female drogan. Its thicker necklace was meant for a man's larger frame.

She ran a finger along the pendant. "When did you get these?"

"Had them made in Tigenne. I saved them for when we finished here. We were both remade on Afthar. If we ever meet any drogans someplace else, they will see we wear their sign. You approve?"

She fingered the drogan pendant in his hand. "I do. And they both are very beautiful."

She gently kissed the side of his face. "Thank you for my necklace. Even more, thank you for what you did to honor me tonight."

He took off his jacket, opened his shirt and smiled. "Would you put mine on for me?"

She did so and the pendant hung just above his gold tattoo. Its diam globe sparkled across the cabin.

He put a finger across her lips to stop what he knew she would next say. "We both know Hari will find some way to make the Veddian offer workable."

"Then what?"

"A family-size ship is the one thing that might entice me to live with other Veddi besides you."

That was only partially true. Even though Yor outwardly resisted, he knew in his core only the innerworlds had the resources to defend mankind. The Veddi must engage with the outerworlds. He was the only one who could guide them.

He pushed away the thought. "Where is your necklace?" He looked for it, lost somewhere in the fabric of Maranth's dress robe. His fingers worked through her upper drapery without success.

His eyes twinkled and his voice grew enticing. "Let me help you get comfortable."

She smiled and enjoyed watching him try to pry her out of her clothing.

Finally, in the midst of a lot of flying fabric, he succeeded. The gown sprawled ethereal iridescence across the bed and floor of the cabin.

Yor shook his head grumpily. "This could only be suitable for celibate people."

Her laugh brought his eyes back up. Maranth now stood before him in only a flimsy white undergarment with her drogan necklace intact against her perfect skin. A tendril of dark hair had escaped down the left side of her face. She kissed his chest where his drogan pendant sat. He pulled her up off her feet against him, skin to skin, and the two drogan pendants intermingled. Then he kissed her the way she liked, slowly and sensuously, before he let her go. He did not have to be telepathic to feel that her desire matched his own. He loosened the rest of her shiny hair and it slipped down over her shoulders and back.

He gently turned her flushed face to meet his eyes. "You have every reason to fear the unknown, with only me there. But now the unknown will also have other Veddi. Will you come with me, with us, to live as Patushah?"

She had dreaded this question, dreaded having to choose. She intended to put off her decision until after they returned to Veddi.

She wanted Yor so much. He knew and maybe that's why he asked her now, when it would be so hard for her to say no. With great difficulty she set aside her feelings, as her father warned her to do.

Yor once explained they were bonded by what he called bro-sou-fire, brothers forged by fire. Was this perception simply an expression of his sexual passion? Yet she also felt a special connection, even before she'd experienced sexuality. Yor was her anchor and she needed him. Perhaps she was his anchor as well.

He had risked himself for others and always told her the truth. His people might be strange and have harsh laws, but they were honorable.

Perhaps she was too young to understand all this. Yet she had stood up to slavers and functioned in risky situations. Her 'special skills' might again cheat death. On her oath as a meddoc, she must go where she was needed. She suppressed a smile. No one in the Medical Ministry would apply the oath to this situation.

Her father and close friends would worry and miss her. She would miss them, miss her father most of all.

Is that reason enough not to go?

She looked into Yor's patient eyes that had read everything she'd just thought.

Her voice was firm. "Aye, I'll go with you. And I'll blend in."

Hari had said the same thing. Yor marveled they both expressed the same childlike confidence. He nuzzled his face into Maranth's thick hair and enjoyed the sensation and hair smell. Most of all, he just reveled in the miracle of the moment.

Meanwhile, a seeming pattern of dancing light approached Afthar from deep space. It stalled a moment. Then it shifted toward the *Beltran* as if riding a slow, invisible wave.

Undetected by any sensors, it broke into sparkles as it diffused into the ship's hull. It made its way through the cruiser unnoticed, then slipped into the *Acacia Glyn* quietly berthed in the shuttle bay. Its pulsing energy shimmered a few inches below the ceiling in the captain's cabin. Suddenly it morphed into a diffuse glow, unnoticed by the two focused on each other below.

Then all trace of it was gone.

ABOUT THE AUTHOR

 R. K. Mann began her full-time work life as an economist, then computer consultant in NY. Later, her hobby screenplay became Vestron's *Backtrack* (*Catchfire*), starring Jodie Foster and Dennis Hopper. She was Associate Producer of the comedy *Round Numbers*, starring Kate Mulgrew, Marty Ingles, and Samantha Eggar. She also co-wrote the novel, *Catchfire*, which was published in several languages other than English. *The Trader* is her first solo novel.

A few years ago, R.K. Mann moved back to her native Florida. She is a lifelong sheller and a more recent kayaker.

Connect with R. K. online:

www.rkmannbooks.com

Facebook:
https://www.facebook.com/rkmannbooks

Goodreads:
https://www.goodreads.com/author/
show/8078691.R_K_Mann

CPSIA information can be obtained at www.ICGtesting.com
Printed in the USA
BVOW07s0807290914

368267BV00002B/3/P

9 780991 594214